"You know what I'm in the mood for? A drink, maybe some dancing, and horrifying my mom. You interested?"

"Depends," a low masculine voice said from beneath the car. "Is that a panties-optional kind of offer?"

Recognition hit hard and Charlotte went completely still. *Jace McGraw.*

The dolly slid all the way out, stopping at Charlotte's feet. Jace's dark chocolate eyes locked on her face and held for a long, weighted second, then slid down to her undone buttons, over her hips, pausing at the hem of her skirt.

The dolly inched closer and Jace's lip curled up wickedly on one side, releasing that lethal dimple. "Actually, I'm partial to the ones you have on . . ."

Reunion in Sugar Lake

A Sugar, Georgia, Novel

Marina Adair

FOREVER

NEW YORK   BOSTON

Forever
Hachette Book Group
1290 Avenue of the Americas, New York, NY 10104
read-forever.com
@readforeverpub

Originally published as *A Taste of Sugar* in mass market and ebook in August 2015
Reissued as *Reunion in Sugar Lake*: November 2024

Forever is an imprint of Grand Central Publishing. The Forever name and logo are registered trademarks of Hachette Book Group, Inc.

The publisher is not responsible for websites (or their content) that are not owned by the publisher.

The Hachette Speakers Bureau provides a wide range of authors for speaking events. To find out more, go to hachettespeakersbureau.com or email HachetteSpeakers@hbgusa.com.

Forever books may be purchased in bulk for business, educational, or promotional use. For information, please contact your local bookseller or the Hachette Book Group Special Markets Department at special.markets@hbgusa.com.

ISBNs: 9781538767108 (mass market reissue), 9781455528691 (ebook)

Printed in the United States of America

BVGM

10 9 8 7 6 5 4 3 2 1

To Luke Bryan, Jason Aldean, and Keith Urban
for writing the kind of music that
inspires my kind of
stories.

Reunion
in
Sugar
Lake

Chapter 1

⌒

Dr. Charlotte Holden took pride in her decorum and her ability to show grace under pressure. As a four-time Miss Peach and current medical director of Pediatrics at Sugar Medical Center, there wasn't much that made her sweat—her mama raised her better than that.

Not that she was sweating. But a distinct, thin sheen of perspiration seemed to be forming on her skin every time her phone vibrated with another message, and that really burned her britches. She was nearing the important part of her tour with a group of potential donors when someone texted her with a Code Silver in exam room 22—which was never a good sign.

"Do you need to take that?" Tipton Neil, chairman of Mercy Alliance, asked when Charlotte looked at her phone again.

The last thing she needed right then was to bring attention to the fact that there was a Code Silver. Not with so much riding on the hefty endowment that was up for grabs.

She'd invested three years and her entire heart into getting the new pediatric ward funded and built. The Grow Clinic—an outpatient center that would provide kids with the therapy and tools they need to thrive in the world after hospitalization—was the final step in realizing her dream. And it was almost ready to open.

"Nothing that can't wait, I'm sure," her father answered for her. Something he did often, and it bugged her to no end. Whereas Charlotte was the heart of the center, Reginald Holden the Third was all about the bottom line.

And the bottom line was—Mr. Neil was their last shot.

She took one last look at her phone, then her father—who was sending her every visual cue possible—and texted instructions to hand the patient off to the other doctor on duty.

"All handled," she said, powering down her phone. "Now, over here is the centerpiece of the new Fairchild Pediatric Center." It was the centerpiece of the entire medical center—a prime example of what made Sugar Medical so special. "Our Grow Clinic."

Tipton took in the massive play center, the brightly colored physical therapy room, and the state-of-the-art equipment. "I was skeptical about what a small rural community could offer, but your new facility and unique approach to medicine could rival the Mayo Clinic."

Well, if that didn't butter her biscuit.

"My Grow Clinic can stand up to any big-city facility. We might be small, Mr. Neil, but we are certainty not backwoods," she said with a laugh.

Her father did not laugh. Dressed in his three-piece suit, suspenders, bow tie, and look of constant disapproval, he was the picture of the quintessential Southern medical director. "What my daughter meant to say is that being a smaller, privately owned clinic has allowed us to stay both profitable and cutting edge."

Actually, she'd meant exactly what she'd said. Being a family-owned clinic allowed them to offer treatments and programs that met their patients' unique needs. It wasn't just a small-town clinic, it *was* the *town's* clinic. And as such, it should benefit all of the town's people, not just the insured ones. But she wisely kept that to herself.

"This is exactly the kind of project Mercy Alliance was created to fund," Tipton said, and Charlotte struggled to contain her excitement. But it was difficult. Almost as difficult as not blurting out, "I told you so."

When she'd reached out to Mercy Alliance it seemed like nothing more than a Hail Mary. No one, including her father, had considered it a realistic possibility. But Charlotte had. Even though their medical center had been labeled "too small" or "too ambitious" by every investor the board had approached, she knew that all it took was one person to see the potential of their idea.

So when a friend from medical school mentioned that Mercy Alliance was pulling its funding from a midsize hospital chain out west, Charlotte contacted them immediately. And now she was about to see her dream become a reality for thousands of kids in the area.

Beating death and living life were two separate challenges, and Charlotte wanted to bridge the gap where insurance left off. Her vision was to create a pediatric rehabilitation clinic where no child was denied treatment based on the family's ability to pay—which was where Mercy Alliance, and their generous endowment, came in.

"But the board feels that at a bigger facility, our funds would go further, help more people," Tipton added, and suddenly all that excitement felt like a big, suffocating knot in her chest.

Why she'd thought that all she had to do was convince

this one man that her plan was good enough she had no idea. But her dad's look said he'd expected this all along. In fact, his grim expression seemed to be doing the I-told-you-so dance all over her morning.

"Paging Dr. Holden to room 22," a slightly harassed voice came over the hospital's intercom. "Paging Dr. Charlotte Holden. Code Silver in room 22. Dr. Holden to room 22."

And just like that, the knot in her chest grew to cut off her entire air supply.

*   *   *

"Please tell me I misunderstood the page," Charlotte asked, taking the medical chart from Dr. Benjamin Clark.

"Wish I could," Ben said, hustling to keep pace with her. He was handsome in that intellectual way that usually got her. And he had gotten her, which made him her ex. They'd dated all through undergrad and then again last summer when he'd been hired at the medical center. He was a bright, rising star in medicine who came from a good family—and was just like her. Which was why they quickly decided they were better suited as friends. "I also wish I could have handled it myself, but the situation requires a woman's touch."

"Chicken."

"Damn right. She took one look at my anatomy and went straight for the boys. I barricaded myself behind the exam table and paged you."

"You always were a little skittish when it came to aggressive women." Ben rolled his eyes at that but didn't argue. "Keep watch and make sure no one comes in."

The last thing she needed right then was to have another patient, or God forbid Mr. Neil, walk by. Charlotte tapped on the door, waited the respectful amount of time, then entered.

And sighed.

Four years of medical school, another three in residency at one of the top hospitals in Georgia, and this was what her life had come to. She stared at her patient, who was on all fours licking the soap dispenser, and allowed herself a quick roll of the eyes before plastering on her most Southern smile, entering the room, and making sure to close the door behind her.

"Mrs. Ferguson," Charlotte greeted, then looked at her patient, who had moved from the soap dispenser to nuzzling the hospital gown on the exam table. "Woolamena."

June Ferguson stood and smoothed down her dress. It was denim with cowhide trim and speckled with fertilizer—which was appropriate since she was co-owner of Ferguson Family's Feed Line and Fertilizer Farm.

The Code Silver in question dropped the gown and bleated a loud *baa-ah* before huddling under the exam table—which was appropriate since Woolamena was a sheep. Not just any sheep, but the reigning sheep scurry champion of Sugar County, who was expected to defend her title at the Founder's Day Fair in a few weeks.

"I know what you're going to say, but it was an emergency," June explained.

"Then you know I'm going to remind you I am a doctor. Not a therapist or a life coach or a veterinarian. And this is a hospital. For humans." They'd had this conversation last spring when one of her prize heifers went into early labor and June tried to convince Charlotte to act as the midwife.

In fact, livestock in the hospital had become such a problem they'd even created a code and a room for such occasions. Silver being the Lone Ranger's horse. The 22 was because Noah filled his arc two by two. Not that the big-city donors would understand that. Which was why Charlotte needed to clear that room stat, before the welcoming tour made their way this direction.

"Your card says family practitioner." June produced a card from her purse as proof and waved it around. "And seeing as Woolamena here is family, I brought her to you." The older woman leaned in to whisper. "I think she needs some of those little feel-good pills you are all pushing these days."

Charlotte choked. "You want me to prescribe Viagra for your sheep?"

"Woolamena. She has a name. And what school did you say you went to again?"

"A very good one."

"Ah-huh." The older woman didn't look so convinced. "I was talking about pills for people who are thinking of *buying the farm*." The woman mouthed the last few words as though the sheep, excuse her, *Woolamena,* could understand.

"You think, uh, Woolamena is a risk to herself?"

"I think that Diablo led her on and now she's got a broken h-e-a-r-t."

"And Diablo is another sheep?"

"No, he is the stud we brought in for the heifers. Paid a farmer from Magnolia Falls a good price to bring him down, but instead of knocking up my cows, he came on to Woolamena, wooed the girl, then left her good and dry. Didn't he, baby?"

At that, Woolamena's ears went back and she wedged herself as far beneath the table as she could get, clearly not open to discussing Diablo—or his leaving. June, however, was just getting started.

"After he went home, she started acting a little off, moping around Diablo's old pen, refusing to eat, tearing her wool out." Which explained the big bald patch on her rump. "Then, last week, I found her standing in the middle of the highway, staring down one of them big Red Bull trucks headed toward Mable's Market. At first I thought she was admiring the sexy bull, but I think she was tempting the devil himself, because today she wandered down to the lake and waded in, and she wasn't taking a bath, neither. The water was already up to her brisket and closing in on her muzzle when my farmhand pulled her out. I said enough was enough and loaded her in the truck and came here."

When June placed a hand to her mouth and gave a few heartfelt sniffs, Charlotte handed her a box of tissue and pulled out her stethoscope. This was in part because any woman who delivered nineteen calves in one evening had more pluck than Charlotte, but also because she was a sucker for broken hearts.

Having suffered from one herself several years back, which she'd barely recovered from, Charlotte understood the delicate nature of loss. She also understood the power of ice cream.

Charlotte poked her head out of the door. "Ben, could you bring me one of those ice-cream bars from the vending machine? A vanilla one without the chocolate shell?"

With a nod, Ben was gone. Too bad dating him had been like dating herself. He was one of the good ones, and between decorating her new house, the stress of the grand opening, and her mother's endless matchmaking—since being single at thirty was a sin in the South—Charlotte could sure use a good man in her life. Not to mention an orgasm.

She could definitely use one of those.

Ben returned, and something about the way he looked at her had every warning flag rising to full mast. They'd been friends too long for her not to notice the way he shifted in his loafers. A sign that he had bad news. "Oh no. They know about the sheep."

Baa-ah came through the door.

He looked down the hall and back at her. "No, I just saw your father load Mr. Neil into his car." *Damn it!* "Reggie was wearing his camo jacket."

Double damn it!

The only time Reginald Holden the Third wore camo was when he was going hunting. Which meant he'd hijacked Charlotte's meeting. Not that she should be surprised. Her father's answer to any professional situation was to bond over a good boar hunt, then get down to business.

He might have appointed Charlotte as head of Pediatrics, but he still believed that the best boardroom in town belonged to the Sugar County Hunting Lodge—a membersonly club that hadn't approved a single female applicant since Ada Bradly "accidently" shot her husband in the backside. She claimed that she saw a figure in the distance, recognized it as the one that had rattled many windows of the ladies on her block, mistook him for the worst kind of dog, and took action.

Mr. Bradly lived, Ada was sentenced to community service, and anyone lacking a Y chromosome knew not to apply. So if Charlotte wanted to finish her meeting with Mr. Neil, she'd have to wait until after the weekend.

If her dad's "backwoods" business tactics hadn't screwed up the deal by then.

"At least they didn't see the sheep," Ben said, knowing exactly where her thoughts were going, and held out not one but two ice-cream bars. "Between your patient load, the meetings with the donors, and now your dad, I figured you hadn't had time for lunch and could use some ice cream right about now."

She eyed the bar, then looked at Ben. Really looked at him, and wondered if maybe it could work, then caught sight of his designer shoes, Sunday-best attire beneath the white doctor's coat, and shivered—not in a good way.

They matched. Even down to the brand of stethoscope. "Nope."

He laughed knowingly. "Would make it easier, though."

It sure would. Unfortunately, her heart had long ago given up on easy, and her other parts only seemed to be interested in courting hard—hard bodies with bad-boy smiles and tattoos.

"Thanks for this." She took both bars—it was well past lunchtime, after all—ushered Ms. Ferguson out of the room and into Ben's care, and closed the door.

Alone with the sheep, Charlotte sat on the floor at the edge of the exam table. "Now come on out."

When the sheep just looked at her, watching her carefully, Charlotte scooted closer and held out the ice cream. "Well, we can talk about it or just plain eat it out, you choose, but moping around and pulling your hair out over a man is just not dignified. And a Southern woman with six titles needs to maintain her dignity at all times."

The sheep let out *Baa-ah* of protest, but the ice cream was too much temptation to ignore. Eyes firmly on Charlotte, Woolamena slowly made her way out from under the table and took a tentative sniff. Then a nibble, and, as though the sheep could recognize another lonely soul, she curled up against Charlotte's side and the two females ate their ice cream in silence.

* * *

It was a rare day in Sugar when Babette Holden graced the morning before the sun, especially when there was no one to bring her coffee in bed. But when Charlotte's mother had her mind set, not even the threat of puffy eyes or lack of a front-door key could sidetrack her.

Babette stood at the counter in a cream pantsuit and enough pearls to accessorize the entire Miss Peach Court, staring down Charlotte's coffeemaker as though waiting for it to make her a cappuccino and irritated that she'd had to wait. "I hit the red button and nothing happened."

"You have to put water in it first." And since Charlotte knew *that* wouldn't happen in her lifetime, she moved into the kitchen, filled up the pot, and hit the red button.

"I prefer mine nonfat. Double shot, please."

"It comes black, with cream or sugar. That's it."

Her mouth tightened. "If you had chosen to stay at home, where all good single Southern women belong, Mavis could have whipped us up a lovely cinnamon latte and delivered it to you in bed."

"Along with my clothes, which you'd pick out and have neatly pressed and laid at the foot of my bed, while you sat next to them staring me awake."

Reason number one that Charlotte had purchased her own home last month. She'd taken one look at the stately antebellum cottage with its pristine white stone structure, original leaded-glass windows, and ornate wrought-iron-enclosed balconies overlooking Sugar Lake and fell in love. That it was on the opposite side of the lake from her mother's only made it that much more appealing.

The lake house was exactly the kind of home she imagined raising a family in. Not that she had a family or even a potential husband, but she still had hope. And for now, that was enough.

"You make it sound as though I smothered you," Babette said dramatically, and Charlotte wisely chose not to comment. Then her mother carefully inspected Charlotte's outfit, a black skirt with cream belt cinching her white cap-sleeved top, and sighed. "Yes, well, you really should invest in an iron, dear. And more pastels. They do glorious things for your complexion."

It was said as though Charlotte needed all the help she could get. And maybe she did.

Charlotte had spent a good portion of the weekend fine-tuning what she was going to say to Mr. Neil. The other part, when she wasn't pulling long shifts at the clinic and should have been sleeping, had been spent staring at the ceiling and waiting for the sun to come up, thinking about things she had no business thinking about.

Sitting there with Woolamena the other day had been like sitting with herself four years ago. And even though the pain had dulled and her heart had healed, the emptiness still remained, and Charlotte was tired of feeling empty. Tired of playing life safe. Tired of her father steamrolling over her career and her mother reminding her what it means to be a lady.

Tired of watching everyone else around her move on, find happiness, while she stayed in the same place.

In fact, she was tired of being tired. So this morning, instead of staring at the ceiling, she'd gotten impatient and decided to fix her life. She was a master fixer, it was what made her such a good doctor. Only instead of fixing her patients, she decided she was going to start with herself and act like the woman she wanted to be, not the woman she had become.

And then she walked downstairs to find her mother in the kitchen.

Babette clapped her hands. "You know what you need?"

A new lock? A good night's sleep? Once again, Charlotte's mind circled back to that orgasm and suddenly she felt like unbuttoning her blouse two more buttons, but resisted. She had a full workload, with the average patient being in diapers or with dentures, and her "need list" was about four thousand pages long.

Yet based on the way Babette was smiling, Charlotte didn't think her mother's idea would even make her extended list. "I need to leave for work."

Babette's face puckered, as well as a face could pucker when the forehead didn't move. "It's Sunday. Who works on Sunday?"

"Sickness doesn't recognize the Sabbath." Her father obviously did, since he'd decided to take a "personal day," choosing to finish up his hunting trip with Mr. Neil rather than work the urgent care unit as he was scheduled to do, leaving a huge gap in patient load coverage. And since the clinic was perpetually short-staffed on the weekends, especially in urgent care, it was up to Charlotte to pick up the slack.

"Well, it should."

Amen to that. "I'm covering a shift."

"That's sweet of you."

Not professional, not ambitious, but *sweet*. As though all of the sacrifice and hard work Charlotte had put into her career was merely a way to pass time until she found herself a proper Southern man and set up a proper Southern home.

"I heard you had lunch with Benjamin."

And there's the reason for her visit, Charlotte thought while pouring coffee into a mug. She slid it across the countertop toward her mother, who looked offended, then tactfully dismissed the beverage with a shake of the head.

"I had lunch with a patient," Charlotte said. And then, not to give her mother false hope, clarified, "A female patient. Ben and I are just friends."

A car horn honked out front. Babette didn't move and Charlotte got a nagging feeling in her stomach that her mother was up to no good. She walked to the window and looked out to find a silver Lexus idling in the drive. Ben smiled through the windshield and waved.

"Mother, why is Ben here?"

"Maybe he wanted to ask you to lunch."

"It's seven a.m. on Sunday."

"Love does crazy things to a person." Babette glided to the window and gave a regal wave, one that could only come from Miss Peach 1977, since the pearl bracelets she wore flashed in the rising sun yet didn't make a single sound.

Ben waved back and opened his car door to walk over to Charlotte's to—look at her tires?

"Why are my tires flat?"

"A handsome man is out fixing your tires at this god-awful hour and you are worried about how they got flat. Honestly, dear, you wonder why you're single?"

Charlotte had never wondered about that. She knew exactly why she was single. Love hurt too much.

"My, he is handsome, isn't he?" Babette fanned herself as Ben fished his phone out of his pocket—most likely to call the local tow truck. "He will bless his wife with such beautiful children."

"I'll be sure to tell his girlfriend that," Charlotte said.

Babette deflated at the news, which was good. Because when her mom sank her teeth into something she was like a pit bull—a pit bull with a diamond-studded collar. And although a good Southern woman needed a good Southern gentleman, no lady poached on marked territory—regardless of how blue his family's blood ran. So rather than clarifying that the closet thing Ben had to a proper girlfriend was

Scarlett Johansson, she let her mother come to her own conclusion.

"Well, it seems as though you have managed to scare off another one." Babette picked up her clutch and strode toward the front door. "What a waste of a morning. And to think I set my alarm for this." Since it was undignified to holler, Babette paused under the threshold. "Don't forget dinner tonight. Your father invited some big-city doctor over. Lionel is a Yankee, midforties, a bit on the pudgy side, but single."

"He is also the new podiatrist on staff at the clinic." But if her dad was bringing a guest to dinner, it meant he'd be at dinner, too, with his new hunting buddy. And although Charlotte wanted to secure the endowment, doing it while her mother passed around her baby photos was not how she envisioned her pitch going. "And has a habit of staring at ladies' shoes."

Babette eyed Charlotte's shoes, then her skirt. "Yes, well, we work with what we have since we can't afford to be choosy, now can we?" And then she was gone.

"Love you, too, Mom. We should do this more often," Charlotte said to the empty kitchen.

Last year, she'd set out to find living arrangements that didn't include sharing a zoning line with her parents and to prove to the hospital board—and her father—that she was ready to head up the Grow Clinic. She accomplished the first and was almost there with the second. Now she was determined to get the rest of her life in order. And that included really living again. Taking chances.

In medicine some of the most amazing advances came from approaching a problem from a different direction, taking risks that others were too afraid to even consider. And she believed life was no different, that if she wanted to enact change then she needed to start taking calculated risks.

A plan that was terrifying and exhilarating all at the same time, because for a girl who mapped out her world down to when her coffeepot started brewing, every little risk felt like a huge challenge. The hope was that several small risks would give her the courage to take some bigger ones, until eventually she would be ready to take life by the horns.

She set her mug on the counter and marched back into her bedroom and riffled through the endless supply of cardigans and pastels, past the tea-length and cashmere forest, to locate the one outfit hiding in the back. It was red, sleek, sophisticated, and said grown-up sexy instead of Sunday tea. And was something she'd been waiting until she gathered the courage to wear.

Not that she had the courage now, but she was willing to fake it for a while. Which was why she'd slipped on her naughtiest pair of panties, mile-high heels, and left the top button of her blouse undone, then marched downstairs to head into work as the new and improved Dr. Charlotte Holden.

Chapter 2

 ~

The sun was setting and Charlotte was still trying to figure a way to get out of going to Sunday dinner at her mother's. Although Mr. Neil was indeed on the guest list, Charlotte knew that if she wanted to be seen as a professional she needed to present her case at the clinic. Not down the hall from her childhood bedroom.

And after ten hours on her feet, a surprising case of chicken pox, and a conversation with Danny Mathews about how eating glue was a bad idea, all she wanted to do was go home, draw a hot bath, eat ice cream while watching high-brow reality television, and be in bed before nine.

But that's what Charlotte did. Boring, ordinary, responsible Charlotte. That realization raced through her chest, and for a moment she thought perhaps she was on the brink of a minor attack. Placing a hand over her heart, she realized that no, it was still beating, the same sluggish beat it had for the past four years. Nothing had made Charlotte hot, bothered, or even a little giddy in all that time. And that needed to stop.

What she needed was a fresh dose of life. A glimpse of this new and improved Charlotte. And tonight, that's what she'd chase. Set on living a life outside of pastels—and other people's expectations—she grabbed her purse, undid one more button, and strutted her way down Maple Street to Kiss My Glass Tow and Tires.

With the busy week looming ahead, she needed her car back, almost as much as she needed a drink. A strong one. And who better to help Charlotte celebrate breaking the mold than the town's own tough girl turned mechanic. Lavender Spencer was a smartass ballbuster who took life by the horns and kneed it in the nuts when it pissed her off—something Charlotte needed to embrace if she had any hope of checking things off her list.

The back bay of the garage was still open and the lights were on. A big engine sat on a workstation, and there were spare parts strewn across the floor like a puzzle that was yet to be put back together. Some kind of redneck rap was coming from the radio, which sat in the back of the garage near a rusted-out shell of a muscle car that was missing all its windows and the passenger door.

Charlotte stepped over an open toolbox and around the engine, careful not to get grease on her shoes, stopping at the front of the car.

"You know what I'm in the mood for?" she addressed the only part of her friend that was visible, a grease-stained ball cap peeking out beneath the underbelly. "A drink, maybe some dancing, and definitely horrifying my mom. You interested?"

"Depends," a low, masculine voice said from beneath the car. "Is that a panties-optional kind of offer?"

It wasn't just the voice that had her heart racing. Nope, it was also the bulging biceps with a familiar tribal tattoo spanning its length that snaked out from beneath the car and had her pulse bordering on dangerous levels.

Recognition hit hard and she went completely still.

Jace McGraw.

The dolly slid all the way out, stopping at her feet and right next to her heart, which had plummeted to her toes when she saw those stormy blue eyes zero in on her. Eyes she'd done her best over the years to forget. They locked on her face and held for a long, weighted second, then slid down to her undone buttons, over her hips, pausing at the hem of her skirt.

The dolly inched closer and his lip curled up wickedly on one side, releasing that lethal dimple. "Actually, I'm partial to the ones you have on."

She jerked back and pressed her hands to her skirt to avoid giving him more of a show. Because the only thing he was going to get from her was a piece of her mind. And maybe the middle finger. She'd never given anyone the finger before, but for Jace she'd make an exception.

"What are you doing here?" she demanded.

"Working," he said, pulling himself up to his full height, surprisingly agile for a man his size.

Because, *Lord have mercy*, at six-foot-four, Jace was all rippling muscle and testosterone. And tattoos, lots of tattoos. Only two were visible, but she knew what lay beneath those low-slung button-flies and fitted ARMY STRONG tee. The memory alone was enough make her thighs quiver.

He was built like a tank, with buzzed hair and a killer smile, and had the confidence of a guy who could handle anything that came his way. A fact that had her good parts fluttering.

And wasn't that just wonderful. Her good parts decided that now was the perfect time to come out of retirement. If she hadn't known him she would have welcomed the flutters, even allowed herself an extra minute to appreciate all that fine, male yumminess.

But she did know him, and all of those warm tingles disappeared, replaced by tension. And a little panic. And a whole lot of something that she didn't want to acknowledge.

"You can't work here," she said, angry that he hadn't called to warn her he was coming home. He at least owed her that.

"Can and do." He grabbed a rag off the hood of the car and wiped off his hand, then stuck it out. "Jace McGraw, Sugar's newest resident mechanic."

She swatted his hand away. "Since when?" Because Jace didn't do home visits. And he didn't stick around one place long enough to be a resident of anywhere.

"Since today." He cupped the bill of his hat and pulled it lower on his head. "Let me guess, you're here as the official Sugar welcoming committee. Where's my pie?"

"What pie?"

"Pie? Something in a covered dish? You know, all those neighborly things people are supposed to do when someone comes to town." He looked at her empty hands and then without a word his eyes dropped to her skirt and there went the other dimple—and her good parts. "Unless there's something I can do for you, *Charlie*?"

The way he said her name in that low, husky timbre, almost whispering it while flattening the vowels, reminded her of a different time, a time when she naively thought he'd meant it. But she wasn't that wide-eyed woman anymore. She knew what he was offering, and what he wasn't capable of giving.

After all, once upon a time she'd been married to him. Yup, Charlotte Holden had fallen in love with and married the town's biggest bad boy. Not that anybody except the two of them knew, since it had ended as fast as it had begun. But those few weeks as Mrs. Jace McGraw had been the most amazing of her life—and what had followed had nearly broken her.

"Yes," she said. "You need to leave." Because wasn't that what he did best?

The briefest frown flashed across his face, and he grabbed some kind of wrench doohickey and busied himself with tinkering under the hood. "Wish I could, but it seems like my services are needed in Sugar for a bit."

Charlotte didn't know what hurt more, that he wanted to leave as much as she wanted him gone—which was ridiculous since him being here, during the most important time in her career, was a disaster waiting to happen—or that, after all the time she'd spent praying he'd come back to Sugar, he finally had. Only it wasn't for her.

"That doesn't work for me," she said.

"Well, this isn't about you. Now is it?" He wasn't even looking at her but tightening some bolt inside the engine. Which was a good thing since she was pretty sure her eyes went glassy at his comment, because at one time he'd made her believe that everything he did was for her. Including walking away from their marriage. "Can you hand me that wrench over there?"

Was he kidding? "No, it's all greasy, and I don't want to get dirty."

He looked at her over his shoulder and cracked a small smile. "Too bad, I always preferred you a little dirty."

She looked at the perfectly pressed skirt, her "daring" skirt, and realized what a joke that was. Maybe once upon a time she'd been more adventurous, more daring, willing to get dirty. But that had been with Jace. He'd made her feel bold, exciting, and, if she was totally honest, alive. Except he took those things with him, leaving her with a shattered heart and a closet of pastels—and not a clue as to how to pick up the pieces.

Somehow she'd managed. She'd channeled that steel Holden pride, stitched herself back together, and moved home to rebuild a life for herself, without anyone knowing what had transpired. And that took guts.

"Well, I've changed," she informed him primly, tilting her chin up a fraction. "And I need to go. So if you could just point me in the direction of my keys."

He ran a hand down his face. "About that. Seems someone chewed off your valve stems. So it wasn't as easy as patching a hole."

"Chewed them off?" Was her mother really that desperate to marry her off?

"See here?" Jace walked over to her car and squatted down. She did her best not to notice the way his jeans cupped his backside—tried and failed. He filled out a pair of Levi's like nobody's business. "Teeth marks. Looks like you got yourself a raccoon or possum problem."

Seems she had lots of pest problems these days. "So can you just throw some new tires on it and I can be gone?"

"You don't need new tires, what you need are new valve stems." And wasn't that just like a man, telling her what she needed. "Which for your sporty, two-door tiara on wheels is a special order. Imagine that."

"So what you're telling me is that I'm stuck here? With you. And my car won't be ready until—"

"Best-case scenario, end of the week."

She let out a completely undignified huff and resisted

the urge to stomp her feet. She'd begged the universe for a way out of dinner, and apparently whoever was in charge of granting wishes had chosen today to listen.

She looked at her phone, considered calling Ben, and then realized she could only handle one man from her past at a time. Plus, he was on a date with the new nurse from radiology, which meant Charlotte was stranded. Something that must have shown on her face because Jace set the tool down and stepped closer—so close he was all up in her personal space, which did crazy things to her emotional space.

"I can take you home." He looked at her buttons and back into her eyes. "Or I can take you across the street to the Saddle Rack and buy you a drink."

Then he did something he hadn't done in over four years, he cupped his palms around her hips and drew her to him, and damn it if she didn't shuffle closer.

"Why would I let you buy me a drink?" she asked quietly, although her brain kicked off a hundred and one reasons on its own. The first being that was how their relationship had started.

Charlotte had been a stressed-out resident in Atlanta, lonely and so homesick it hurt, when she'd walked into a bar and seen Jace. He flashed her that bad-boy smile, bought her a drink, then another, and before she knew it he had sweet-talked her into his bed, then down to the Justice of the Peace.

"Because I think you could use a shot of something strong right now," he said. "And we need to talk."

"You lost the right to tell me what I need a long time ago. As for that talk you want, you're about four years too late."

"Not according to the great state of Georgia," he said, and her stomach dropped. "Since legally we're still married."

*   *   *

Jace McGraw had spent most of his life fighting—in his youth for fun, more recently for his country, but right then the only thing he was fighting was the insane urge to pull Charlotte into his arms and tell her it would all be okay.

But since that would be a big, steaming pile of BS, not to mention her body language was giving off that *don't look and don't even think about touching* vibe, he grabbed a clean mason jar off the sink and a bottle of Johnny Walker out of Spencer's bottom desk drawer.

Pouring two fingers, he handed it to Charlotte, who was still leaning up against the charred remains of one of his favorite vintage muscle cars of all time, a '61 Stingray, which he'd been conned into restoring since the resident town mechanic didn't specialize in complete rebuilds. And this was a ground-up kind of job, which required a clear head and lots of finesse—two things that were impossible for him with regard to this car. And apparently this woman.

This was a mess. And he hadn't even told her the worst part.

Silently, she took the glass. Besides telling him she was going to be sick, which hurt more than he'd anticipated, she hadn't said a single word. Not that he expected her to hold an in-depth conversation after that bomb. If there was one thing he knew about Charlotte Holden it was that she was as tough as they came. Not much fazed her, but when she needed to process a situation she went radio silent.

This silence was different, though. It was the kind that demolished her cool-as-a-cucumber exterior that used to drive him batshit crazy.

Used to? Hell, it still did. Even after all this time, seeing Charlotte upset brought out this insane need to comfort her, help make her world better. Except Jace had learned a long time ago that the only thing his help had ever brought others was pain. And the best way to help the people he loved was to keep his distance.

"That's not possible," she finally said after staring at the glass for a good, long time. "I filed the annulment myself."

"Unfortunately, the traveling notary I used notarized the annulment on an expired commission." He repeated what the woman at the clerk's office had told him. "I guess they tried to contact me when they discovered the mistake, but I wasn't in one place for long enough."

"Why didn't they contact me?"

He shrugged. "I have no idea, but I learned that the person in the clerk's office who handled this kind of thing passed away shortly after we filed. So I am guessing we got lost in the shuffle, or someone dropped the ball."

"Wait." Her eyes went cold. Cold enough to freeze off his nuts. "How long have you known and kept this from me?"

He held up his hands. "I only found out last week, when the bank denied me a business loan due to my debt-to-earning ratio." When she only frowned he added, "Seems we bought a house on Sugar Lake last summer, so buying an engine shop came off as greedy."

Atlanta Motorsports was more than an engine shop. It was the premiere high-performance facility in Atlanta. Hell, in all of Georgia. Known for their high-performance chassis, drivetrain tuning, and a magic touch with the world's rarest exotics, it didn't get more elite than that.

And Jace had a once-in-a-lifetime opportunity to make it his.

The owner needed to sell fast, so Jace needed to secure that loan by the end of next month or his dream shop would go to another buyer.

"*We* didn't buy anything," she snapped. "I bought my own house, thank you very much."

·"Explain that to the bank, because as far as they're concerned, since we're married, your home loan was listed as a liability on both of our credit reports. Which means we have thirty days to figure this out and untangle our lives."

If not, then he was going to miss out. Big-time. And he'd worked too damn hard for this.

"Can't your brothers help you?"

The easy answer was yes. Between Brett and Cal, his brothers had enough money to buy the shop and all of its competition outright, but Jace didn't do handouts. And he certainly didn't do pity loans. His brothers had helped him enough over the years, and it was time for Jace to grow the fuck up and figure his shit out.

Which was what he'd been trying to do when the bank had called him with their regrets.

"Not an option," he said, crowding her a little. He knew he was a big guy, knew that his proximity usually made people bend to his will. And he needed Charlotte bendable right then, because if she wasn't on board then he was screwed. "I have an appointment for our case to be heard a week from Wednesday in Columbus with the county judge, but since this is a special case we need to see the county recorder first," he explained. "I have an appointment with the recorder's office this Tuesday in Atlanta, and both parties need to be present."

"Oh no," she said. "I am not going with you to Atlanta."

"Afraid you won't be able to control yourself?"

"No." She crossed her arms. "The new Grow Clinic is opening next month, and my appointment schedule is booked weeks in advance. Plus, last time you sweet-talked me into going to the courthouse I wound up married to the town bad boy."

Jace flinched a little at the reminder. His misspent youth had been a dangerous mix of anger, self-loathing, and guilt.

He'd made a hobby out of straddling the line, but after his parents' deaths he'd channeled all that pissed-off rage into making trouble, the wrong kind of friends and the wrong kind of choices.

He packed up and moved to Atlanta—where he ran into Charlotte.

And man, one look at his hometown's own Southern belle, tossing back tequila shots in a big city honky-tonk, and Jace was a goner. Only, as luck would have it, this time his past decided to follow him, and it wasn't just his future in jeopardy. Charlotte had made the short list for a high-profile pediatrician position at a big hospital in Atlanta—where reputation was gold. So he'd done the best thing he could, filed for an annulment and got himself as far away from her as possible.

Only he'd still ended up hurting her—and turned out they were still married.

"Then take a sick day or a personal day, I don't care. But I need you there." Something that Jace didn't say often— and Charlotte knew it. She also knew he was using her superhero, fix-everything complex against her. And it was working.

She ticked her manicured nails against the side of the car and expelled several deep huffs, a telltale sign she was trying to control her temper. Too bad her eyes were shooting daggers through his chest. But he wasn't scared by a pissed-off female. He'd spent enough time with his hormonal teenage niece, who made a living off mood swings and hysterics, to be intimidated.

So he scooted closer, his expression making it clear that "no" wasn't going to cut it in the answer department, and waited her out.

Problem was, Charlotte was as stubborn as he was, and

after a long standoff he realized just how close they were to each other. So close that he could feel the evening heat roll off her body, smell her perfume, a real look-but-don't-touch scent, which for a guy who lived to defy the rules had him wanting to touch her all over.

Starting with those full lips of hers that were lush and glossy and damn tempting—and working his way down to that collar she left open, showing off enough creamy cleavage and white lace to have everything below the belt man up.

She was staring at him, too—his mouth to be exact—and although her expression gave nothing away, he could tell she felt it. That undeniable heat that went from zero to mind-fuck whenever they were within fighting distance.

Or kissing distance.

"Stop crowding me," she snapped, placing her elegant hand in the center of his chest and shoving. Not hard enough to move him, but being a gentleman he obliged and stepped back—an inch. Then it happened. The queen of cool stomped her foot—right on his. "You're getting your army of one stench all over me."

"You used to like my army of one all over you."

"That was when I thought you'd still be there come morning," she said, and—message received—Jace stepped back. All the way back.

"One day, Charlie. That's all I'm asking for. I leave town, and then we both go on with our lives." A plan that didn't have as much merit as it had ten minutes ago. The idea of walking away from something he'd never deserved to begin with had seemed easy, yet suddenly he couldn't remember why he had been so sure they wouldn't work.

A bad sign, so he stuck out his hand as though he was okay with the arrangement and wanted to shake on it.

She looked at his hand and back to his face. With a grim

smile she said, "I'll think about it," and strolled right past him and out of the shop, gifting him with a unique view. And he wasn't just talking about the way she swished her perfect ass all the way across the garage until she disappeared through the bay door.

Jace had made sure he'd always been the one to do the walking. Watching it from the other direction stung like a bitch.

Chapter 3

Ending the day at her parents' house for Sunday dinner was not an option. Babette Holden could sniff out a scandal like a bloodhound with wounded prey. Her mother would take one look at Charlotte, smell the scent of impending divorce, and before Charlotte could explain the situation a traditional Southern wedding fit for a former Miss Peach would be planned and executed. Because the only thing worse than Babette Holden's only daughter eloping with the town bad boy was divorce.

Admitting her marriage had been over the first time had nearly killed her. The fact that she had to face it again was starting to give her hives. She didn't need her parents influencing her decision.

Nope, Charlotte was going to go home, open a bottle of champagne, and finish it in one chug while wearing her sexiest nightgown. Then she would fall into a drunken sleep, convince herself that her life wasn't rapidly spiraling out of control, and if that didn't work, break into the ice cream she'd been hiding in her freezer.

That had been her plan.

Until she realized she was stranded in town, with no car, in a pair of adorable yet impractical heels, with only two options. Ask her ex-husband, who had apparently messed up filing for the "ex" part of the title, for a ride home, or see just how far stubborn pride could carry her.

When the blister on her right pinkie toe grew to the size of the Mississippi, Charlotte went for option three. Which was how she ended up seated at her parents' formal dining table, across from a potential investor, while on a blind date with a bald man who kept dropping his napkin—on her adorable heels—only to retrieve it slowly, while her mother smiled on.

"Disposable inserts," Babette mused, as though Lionel had discovered the solution to global warming. "Just fascinating. Isn't that fascinating, Charlotte?"

And because Charlotte was a classy Southern woman, she smiled generously before hiding an eye roll behind her wineglass as she took a generous swallow. Her mother would think that growing grass was fascinating if the man was loaded, connected, and interested. And based on the way Lionel's fingers grazed Charlotte's arch every time he dropped his napkin, he was interested.

"The bottom line," Charlotte heard Tipton Neil say to her father, "is you are just too small for the board's comfort. We recently had to pull funding from a midsize project out west less than a year into the partnership because the local support dried up after the clinic received our endowment. Since then, the board is hesitant to invest in smaller companies."

"You have my word that won't happen here," Reginald assured him. "Sugar Medical Center has been owned and operated by the Holden family for over ninety years. And for ninety years we have served this community with dignity and pride."

Huh, no wonder Charlotte had a perfection complex.

"And the town realizes that," Babette said in a regal tone, which, combined with her entitled pearls and heirloom attitude, made her appear the lady of the manor speaking of her serfs. Not the modern-day image of teamwork Charlotte wanted to portray.

"We're not just a town clinic, we are *the* town's clinic, and we work hard to be a positive part of the community," Charlotte explained. "When we announced the need for a new pediatric ward and the Grow Clinic, the town came together to raise the million dollars needed for the expansion."

"It was lovely," Babette said. "They hosted bake sales and potlucks, even a fish-a-thon."

"A fish-a-thon?" Mr. Neil did not sound impressed. In fact, he sounded as if her mother's attempt to help had only helped reconfirm his original concerns—Sugar was a small town with a small clinic. Too small a fish for Mercy Alliance to do anything with but let go.

That's what got to Charlotte most of all. She was tired of being tossed back, wanted the chance to prove Sugar was worth the investment, worthy of Mercy's time and commitment.

"Here in Sugar we believe that it takes a village to raise a hospital, and it takes a whole lot of love to save a child," Charlotte explained. "We may be short on census numbers, but we have enough support and heart to make a difference. To these kids and the families in this county, the Grow Clinic is the difference between life and really living. We've built the clinic, the doors are nearly ready to open, and now we need Mercy's help to make sure that all the patients have access to the treatment they need. Regardless of insurance."

Tipton put down his knife and studied her—really studied her—and Charlotte knew that she was getting through. It wasn't about numbers, it was about people and saving lives. That was why Mercy Alliance was founded, and that was why Charlotte did what she did.

"Which is why the town decided to dedicate this year's Founder's Day Fair in support of Sugar Medical," Babette lied, and Charlotte choked on her own spit.

"Mom," she whispered, but Babette wouldn't be deterred.

"There will be local booths selling wares, the annual Sheep Scurry and Trials, and a televised parade hosted by our homegrown golf royalty, Brett McGraw."

"It's only a local access show," Charlotte clarified, while giving her mother a gentle nudge under the table to cool it.

Unfortunately, Babette was raised to believe that the most important skill a woman could possess, other than the ability to glisten instead of perspire, was hosting a dinner party that would be talked about. So, if it made the company more exciting, then it was not a sin to embellish the facts. "I heard that they are holding it in the medical center's parking lot."

"Actually," Charlotte said, trying to hide the panic creeping around her neck, because everyone knew that Babette would tell Mr. Neil that Sugar Medical had discovered the cure for cancer if it meant her dinner would be the talk of someone else's table for weeks to come, "the Founder's Day Fair has traditionally been held on Maple Street since the first general store and post office opened its front doors back in 1846."

Tipton looked perplexed. "And this year they are holding it at the medical center?"

"Well, I don't see why not," her mother said, raising her

glass as though it were a wonderful idea. As though it had been decided. As though they could just change the location of a 169-year-old tradition.

"And Charlotte is heading up the entire event," her mother said, then whispered to Lionel, "Knows how to keep her house in order, just ask anyone."

Yes, because after achieving a doctorate and dedicating ten years of her life toward the advancement of medicine, the most impressive thing about her is her super-fantastic party planning skills.

"That is a lot to take on with your practice and the Grow Clinic," Mr. Neil said, now sounding concerned.

And since the last thing she needed Mr. Neil thinking was that the head of his potential investment would be too busy polishing her pearls to head up the clinic, she said, "The Grow Clinic is my focus."

Her mother sighed heavily, then whispered to Lionel, "Which is why she's single."

"I am just helping out with the event," Charlotte clarified over her mother's comment. "It is really the Sugar Peaches who run the show."

"The Sugar Peaches is an exclusive local woman's organization dedicated to upholding our county's rich tradition of giving back to our community," her mother added, as though anyone cared. "And Charlotte is the current regent."

"Dad," she whispered as her mother outlined the complete history of the social organization in the same way one would explain the three branches of government. "We can't move the fair."

"You're a Holden," he whispered back. "You can do anything you set your mind to. You want this Grow Clinic to include pro bono treatment? Then get that endowment secured or we go back to my plan."

Which meant no insurance, no treatment.

"You want me to lie?" Her father might not be known for a warm and fuzzy bedside manner, but he wasn't a liar.

"I want you to finish what you started," he said. "Plus it's not like they're going to come to the parade."

"What was that, dear?" her mother asked.

Her father cleared his throat and smiled. "Charlotte was explaining how most of the proceeds from the fair will go toward the Grow Clinic and its patients. It should cover the remaining funds needed to purchase the pediatric physical therapy machines and install the wireless network for the research center."

And because nearly every one of Charlotte's decisions were influenced by two factors, making her father proud or horrifying her mother, she gave her brightest smile.

Neither confirming nor denying her father's big fat lie.

"That is the kind of commitment we are looking for, Reggie," Tipton said, clapping her father on the back. "Mercy Alliance wants to pursue organizations that exhibit the same dedication to medical care as our company."

"Ninety years," her dad repeated, and just like that the conversation was over in his mind. He pulled out the proposal Charlotte had sent him. The one she'd spent the entire weekend reworking, only to have him reject it on the grounds that it "needed work." *Now* it seemed to be fine, since he handed it to Mr. Neil. "Take a look at this, and let my office know if there is anything else you need. I'd like to wrap up the paperwork before the end of the month, so we can announce the endowment at the Founder's Day Fair."

"You're a hard man to say no to, Reggie."

Preaching to the choir, Charlotte thought, because by "my office" he meant Charlotte, since no one knew as much, or cared as much, about the Grow Clinic as she did. Sure, he hadn't implied that Charlotte was his secretary, as he'd done in the past, but he'd passed off her hard work as his. She could have said something. Should have. But she didn't—an annoying character flaw she was determined to work on.

But then Mr. Neil smiled and said, "Let me take this to the board and see what I can do," and Charlotte decided she'd work on it tomorrow because Lionel dropped his napkin again, and Babette looked delighted at the outcome of her dinner.

* * *

When it came to family and favors, Jace knew that doing the right thing would likely come back and bite him in the ass. And this favor was going to leave marks. Hell, just standing there in the garage at Kiss My Glass and looking at the burned-out hull of the car his family wanted him to rebuild was already pissing off his chest. Even worse, it was bringing some pretty intense feeling that he'd thought he'd buried years ago.

"Christ," he mumbled, running a hand over his face and heading for the door—and space that didn't reek of the past.

He stepped out into the crisp autumn night and watched a couple of maple leaves blow down the empty cobblestone sidewalk and into the street. The cool air filled his lungs, and he did his best to get a handle on all the emotions threatening to take him under. When that didn't work, he decided to ignore them.

There had been a time in Jace's life when he couldn't imagine leaving the wide-open plains of Sugar, but that was before. Before that summer. Before the fire. And before he cost his family everything.

But no matter how far he ran, how many shitholes he was

sent to, how many battles he fought, he couldn't seem to out-
run the slug-size hole growing in his chest. Until he'd met
Charlotte, and in typical Jace fashion, he'd destroyed that,
too.

Now he was back in the only place that had ever felt like
home, surprisingly still married to the only woman he'd ever
loved, and he was going to walk away. Again.

And wasn't that fan-fucking-tastic, he thought, crossing
Maple Street and bypassing his truck—not to mention the
dozen texts from his brothers telling him to get his butt to
dinner. And since sitting at the family table surrounded by
his brothers and their ball-and-chain bliss required a few
drinks, he headed for the swinging doors of the local honky-
tonk.

He was happy for what his brothers had built. Happy that
they'd found that same insane connection and undeniable
love that their parents shared. He really was. But being surrounded by everything he wanted, everything he'd once had,
knowing he was never going to get it back made his chest
hurt.

And tonight he'd let his own selfish needs take prece-
dence, because his family didn't ask him for much, which
was why telling them no was going to suck. This was one
favor he couldn't come through on. And even if he could, he
wouldn't be around long enough to rebuild that car.

Hell, all the time in the world wouldn't be enough for him
to rebuild that car, and he only had two days.

Jace took a deep breath and entered the Saddle Rack. Stepping inside the bar was like wading neck-deep in his past,
literally. The dark wood dance floor, neon beer signs, and
mile-long bar top was exactly the same as when he'd left. Even
worse, there wasn't a face he didn't recognize—and they all
seemed to recognize him back.

Tipping his ball cap at half the town, Jace headed straight for the bar, passing the other half, it seemed, and stopped.

Well, shit. His brother Brett was seated in their old spot at the far end of the counter. An empty stool on one side of him, two frosty longnecks on the other. And he was waiting. The smug, brother-knows-best look said he was waiting for Jace—that he knew he'd bail on the family dinner and come here instead.

Locking eyes, Brett lifted his beer and saluted—challenging Jace to avoid him now.

He considered just that, except Sunday night football had taken over the Saddle Rack, so there wasn't another spare seat in the joint. Otherwise Jace would have taken his beer and found somewhere that didn't stink of "projects" and disappointment. Jace took the stool next to Brett, making sure to jab him a few times while getting settled. "Shouldn't you be at home eating dinner?"

"I could ask you the same," Brett said, sliding a beer in front of Jace.

"Was going to grab a drink then head on over," he lied, and Brett knew it but didn't call him on it.

"Cal bet you were just running late."

"Cal's always been my favorite brother."

"That's because he didn't know half the shit you pulled growing up. Which is why I put twenty on you hiding out here instead of facing Grandma." Brett clinked his bottle against Jace's and lifted it in a toast. "Here's to you being a total pussy." Then took a long pull.

Unable to argue that, Jace joined him, the cold liquid doing not a thing to help his breathing.

"Now that that's settled, why don't you go thank your wife for making that fancy dinner?"

"You say that like I didn't already try." Brett eyed him—

hard—then toed the brown paper bag at his feet. A little puff of heavenly smelling steam escaped. "Mom's meatloaf, garlic mashed potatoes, Hattie's green beans, and a whole pecan pie."

"You brought me dinner?"

"Hell, no, I brought you this." He gave Jace a swift punch to the shoulder.

"Ow!"

"That is from Joie," Brett said, going back to his beer. "When you didn't show, she packed up two helpings and a whole pie to go. Said I couldn't have dessert until she knew you'd been fed. The mommy flip was switched and she can't do *anything* until everyone is taken care of now. So take the damn food. Eat it, and fast. Then call Joie and tell her how delicious it was, so she'll give me my dessert before one of us falls asleep."

Jace leaned over and peeked inside the bag. It looked good and smelled even better. Like garlic and grease and his childhood—and home. God, it smelled like home. "Hey, there's a piece of pie missing." He eyed Brett. "Like a half-the-pie piece."

"You're lucky I left you anything. Do you realize my daughter is fed and bathed and fast asleep?" Brett looked at Jace with the eyes of a man who hadn't seen more than four hours of sleep a night in the past nine months. "In her crib, man. Not my bed. Her crib. And instead of me getting my 'taken care of time' I am here. With you."

Brett dropped his head on the bar top with a thunk, and Jace actually felt for the guy. Little Lily Anne McGraw, with her blonde curls and Daddy-do eyes, came out swinging. It was amazing how a kid smaller than a gas can had the ability to wrap a PGA superstar around her pudgy little finger with one coo.

"Yeah, well, I spent most of the day trying to figure out how the hell you got ahold of a '61 Stingray just like Dad's," Jace said, the last few words getting caught in his throat, making it hard to breathe. *Jesus*, he hadn't felt this kind of slow suffocation since he was a teenager. "By this evening I realized it *was* Dad's."

Which seemed impossible. Jace had come to terms a long time ago that the car he'd spent two summers rebuilding with his dad was gone. His dad had sent it off to be re-painted, cherry red like Hattie had wanted, then the fire had happened, and when none of the local shops had a record of the car, he'd considered it lost.

"Are you pissed because I didn't tell you or because it was Dad's?"

Jace wisely didn't respond, taking another pull of his beer instead. Only three people in the world had the ability to read Jace like a book. One was gone, the other wanted him gone, which left his brother Brett. "Where did you find it?"

"When the crew was demoing what was left of the old farmhouse, they found it under the collapsed boathouse," he said, referring to the small garage that had been near the lake on their parents' property.

Last year, Brett had retired from the professional golf circuit to raise a family in Sugar—and he'd chosen to build his home on their parents' property. Kudos to Brett for making himself and his family a home, but it's not what Jace would have done with the property. Not that anyone asked Jace how he felt about it—just like they hadn't asked him how he felt about rebuilding his dad's old car.

"What was it doing in there?" The shed was near the water, and that was the last place to keep that kind of car.

"I don't know, but Hattie's already been telling folks that she's going to ride in it with her new granddaughter for the

Founder's Day Parade. Excited about there being three generations of McGraws," Brett said, making what Jace was
about to say that much worse.

Hattie cruising the Founder's Day Parade in the Stingray
was a family tradition. It started the year she'd married Ray
McGraw and continued with her sitting beside her son, years
later her new daughter-in-law, then again every year each
of the boys had been born. It was a rite of passage in the
McGraw family, her way of making a public declaration that
this was her family. These were her people.

Then, the summer before Jace turned fifteen, they lost his
parents and the car to a fire, and with it the tradition.

"I told Dale I'd be back in Atlanta by Tuesday," Jace said.
"There is no way I can get that fixed before I leave."

"Use some of that vacation time you've been accumu-
lating," Brett said, as though it were that simple. Jace was
secretly relieved that it wasn't. And didn't that make him a
prick. "If Dale knew it was for Hattie, he would give you the
time off."

And here was the second conversation he'd been trying to
postpone. "Dale needs cash to expand the Beverly Hills location, so he's selling the Atlanta shop."

Brett's eyes went wide. "He's selling? Wow, he's been
talking about it for years, but I never thought he'd actually
do it."

"He's selling the Atlanta shop to me."

There was a long, weighted silence as Brett took in exactly what that meant. Jace knew the minute Brett put it
together—Jace buying Dale's shop meant he was finally
putting down roots. A safe two hundred miles from his
family.

Two hundred miles away from watching his nieces grow
up. From his brothers. From the past.

"I'm happy for you, bro. I wish it was closer to us, but I get it," Brett said, and Jace felt his chest relax a little, because if anyone could understand Jace's need for space, it was Brett. Before he'd met Joie, Brett had done his fair share of running, too. Sure, now he was happily living the domesticated dream in Sugar—he deserved it. But even if Jace had thought he deserved that life, it wasn't his dream. Not anymore.

"Does Hattie know?" he asked.

Jace shook his head. "I haven't told anyone yet." *Except Charlotte.* "There is some paperwork I have to get finished up before we can finalize the deal, but Dale is determined to close by the end of October. Which is why I have to head back to Atlanta in a few days."

Even if he couldn't get Charlotte to agree to come, maybe he could get her to sign some kind of official statement saying she wanted the annulment to go forward. Or maybe he'd just throw her in his truck. Either way, he wasn't missing his meeting with the recorder.

"Congratulations, I know this is what you've wanted." When Jace didn't say anything, Brett added, "This is what you want, right?"

"Owning a garage like Atlanta Motorsports?" Jace snorted. "It's been my dream since I was eleven and Dad took me to that car show in Atlanta and I got to sit in that '65 Le Mans Ferrari."

Brett's smile stayed in place, but there was something about that felt forced. "What are you going to do about Dad's car?"

Guilt rolled through him, pinching his skull. "I know a guy who does clean work and owes me a favor."

Brett let out a low whistle and shook his head. "Make sure I'm there when you tell Hattie that *you* aren't doing the work. I'd like to see what that looks like, because ever since she saw that article on you in *Car and Driver* she's been telling anyone who'll listen how you're going to use all those fancy skills to get the Stingray looking like the day she came home."

Last month, *Car and Driver* magazine had done a spread on the top ten up-and-coming exotic car specialists in the country, and Jace had damn near topped the list. It was what had finally convinced Dale to sell. Jace's reputation as an engine specialist had put him in high demand, keeping Dale's shop booked months in advance. When that article was published, offers flooded in and Dale knew that if he didn't sell the shop to Jace then Jace would eventually move on and open his own. He was practically running Dale's as it was.

"I said I'd look at the car," Jace defended, his stomach feeling squirrelly. "I did, and there is no way I can get that fixed before I leave."

"Did I mention she cut out the article and showed it to her knitting group?" Brett said, and, yup, he was going to be sick. Or his heart was going to explode right out of his chest.

Jace came back to Sugar with a clear goal: get in, get a signature, and get back to Atlanta to open his shop. No detours, no pit stops, just a straight shot toward something good. But to let down the woman who had sacrificed so much to make sure he had a loving home after his parents passed? Who could do that?

He sure as hell couldn't, not when he knew what parading through town in that car meant to her.

"Then she hung it on the fridge. It's next to Payton's report card," Brett added, and Jace wanted to punch him.

Chapter 4

⟿

In the South, the difference between voicing a concern and staging a coup wasn't always clear. But Charlotte had faced off with enough entitled debutantes to know the difference. And Darleen Vander, with her couture smile and holier-than-thou pearls, was gunning for Charlotte's job. She wanted to be the regent of the Sugar Peaches. Plain and simple.

Not that it was a surprise. Darleen had been trying to steal Charlotte's thunder ever since pre-K when Charlotte snagged the role of Dorothy in their school's performance of *The Wizard of Oz*—leaving Darleen to play Toto. That the woman was doing it in Charlotte's house, though, in the middle of *her* emergency Sugar Peaches meeting, while helping herself to a second glass of Charlotte's sweet tea, took this from a silly competition to a feud in the making.

Charlotte never backed down from a challenge, and a feud with the Vanders didn't scare her. In fact, she had spent all last night coming up with the perfect plan to secure that endowment, and she needed the Sugar Peaches on her side.

All of them. And losing her cool, even though she was boiling mad inside, wouldn't help win friends and influence the right people.

"The last time this leadership took it upon themselves to buck tradition we ended up with the entire Miss Peach court in cuffs," Darleen said, and a collective gasp filled the room. Because everyone knew that by "leadership" Darleen meant Charlotte.

"Cuffs are a bit of an exaggeration," Charlotte clarified. The girls may have spent the night in the sheriff's drunk tank, but no cuffs were involved. "And it worked out in the end. The skills they learned during their community service were priceless, and the experience gave two of them something to write about on their college entrance essays."

Not to mention Charlotte gained four extra interns for the pediatric ward. As far as she was concerned, it was a good experience had by all.

"And I am not suggesting that we buck tradition." She looked at the over-sixty group since they were the ones who had the hardest time with change, and she let loose a slow, serene smile that had the silvered ladies smiling back. "I want to expand on what our town's founder envisioned. Our community has grown, and our Founder's Day Fair needs to reflect that. This new parade route allows for twice the amount of premiere seating for spectators and more booths."

"We don't need more seating or more booths." Darleen stood, pressed her skirt down, and shifted to face the crowd—transforming Charlotte's meeting into a cohosted event. "What we need is to go one year without some kind of scandal. The Sugar Peaches is one of the most honored and respected societies in town. People look to us with regard to standards and tradition, and we need to remember that as we consider *other* options. Each of these small concessions might lead to an unraveling of what we hold dear."

"No need for the dramatics," Hattie McGraw, the most dramatic woman in town, said. She was also the eldest member of one of the founding families—and Jace's grandma. "The girl's talking about adding three lousy blocks to the parade, not challenging the moral fiber of our organization. Isn't that right, dear?"

Charlotte nodded, feeling the sudden need to obtain her grandmother-in-law's approval. Which was ridiculous since no one knew about her marriage to Jace. "No, no moral fiber being challenged, just the location."

That got a few chuckles, and Charlotte found herself relaxing.

"And I'm not going to pretend that these changes wouldn't help the Grow Clinic, but it also addresses some of the problems we've been facing. Having the parade end at the Medical Center, and having the fair in the parking lot, will give us more space. That way spectators and vendor tents won't be fighting for the same locations. Placing the booths at the end of the route leaves all of Maple Street for the families who want to watch the parade. We can even add ten percent more booths this way. More booths mean more money."

"Well, isn't that interesting," Darleen said with so much sugar in her tone Charlotte felt herself forming a cavity. She held up a copy of the day's agenda. "Since according to this, the next topic of discussion is this year's benefactor for the Founder's Day pot. As our current regent, what organization were you going to propose again?"

Every year, a portion of the profits was allocated to the Miss Peach college scholarship fund and the remaining portion was given to a local organization of the group's choosing. They had yet to officially decide who this year's recipient would be, but everyone in the room knew that Charlotte was going to nominate the Grow Clinic. It had been the center of her campaign platform when she was running for regent. But with the way Darleen was presenting the Grow Clinic now, it would appear as though Charlotte was capitalizing on her position in the Peaches to benefit her charity.

But this was bigger than Charlotte. Bigger than Darleen's grudge. The Grow Clinic was almost there, so close Charlotte could finally see how many kids would benefit, how many local families they could help, and she just needed to convey that to the board.

"I would like to propose to the board that the pot go toward the Grow Clinic."

"Of course she would," Darleen said under her breath, making sure to give her words enough air to filter through the crowd.

The other night at dinner, Charlotte had feared that she would receive some opposition, but now that Darleen was spearheading what was turning out to be an inquisition, Charlotte would be lying if she said she wasn't a little rattled.

"The Sugar Peaches have played a huge hand in the building of the new pediatric ward and clinic. There are hundreds of children, brave children, who need a place like the Grow Clinic to heal. A place that supports and gives them the tools and care they need to transition back into living a full life. These funds will help provide that safe place, ladies. And we are almost there. With this pot we should be ready for business."

"We've almost been there for three years," Darleen argued, and a few women nodded in agreement. "Which is why I propose that, this year, the board consider something different, something that will benefit everyone in the community. Not just the patrons of the Holdens' hospital."

Charlotte wanted to argue that her Grow Clinic would benefit everyone, because helping these kids only made the community that much stronger. But Darleen was already on her soapbox. "Something that, if done right, could cement the Sugar Peaches as the most prestigious and respected organization in the history of the county."

Darleen gave a long, dramatic pause, and Charlotte rolled her eyes. All of the other eyes in the room were too wide with anticipation to do any kind of rolling.

When she had every strand of pearls in the room clicking with excitement, Darleen said, "I propose that we use the pot to resurrect"—she snatched the Golden Peach off the table, which was a sign that she was taking the floor—"Bluebell Hall."

As though on cue, Summer Sheen, Darleen's sister debutante in crime, yanked the covering off an easel holding a poster board to expose a blown-up picture of Bluebell Hall in its prime.

Several gasps escaped, including one from Charlotte herself—because this glossy presentation, with its high-resolution images and symmetrical design, was too slick and professional to be anything other than a premeditated strike on Charlotte—and Darleen had used the perfect weapon.

Bluebell Hall was not only one of the oldest buildings in Sugar County, in its day it was the heart of entertainment for the area until it was destroyed by a tornado that blew through Sugar back in the forties. In fact, John Wilkes Booth had once performed on its stage, accidently stumbling over a warped board and cutting himself with his own sword, an event that was later considered to be a symbol of the hall's patriotism. So when it toppled over on the same day as the attack on Pearl Harbor, the citizens believed it was confirmation of the landmark's patriotic roots, and the Bluebell Hall debacle of 1941 became known as the day that would live in infamy—and the town would never rest until Bluebell Hall was standing proudly again.

Over the years, developers, local organizations, even the town had tried their hand at restoring the old hall, but between pleasing the historical society's stringent guidelines and Bluebell's stubborn pride, every single attempt had ended in bankruptcy—even death. Bluebell Hall was not only the biggest money pit in the history of Sugar County, it was the chupacabra of philanthropy—history, patriotism, and centuries of local folklore.

And everyone in the room knew it.

If the Sugar Peaches could resurrect what no male organization had been able to do, they would gain a new respect in the eyes of the town. If they failed, Charlotte would be seen as the only Peach regent on record to ruin the Miss Peach pageant *and* fail old Blue herself.

"I think that is a great idea," Charlotte said diplomatically. "But I believe that a project that ambitious, that means so much to the town, would be risky to jump into without really coming up with a plan." Because once they made the announcement, there would be no going back.

"Maybe it's just too ambitious for the current leadership," Darleen challenged, then leaned in so that only Charlotte could hear her. "Or maybe you're just scared because you are one little scandal from being *im*-peached."

Charlotte opened her mouth to speak, then thought back to yesterday at Kiss My Glass and swallowed hard. Surely, the reemergence of a secret husband wasn't scandal material. It wasn't as if she'd be married to him forever—that dream had sailed a long time ago, and the disappointment barely even bothered her at all anymore.

She needed this annulment to happen and hoped beyond hope that its finality would be the closure she needed to finally let go and move on. She just didn't think she could make it happen in Jace's time frame. After the fair she'd be more capable of finding the time and, more importantly, the emotional capacity to go to Atlanta.

One look at Darleen, though, and she knew that if she didn't get that annulment, and soon, it might turn into the biggest news to hit Sugar County since, well…since the entire Miss Peach court was arrested for B&E and public intoxication of a minor.

* * *

The next morning, Jace hadn't even gotten out of his car, and already he knew he'd made a mistake. Then again, whenever it came to Charlotte, mistakes seemed to be his specialty.

When she had called earlier, asking him to swing by on his way out of town, he'd honestly assumed it was to check on the status of her car—or ask for a ride to work. But one look at her sitting on the porch swing with her well-manicured hair, hoity-toity dress, and PhD heels and Jace knew that she was finally going to give him what he wanted.

"Morning, Dr. Holden," he said, unfolding himself from the car.

"You're late." Charlotte stood and swished her way down the steps toward him. No *good morning,* no *thanks for coming,* just a *you're late* as though they had plans, as though he'd disappointed her again.

"Sorry," he said coolly, tapping the face of his watch. "Forgot to set it to Charlotte Standard Time."

She stopped a few feet from him, and he could see the hesitation in her expression. Hesitation and something else. Something that looked an awful lot like vulnerability. Oh, there was a good portion of irritation and hostility glaring at him through those baby blues, but behind it all was definitely vulnerability. Interesting.

"You're the one who said we had to go to Atlanta today."

"I believe you told me you were too busy to make the time," he said, not sure how he was going to handle six hours in an enclosed space with her. Just standing downwind taking in her floral scent was making him hard.

"I changed my mind."

Jace looked at her for a long moment, then laughed. She was serious.

"Darling, you don't change your mind. Ever." Charlotte Holden might be a Southern belle, but her Kevlar wall of stubbornness could rival a Southern granny's—and having been raised by the most mule-headed granny in the world, that was saying a lot. Oh, he believed that Charlotte had changed her mind, he just didn't know why. "So what happened with your debutante sisters yesterday that has you desperate enough to call me?"

"Sugar Peaches," she corrected. "And since when do you keep up on Sugar gossip?"

"Since you started calling yourself a Sugar Peach. I mean, weren't the Peaches your mom's thing?"

Charlotte had once confided in him that she moved to Atlanta to escape the pressure of following in her mother's footsteps. The pageants and parties and social ladder climbing were Babette's dream for Charlotte. Charlotte's dream was to save lives—and she was a master at it.

"Well, it's my thing now," she said, and he couldn't help but notice the resignation in her voice. He wanted to know what else had changed, then realized it didn't matter anymore. "And that means I have to be back as soon as possible. Founder's Day is only three weeks off, and I have a lot to do."

"Yeah, me too." He had to get an annulment, convince his buddy to fix Hattie's car, *and* secure that loan before Dale pulled his offer.

"Good, because as the current regent of the Sugar Peaches it falls to me to plan the Founder's Day Fair, so this trip needs to be a quickie," she said, her bossy, take-charge tone making him smile.

"Quickies aren't really my specialty," he said. "But who am I to argue with a lady?"

"Easy and discreet, Jace. The last thing I need right now is to explain this to my parents," she clarified as though he was slow, as though he didn't know just how anxious she was to put the past behind them. Which shouldn't have pissed him off, because that was what he wanted, too. But it did.

"Easy and discreet? Kind of like our marriage?" he mused.

She looked at him for a long moment and then slowly shook her head. "Nothing about our marriage was easy, Jace," she said, and the absolute certainty in her voice made him want to prove her wrong.

"There was one easy thing between us," Jace said, stepping into her and closing the distance, trapping her between the car and his body. He reached behind her neck, crushed his mouth to hers, and kissed the hell out of her.

Only one touch, and she was kissing him back. No hesitation, no second-guessing, just—*pow*—debutante to seductress. *Not interested* to *tongue down his throat* in two seconds flat.

And holy fucking God, it was perfect. The way she felt, the way she tasted, the way she crawled up his body and demanded more...How had he forgotten this side of her?

Charlotte hadn't accidently stumbled and caught herself on his mouth, which was the only way Jace would have imagined this miracle taking place even a day ago. No, Charlotte Holden, the woman who had done her best to avoid him for the past four years, was pressing her elegant, bombshell body so firmly against him she couldn't possibly get any closer. And her hands? Yeah, those were wrapped around his middle, making these insane little strokes under his shirt.

His hands? They didn't waste a minute, working their way around to cup her ass—and what a spectacular ass she had. Soft, round, and custom-made for him.

Her mouth, that was made for him, too, and the way she was melding it to his had him wondering what the hell he was doing.

That insane pull between them, which he'd convinced himself didn't exist, wasn't only burning a hole through his clothes—and his mission—it also wasn't one-sided. Which told him that he should a) back the hell up, and b) immediately cancel this field trip they had planned. Before things got crazy.

But then she made this sexy little sound in the back of her throat—the one that used to drive him batshit crazy, that still drove him batshit crazy—and he was a goner.

So he deepened the kiss, because why the hell not? Charlotte had her prim and proper hands all over him, and he was certain that this was the best kiss he'd ever had. Hot and needy and raw and so damn desperate it was like driving down the track at three hundred miles per hour with no breaks.

Then he realized that this was not only the best kiss ever

but probably also their last kiss ever, and he slowly pulled back, tugging her lower lip between his teeth as long as he could until the connection finally broke. And damn, he wished he hadn't stopped.

That one second of uncharged air was all Charlotte needed. Sure, she was breathing heavily, and her gaze was dazed and confused. A mirror image of his own. But within a split second her eyes frosted over and that unflinching fortitude was back.

Not that he was fooled. Jace knew that they had chemistry, remembered how electric they were together, but what had arched between them just now floored him. And it had floored her, too.

Charlotte cleared her throat. "This changes nothing."

Jace lowered his gaze to her hands, which were resting on the buckle of his belt. "Oh, it changes something."

Charlotte jerked her hands back and stuffed them into the pockets of her dress. "I go with you to Atlanta, we get the annulment straightened out, then you leave. That's the plan."

He knew the plan, had come up with it himself. Yet after that kiss he was reconsidering if there weren't a few road stops that were missing. Like another mind-blowing kiss with his wife.

Charlotte stepped back—way back—putting a good *even if hell freezes over* distance between them. "If this is going to work, then we have to set some guidelines."

"Sugar, the only lines in my world are at the end of a track," Jace said, tipping the bill of his FERRARI PIT CREW ball cap. "And the guy who crosses them the most in the least amount of time wins."

She ignored this and held up a finger. He was surprised that it wasn't her middle one. "First rule. No kissing."

He leaned a hip against the door of his car and tsked.

"Yeah, we already broke that one, so that rule doesn't work for me."

"Too bad. Second rule." There went another finger. Long and sleek and elegant—and about two seconds ago they'd been two inches from dropping him into third. "No touching—"

"Please refer to my earlier statement," he argued.

"—no flirting, and absolutely no talk of the past."

There was no point in arguing the last one. The last place he wanted to revisit with this woman was the past.

"Oh," she said, snatching his keys right out of his hand. "And I get to drive."

"There are too many horses under that hood for you to handle." He snatched them back, holding them out of reach to be safe.

"You don't know what I can handle, Jace," she said, and he knew that one would leave a mark. Charlotte might look like a debutante, and she was persuasive as hell, but when she couldn't negotiate herself into the winning chair, she fought dirty. And that comment was below the belt, probably only because it was true.

"Yeah, well, the no-touching rule still extends to my keys," he clarified.

"You can't extend a rule that you rejected."

"Are you saying that the touching rule is out of play?"

"What?" She smacked his chest and he flexed a pec. She jerked her hand back. "No!"

Jace leaned in, and in that tone that usually had women melting like putty said, "You sure? Because you said no, then groped me, so I was a little confused." When she didn't even blink, he flashed his trademark grin, the one that had been passed down from McGraw father to McGraw son. "Then I drive."

He gave her a quick pat on the ass and walked toward the passenger door. Opening it like the gentleman his mama raised him to be.

Charlotte stood there for a long, tense moment before releasing the huff to end all huffs and stomped over to the car. "Fine, but I get to pick the station." She looked at his car, sleek and muscled and zero to speed-of-light in two seconds flat. Then she took in his backseat, custom leather that was butter soft and built to impress, and smiled.

Her smile was just wicked enough to have him wondering what ideas Charlotte had with regard to the backseat. And that got him thinking what the two of them could do in that backseat—what they'd already done a time or two. And suddenly all of the possibilities loomed in front of him.

All he had to do was lean in for the kiss and get this party in motion. Within minutes, maybe even seconds, he could have them both sprawled out in the back—although he was a big guy and it was a tight space, he could manage—and he could remind her what else was easy between them.

The memories had a wicked smile of his own forming.

"No staring," she said. "Or smiling like that."

"Darlin', those weren't in the agreed-upon rules."

"Fine, stare all you want," she said, climbing into the passenger seat. "But that smile counts as flirting, and you know it."

He did. Which is why he released the double dimples her way before walking around the back of the car and sliding behind the wheel. He started the car and noticed that Charlotte was turning her body to look out the window, avoiding eye contact. Fine with him, since the twisty motion she was executing caused her dress to ride up, showing off a good three inches of creamy white skin.

He looked his fill, then started the car and let it idle for a few minutes while he flipped through the stations.

"What are you doing?" she asked.

"Finding some mood music," he said, stopping on a smooth, sexy jazz station.

"Mood music?"

He looked over at her and smiled. "You never said anything about fantasizing on that extensive list of yours." Then he dropped the car into gear and gunned it.

Chapter 5

⌐

The county recorder was out sick.

Of course. Because of all the days for the one person who could fix this mess to be sick, it had to be today.

"But we had an appointment," Charlotte said.

Jace took one look at the OUT OF OFFICE sign, gave an unfazed shrug, and started walking toward the exit to go God knew where. That was it, one little unexpected hardship and he was already walking away, leaving her to figure it out. "Wait, you're really leaving?"

Jace stopped to look around. He looked at the security guard standing by the metal detector, at the endless row of people in the Social Security line that stretched on forever, at the very unwelcoming woman in the I HEART JOHNSON T-shirt who sat behind the welcome counter, then back at Charlotte. "Oh, are you talking to me?"

Heat flooded her cheeks at his comment. Charlotte had feigned sleep for close to two hours in the car. She couldn't remember the last time she had worked so hard to ignore someone. Not that Jace complained. Nope, he just turned up the radio, took a peek at her thighs, and then grinned, the big jerk.

Every time he'd look her way, she'd pretended to be asleep. But the moments when he was concentrating on the road gave her the chance to look at him, really look at him for the first time since he'd come home without the fear of being caught breaking her "no staring" rule.

Only looking led to thinking. About how good those tattoos looked peeking out from under that soft shirt. About his incredible, sculpted, "I lift car engines out by hand" chest. Even worse, thinking with that "mood music," as he called it, led to fantasizing. About him. That kiss. And what might have happened after that kiss if he hadn't pulled back.

After four years of missing him, Charlotte had earned a PhD in fantasies, with an emphasis in creativity—especially when it came to a tattooed army of one bad boy. But that kiss had been seven thousand times better than any fantasy she'd ever conjured.

Crapcrapcrap, she still wanted him. Despite every logical reason for her to hate him, she still wanted him. If not, she wouldn't have kissed him back. Right?

At least not the way she did—as though she'd been starved for his touch. God, how embarrassing was that? One little smooch, which was his way of proving a point, and she'd caved. Forgotten that he'd walked away from them. Broken his vows. And her heart.

Forgot that he'd broken her world.

Which made her the biggest loser in the history of failed marriages. Because beneath all of the hurt and heartache, Charlotte still wanted him.

Him. Jace McGraw.

Instead of being wildly attracted to some normal suit type who lived in Sugar and wanted to get married and have a litter of kids, it was the mysterious, tattooed engine specialist who also specialized in taking it from "I do" to "outta here" in two-point-two seconds that flipped her switch.

A humiliating fact that she'd rather die than admit. Jace hadn't just been her husband, he'd been her everything, and if she wasn't careful he could easily become that again.

And that terrified Charlotte.

She'd managed to fool her entire family for the past four years, she reminded herself. She could manage four hours with Jace.

If she tried really hard.

"You know what?" Her gaze went to the woman behind the welcome counter, who was managing her cell, Facebook, and Instagram all while sucking down a Slurpee. "I'll handle this."

She'd handled a hell of a lot more in the past few years without him.

Charlotte waited patiently for Val, at least that was what her name tag said, to finish her text. Only Val must have been transcribing the Bible because her fingers never once left her phone.

"Excuse me," Charlotte finally said, going for sweet. "I was hoping you could help me."

Val had spiky orange hair, a barbell jammed through her nose, and Slurpee-red lips. She jabbed her finger at the OUT TO LUNCH sign and then went back to her cell. If Charlotte were to hire a gatekeeper she'd hire Val. It would take a master to sweet-talk or BS their way around her.

Good thing Charlotte aced the BS portion of med school.

"Right. And I am so sorry to interrupt your meal, but we are in a time crunch, and I was hoping you could help."

Val set her phone on the desk and leaned forward—way forward. "Then we're both sorry, because I can't answer your question." Then she speared Charlotte with a look that would have had most women in tears. But Charlotte wasn't most women. And she didn't do tears. She might be a former Miss Peach, but her backbone was all steel magnolia. Oh, Charlotte always handled herself with class and decorum, and a friendly smile always helped things along, but she absolutely did not like to take no for an answer.

And after her week, she wasn't going to start now.

"You're the welcome desk," Charlotte joked. "Besides, you don't even know what I was going to ask."

"Don't need to," Val said, leaning back in her chair, taking a long slurp. "Now, if you ask me in, say, thirty minutes, when my lunch break is over, I might have a different answer for you."

"It's just a quick question."

"Great, then it will be a quick answer," Val said, putting down her Slurpee to pick up her cell. She started clicking away. "In thirty minutes."

"We had an appointment with the county recorder ten minutes ago. And it is a really important appointment."

Val paused in writing her post, which no doubt said something derogatory about the demanding customers she had to deal with, to look up at Charlotte. "The county recorder is out today. She comes back tomorrow."

To an onlooker it would seem as if Welcome Gal Val was full of cheery customer service, but her tone was pure *eat shit and choke on it.*

Charlotte ignored this and flashed a friendly smile, instead choosing to focus on the fact that they were headed in the right direction. Obtaining information. "Unfortunately, tomorrow doesn't work, and I have driven three hours and taken a day off work to make this meeting. So is there anyone else who can help me? Today? Please?"

Val picked up her Slurpee again. "No."

Knowing that sometimes even the most sour grapes just needed a little sugar, Charlotte asked, "Was that a 'No, there is no one else who can help me?' Or a 'No, because it is still your lunch break?' "

Val smiled back. Reached her hand forward and pinched the edge of the plastic partition—only to slam it shut, nearly taking off the tip of Charlotte's finger.

Slurrrrp.

Charlotte took a fortifying breath, then reached into her purse and pulled out her grandfather's business card and slid it under the partition as though it were an FBI badge. "I hoped it wouldn't come to this, but my grandfather is the honorable Judge Holden of District 4. And I need to speak with the county recorder in regard to a time-sensitive matter, so if you could give me a moment of your day to direct me to someone else who can help me, that would be much appreciated."

Any second that partition would slide back open, because when someone in the South said they were related to Hang-'em-High Holden, people got right neighborly.

As expected, the partition opened and Val slid the card back across the counter. Then—

Slurrrrp. Slurrrrp. Slurrrrp.

Charlotte felt her friendly smile fade and feared that Val was one slurp shy of tossing her Slurpee in Charlotte's face. Jace must have noticed, too, because he flashed that grin of his, the one with the double dimples, as if he thought that was going to work on Miss Tude. Then he rested his forearms leisurely on the counter top, and Charlotte couldn't help but notice the way his biceps budged at the motion. "Val. That's a pretty name. Is that short for Valerie?"

And to Charlotte's surprise and irritation, it worked. Val smiled, shy and giddy, Jace's biceps not going unnoticed. "Valentine," she said. "I was named after my grandfather."

"Small world." His drawl got thicker and Val's eyes got wider. Charlotte threw up in her mouth a little. "I was named after my grandpa, too."

He reached out his hand and Val leaned forward to take it. "Jace McGraw."

"Valentine Sharp." She looked Jace up and down, not even bothering to hide that she was checking the man out in front of his wife. Granted neither of them had a ring on, but still, they had walked in together. "You a Johnson fan?"

Talk about a personal question, Charlotte thought, but Jace tipped his hat in Val's direction and whispered in that bedroom voice of his, the one that used to have her melting, "What do you think?"

Oh, for God's sake. "Jace is more of a boob man," Charlotte said. "Now that that is cleared up, how about our appointment?" Because she had enough to deal with without adding another four-hour car ride with Jace to her calendar.

Jace looked at her and grinned. Big and smug and she knew he was laughing at her. "Actually, I'm more of an Earnhardt fan, but I know Jimmie. Used to be on his crew."

"Omigod," Val said in one big screech. "Jimmy Johnson? Are you serious?"

"Do you think I'd lie about NASCAR?" he asked, and Val shook her head, mesmerized by Jace's charm.

Charlotte didn't blame the girl. She's been that young, impressionable woman before, too. Only she knew better now. At least her heart did. She wasn't so sure about her body.

"I work on exotics now," Jace went on. "But I still have a few friends in NASCAR. I bet I could make some calls and see if I can get you and Grandpa Valentine some seats at this week's race." Jace leaned in, getting up close and personal with Val, those worn Levi's stretching at the seam across his incredible butt, and Charlotte knew what was about to happen. He was going to use his eyes, those flirty baby blues, to land them an appointment. "I could drop them off tomorrow when I set up that new meeting with the recorder."

And even though Charlotte couldn't see his face, she knew the moment he unleashed the McGraw wink on her: Val's smile went full watt. So did that blush she'd die if she knew she was sporting.

Val looked around and lowered her voice. "I shouldn't be telling you this, but Elvina Larson is the county recorder. Her schedule is booked until next week, but she comes in a half hour early every morning so she can drink her coffee without her kids driving her nuts. If you show up early with chocolate doughnuts and an extra set of tickets, I bet she'd see you."

"Chocolate doughnuts, four tickets, and a cherry super-gulp. Got it," Jace said, laying it on so heavy Charlotte could actually hear Val's heart flutter. "See you tomorrow, Valentine."

Then with one last wink he took Charlotte by the elbow, and before she could remind him that tomorrow didn't work for her, that she couldn't last that long, he leaned and whispered against her ear, "And for the record, Charlie, I'm not a boob kind of guy. I'm a you kind of guy."

And damned if Charlotte didn't feel a little flutter of her own.

* * *

"Twenty-four hours," Charlotte said, taking a seat on the hotel bed because her stomach gave that familiar little twist she hated. If this conversation went anything like the one she'd had only in the car, she'd need to find a bar—one that served by the shot. "I am only asking for twenty-four hours."

Her dad sighed into the phone as if she'd asked him to cure cancer, when in fact she was only asking him to reschedule the call with Mercy Alliance, *her* call with Mercy Alliance, for tomorrow afternoon instead of today.

"Tipton was expecting a virtual tour *today*. His board is expecting it *today*, Charlotte." She closed her eyes and swallowed past the thickness in her throat. She hated when her dad said her name that way, as if he believed her name directly translated into disappointment. "I meant what I said to Tipton, Sugar Medical was built on dignity and pride," Reginald said. "Which means we uphold our obligations."

"I know, and I'm sorry, but like I said, something important came up," she said, suddenly feeling like a little girl asking her daddy for permission, instead of the capable and competent head of pediatrics she'd become.

"Do you want me to explain to a group of men who are considering investing their money and reputation in our family that my daughter's something was more important than this meeting?"

Charlotte silently nodded and blinked several times against the choking burn. That was exactly what she wanted. For her dad to come through the phone. To hold her and tell her everything would be okay. That she wasn't a complete disappointment and that this weird, lingering restlessness that she didn't even realize she had until Jace came home would pass.

But he couldn't. Reginald hadn't bothered to ask Charlotte what was so important that she had asked Ben to pick up her patients today. Ben knew something was wrong, because he knew that Charlotte would never skip out of responsibilities unless she had a good reason. A really, really good reason.

And she did. Charlotte needed today to go smoothly so badly that she'd nearly lost it when Jace told her it would be smarter to stay in Atlanta overnight than to have to drive back again tomorrow. And he was right, but Charlotte couldn't get past the fact that she would have to make it through an entire night sleeping with only a wall between them. She'd have to put off her annulment once again and act like she wasn't slowly losing it.

Part of her had called her dad instead of rescheduling with Mercy Alliance directly, hoping he'd ask what was wrong, what he could do to help. And who knows, Charlotte might have even told him the truth. Because after all these years, she was still as confused as the day Jace asked for an annulment, and she still wanted perspective, someone to talk it through with her. Be the voice of reason.

But her father hadn't even cared. And if she let him hijack her meeting again, it would be like telling him that that was okay. That she was open to being ignored and walked over. That he was right, and she was a silly little girl with silly little problems.

A disappointment.

"You know what, Dad? I have put the last three years into making this center a reality. I know more about the project and Mercy Alliance than anyone else. This is my project, and I'd like to close this deal. All I'm asking is to see if we can look into pushing the call to tomorrow."

"And I am the director, and tomorrow doesn't work for me."

That twist in her stomach got worse, making it hard to

breathe, because Charlotte had heard that statement so many times in her life, most recently from her own mouth. And she'd said it to the person who was actually giving her the chance to finally get closure on the past. And it didn't just hurt, it was the kind of sting that got worse with time.

The realization weighed heavily in her chest, so heavily she lay back on the bed and closed her eyes. She had spent the entire afternoon ignoring the one man she'd vowed to love for eternity.

Proving she was more like her father than she thought.

* * *

A couple hours later, Jace stood at far corner of the bar with a bag of women's lotions and potions in his hand, telling himself that this wasn't his problem and to go back to the hotel room. Due to the Vegas-style decor, lack of plasma screens, and ridiculous pricing, the hotel bar was completely empty.

Except for Charlotte.

Jace wasn't sure how to handle the situation, or if he should handle it at all. Charlotte had made it more than clear she wasn't interested in his company, yet she'd been sitting at the bar picking at a basket of fries for what had to be the better part of the evening. Jace had first spotted her during happy hour when he'd come down to grab a cold one and maybe some wings. Sensing he was the last person she'd want to see, he'd driven into town to pick up dinner and some personal items they'd need for tomorrow.

Now it was past dinnertime and she was still there in the same dress with the hundred little buttons trailing down the front that he'd love to undo—one by one. Ever so slowly.

Then he noticed the sunken posture and the empty ice-cream bowls and wanted to hug her. As if that wasn't a train wreck in the making. So he settled on buying her a drink.

"Two Dirty Girl Scouts and a pint of whatever you have on tap," he said to the bartender when he reached the bar.

Charlotte didn't look up, didn't offer him a seat, didn't even make some comment about his ridiculous drink order. On the plus side, she didn't tell him to go fuck himself, either. So he'd take it.

Still standing, he extended the paper bag. "I stopped by the drugstore. Picked up a few things I figured you might need."

Charlotte looked up at the bag and eyed it skeptically, then eyed him skeptically, as if waiting to see what the catch was. Oddly enough, right then, Jace didn't have any ulterior motives.

"You going to take this?" he asked, still holding the bag.

"Does it contain condoms, lube, a G-string, or something else you think would be funny?" she asked.

"Nope, just a toothbrush, hair spray, and a T-shirt to sleep in. The essentials," he said, making a mental note to swap out her LOOK AT THEM PEACHES tee for the standard black one he'd gotten himself.

"Nothing cute to break the tension?"

"Does a box of Peppermint Patties count?"

"Thank you," she said, snatching the bag without hesitation, but her voice sounded tired. The kind of bone-deep tired that comes from years of disappointment.

The bartender returned with his order. Jace dropped a couple of bills down and slid one of the shots in front of Charlotte, then picked up the other and raised it. "To Peppermint Patties."

She paused, clearly weighing the cost of sharing a drink with him. "It's just a drink, Charlie."

She picked up the shot glass and took a tentative sniff, watching him over the rim the entire time. "It smells like ice cream."

"Mint chip ice cream." Her second favorite addiction. "You looked like you could use something a little stronger than vanilla."

She nodded gently, then to his utter horror, her expression went from blank uncertainty to something a hell of a lot rawer. She was looking at him as if she didn't know how to handle the fact that he'd paid enough attention to know her favorites. Which turned his stomach, because knowing he'd hurt her when he left was one thing, seeing that hurt with his own eyes broke something deep inside of him.

"Shitty day?" he asked.

"I don't want to talk about it," she said quietly.

"If you don't, it will just build up, and then you'll start missing sleep and your eyes will get all puffy," he said. "You hate puffy eyes."

"I don't want to talk about it with you," she clarified, and, man, if she could have said one thing guaranteed to leave marks, that was it. "At least not right now, anyway."

Jace hadn't come back to Sugar to make her life more difficult or dredge up the past, he'd come to finally set her free. To set them both free. And, okay, he'd come back to see her one last time before he officially put down roots in a town that wasn't home, in a house that wasn't theirs. But it wasn't going as planned. He never expected his heart to feel this heavy.

Maybe he had been wrong before. Maybe in order to move on they had to first go back. Clear the air so all of the pain and disappointment would disappear and the memories wouldn't hurt so bad.

"Maybe now is the perfect time," he offered. "We've been

skating around things for four years, and tomorrow might be too late."

"I know," she said, sounding more upset and, *okay*, back to looking like she was about two seconds away from tears.

"How about just one drink," he suggested, because suddenly he wasn't all that far from tears himself, which made not an ounce of sense. "We drink, we talk, we try to figure things out, and when the glasses are empty you can make the call to continue talking or go to bed. No pressure."

"All right." She picked up the shot. "To Peppermint Patties." Then the woman who was notorious for leisurely sipping her Baptist cocktail with her pinkie in the air threw back the entire shot in one swallow.

With a big gasp, she went to slam the shot down, right as he slid her second glass in front of her. She blinked, no doubt wondering if she was already seeing double. "What's this?"

"Plan B," he said. "In case you tried to do, well, exactly what you did." He took a pull of his beer. "And I'd go slow with that second one. They might be sweet, but they don't call them dirty for fun."

Chapter 6

Y ou're drinking too slowly," Charlotte chastised, taking dainty sips of the coffee she'd ordered after she polished off shot number two. It wasn't helping. Jace sat there, so close their knees brushed every time she so much as moved, looking sexier by the second while he slowly spun his glass between his oh-so-capable hands.

"And you're stalling. Again."

Charlotte raised her gaze to meet his, and what she saw there had her mouth going dry. Genuine interest. In every word she said. "At least take a sip. And stop spinning the cup, it's driving me nuts."

"Deal. As long as you finish the story about your dad."

"That was really it," she said. "Before we hung up I finally got him to agree to ask if moving the virtual tour would be an issue, then he never called back. My guess is it happened without me."

"I'm sorry that coming here put you in that position," Jace said, and she could tell he meant it.

"That's okay, I think it would have happened regardless," she admitted. "Even though I have sacrificed everything for this project, I don't think he sees what I bring to the table."

"Then your dad is an idiot," he said.

"I don't know," she lied, because she did know. Her dad couldn't see past his own ego to realize how much Charlotte had put into the hospital's expansion. They had a long habit of him completely discounting her achievements and Charlotte smiling through the disappointment and putting the needs of the hospital above her feelings.

In fact, defending her family was so ingrained that she found herself saying, "It was just a virtual tour, and my dad really is good at what he does. And this endowment will be huge for the hospital."

"You're really good at what you do, Charlie," he said quietly, resting his hand on hers in a show of support. "And this endowment is huge for *you*."

Panic bubbled up inside, tightening around her chest, because somehow he knew, saw what everyone else overlooked. Gaining this endowment wasn't just huge, it was everything. Those four walls and the people inside them represented who she was and, more importantly, who she aspired to be. Most people just saw the building, patients in need, the fancy medical equipment. But someone who knew what to look for, who took the time to look deeper, would see that this center was all she had.

Her panic must have shown because his smile softened, to the point that it was hard to breathe. "This Grow Clinic has been your dream since grad school, when you interned for the sports medicine pediatrician and helped that kid take back his life."

Will Harper had been eleven years old when he lost the use of his legs and with it his sense of self. Insurance covered the surgery and physical therapy, even the new wheelchair ramp to his house, but it didn't provide any solutions for how he was supposed to fit back into a life that didn't fit his new body. That's when his mom brought him to the center in Atlanta, and through experimental techniques and a lot of love and support and hard work, Will finally found his place, found a way to adapt and excel and, most importantly, connect with others. The first time Charlotte saw him race in a local marathon, she knew she'd found her calling.

That Jace remembered was touching.

"It's your way of giving kids the tools they need to really live life. The way they want to. Not limited by a wheelchair, or a doctor, or preconceived ideas." *Or their parents*, went unsaid but hung between them, thick and real. "The center gives them the freedom to live the life they dream of and the life they deserve. But you, Charlie," he interlaced their fingers, "with you, they gain the courage to live it. Your dad needs to stop, for just one second, and really see what you bring to the table."

A familiar tenderness washed through her. Jace had always been the one person Charlotte couldn't hide from. He had this way about him, an intensity, that when focused had the ability to cut through her facade and fears and speak to what was important, her truth. He got her in a way that no one in her life ever had, and he gave her the courage to live life without apology. With Jace she had always felt as though she was wanted. As though she was enough.

He was perfect in every way except for the one that mattered most.

"If I bring so much to the table then why do I find myself setting it for a party of one?" the alcohol asked, because there was no way sans the shots that those words would have ever left her mouth. Oh, she thought about them every day, but never dared voice them.

Until now.

"I don't know." His hand rested on her knee, then slowly moved up, just an inch, but enough to tease under the hem of her skirt, and a deep pulsing started in her core. "Why aren't you seeing someone?"

There were a lot of reasons she could give, work being the most common excuse she'd used in the past. But she was tired of being bound to misery by excuses. "I don't know, Jace, the last time I opened myself up to someone I thought really *knew* and *loved* me, he bolted." Her stomach hurt. "Can we talk about something else?"

"Aw, Charlie," he whispered, and the flare of hurt in his eyes made her stomach twist.

"Don't *Aw Charlie* me with those bedroom eyes of yours. You walked out, Jace. You promised to love me forever, no matter what, and you walked out. It didn't go how you wanted, and you just left."

The first time Jace had talked about leaving, she'd thought he'd just been reacting to the news that a story was going to run on him assaulting the golden boy of NASCAR. But the next morning she'd woken up alone, next to a stack of papers resting on his pillow with one little sticky note that said sorry and another pointing to where she needed to sign as though he wasn't asking her to annul her happiness. That was it, one minute she was married to the man of her dreams, talking about kids and the future, their future. And the next she was signing on the dotted line as if her entire world wasn't ending.

The worst part was that it hadn't ended. She had to pick up the pieces and move on, without Jace. With no closure.

With the knowledge that no one out there loved her for exactly who she was.

"I walked out because I knew that staying would ruin your life, too," he admitted. "That story was going to blow up, and Dylan fucking McAdams was talking about suing, and you had worked so hard to get that job at Atlanta Memorial, I didn't want you to lose out on it because of me."

"I quit that job anyway," she reminded him, her frustration as sharp as it was four years ago. Less than a year after he left, she resigned when she realized she couldn't stay in Atlanta.

Giving up that job and admitting it was over, that he wasn't coming back, had been hard. Going home and pretending as if their marriage had never happened had been harder. But she'd done it, she'd found some kind of peace in her job, and when that wasn't enough she went after her dream, throwing her heart into the Grow Clinic.

But even though she'd accomplished what she'd set out to do, she was lonely. So lonely at night when she came home that sometimes it was easier to go to bed than listen to an empty house settle in for the night.

"That job meant a lot to me, but you meant more," she admitted quietly. "I would have walked away from everything if it meant you would have stayed."

"You hadn't even told your family and friends about us because you were so scared of the drama it would cause," he said, the anger in his voice clear. "How were you going to handle explaining to them or your new boss that, oh, yeah, my husband, the one I never told you about, might be sued for assault? Oh, and the prick suing is some bigwig so it's going to be everywhere."

"But he didn't sue. It was all for nothing."

"Only because Brett paid him off. Settled it quietly out

of court." Something that she knew bugged him. Jace was too stubborn to admit he needed help, which was the core of all of their problems. He was so set on taking care of things himself that he didn't stop and talk things through. He just made what he considered was the right decision and went with it, never realizing that love was about partnership, facing the world together.

"And when Brett came to the rescue, did you tell him about us?"

"Why? So he could know that I'd lost yet another person I loved?" Jace said, removing his hand from her thigh. Then he looked down as though he hadn't meant to say that, and Charlotte's heart swelled from the honesty in his statement and then broke all over for him. It broke for the boy who believed he killed his parents, and for the man who didn't believe he deserved to be loved. That he deserved her.

Charlotte reached out and cupped his face, tipping it until there was nowhere to look but at her. "I never told my parents about you because I wanted you all to myself. For just a little while. You were *my* choice, Jace. The one thing in the world I wanted enough to go after on my own. And I didn't want my parents to weigh in, not yet."

"And I didn't want you to have to defend me to everyone."

"But that was *your* choice." She wanted to make this clear. After all, he didn't lose her, he'd left her. "You chose to handle it on your own and then made my choice for me, deciding what I could or couldn't handle. Because I would have chosen to stay by your side. I would have chosen us."

Jace was quiet for a long, painful moment as his hand came up to tangle with hers. "You could still choose us."

Charlotte wanted to cry for all they'd lost. Because the "us" that she would have fought for, would have stood against the world to protect, was gone. "You are opening your dream garage in Atlanta, the Grow Clinic is finally happening, and come tomorrow there will be no us, Jace."

"Maybe." Jace tugged her hand until she stood, then slowly drew her closer until she hit the edge of his bar stool, his legs on either side of her. "But there's still tonight."

Four words, and Charlotte felt her resolve crumble, felt herself lean into his offer and taste his lips, because she knew that no matter how hard she wanted to, she couldn't change the past. Neither of them could. But fate was giving them a second chance to do what they should have done all those years ago.

Tonight she wanted her good-bye.

* * *

Jace McGraw: luckiest son of a bitch to walk the earth. That was what his next tattoo was going to read. Because never in a million years would he have imagined a reality in which Charlotte didn't hate him. In fact, it appeared as though she still liked him—a lot.

It took about three seconds and a shot of Naughty Girl Scout for it to register that while Jace sat there on a vinyl bar stool, beneath a blinking neon Lone Star sign, Charlotte Holden, queen of discreet, was kissing him.

It wasn't the casual peck or the simple brushing of lips that one might expect to see two people exchange in such a public forum. Nope, it was a hot, openmouthed, hand-in-his-hair, real fireworks and fuck-you kind of display. It was a kiss to end all kisses, a kiss that left no room or question of exactly where this would lead.

And Jace decided right then, in that hotel bar, that when it came to this woman, she could lead him wherever the hell she wanted. No questions asked.

All this time he'd been terrified that addressing their past would hurt too much. Convinced himself that avoiding the hard conversations, loving her from afar, was for the best. Man, was he wrong. Because nothing could be better than this.

Well, okay, he amended as she slanted her mouth so that he could nip and tease at that lower lip of hers, there was one thing. But he was pretty sure by the way her fingers trailed down his chest to fiddle with his belt buckle that this was just the prequalifier. The real race, the one with the waving flags and exploding champagne bottles he'd been dreaming about since that last night, when he'd stayed up to watch her sleep, memorizing every detail about her, if that race happened it would be a direct result of him instigating the conversation he'd been so adamant to avoid.

Hell, if this was the result of talking it out, Jace was going to take a class on how to converse like a pro, because this was, by far, the best conversation he'd ever had. Deep, intense, passionate, a real give-and-take kind of situation.

There was a lot of heat—and a whole hell of a lot of emotion. Emotions that he'd worked hard to hide. And it was coming from both sides, because Charlotte was pressing closer, burrowing into him as if she, too, couldn't stand the distance a second longer.

He could feel her pulse pounding as he kissed down her neck, then her hands got creative, sliding down his zipper to cup him gently, then not so gently, then *holy shit* she took one more lap over the hard ridge, this time looking for the finish line in his pants.

They were in a bar, a freaking public bar. Sure, there was only the bartender and a single television playing *Dancing with the Stars* in the background, but Charlotte had those elegant fingers of hers, the ones she used to play the pi-

ano and do all of the refined things debutantes with the last
name Holden did, wrapping around him, and, mind blown,
he bucked into her hand.

One little stroke and he could see the finish line. And at
the end, waving the big checkered flag, in nothing but skin
and those sophisticated heels she loved, was Charlotte. Oh,
not the sweet, cultured, cool-as-ice Dr. Holden, but Charlie
McGraw...his wife.

He pulled back because—*hello,* they were in a bar and
his hands were playing with those buttons, those sexy little
buttons that had been begging him all day for release, and he
was about to release them, right there. One by one.

Undoing the dress.

His wife's dress.

His wife, who stood there, looking up at him with questioning eyes. And he had just the answer for her. But then
she picked up his mug, downed the last little swallow, and
said, "The glasses are empty. Which means this talk is over.
And I want to go upstairs."

Jace must have been breathing too hard, because he
thought that she said the talk was over. As in they were not
going to rev their engines, speed down the track, or even go
one lap.

"Alone?" he asked, telling himself to let go, because
that was their deal, right? Even though she'd stuck her
hand down his pants and kissed him like he was her lifeline, it was her call. And she'd made it. Even if it was the
wrong call.

Then, *thank you, Jesus,* she smiled, sweet and a little
naughty. "With you, Jace. I want to go upstairs with you."

Um, yes. Hell yes. This is the best day of my life yes. They
were all acceptable responses, yet none of them really en-
compassed the sheer amount of enthusiasm, eagerness, *how*

fast can we fucking get there? feelings he was having. He really needed to enroll in that communication class, because he took too long to respond, and that animated expression she wore vanished, leaving behind one that was full of vulnerability and uncertainty.

And if there was one thing he wanted her to know, it was just how badly she got to him. How badly he wanted her. So he leaned in ever so slowly, keeping his eyes firmly on hers, and teased the seam of her lips, his hands tightening possessively on her hips, steering her into him.

When she was good and clear on just how enthusiastic, he took her by the hand and said, "Let's take the stairwell. It's quicker."

Charlotte nodded, not saying a single word other than "hurry up" as he pulled her through the lobby, past the lady with the fire-engine red hair who had looked surprised when he asked for two rooms—she knew they wouldn't be using that second one now—and into the stairwell.

They lapped the first level, the second, and were going into their third flight—why the hell hadn't he asked for a ground-level room?—when Charlotte stumbled a little in those heels.

She fiddled with the sexy clasp at the ankle, then tried just yanking it off. Jace considered picking her up and carrying her up the rest of the stairs. But he couldn't wait, needed one of those detours he was so adamant about avoiding, so when his wife placed those delicate hands of hers on his chest to gain her balance, he led her to the wall.

Pressed her against it without warning, crushing his mouth to hers. He felt the surprise in her sexy little gasp turn to excitement as she rose up on her tiptoes to meet him halfway. God, she tasted incredible, like Miss America and mint chip or something. All he knew was that she tasted incredible. Better than incredible. Like she could end world hunger and create world peace with a single kiss.

He figured this was a little pit stop, a little grope and a little loving, so that they had the motivation to get up the next three fights. But she pulled back, her face a pretty shade of pink when she asked, "You know what else I love about stairwells?"

No, he didn't. Jace might not be an expert communicator, but he knew when to shut up. And this, his head was telling him, was one of those times.

Charlotte looked at his zipper, then back to his eyes, and she flushed. "They're also less crowded," she whispered, and he could hear the excited nerves shake in her voice. See the uncertainty in her eyes. Feel the way her heart leapt when he offered up an encouraging smile.

"Are you saying that you wanted to get me alone, Miss Peach?"

She smiled back, flirty with a hint of naughty, and it was hot as hell. So Jace, always the gentleman, gave the lady what she wanted—the kind of kiss that required privacy. That was all it took. For him to make the first move. Because Charlotte crawled up his body, shrink-wrapping herself to him to gain leverage.

His mind went ballistic, trying to reconcile all of the emotions and pent-up tension from the past week that had twisted into a really freaking complicated hot ball that settled right in his groin. Especially when her hands smoothed down his chest, teased across his stomach, and—bingo—his zipper was down in record time and before he could remind her they were in a stairwell, less crowded or not, his pants were around his hips and her warm hands were firmly wrapped around him.

Two strokes that had his eyes rolling to the back of his

head. and then he was somehow back against the wall and she was on her knees.

In. Front. Of. Him.

Officially blowing his mind. Which was the only excuse he had for forgetting about the stairwell, forgetting that at any moment someone could walk through that door, right in on them. Because Charlotte was one of the most talented pianists in Sugar, hers fingers were deft and sure. But her mouth? *Ah man*, her mouth was something of legends, a fact that was confirmed as she moved from base to tip, tightening a little more every time the motion was repeated, driving him closer to the edge with each pass.

"Charlotte," he said, taking her hands and helping her up, because even though a part of him cried at the thought of her stopping, another part of him knew that he was one lick from done. And in his world it was always ladies first. "Just a few more flights."

"Charlie," she whispered, her mouth wet and her hair a beautiful mess. "I like it when you call me Charlie."

And before he could tell her that he liked it when he called her Charlie, too, that it was *his* name for her, for the woman she was behind closed doors, and now apparently the woman she was in stairwells, her mouth was on his, hot and demanding.

And everything else faded. His plans, his garage, his entire reason for coming. Jace no longer wanted to get those papers signed then get the hell out of Sugar. All he wanted in that moment was Charlie. *His* Charlie, kissing him as if he were her lifeline.

Her life. And even though he knew she was caught up in the moment, and hell, maybe he was, too, he couldn't get past how perfect it all felt.

She started using her teeth to nip and tease and Jace

gave up. More like gave in to what he'd been too afraid to admit until now—when it came to Charlie, he was unable to resist.

He flipped them around and pressed her to the wall, pinning her with his hips, and freeing up his hands to do some exploring of their own. He ran a palm down her breasts, over her stomach, and, following her lead, right down her skirt and—holy hell.

Jace pulled back.

"You aren't wearing panties," he said.

She bit her lower lip, a little nervous and a little brazen. Great combo on her. "It's today's risk."

"Risk?"

"Yeah, Sunday it was red lace. Yesterday, I wore my hair down. And today." She looked down to where his hand had disappeared beneath the hem of her dress and shrugged.

"Tuesday is now my new favorite day of the week," he admitted, pulling a condom out of his back pocket. One he'd bought earlier as part of a gag and slipped into his pocket when she was sipping her shot. "This was my risk."

"That, Jace"—she said, taking the condom in his fingers and smiled—"is my kind of risk."

He wasn't sure how he felt about being one of her risks, but he was pretty sure it was a green light all the same. So Jace ran his hands down her sides and mile-long legs until he met the hem and reversed, touching every inch of skin she'd kept hidden beneath that dress. Mapping it and memorizing it as her breaths became shorter and shorter.

"Now," she said, and Jace was nothing if not a gentleman.

He palmed her gloriously naked ass and lifted her until she was so flush with him she had no choice but to wrap her legs around him. Which she did, then tightened, creating enough friction that would have brought him to his knees if he hadn't been pressing them into the concrete brick wall.

"Oh God, baby." She was wet. He could feel it even through the soft cotton of her dress. She was wet and so primed, her body shook when he slid his hand beneath and pushed one finger in to see if she was ready.

Lucky guy that he was, she was more than ready. Her whole body was humming, begging for release, so he shifted her skirt up and positioned himself, pausing to look her in the eye. To see the truth. He'd known what it was like to be her biggest regret. He didn't want to be that guy ever again. "You sure?"

She unwrapped the condom, rolled it on, and, giving him a stroke or two to insure it was applied correctly, she kissed him gently on the lips. "Never been more."

That was all the confirmation he needed. In one long push he was inside her and they were both moaning at the sensation. It felt familiar and completely new all at the same time. It was like coming home.

"You feel so good," he rasped as she arched, causing him to sink even deeper until he was so deep it was enough to drive a man insane.

Slowly, he started pumping, and slowly her hips shifted to deepen the friction. She pressed forward, her body tightening around him, and things got serious real fast. Breathing turned nonexistent, his chest felt too big for his skin, and he knew he was close.

"Jace," she moaned, and man, he loved hearing his name on her lips. He loved it even more when he felt her tighten further, felt her body start to shake, and—

"Fuck." He hit the right spot, he could tell. Charlotte screamed out and her body exploded, just like that. Just like he remembered. Just like he knew she would. And then he let himself fall. And he fell hard. Or maybe it was that he'd never gotten back up. Either way he knew he was in trouble, because this wasn't just the best conversation of his life.

It was the only conversation he cared to continue.

Chapter 7

W ell, it seems that both parties are in agreement to annul
the marriage," Elvina Larson said, her bifocaled eyes peer-
ing over the box of doughnuts Jace had brought. "You are
both in agreement, correct?"

Yes, of course she was in agreement. It was why she'd
skipped work, disappointed her father who'd in exchange
disappointed her, forfeited her last chance to talk to the
Mercy Alliance board before they decided, and had sex with
her estranged husband—in the stairwell.

Yup, she was all about agreement at this point. Twenty-
four hours of playing Mrs. McGraw had nearly cost her
everything she'd worked so hard for. It had also reminded
her what it felt like to take chances, to be spontaneous and
really live in the moment.

To really live.

"Charlie," Jace said in gentle question, resting his hand
on hers. The simple contact sent a warm tingle of awareness
up her arm and right into her chest, settling above her heart.

"What?" She looked up, surprised to find all eyes on hers. As though she hadn't already answered the question. Then she realized that she hadn't. She'd thought it, but for some reason saying it out loud was harder than she imagined.

"Are you in agreement?" the recorder repeated, and Charlotte noticed just how much Elvina looked like a Keebler elf. She was a pocket-size woman with short, bottle-orange hair, and kind of pointy ears. "You need to state it for the record."

Jace looked right at her, and she was momentarily distracted by his eyes. They were the perfect shade of blue, not cool or icy but the color of twilight, warm and comforting and twinkling with intensity. Today they also had a sparkle of hope in them, and more than anything Charlotte wanted to drown in that hope.

If she wasn't in agreement. Which she was. So Charlotte refused to acknowledge that small tug in her heart that told her his kind of hope was just what she needed, because she knew better.

And wasn't that the right decision? Because Elvina said, "That way I can send a preliminary letter to Mr. McGraw's loan officer explaining the situation," reminding Charlotte of why they were there to begin with. Not for hope or second chances, but so they could both move on with their lives—separately.

As in two hundred miles apart.

Charlotte pulled her hand back and sat straighter in the chair. "Of course I'm in agreement."

"Great," Elvina said, setting down the doughnut to lick the chocolate residue off her fingers. She picked up her pen, which meant that Jace was in agreement, too, and even though that should bring relief, it only seemed to bring on a strange sense of sadness.

"Great," Charlotte repeated, clasping her hands in her lap.

It felt strange sitting on the arm of the chair, so close to him, yet not touching.

Elvina jotted down a few notes in the back of a very full notebook, and Charlotte was tempted to ask if that was the Tried and Failed notebook or one that she used on all of her cases. Not that it mattered, but it would be interesting, from a simple research standpoint of course, to know how many people failed at what should be the easiest part of their lives.

Elf slid the glasses down her pert nose and peered at Jace and Charlotte over the wire rims. "I will write up a quick letter explaining what transpired and then send it to the presiding judge. It shouldn't take long at all to receive his ruling."

Made sense, Charlotte thought, they'd actually only been married three months, one week, and nine days, so of course the resolution of such a small blip in their lives wouldn't take long.

Glasses perched in place, Elvina wrote one last thing in the book then set her pen down with a smile. "Three weeks or so and everything will be handled."

This was *not* what Charlotte wanted to hear.

After her catastrophic failure yesterday with her father, then her decision to do the stairwell hustle with her husband, who was supposed to be her ex-husband by now, Charlotte needed something to go her way. And three weeks was not her idea of quick and easy—not when it would be spent trying not to dwell on the what-ifs.

"I'm sorry," Charlotte said, noticing that swallowing had become difficult. "I was under the impression that we would come here, explain the situation, and it would be handled."

She would walk out that door a single woman. Go home with the closure she needed to really start living her new life. It was to be her grown-up, sexy era. She'd even named it:

Charlotte 2.0. That was the plan, the reason she'd agreed to last night, gone after her good-bye. And now someone was messing with the plan—and she was pretty sure she was going to be sick.

"You okay?" Jace asked, that concern he was so famous for bracketing his mouth.

"Fine." She was fine. Everything was going to be just fine.

Fine, fine, fine.

She would go home, land that endowment, and in three or so weeks she'd be single. Completely, officially, according to the great state of Georgia, single. And then she'd go back to being grown-up sexy. It wasn't as though she'd still be Mrs. McGraw with Jace around—reminding her of what they'd done, what she'd be missing out on, or what she'd lost.

Nope, she'd be fine.

"Where should I mail the final paperwork?" Elvina asked, slipping her glasses back on and opening that notebook again to their page. *God, they had a page.* "You'll both need to sign it and mail it back to my office. One business week after receipt, you will receive an email that it is official."

Charlotte opened her mouth to give Elvina her address when Jace spoke. "You can just mail it to me, since I'll be staying in Sugar until the Founder's Day Fair."

* * *

"You can stop pretending to be asleep," Jace accused, and Charlotte could feel his stare even though her eyes were closed, like they had been for the past three hours. "We're here."

Charlotte opened her eyes and, since ignoring had become her new way of life, she blinked a few times against the early afternoon sun that reflected off the glass walls of Sugar Medical Center and then, for added affect, feigned a stretch.

She was good, Oscar-worthy really, and not at all grown-up sexy. Which was fine with her since talking with Jace seemed to lead to sex with Jace, so Charlotte decided ignoring him was the safest solution. Not that she wasn't interested in sex with Jace, quite the opposite. Sex with Jace had been a religious experience, a whole body-and-soul transformation, complete with the hallelujahs and amens. But if talking led to sex, then she was certain that sex would lead to feelings. And wasn't that a way to complicate everything?

"Thank you for..." She stopped, unsure how to proceed.

Did she thank him for giving her the annulment she never wanted but now couldn't move forward without? Or maybe she should just thank him for the amazing sex, because that's what grown-ups did, right? They had sex, they enjoyed it, and they moved on. But she knew if she brought up the sex, they would only move on to what she'd been ignoring successfully since they left the recorder's office: Jace was staying. In Sugar. Until Founder's Day.

And she was going to have to pretend that there was nothing between them, that they weren't still married and hadn't rekindled more than a few flames last night, with him living right across the lake.

"Thank you for the ride." There, polite and sincere, with a definite period on the end. As in, end of conversation.

"We're going to have to talk about it," Jace said quietly.

Panic reached up and grabbed her by the throat, making talking a nonoption. She picked up her purse and fished though the grocery bag full of supplies he'd brought her, not wanting to face him. She knew if she did, she'd see that hope of his that was hard to ignore. See the man she'd once loved enough to marry with his good old boy swagger and soothing blue eyes that had a way of looking at her until she felt as though she were enough.

"I know we do, but I can't right now." Because right now she conveniently had to get into work, see what was so important that it warranted six texts over the past two hours, and do what she did best. Fix other's people's problems.

It was a lot safer than fixing her own.

Jace didn't say a word, but she could feel disappointment and concern radiating off him, drawing her in. Then he unfolded that big, badass body of his until he was leaning across her. Pressing against her. And for one stupid, idiotic, gloriously amazing moment she thought he was going to kiss her.

Her good parts were the first to get on board, followed by her heart, which began to pound when his arm—the one that had hoisted her up last night—brushed up against her.

To grab her door handle.

He didn't open the door, didn't move his arm any farther, didn't move at all, just sat there, his upper body acting as a safety belt across hers, his hand securing the door closed. She turned toward him and—big mistake. He was close, so close his broad shoulder and mighty fine chest filled her view, as though blocking out the rest of the world. He looked so big and safe and familiar, and Charlotte wanted to lean right in and make herself at home. But she had places to go, people to fix.

Then his other hand was on the move, sliding down the seat back—and into her purse.

"What are you doing?"

Ignoring this, he pulled out her cell, fiddled with it for a second, one-handed because he was that cool, then handed it back to her. She noticed he'd programmed in his number.

"For that talk we're going to have" was all he said, but it was accompanied by a look that told her he was as serious as a bullet. Then he flung the door open and smiled.

Charlotte might have smiled back, she wasn't sure, she was too busy grabbing her things and sprinting for the medical clinic so as not to be tempted to do some of that "talking" he was so good at in his backseat.

It wasn't until she was on the elevator, riding up to the ER, that she felt herself breathe. Although the reprieve was short-lived, because the second those doors opened Charlotte understood the reason behind all of the texts.

The waiting room looked like a scene from one of those end-of-the-world movies her grandfather was so fond of. It was at standing room capacity, with a line of jars, jars, and more jars held by arthritis-riddled fingers, winding their way down the hallway and toward the nurses' station. Not specimen jars, but jelly jars. All with red-and-white gingham labels that read THE GREAT SUGAR JAM-OFF.

Which was today, and she'd completely missed it. Not good since it was a Sugar Peaches' event that was applied to the Founder's Day Fair collection, and as current regent it was Charlotte's responsibility to make sure it ran smoothly.

Before Charlotte could sneak back inside the elevator, go home, and eat a gallon of ice cream, Glory Mann, pediatric nurse and one of Charlotte's closest friends, was by her side—blocking her escape.

She was wearing dancing armadillo scrubs and had a stack of files in one hand and a cup of pencils in the other. Both nurse and scrubs were covered with a thin layer of what Charlotte assumed to be peach jam.

"Going somewhere?" she asked with a knowing grin, as

if half the county's Social Security recipients hadn't staged a jam tasting in her ER. Glory was sharp, had a huge heart, and wasn't afraid of hard work. That she spent quite a bit of time with her grandmother's friends meant she was also immune to drama. That she was a soon-to-be stepmom to Cal McGraw's teenage daughter meant that the calm demeanor wasn't for show. Nope, under those bright pink scrubs was one of the most skilled professionals Charlotte had ever had the pleasure of working with.

"Are you kidding? I leave you for one day and you destroy the ER."

"Your Sugar Peaches destroyed the ER and..." Glory trailed off, her skilled gaze assessing. Her forehead puckered in on itself, as if perplexed. "You look different."

"I do not," Charlotte argued, refusing to acknowledge the heat creeping up her neck.

"Yeah, you do. You look..." *Relaxed, blissful, giddy?* "Guilty." *Or that.* "Right there," Glory pointed to Charlotte's lips. "That serene smile. You only get it when you're hiding something."

"I am not hiding anything, I just feel bad that I got here so late and you had to deal with all of this."

"Ah-huh," Glory said, so not believing a word Charlotte said.

Even worse, neither was Charlotte, so she did the next best thing, took the stack of files from Glory and started walking. "Please tell me that the riot squad didn't bring out the hoses at the Jam-Off again."

That was all the ammo Darleen Vander's im-peachment campaign needed.

"Worse." They rounded the corner, and—*Lord have mercy*—there were people sitting in the chairs lining the hallway. "It seems that someone didn't seal their jars properly. We have one of the attendees claiming botulism poisoning."

"It was bad jars," Darleen Vander said, standing up from one of the chairs with a grin. The woman was dressed in a cashmere sweater set and pumps—all daffodil yellow—her hair so teased it was three inches from God. Made complete, since the woman was standing as though in the pulpit, holding three jars of jam in her hands like they were stone tablets. "It didn't specify on the entry application the kind of jars." Something that she'd brought up at the last meeting. "And entry number 332 used those fancy jars off the Internet, which we all know come from China. You need to get Kerr jars if you want to be safe, because they make the *pop* when they seal."

Darleen pursed her red lips for effect and popped her mouth, while holding her hand out like a gun and pulling the lethal trigger. "*Pop*," she reiterated. "Probably, Brett's new wife. Poor thing is a Yankee, and without proper instructions she wouldn't know any better. "

"We don't know if it was Joie's entry," Glory defended. "In fact, we don't even know if there is tainted jam. Only one person has symptoms that are consistent with botulism."

"Then why is my ER filled with half of Sugar Baptist's congregation?" As soon as she asked the question, she knew she was going to dread the answer.

"Because Rooster showed up at the church, screaming to stop the sampling because he had been poisoned by bad jam," Darleen said with great theatrics. Then, resting a hand on her chest, she raised her voice so it could be heard down the hall. "Right as the judges were getting to my entries. He tried to throw my jam in the trash, so I reacted. Any man knows not to touch a lady's jars without asking first."

"Rooster is in exam room nine." Glory smiled and Charlotte rolled her eyes. "To make things more interesting, Rooster vomited right on Pastor Hal's shoes. Within ten minutes people started showing up. A good portion came volunteering their jam for testing to prove that they aren't killers."

Making jam was a serious pastime in Sugar, and a woman's reputation could rise or fall based on her most recent batch. Serving a tainted batch to a panel of jam experts—well, that would be cause for a public stoning.

"And the rest of them?"

"Didn't want to be left out of what is to be front-page news tomorrow." She tapped the files in Charlotte's hand and rolled her eyes. "These are the people complaining of symptoms consistent with Wikipedia's diagnosis."

"Glory, if you could take those jams to the lab and see if they are tainted, then get Ms. Vander's copy of the entry list so we can see who entered what jam, that would be helpful."

Darleen clasped her hand to her chest, her pearls rising as she gasped. "That list is sealed in a safe at the bank. Opening it before the winner is called would mean canceling the ninety-second annual Jam-Off."

"Yes, well, that is the only way to contain this possible botulism outbreak."

Darleen's smile was big and smug, and Charlotte wouldn't be surprised if Darleen hadn't entered tainted jam herself. "I'd need the regent's permission to do something so...against the moral code."

Charlotte was more concerned with a possible food poisoning outbreak than her position as regent, so she smiled back—equally smug. "Just do it."

Charlotte started walking and Glory followed, lowering her voice when she asked, "Why do I get the feeling Darleen just won?"

"Because she did." Once the board heard about Charlotte's most recent decision, there were going to be gripes. With a frustrated sigh she headed toward her office. "Explain to me how Rooster got access to the jams?" Although Rooster wore many hats in town, they were all grease-stained and said ROOSTER'S ROOFING AND REMODELS: REDNECK WITH A TOUCH OF (CL)ASS. The only thing he knew about jam was that he liked it on his toast.

"His dad is a judge, and Rooster admitted to breaking into his restaurant late last night and sampling a few of the entries," Glory said as Charlotte unlocked her office door and walked inside. "He also sampled some of that Fairchild House moonshine his dad keeps on hand."

Charlotte flicked on the light, and she set the files on her desk. Grabbing a pencil from Glory's cup, she twisted her hair up into a bun, speared it, and was back to being Dr. Charlotte. "So patient zero was consuming stolen jam and moonshine all night?"

"Yup." Glory laughed. "We ran a blood panel and should hear back from the lab by tomorrow. But my professional opinion tells me that the double vision, cotton mouth, slurring, and vomiting have nothing to do with the jam."

"I will check on Rooster first, then go see if I can weed out the rest." Plan of action in place, Charlotte grabbed her stethoscope and put it around her neck.

"Why were you in Atlanta again?" Glory asked.

"I had some paperwork to finish up with regard to the house." Which was not a total lie. It was her purchase of the house that started this whole mess. Actually, she thought looking down at her bare ring finger, it was her rash decision to marry Jace.

"Funny, Jace was in Atlanta finishing up some paperwork, too."

Charlotte went still. "Imagine that."

Glory laughed and, *oh boy*, she knew. Charlotte didn't know how Glory knew, but she knew all right. Her friend was the only person in Sugar who was privy to her and Jace's history. It was the result of an unfortunate slip Charlotte had made when Glory first started seeing Jace's older brother Cal. At the time she didn't want Glory thinking she'd slept with Cal, so she came clean. Not with everything, but enough to know they had a past—a sizzling past.

This was not good.

"I can imagine all kind of things, so you might want to spill since I am sure what I'm imagining is way worse."

"Worse than stairwell sex with Jace McGraw?" Charlotte whispered, feeling her entire body tingle at the memory.

"Oh my God!" Glory's face lit with excitement. "Stairwell sex with the bad boy of the family? I gotta say I am impressed, Doctor." Charlotte wanted to argue that Jace wasn't the bad boy. He was sweet and attentive—in and out of the bedroom—and wonderful. And he was bound to break her heart again if she gave him the chance.

After a long, intense moment, Glory's grin faded and she sank into the chair. "I know that look."

Charlotte was terrified that it was the same look Glory had worn when she'd realized she was falling for Cal. Not that Charlotte was stupid enough to fall, but when it came to her and Jace, there was always the potential for stupidity.

"Hang on." Glory fished through her pocket and came up with a quarter, a pulse oximeter, a folded-up magazine page of a wedding dress, and a breath mint. She unwrapped the mint, broke it in half, and offered part to Charlotte. "It's not chocolate, but it's the best I have. Now, spill."

Charlotte popped the mint in her mouth and sat down on the edge of her desk. "I don't know where to start."

She was so confused about what had transpired over the

past twenty-four hours that she desperately needed some female advice. Especially from a female who had intimate knowledge of how to deal with those stubborn McGraw men. She couldn't start at the beginning, as mentioning the annulment to a soon-to-be McGraw would feel like a betrayal of Jace, but she could certainly talk about last night.

"We had amazing sex in the stairwell of a cheap hotel, and I mean amazing."

"You don't have to convince me. I am fully aware of just how talented the McGraws are." Glory wagged a brow, then her face went soft. "I'm also aware of just how difficult they can be when they meet the right woman."

"I'm not the right woman." Because if she were he wouldn't have walked away all those years ago.

"Right enough for stairwell sex."

"Yes, but the plan was he'd go back to his life, and I'd go back to mine. But now he is staying. In town." Only to leave after the parade. Which would be harder than if he just left now. "That wasn't part of the plan. He's totally screwing with my plan."

"That's what McGraw men do," Glory said, then sat back, then her eyes went wide with astonishment. "Oh my word! You *like* him screwing with your plans."

There was so much truth in that statement, it terrified her.

Chapter 8

⟳

In the South, the difference between being sweet-talked and strong-armed wasn't always clear. But Jace had been with enough women to recognize the signs, and he was being strong-armed. The embarrassing as shit part: he was actually scared. That she was five-foot-nothing and named after a flower only made the experience that much more embarrassing.

"It's up to you," Lavender Spencer, owner of Kiss My Glass Tow and Tires, said as though he *really* had an option in the matter. "Either you teach the next few Saturday classes for me or clear out of my garage."

Jace slid the mechanic's dolly out from under the car and looked up at the owner of those steel-toed boots. "I'm the last guy you want teaching a bunch of old ladies about car maintenance."

"You say that like I'm a better option. My last date ended up in the hospital," Spencer said matter-of-factly. "He kept asking me questions—about my hair, what I liked to eat, what my hobbies were—so I pulled out my favorite hobby, unloaded my entire magazine, and ruptured his eardrum."

"You shot your date?"

"He was deaf for the night, not dead." Right, because if she shot at him she wouldn't miss. "And don't look at me like I'm crazy, we were at the shooting range, and he didn't get his ear protection on fast enough."

"You go on dates to the range?"

"What's wrong with the range?" Since his last date took place in a stairwell—and Spencer's boots were inches from his head—he figured it best not to argue. "And it wasn't like I meant to injure his hearing, I just wanted him to shut up. Who talks while someone is shooting?"

"Maybe a guy who thought he was on a date," he said, standing up—and out of striking range.

She blinked as though just realizing that the poor guy was trying to get to know her. "This is the exact reason why I can't teach this class. If I shoot at anyone I'll lose my county contract, which means I'll lose my shop. And I am bound to shoot at someone, since half the Sugar Ladies choir signed up, and we all know how they like to nag. And wouldn't that make Sheriff Duncan's day." A weird, and quite frankly unsettling, twinkle lit her eyes. "I hate making the sheriff's day."

"Did you say the class is on Saturday?" He flashed his trademark grin, the one that had been passed down from McGraw father to McGraw son. "Sorry, darling, but that's family dinner night." Not that he was going, but she didn't need to know that.

"I'm sorry, dickhead"—Spencer looked at her black tank top—"what does my shirt say?

Jace swallowed. "Lug-Nut Crusher."

"Thank God, the way you were treating me to that smile,

I thought I accidently put on a 'Hey, I've got boobs so I must be stupid' shirt. Because family dinner night at the McGraws' is Sunday, and you haven't gone to a family dinner in years, which explains the stupid look on your face. Plus Hattie is on the list for the class."

Eyes locked on his, Spencer pulled a doughnut out of the pink box that sat on the workbench next to her. She inhaled half of it in one bite, wiping her mouth off on the shoulder strap of her tank top. "Here's how I see it. You dropped this car off over a week ago and I have been pretty damn neighborly about it, never once saying a word."

"Brett dropped the car off, not me."

"Brett, Jace, same thing. A McGraw is a McGraw." Unconcerned, she shoved the other half in her mouth. "Point is, my garage looks like an automotive graveyard. There are more parts on my floor than in the cars, and it is starting to piss me off. Almost as much as having to do this stupid class for the community in order to keep the towing contract I have with the sheriff's department. So unless you want to explain to your grandma why her car is having a sleepover at the junkyard, then I suggest you get your little crowbar ready and figure out how to teach women with hip replacements how to change a tire."

Jace looked at the calendar on the wall, at the number of days that had passed since he'd last seen Charlotte—two. Receiving the silent treatment after what they'd shared the other night left him feeling agitated and confused. Okay, sure, so it had started out as a long-overdue farewell, a way to find some kind of closure, he knew that. But then she'd kissed him as if she couldn't breathe without him, and in that second everything shifted. For him, it was no longer a hot and heavy good-bye, only he was afraid that was exactly how Charlotte had seen it.

With a frustrated groan, he looked at the remaining number of days until Founder's Day—twenty-one—and felt that suffocating panic he was so good at burying rise up and expand until he thought his ribs were going to burst.

But being here, in the place that reminded him of all he'd lost, knowing that Charlotte was just across the lake, within reach but completely untouchable, was going to be hell. So maybe this was a good thing. Maybe working on that car might be the distraction he needed, since Charlotte wasn't following through on having that talk she promised him. Hell, she couldn't even follow through with returning his call.

Jace looked at his dad's car and sighed. It would be one hell of a push, but if he pulled a few all-nighters he could get the car done before he left, get it running and polished in time for the parade. And when he packed up to start his new life in Atlanta he could walk away knowing he'd done something positive with his time here.

"I'll do it," Jace said, cupping the bill of his hat and pulling it lower on his head. "And Hattie's car will be done before I leave town."

"Good answer." Spencer shoved a flyer at him. "The first one is tomorrow. Don't be late." Spencer snagged the last jelly-filled and headed toward the office.

He lifted his head to see what else he'd signed on for. "Hey," he hollered. "It says my name on the flyer."

"So?" came through the wall.

"So?" He walked over, opened the door, and leaned against the doorjamb. Spencer was already pushed back in her chair, steel toes up on the desk, enjoying the hell out of her breakfast. "What would you have done if I'd said no?"

"I would have called Charlotte back and explained that her car, the one you hijacked, has been sitting in my garage, ready to go, for two days, and you haven't told her."

"She called? Asking for me?" Jace looked at the shop phone on the wall, then he smiled. He couldn't help it. It was big and stupid and he didn't care.

"She called about her car." *Yeah, but she called.* "And she sounded all put out."

"It's not like I was holding it hostage or anything." Spencer made a sound that translated into "bullshit." "What? I was waiting for her to call back so I could give her the good news." After they had that talk, of course.

"You were waiting for her to come to you."

"No, I wasn't."

Spencer stood up, then narrowed her gaze on him for a long *are you fucking with me* moment, and Jace narrowed back the best he could, then glanced at his cell to see if he'd missed any calls and—

Ah, shit, Spencer was right. He'd been sitting around waiting for Charlotte to come after him, have that talk, and tell him…what? That she'd changed her mind. That she didn't want the annulment. That what she really wanted was him—in the stairwell again and maybe this time in her bed, too. Because that's what he wanted. Her in his arms for another night, because one wasn't enough. Two wouldn't be, either, but he'd take what he could get.

Jace ran a hand down his face, unconcerned if he was smearing more grease along his scruffy jaw, and let out a soul-deep breath. It didn't help. His ribs felt even tighter, so he sat down on the workbench.

"Yeah, that's what I thought," Spencer said in a smug tone while clapping him on his sorry back. "How I see it, you have two options. Grow a pair and tell the pretty doctor that you want to look under her hood, or sit here with your dick on your sleeve and wait for her to come to you. Your call." Handing him a half-eaten doughnut, she shrugged, a sign that their kumbaya moment was over. "Either way, by the end of the day if her car is still here I'm having it towed."

* * *

Later that afternoon, Charlotte headed toward her office, desperate for a few minutes of peace and pleased as punch that she had successfully avoided Jace for two entire days. A difficult task in a town with only two blinking lights. Yet amazingly enough, between pulling double shifts at the clinic and volunteering to cover the urgent care overflow today, she had kept herself too busy to do something stupid.

Like return his calls.

That didn't mean that she hadn't thought about it, though, damn the man. Because while she spent her days consciously avoiding him, which led to thinking about what might happen if she stopped avoiding him, and ultimately to why avoiding him was so imperative, she'd spent her nights dreaming about the sexy mechanic with nimble hands and a devastatingly talented mouth.

So when she rounded the corner to her hallway and saw Ben standing by her door, waiting with a stack of patient files in hand, she turned right back around and headed straight for the vending machine to have a moment alone with an ice-cream bar.

She made it as far as the entry to the waiting room when Ben caught up to her. "I wouldn't go that way."

"It's the quickest way to the ER." And the vending machine.

"And half the JV Sugar High football team who miscalculated the length of the wick on the M-80 they stuck in Mr.

Ferguson's cow chip pile." He flapped the file in his hand. "And right here is one measly patient."

"If it was measly then you wouldn't be trying to hand it off to me." But she took a hard left anyway, heading through the ob-gyn ward. Charlotte knew every possible route the hospital had to get to that vending machine.

"The Jam-Off contestants cleaned out the machine. It doesn't get refilled until Monday."

"Lord help us." Charlotte stopped and let out a deep sigh. When she opened her eyes Ben was standing in front of her. "I really wanted an ice cream."

"And I really want to make my tee time." That was when she noticed that Ben wasn't dressed for the ER but for playing golf. And because he was sporting a pair of khakis and a fitted polo that stretched over his broad shoulders, every woman in the area paused to check out his goods. "And it's my day off. My only day off in two weeks since I covered for you Wednesday."

"Which I thank you for." Charlotte started walking back toward her office—and the roll on mini-doughnuts she kept stashed in the back of her desk.

Ben fell easily in step with her. "Lester Koozner is in room 6. He picked up some Viagra on his recent trip to Mexico and he and the missus wanted to see if it worked."

Charlotte slid Ben a sidelong glance. "Did it?" He handed her the file and she read the nurse's notes. "Wow, he took it two days ago."

"Yeah, his wife is in room nine suffering from dehydration, exhaustion, and a mysterious rash she won't talk to any man about."

Charlotte looked at Ben, then at his cleats, and sighed. This is what she signed on for when she moved back to Sugar. She knew that she'd be leaving behind her position at the forefront of medical advancement for snakebites, poison ivy, and the occasional Viagra overdose. But she'd also left behind all of the pain and disappointment that came with living in Atlanta. Sugar helped her heart heal at a time when Charlotte wasn't sure how to go on, and now it was her turn to repay that kindness.

"I'll take Mrs. Koozner, but page my dad. If Lester is here he'll want to see my dad, not me."

Ben gave Charlotte a concerned look that hit her straight in the chest. Taking her arm and steering her into the hallway, he lowered his voice. "Your dad's not here, Charlotte, which is why I was called in."

It also explained why she'd been double-booked, and why she hadn't seen her father once since her return from Atlanta. In fact, she hadn't seen or heard from either of her parents since their phone call.

"He called in sick?" Even as she said the words she knew that answer. The great Reginald Holden never called in sick—that would be admitting weakness.

Ben's face went soft—too soft. "He left yesterday for a business trip."

The pounding in her chest stopped. Her heart? That stopped, too, because her father never booked out-of-town meetings in the middle of the workweek. God forbid he left the clinic to someone else's care. And there wasn't anything on the calendar, which could only mean it was a last-minute meeting. And Charlotte had a terrible feeling just who that meeting was with. But she heard herself asking anyway. "Where did he go?"

Ben's face curled in on itself in anger, because if there was one person who had worked as diligently as she had this past year to get the Grow Clinic up and running, and who understood what it meant to Charlotte, it was Ben. He also had firsthand experience with just how difficult Reginald Holden the Third could be. "He went to Nashville."

Charlotte's expression must have been as shattered as her heart, because Ben swore, then pulled her away from prying eyes and toward her office. "Son of a bitch, he didn't tell you, did he?"

"Nope," Charlotte said, holding the file against her chest so that he wouldn't see her hands shake. "He didn't. He took over my call Wednesday with Mercy Alliance, and I guess he forgot to mention to me that there was a face-to-face meeting that came from it."

It was a lie and they both knew it. Reginald had not only intentionally kept her out of the loop, but he also completely hijacked her project. She didn't know if it was because he liked to be in control of his world or if he did it out of sheer habit. Either way, it proved that her father didn't trust Charlotte's ability to do her job. And after everything she had sacrificed to come home and work in the family clinic, and the lengths she'd gone to prove she was good at what she did—including giving up any kind of real life—his lack of faith in her stung.

"It is because of you that the meeting even happened," Ben said softly. "But your dad knows what he's doing, what this endowment means, he won't blow it."

Yeah, but Charlotte knew more, understood that the way to break through peoples' hesitations was through their heart. Which was why she should have been the one to go. Only she had been too busy ending her marriage to even know there was a meeting scheduled. "I know. It was just bad timing. My trip took longer than planned." Everything was taking longer than planned. "I was distracted, and my dad jumped in and took over."

Story of her life. Her old life, that was, because Charlotte was tired of men screwing with her plans. This was her endowment, her center, her future. And she needed to start acting like it.

"You never said why you went to Atlanta," Ben said as she opened her office door.

"Yeah, Doctor. Why were you in Atlanta?"

Charlotte's heart leapt into her throat at the sound of the deep male voice coming from her private office. The door swung open and a hot flash of irritation rose because there, not even ten feet away, leaning back her chair, boots kicked up on her desk, acting as though he owned the place, was Jace McGraw looking bigger than life.

Maybe it was the way his eyes twinkled with challenge under the brim of his ball cap. Or maybe it was the battered jeans and black tee that clung to his broad chest with the day's work in that *real men get dirty* kind of way. But one look at him sitting there with that easy smile and a different kind of heat altogether skittered through her body.

"What are you doing here?" Charlotte asked with her most intimidating glare.

The man didn't seem intimidated in the slightest. He just gave her a deceptively playful smile and said, "Wanted to follow up with you. The lady at the front desk said I should make an appointment. I thought about you walking into the exam room with me in nothing but one of those little robes you all hand out, that never seem to cover enough." He lifted a single brow. So much was said in that one movement that her thighs quivered. "But you were booked solid until next week, so I decided to come and find you."

Ben's eyes narrowed at Jace and then he took a step forward in a clearly territorial move. "Well, Mr., um..."

"Jace." He stood, all his six-foot-four inches of masculine intimidation, and crossed his arms over his impressive chest.

He was the poster boy for laid-back and unaffected, but there was a lethal edge to his stance that was tangible if you really knew him. "Jace McGraw."

"Well, Mr. McGraw," Ben said, studying Jace, every muscled inch, and Charlotte had to give the man credit, he didn't back down. Although she could tell he was a little nervous. "You should make that appointment, because patients aren't allowed back here."

"Oh, I'm not a patient."

"Then what are you?" Ben demanded.

Jace's eyes twinkled as he lifted them to Charlotte. Then he leaned against the desk and raised a brow as if saying, *You want to take this, darlin'?* Which really chapped her hide. Not because he was letting her take the lead, that was actually sweet and thoughtful. But because he knew she hated it when he called her darlin', and that cute brow raise always translated into darlin'. So she chose to say nothing at all. Except the men in Charlotte's life were never big talkers, so it was no surprise when both men got comfortable, waiting for her to speak.

"Oh, for God's sake," she said, walking farther into the room and dropping the file to her desk. The escalating level of testosterone was giving her a headache. "Jace, this is Ben Clark, a doctor on staff here at the clinic."

"Right, Ben." Jace drawled because Jace knew all about Ben. Knew that they had dated in medical school. Knew that her mother had taken one look at Ben's last name, his strong Southern family with deep roots and deeper pockets, and started picking out wedding dates.

"And Ben, this is Jace, he's my . . ."

My what?

My friend, my ex, my husband?

This was the first time she'd ever been in a position where

she had to explain what Jace was to her. And Charlotte wanted to explain, she really did, if anything for her own clarity, only none of the previous titles seemed to fit.

And wasn't that the problem?

Jace was her ex *and* her husband *and* the biggest unanswered question in her life all at the same time. He was also so much more. And no amount of explaining could make sense of how they'd ended up here, but she could tell by the underlying challenge in his eyes that was exactly what he wanted her to do, and a deep disappointment welled up at the realization before she quickly pushed it back down.

This wasn't her situation to explain, it wasn't her choice. Charlotte had made her choice, she'd chosen Jace and he'd chosen to walk away. So Charlotte went with the one title she could stomach. "He's my mechanic."

There, cut and dry, clearly stated and no room for misinterpretation. For herself or anyone else.

She could tell by the way he held his shoulders that she'd hurt him, but she couldn't worry about that right now.

"I'm more of an engine specialist," Jace said, his comment sounding more like a promise.

His eyes never leaving hers, he held up her keys by two fingers and shook them for added emphasis, and a small part of her sank inside.

"Thank you." She grabbed for the keys as he lifted them out of reach. But Charlotte was no delicate flower, she had long legs, longer arms, and deadly elbows. Not to mention years of working in pediatrics had given her quick reflexes. Only Jace was quicker, so when she went for the one-two to the ribs then grab move, he deflected her easily and moved the keys to his other hand.

"Give me the keys, Jace."

She was so close she could give him a kiss, something

that didn't slip Jace's attention because he leaned in farther and whispered, "That's Mr. McGraw, certified engine specialist, and first, I need to talk to you about that last tune-up I performed."

They both knew he wasn't talking about her car, but about his skill in revving her engine, and Charlotte felt her face flush. Jace's grin widened at her unease, and he stuffed the keys in his pocket—his front pocket—then put his hands up in surrender as if to say, *You want 'em, come and get 'em, baby.*

Because the big jerk knew that the only word Charlotte hated more than *darlin'* was *baby.*

A weighty silence pressed in on the room as he waited until she was good and flushed and she'd retracted her hand before looking to Ben, who was staring at Charlotte as though she'd grown a third eye.

"If you could give us a minute," Jace said. When Ben didn't budge, he nodded to the open door with his chin. "In private. What with doctor-patient confidentiality being what it is."

"I thought you weren't her patient," Ben challenged.

"Oh, I'm not," Jace said, and the way he pitched his voice, low and assertive, had her thighs tightening. "But she's my doctor."

Ben was smart enough not to push any further, because they all knew there was a big difference between him being her patient and her being his doctor, especially when Jace waggled a brow.

"Ben, could you go check on Mr. Koozner? And tell Mrs. Koozner I will be there momentarily." Ben still didn't move, except to cross his arms defiantly. With a sigh, she placed a hand on his shoulder. "I need a minute with Mr. McGraw to discuss a sensitive, um, automotive matter."

"Uh-huh" was all he said, but after a final stern look at Jace he left—stationing himself right outside the door, which Charlotte closed with a gracious smile. Or tried to, only Ben grabbed her by the wrist, pulling her halfway into the hall.

He studied her for a long, hard minute, then his face softened with understanding. Whatever epiphany he'd had Charlotte didn't know, but she'd do just about anything to find out. Because the smile he gave her had a lightness to it that she hadn't seen in a long time.

"Holy shit. That's him," he said, then gave a low whistle.

"Him, who?"

"Him." Ben looked at her again and shook his head, his smile turning so big Charlotte wanted to ask him what was so funny. "The reason we never worked out."

* * *

Well, shit. Jace knew this was going to be a challenge, but he didn't expect Dr. Fucking Perfect to be here. In Sugar. With Charlotte. Situating those fancy letters and starched degrees right between Jace and his goal.

Even worse, he didn't know what Ben being here even meant. From what Charlotte had told him about Ben, and it wasn't a lot, he knew that the guy could get a job just about anywhere in the country. The only reason someone like that would work in a small town like Sugar was if it were for a woman like Charlotte.

Too bad for Ben that Charlotte was Jace's woman.

At least for another three weeks.

Jesus, even thinking it had his stomach knotting and his soul sweating over what would happen when he was gone. Down in Atlanta, running his garage—and from his mistakes—with the taste of Charlotte fresh on his lips. Because she would be here, in Sugar, working herself ragged to prove to her father that she was enough, when she was already so much more than they even realized. Only he wouldn't be here to remind her of that, but some other guy would. Some smart guy. Probably some educated, manicured guy who didn't have a messed-up past, wore pants without grease stains, and had no problem living here in Sugar.

A guy like Ben, who could give Charlotte everything she wanted, everything she deserved—everything that Jace couldn't.

Fuck!

"What are you doing here, Jace?"

Jace looked up from his hands, calloused and rough, to the primly dressed Charlotte in a white lab coat, with her hair pulled artfully back in one of those fancy little twists women like her mastered by age six, and wondered the same thing.

"I came to bring you your car," he said.

"You could have left me a message."

"I did. You never called back."

"A message about my car," she clarified.

She had him there, and sure, maybe he should have, and then he wouldn't have had to witness firsthand everything that Charlotte's life had become. She was exactly what he always knew she could be and more. Amazing, successful, and so damn beautiful it tore him up. She'd done it, gone after her dreams and created a future all on her own, and he was damn proud.

In his heart he knew she deserved that—deserved her life to be amazing. Deserved a good guy like Ben who shared her passions and understood her world. But even though he knew all of this, he couldn't seem to walk away, not yet. Because beneath the formal tone was a spark of hope and what he was pretty sure was heat.

For him.

Somehow, beyond all logic, Jace in his worn-out shitkickers and lived-in attitude turned the pretty doctor on. To test that theory, he pushed off the desk—sure to flex his arms a little in the process—and moseyed a little closer, biting back a grin when she backed up—right into the door.

And just like that, Jace wasn't worried about Ben, or not being cut from the same cloth, because even though Dr. Fucking Perfect was a good guy, Jace's brothers were the best men he knew.

Had to be, because they were just like Jace's dad, cut from McGraw cloth. And even though a lot of that didn't transfer to Jace, he knew that he had to have some of his dad in him, the good parts as well as the stubborn ones, and this was the time to dig deep and go McGraw.

"I didn't come here because of the car," he said, stepping even closer, and pulled out her keys because Spencer had been right. Jace had somehow convinced himself that holding on to her keys was like holding on to her. And it wasn't even close. Because he had learned that the way to Charlotte wasn't to take away her choices, it was to empower her with information and let her make her own decision. And he could only hope that she chose him. "I came here to let you know I can't stop thinking about you—or that night. And I want more time."

"We had a deal," she said, reaching behind her to grip the doorknob, conjuring up some kind of escape plan in that gorgeous head of hers. "One night, and then we walk away satisfied."

"That's the problem, Charlie," Jace said, closing the last

bit of distance until he could smell the light floral scent that was Charlotte. "I'm not."

"Well, I am," she said, right as he reached out and slowly slid the keys inside her coat pocket, noticing the little quiver that ran though her body at the gentle contact. He slowly pulled his hand back out, and when she caught his grin she sighed. "Okay, fine, it was amazing. Sex with you, it's always amazing, but that was never our problem. It's what happens after sex that gets tricky."

"I agree, then let's simplify things." He placed his hands on the door on either side of her head, then looked down into those eyes that he knew were so easy to get lost in. That they were dilated told him she was getting lost, too. "Have dinner with me, Charlie."

She licked her lips as though contemplating life's meaning, then firmly shook her head. "I don't think dinner with you is a smart move."

He faltered. "Dinner. With me. Isn't a smart move?"

And then because she couldn't lie to save her life, she said, "Sex isn't a smart move."

Jace let that settle. It was a direct hit he hadn't seen coming, and the implication burned deeper than he could have imagined. "I didn't say, 'Hey, are you free tonight for sex?' I wanted to take you out to dinner." He caressed her cheek then stared into her eyes, hoping she could see how serious he was. "To talk, Charlie."

He watched her throat work as she swallowed. "With us isn't it the same thing? You ask me to dinner, we talk, have a few drinks, then end up naked in a stairwell."

Jace dropped his hand and took a small step backward because she was serious. And mad. And truth be told, she was right. But not completely. He *did* want to spent time with her, see where this insane connection between them could go, and, yeah, if it led to sex, he was game. But that wasn't the only reason. The other night something between them shifted. Things he'd assumed were long ago forgotten somehow resurfaced, and even though he had zero ideas at the moment on how this could work, he couldn't let go of just how perfect it had all felt. Couldn't let go of the idea that maybe this time they could make it work.

"Are you saying that you don't think I'd want to take the woman I married out to dinner, to talk and catch up, hear about her day?"

"I think what happened in Atlanta was amazing. But we're home now. Back to our real lives. And I think we need to be real about this."

"As opposed to our pretend lives?" Jace said, maybe a little louder than he should have. But every fucking second of it had been real to him. More real than anything that he'd experienced in the last four years. And he'd thought it had been real to her, too.

"Don't get me wrong, it was fun and exciting." *Fun? Exciting?* His stomach burned at the words. It had been a hell of a lot more than that. And he'd thought she felt the same way. "And it was the closure we both needed."

Jace stopped. Brakes pushed so far into the damn floor he felt his body jerk. Obviously, he was wrong. On so many things. "So that's all it was. Closure?"

It was. *Holy shit*, to her that's all it was. Charlotte had the worst poker face, something he used to think was endearing, but right then it was like a fucking wrecking ball to the gut. What he'd thought of as a start to something, she chalked up to closure. And why should she think any differently?

"So what was I?" His voice sounded bitter. Angry. But he didn't care. "Some check in your Risk List?"

"No, of course not," she said, and rested a hand on his

chest, but he didn't believe her. "I just think that what happened is best left in Atlanta."

It took him a long moment to speak. To find the words past the ache, because he was the one used to doing the walking. Being on this side of it sucked, because everything inside him was fighting the good-bye.

"I disagree," he admitted, looking at the confusion in her eyes. "And I think deep down you do, too."

She studied him so intensely Jace felt every bad decision, every regret, every mistake he'd ever made bead up on his forehead. Because she was looking at him as though wishing beyond all wishes that she could find that one thing she needed to say yes. And he hoped to God that she found what she was looking for, because there was something about her that got to him, made him feel things he'd stopped feeling when his parents died. And he didn't want it to stop. Didn't want to go back to feeling hollow.

Didn't want to go back to being that waste-of-space shithead punk that everyone else saw. He'd busted his ass to become a better man, and he wanted Charlotte to see that man. To be proud to be seen with that man. "All I'm asking for is to take you to dinner. Have that talk you promised me."

Now she was pissed off. He could see it in her expression, the way she primly pursed her lips. The softness he'd seen swimming in her expression was replaced by a distant and resigned smile.

"And you promised me forever." She scooted out from under his arms, and even though she only walked the few feet to her desk, it was as though she'd just moved to another state. "But since I follow through on my word, let's have that talk." She spun around to face him, that steel magnolia facade back in place. "I'll start. I just have one question. Are you opening your shop in Atlanta?"

"If the loan comes through." Which was why they couldn't waste any more time playing games.

Unfortunately, for him, Charlotte didn't agree. She was making an escape plan all right. One that would include scheduling all the overtime she could, taking inventory of what was in her pantry so she wouldn't have to go into town, could insure she wouldn't have to see him, would be able to ignore what was happening between them until he left.

Then her eyes narrowed. "Let me get this straight. You come in here, interrupt my workday, insult me, wanting, what did you say? More?" They narrowed even further, until they were two slits of pissed-off female. "Well, you know what, Jace? You don't get more if you aren't willing to put in the time."

"First off, Atlanta is a few hours from here. And second, we still have a few weeks." Which as far as Jace was concerned was the perfect amount of time to see where this could lead. To figure out how to make this work. Because he was certain now that being together was the only way either one of them could ever find happiness.

"I'm not looking for a drive-by relationship, especially with a guy who already has one foot out the door. Been there, done that, have the skid marks on my heart as a reminder," she said, and the quiver in her voice ricocheted around Jace's chest.

"Actually," he stepped forward, "I have both feet firmly planted. Right here. In your office."

"For how long?" she whispered, looking up at him in a way that tore open his damn soul. "A few weeks. Then you'll be, what? A few hours away." She shook her head. "I'm not interested in a *few* of anything."

"So you're not interested in a few," he asked, equally as soft. "Or you're not interested in more?"

Her gaze leveled him. "I'm not interested in starting something that is going to be hard to end or opening myself up to be…"

He waited for her to finish, for her to finally say how she felt, even though, sick bastard that he was, he already knew. It was in the way her face creased as though trying to hold it together and how her glossy eyes flooded with sadness. He'd hurt her, the kind of bone-deep hurt that never really goes away. Something he'd always known, had struggled with since walking out that door, but seeing it firsthand was painful.

Rather than hurt him back, she smoothed her hands down her coat and with a steel gaze said, "Frustrated."

An emotion he knew intimately.

Jace wanted to stay with Charlotte, but her home was here, in Sugar. And even though he couldn't imagine walking away from Charlotte again, he couldn't survive living in a place where there was a different set of expectations for behavior placed on him that other people didn't have to overcome.

And wasn't that a fucked-up scenario? Brett had said the shop was his dream, but Jace had lots of dreams. The most important one being Charlotte, whose carefully constructed life was here. And yeah, he knew that the potential for one, if not both of them, to wind up hurt was high. But after Atlanta, he knew that walking away would slowly tear them both apart.

So, he might not be able to live in Sugar, but that didn't mean that they couldn't find a way to make this work. People did long-distance all the time.

Charlotte was already back to looking at the file on her desk, not so subtly dismissing him, a clear sign she was not ready to admit that.

Fine with Jace, since he was more of an action-oriented guy anyway. So he walked over, getting so close she had no option but to look up, and when she did—man oh man, he felt everything inside of him come to life.

He reached out and cupped her cheek. "It doesn't matter if I open my shop, or if you pretend that this is going away. It's not. Not anytime soon." And to prove his point, he traced her lower lip with his thumb, which trembled slightly under his touch. "And neither am I."

Chapter 9

~

I just have to try harder!"

Hattie McGraw choked up on the lug-nut wrench, pulled back, and was ready to swing when Jace stepped in. He grabbed the top of the tool a mere second before impact.

"The only thing you'll accomplish swinging like that is to throw out your back or destroy the rim," Jace said, holding firm when his grandma tried to finish her swing, which was likely to take out the back tire and a good chunk of his new paint job.

"Throw my back out," Hattie scoffed, straightening to her full height of five-foot-nothing. "I hold the town's Mail Box Baseball record in the sixty and over category." Since Jace was not exactly sure if she meant speed or age, he quickly relieved her of the wrench. "Even got my bat bronzed."

"Which means you know it's not about brawn, it's about the using the right tool," Jace said, taking Hattie by the hand and escorting her to her seat. "Because the first rule of car care is being safe. And if you're on the side of the highway your phone isn't getting reception, you want to get out there and get the tire replaced fast. Plus, if you're looking as pretty as you are today, you wouldn't want to dirty your favorite tracksuit, Grandma. Not if you don't have to."

"Well," she flushed, giving his hand a little pat, then taking her seat and running a hand over the leg of her still clean fuchsia tracksuit. "I guess you have a point."

"Which is why I suggest that every one of you go out and buy one of these." He grabbed the electric lug-nut remover he'd borrowed from Brett, who was sitting in the back of the garage next to Cal, both of them sipping sweet iced tea and wearing shit-eating grins.

"Is your tool battery operated?" Brett asked, and Cal smiled even bigger.

The second word spread that Jace was indeed the instructor of the month, both of his brothers registered for the class. So had every single lady in town—and several of the married ones as well. Which was why he shouldn't have been surprised when he was walking back to his Camaro that someone goosed him, or that when he bent over to demonstrate how easily it fastened to the lug nut someone yelled, "Nice bumper!"

This came from MeMaw Wilkes, owner of the local feed and pet store and his grandma's poker buddy, who was seated front and center, although she hollered as though she was standing at the bottom of the Grand Canyon.

Jace ignored the catcalls that her comment provoked and said, "Now, to prove just how easy this is to use, can I get a volunteer?"

Every hand in the room went up, except for Hattie, who was still eyeing her wrench.

"I'd love to check out your tool, Jace," a honeyed voice came from the back, and before he could answer or anyone

else could approach the car, Darleen Vander sauntered her
way to the front in her mile-high heels and pearls. Red hair
swinging, hips swaying, boobs jiggling, she was there to
be noticed—and since she was currently on the hunt for
husband number four Jace took a good step back. Because
Darleen wasn't just looking for any man—she'd made it
clear to anyone who would listen that she wanted a McGraw.
And Jace, the last remaining McGraw, was apparently her
target.

She'd done everything shy of writing her number on his
forehead in the past forty-five minutes. So, ignoring the bla-
tant invitation in her smile, Jace squatted down and placed
the tool on the lug nut. "All you have to do is situate it like
this, then press the button."

"Let me try." Darleen flashed him those pearly whites and
a little cleavage as she took the tool and did as instructed. A
second later she said, "Oh my. Look at that. Easy as pie!"

"She cheated," Hattie, the most competitive woman on
the planet, called out. "Either that or I loosened it first."

"Sorry, Ms. Hattie. I just have a soft touch when it comes
to a man's lug nuts." Darleen straightened and dropped the
lug nut into his palm and smiled up at him. "Wouldn't you
agree, Mr. McGraw?"

Normally, Jace would have said yes. A woman like Darleen, stacked, sexy, and ready to go, was right up his alley.
Only Jace wasn't looking for fun, he was interested in something deeper this time around. Sure, he had a thing for
leggy debutantes, but there was only one leggy debutante he
wanted anywhere near his lug nuts. And wouldn't you know
it, she was the only woman in Sugar who hadn't shown.

Not to mention that, although Jace and Brett shared a lot
of things, similar taste in cars, sports, and fishing, the one
thing they never shared was women. And since Darleen had

done this whole song and dance with Brett years back, Jace had zero interest.

"I would agree that every person in this room should order one of these tonight," he said diplomatically. "In fact, for being a good sport," and because it belonged to Brett, "you can have this one."

Darleen gave her best pageant smile.

Jace shot Brett a big-ass smile. Brett shot him the bird.

In spite of himself, Jace laughed and felt that smile turn genuine. He was looking out at a few dozen familiar faces who all knew his past, his parents, his loss, and instead of feeling that painful ebb of remorse, he felt surprisingly light.

"Next week we'll cover how to safely jump-start your car."

"Do we need to bring our own cables?" Jelly Lou, his old Sunday school teacher asked. "Or do you come prepared?"

"Look at him," MeMaw said on a dreamy sigh. "The man was born prepared. And I bet he doesn't need a jump to get started, either."

And on that note: "Thanks for coming, folks."

Before someone else could ask about his tool or jumping techniques, Jace gave a general wave to the room, narrowly avoided MeMaw and her octopus hands, kissed his grandmother's forehead, and finally made his way to the back office—hoping to quietly slip out the back door after everyone cleared out.

Only someone followed him to the office. Darleen. She had taken off her sweater and stood in the doorway in just her red dress, a clipboard in her hand and a flirty smile on her lips. "You forgot the sign-up sheet."

Standing firmly in place, she held up the clipboard and waved it in the air as though asking him to come closer, which would be as stupid as approaching a cornered cougar.

"You could just leave it over there." He gave a wave him-

self, more of an *anywhere but near me is fine* flick of the
wrist. "Spencer needs a head count to report back to the
sheriff's department."

"I could," she took a step closer, her perfume reaching
him before she did. "But then I wouldn't be able to tell you
that I won't be able to make it to next week's class."

"Sorry to hear that," he lied.

That got him a smile. "Me too. Tribble has a mini-mites
golf tournament that day, but Sunday he goes to his dad's,
and I was hoping that you could come and give me a private
lesson. Maybe around dinnertime?" She batted those lashes
his way. "I would hate to need a jump and not know how to
get the engine going, if you know what I mean?"

Oh, he knew exactly what she meant. And if the *let's get
busy* purr in her voice wasn't enough to confirm what kind of
jump she was after, the possessive way she rested her hand
on his arm, tracing his tattoo with her painted nails, left no
question.

"Everyone in Sugar knows that Sunday night is family
dinner at the McGraws'. Isn't that right, son?" Hattie asked
from behind, and although Jace had been desperately skirt-
ing around the topic of attending family dinners, especially
this week's dinner since it was at Brett's place, the interrup-
tion was welcomed.

"Yes, ma'am." He took the clipboard from Darleen's
clutches and set it on the desk. "Wouldn't miss it."

"Good, because missing Sunday dinners is as sinful as
fibbing," she said dryly, and Jace felt the walls start to close
in, because now that it was out there, and he'd said yes, it
was as good as done.

Jace was going to Sunday dinner at Brett's. Which was
pretty much like going to dinner at his parents' house since
his brother lived on his parents' old property. Sure, the house

had been demoed and a new one put up in its place, but gathering around the family table, looking out at Sugar Lake, being surrounded by all of that love and the memories was going to be rough.

"Good to hear it." Hattie gave him a sweet smile, one that was full of gentle understanding. His grandma might be stubborn, and she sure loved to get her way, but she also knew dinner would be hard on Jace. Not that she'd let him off.

Then the sweetness left and she was all judgment and condemnation when she shifted her attention to Darleen—and her hand on Jace's arm. "Missing dinner is almost as sinful as coveting a woman's grandson in front of God and witness."

"Oh, Ms. Hattie, I was just being neighborly," Darleen said, and sent Jace a sly wink—which he did not return, sly or otherwise.

"I know, dear," Hattie said, cupping Darleen's elbow and guiding her away from Jace and toward the exit. "But last time you welcomed home one of my boys, he nearly lost his career and his girl." Jace didn't bother to point out that Hattie and her busybody ways had caused more problems than Darleen selling confidential information to the papers about Brett. But since he wanted Darleen gone, before lips started flapping, he just smiled as Hattie went on. "So why don't you go look after your boy, while I look after mine."

Without so much as a *Night now*, Hattie shut the office door on Darleen's stunned face and turned to stare him down. "Now, you want to tell me what this nonsense is about?" She pulled an envelope out of her purse and walked forward so she could slap it against his chest. "And remember what I said about fibbing."

Jace took one look at the return address belonging to the County Recorder, then the opened seal, and felt his chest hollow out. "You opened my mail?"

Hattie walked over to the leather couch in the corner and took a seat. "Opened it, read it, reread it, even called you a few names that if they weren't true God would have struck me dead right where I stood."

"This is private," Jace said, feeling his palms start to sweat.

At first glance, Hattie, with her apple cheeks, round bifocals, and spiky white halo of hair looked like your run-of-the-mill, sweet-as-pie grandma. Only she was like a ferret when it came to other people's private business. Her family was no exception.

So if Hattie read the letter, then she knew about the annulment. And if she knew about the annulment, she had to know about the marriage. Which meant the entire town of Sugar was bound to be buzzing with marital bliss by morning.

"Honey, private ended when I changed your first diaper. And you can guess where I think your privacy can stick it, since I watched as you burned rubber across the South, stopping everywhere but home."

"I go where my job takes me," he defended.

"You're going to crack hell wide open with that lie," Hattie said, but her voice held no real steel. In fact, his grandma sounded sad. And if there was one person Jace hated to disappoint, it was Hattie.

After the fire, she had given up everything, buried her grief and pain over losing her son, to help them rebuild some semblance of family. Hattie never judged, never laid blame when the laying would have been easy, put up with his shit, and loved him even though he was pretty hard to love back then. "I'm tired of waiting for you to come to your senses," she said quietly. "So I hope you're tired of running, because

I'm too old to chase you. Now come over here and sit down, tell your grandma what's going on."

Jace sank into the couch and closed his eyes. It wasn't just a letter from the county recorder's office, it was a letter confirming that the annulment had been filed and sent to Columbus, and now they were just waiting for the judge's signature. When that happened it would be mailed to Sugar and would require two additional signatures.

A signature he wasn't happy about providing anymore.

"How much did you read?" he asked.

Hattie rested a hand on his knee, and when she spoke it was in that tone she'd used when he'd decided it would be funny to pick up his prom date in Mr. Harper's hearse. "Enough to know that you're flushing away what might be your last chance with that sweet doctor. No woman will forgive a man for walking out twice, I don't care how handsome you are."

He straightened. "Twice? You knew about the first time?"

"Who do you think signed for the certified letter the first time, telling you there was a mistake in the filing?"

Well, shit. "Why didn't you tell me?"

Hattie smiled as though he was the slowest man on the planet. And maybe he was. "I figured that if you loved that girl enough to make her a McGraw then she must be someone pretty special."

Jace looked Hattie in the eye and went for bone-deep honest. "Charlotte is beyond special." She was everything to him.

"I can't believe you made me miss my favorite grandson's wedding."

"We eloped," he explained. "And Cal's your favorite grandson."

"Actually, Brett is, but he already has it so easy with

women I pretend it's Cal." Then she lowered her voice, serious and thick with emotion. "But you were so young when your parents went, so hard to reach but so easy to love, I've always considered you mine. And the boy I raised wouldn't walk out on love."

Jace swallowed hard past the emotion clogging his throat. "If I had stayed I would have ruined everything for her, and she has worked so hard. I couldn't do that."

Jace explained the position Charlotte had been up for and how the lawsuit would have ruined everything.

"I hear what you're saying, son," Hattie said when he finished. "You were young, scared, made what you thought was the best decision. But why are you filing this time?"

Jace stumbled. Unsure how to answer *that* question, because the reasons seemed so clear to him now. "Because it was over. Dead and buried."

"Was?" she said, her eyes were zeroed in, dilated and assessing, and flashing with amusement, making Jace want to ask what was so damn funny.

"I asked her if she wanted to refile. She said yes. I'm giving her what she wants."

"And what do you want, son?"

Her. No hesitation, no question. He wanted Charlotte. For as long as he could have her. Period.

"You still love her," Hattie stated with so much conviction, Jace had to wonder just how bad his poker face was.

"So much it hurts to breathe sometimes," he said, knowing that it would only get worse if he walked, but terrified that if he stayed and blew it, it would be game over. Forever. "What if love isn't enough?"

"Love is never enough," Hattie said, as though it should be adopted as Hallmark's newest slogan for greeting cards. "It takes love and trust and a whole lot of elbow grease to go the distance. Marriage is hard work, all relationships are. And sometimes we make mistakes, get scared, but how you deal with your own devil shows the character of the man. And I like to think I raised me three strong McGraw men."

Whether it was the honesty in Hattie's eyes or the simplicity in her smile, Jace realized he couldn't walk away again. He had to do whatever it took to prove that what they had was worth fighting for. More importantly, let Charlotte know that she was worth fighting for.

Taking things slow, giving her the space she needed to distance him right out of her life wasn't the answer. Not when the final papers would be arriving in a few weeks and the woman he loved was on the line.

"Looks like I won't be needing those spare sheets you just put out," Jace said, his heart giddy over how incredible it would be to be back under the same roof. To start and end the day watching her from across a home-cooked meal. "Seems I have a set across the lake."

Hattie cupped his face and got eye to eye—which was pretty funny considering she was standing and he was still sitting. "You telling me that you're going to ask your woman for a key?"

"Who needs a key when boots work just as well?"

* * *

"No risk, no thrill," Charlotte mumbled.

It was the same mantra she had embraced last night over a pint of vanilla-bean ice cream when, tired of people stomping all over her plans, she'd decided to toss the demure debutante attitude right into the hamper and crawl into bed in nothing but what God had given her. After her mother had guilted her into coming over tonight for Sunday dinner to hear her father out, Charlotte had slipped on a new set of silky sheets she'd ordered off the Internet, part of her grown-up sexy plan and part of her horrify her mother plan. Then she decided it would be a shame to put a matronly cotton gown between her and the 1,500-thread count. So she'd gone the full monty on life, and now that the sun had risen she was questioning her sanity.

Because although Charlotte felt very grown-up and sexy, she was also one hundred percent positive that although she'd gone to bed alone, she had woken up to a party of two.

In her bed.

"I have to be honest and tell you that your risks are thrilling as hell," a smooth voice drawled, way too amused and happy for the early hour. Charlotte hadn't forgotten that bedroom voice, she just hadn't expected to hear it again while in bed—and naked.

Ignoring the way her toes curled, she opened her eyes. Blinded by the gleaming white teeth and smug face sitting next to her—on her bed!—she immediately closed them. "I must still be asleep, having some kind of ice-cream-induced dream."

"I've been telling myself that for the past hour, then about fifteen minutes in, you got hot and kicked off all the covers and I considered pinching myself to make sure." She opened her eyes to find Jace propped up against the headboard reading a copy of *Hitched* magazine that advertised "Ten Ways to Keep the Sizzle after Singlehood." He was on top of the covers—thank the Lord—wearing a blue flannel shirt, a pair of well-worn jeans, no socks. "But if you're that concerned, I can pinch you."

His hand went to lift the sheets and Charlotte smacked him away. "What are you doing here?"

"Besides bringing my wife her morning cup of joe?"

He reached over and grabbed a mug off the nightstand and wafted it under her nose.

"I'm not your wife, and..." The mug took one more pass beneath her nose, filling it with the bitter and rich scent of coffee, and she took one more heavenly sniff. Peppermint latte. The man was playing dirty.

She slipped her hand out from beneath the covers, just enough to grab the mug without showing the goods. "Thank you." She snatched the cup. "Now go home."

Jace looked up from the magazine and slid her a smile. "According to the great state of Georgia, I am home." He flipped the magazine around and pointed to number five on the list. "And according to *Hitched* magazine, couples who have little rituals together, such as sharing their morning cup of coffee, often have more spontaneous sex."

Charlotte choked on her coffee. "Me drinking this does not mean we are going to have sex. Spontaneous or otherwise." Charlotte had worked for years to get her life back in order, and she wasn't about to let him walk back in and wreak chaos again.

He folded the magazine and shrugged, as though unconcerned with her statement. "Sharing a drink led to stairwell sex, so who knows where a few more of these coffee-in-bed mornings will lead?"

"Nowhere. Because this is the last coffee we will share in this bed or any other. Because there is no way you are staying here."

He let out a low whistle. "Thing is, I already gave my notice at Cal's, Brett's house is full of baby crap, and the B&B is booked until Founder's Day. So I don't know what to tell you, Charlie," he said. "Except to point out the fact that, while it may take some getting used to your snoring again, you did offer."

"It is not a fact, because I never offered for you to stay here," she countered, sitting up on her elbows. "And I don't snore."

Jace raised a disbelieving brow. "Ah-huh, and you did," he said. "Right there in that official government office. You went on record saying that you understood it would take three or so weeks for the marriage to be absolved. And darlin', I want my three or so weeks."

His eyes drifted to the sheets, which had shifted slightly, and he grinned. His smile was crooked and a little naughty around the edges, and her heart fluttered. Four years, and he still had the ability to send her into a free fall with one smile. "You can be such a jerk."

"True," he said, meeting her gaze when she tucked the sheets around her neck. "But part of marriage is accepting your partner for who they are, so I would hate to deny you part of myself. That's number three on the list." He went back to the magazine and turned the page. "But I have to admit that I'm looking forward to number seven the most. 'Naptime Shenanigans.' "

"There will be no naptime, because you aren't sleeping here." She snatched the magazine and threw it on the floor.

He rolled to his side so that he was facing her. She had to admit that being this close to him when he had that mischievous twinkle in his eyes was tempting.

"I like naptime when we're awake better anyways."

Charlotte rolled her eyes, because grown-up sexy women didn't give into temptation, they harnessed it. "I meant that you need to find your own bed."

"Already did." He patted the mattress a few times, then went about snuggling in, getting his massive body comfortable, purposefully grazing her thighs with his in the process.

"This," she spread her hand out to encompass the entirety of the bed, sure to hold the sheets tight with the other, "is my bed."

"This," he took her hand and a jolt of something familiar and heated slid through her body as he moved it to the middle of the mattress, "is your half. And this is mine. You can use the big pillow I have down in my car as a wall if you're afraid you might be tempted to spoon. But don't blame me if I cross the line tonight. You know me, I like to be the big spoon."

He also liked to hold her close, as though even while asleep he wanted her to know she was completely adored. Treasured. Cared for. Three things that she desperately wanted but was terrified to reach for. It had taken her a long time to get used to an empty house. Having him stay only to leave again would make her house seem even emptier than it already did.

"There is no way in hell...wait." Her heart, which was already beating irregularly due to being naked in the presence of the best lover she'd ever had, kicked into high gear. "Did you say your car is here? As in out front?"

"That a problem?"

"Yes!" Charlotte sat up so fast little dots of anxiety spotted her vision, then she nearly lost the sheet completely. Jace smiled, so she tugged harder. It didn't help, the big ox was too heavy to budge. "You know how Sugar is. Brett spent one night at Joie's place and stories of the *big city Yankee polishing PGA playboy's five iron* was all anyone talked about for months."

And Jace's big blue muscle car with black racing stripes in her driveway was a problem of epic proportions. The thing was so noticeable, so identifiable, having it at her house would be worse than hanging a neon DR. HOLDEN SHACKIN' UP IN SIN AND SCANDAL sign from her front porch. One night and the gossip mill would shred her reputation.

And Darleen Vander, Lord help them all. That woman would take one look at Sugar's fastest ride making cozy with Charlotte's Sunday school sedan and Darleen would have the *im*-peachment campaign locked down before Monday's meeting. And Charlotte would be out of office before Founder's Day. Which would mean any headway she'd made in moving the fair to the clinic's lot would vanish. Poof. Just like that.

One night, and Charlotte would be back to ground zero.

Her chest started tightening, and Charlotte was pretty sure that the bed was spinning.

"Five iron, huh?" Jace shook his head empathetically. "Poor guy, at least they could have said nine iron."

"Jace, I'm being serious, you need to move your car. Now," Charlotte demanded, pulling a pillow up to her chest as though *that* was the same as wearing clothes. Then she gave him her most intimidating look, which was difficult considering she was afraid she'd flashed a little skin in the process. When he didn't move, didn't even blink, she figured all the important parts were covered and went for honest. "Look, I know you're mad about me avoiding you and not returning your calls and that you want to talk about Atlanta, but—"

"I am so past talking."

"—if anyone sees your car here they will assume we're"—she looked at his mighty fine body sprawled across her bed, then at her mighty naked state, and whispered—"you know."

"No, I don't know," he whispered back. "I have a pretty good idea, but why don't you explain it to me so we know we are both on the same page and I can get the visual?"

She ignored this. "If anyone sees you here, at my house, it will ruin"—her position with the Peaches, her position at the hospital, her position in the community—"everything."

"Everything, huh?"

A flash of hurt crossed his face at her statement, and Charlotte found herself wanting to explain, wanting to say that she didn't care if anyone knew, that once upon a time she was proud that he was her husband. But so much had changed since then, and so much was on the line now, she held her ground. "I am serious."

"Baby," he said, sitting up and leaning over her until she was pressed against the headboard, and the only thing between her and his big, muscled body was a few measly feathers wrapped in cotton. He smelled of warm sheets, sweetened coffee, and pissed-off male. It was a complete turn-on. "You have no idea how serious I am. You want to keep all of this quiet? Fine," he said, and nothing about his tone or the way he flicked that *F* sounded fine at all. "But this time around, I want something, too."

Charlotte swallowed, hard, because his look was fueled by anger, sadness, one hundred percent bone-deep determination. And the last time he'd been so set on something was the night before he walked out, when he'd been adamant that his reputation would ruin her chances at Atlanta Memorial. And too concerned over her family's opinions, she didn't fight hard enough to convince him otherwise. "I'll play your game, but you'll have to play mine. I want three weeks. Three weeks of morning coffee, talking about our days, you being the last person I see before I go to bed."

"Jace," she said on a broken whisper, her chest so tight it hurt to breathe, because she couldn't give him what he was asking for. Couldn't go there with him again only to lose him in the end. She'd been there before, and it took years for her to finally heal enough to move on. Sure, she knew the sex would be magical. Just like she knew his leaving would open up old wounds that would never properly heal. "Three weeks of pretending that this is real—"

He put a finger on her lips, silencing her. But when he spoke his voice was low and gravelly and caused something deep in her soul to warm. "I want to hear what you have to say, I really do, baby. But I'm not done talking, and I need to get this all out, okay?"

"Okay," she finally breathed against his finger, because although she was terrified to hear what he was going to say, she couldn't live with herself if she didn't let him finish.

"I walked out. I got scared and I walked and I hurt you, so damn much I can still see it every time you look at me." He tucked her hair behind her ear and let his finger trail down her jawline and she felt the tears she'd buried long ago begin to rise. "I am so sorry for being that guy to you, for letting you down, and I know that no matter how much I apologize it will never be enough. Never make it right. That's why I need three weeks of naptime shenanigans and holding hands and marriage. To prove to you that I'm not that guy, that we can make this work somehow. No pretending, Charlie, real and raw and honest. Like how it used to be."

He closed his eyes, and when they opened Charlotte forgot to breathe. Because there looking back at her was enough longing and loneliness and earth-shattering desire to break her resolve—and her heart. Even worse, it was like looking in the mirror four years ago. "I want three or so weeks of you, Charlie, so please don't say no."

Chapter 10

Charlotte studied the man who had once been her whole world and wondered how her life had veered so far from the plan. Then she saw those intense blue eyes looking down on her as though she was everything and she knew. The woman who had a ninety-two-checkpoint life plan by age sixteen, who never took a road trip without a highlighted map, had slept with her estranged ex-husband. Except now he wasn't so estranged and he wasn't even her ex.

And his plan was to move in with her and pretend like the last four years hadn't happened.

Charlotte wouldn't allow herself to think about what that could mean, or even how wonderful it would be to go back to the way things were. Because wondering led to wishing, and wishing wasn't a risk she was willing to take—not with so much to lose. "What if I say no, that I can't right now, then what?"

He shrugged, as though expecting her to say that. "You

do what you need to do and I'm going to do what I need to do."

"Which is what?"

His eyes went darker, laser sharp, and she knew that Jace had his end goal in sight—and she was it. "Prove to you that I'm worth the yes."

Her heart ached at his raw statement. Made her want to tell him he was worth so much more than a yes. But things had changed. She had changed. The world had moved on and life had taken them in different directions, and no amount of wishing could change that. Which should have made saying no that much easier.

But it was obvious Jace had changed, too. For the better. Sure, he was bigger, broader, sexier—if that was even possible—and the hard edges had softened a little with time, but it was something deeper. Jace was more comfortable in his skin, more grounded and focused. There was an ease to him now that was compelling, that drew people in. Drew her in.

All excellent traits for someone opening their own business—in Atlanta.

"It's not that easy," she said to the both of them. "I have a list a mile-long of things that need to happen. And if they don't, or I get distracted, then everything that I've worked for since leaving Atlanta will be for nothing." Which would leave her with nothing—and wasn't that a terrifying thought. "There isn't room on my list for this."

Silently, he stared down at her, taking in her eyes, her lips, then tucked a strand of hair behind her ear. "This wasn't on my list either, Charlie, but we're both here with a second chance to get things right. And I promise you that I won't make your life any harder."

"But just you being here will make it harder." Already she

felt like she was drowning in expectations. "Between work, the Founder's Day Fair, and the endowment, my life is crazy. You being here will only make it crazier." But even as she said it she wondered if that was true. Wondered what these next few weeks would be like knowing that she had someone in her corner. Even if it was temporary. "How would I explain your car or you or *us* to people? They would be so focused on what was going on in my personal life, it would overshadow what I bring to the professional side."

And by people, she specifically meant her father. He was already encroaching on her job, challenging her ability to get things done. If he found out she was secretly married—to the town's most notorious young gun—she had no idea what he might do. But she could guarantee that it wouldn't end well for her—or her job.

Because if she let herself belong to Jace, even for a moment, she feared she'd lose the life she'd fought so painfully hard to create. Just the thought terrified her and made the broken spot in her heart that still belonged to Jace throb a little.

Charlotte had already let go of her dreams for marriage, children, a family. She couldn't lose her Grow Clinic, too.

Jace knew what she was worried about, it was obvious by the protective undercurrent rolling off of him. She could also tell that he was disappointed—in her. Not that she blamed him. If Charlotte hadn't been so adamant about keeping their marriage a secret back then, none of this would be an issue now.

"You don't have to explain anything to anyone if you don't want to," he finally said. "I won't park my car out front, I won't interfere with your job or life outside these walls, and no matter what you decide, it stays between us."

"So no one has to know?" she asked hopefully.

Jace's hand, which had been gently stroking her shoulder, faltered for a moment. "If that is what it takes," he said, so full of understanding it made shame rise up and take hold. Because it shouldn't matter what everyone else thought, but apparently to her it did. "Regardless, I'm not giving up. I was given three more weeks of being your husband, and I am going to be the kind of husband my dad was, the kind of husband you deserve, the kind of husband I should have been before."

Charlotte swallowed at his statement, let those words slide into her heart. Resisting laid-back Jace was hard enough, resisting him when he was all in would be impossible. "The last thing I want to do is complicate things more for you, Charlie. We both know that things are already complicated, but between us they doesn't have to be. Please, just give me the chance to prove that."

The thought of eliminating one what-if from her life was enough to give her pause, but it was the quiet steel behind his statement that had her reconsidering. Jace would find ways to put them in close proximity regardless of what she said. At least this way she could control some of the fallout when he left.

"Fine," she said, hoping she made the right choice. "You can stay. Downstairs on the couch. No sneaking in my bed, no naptime shenangians, and no sex."

"We'll see."

"And at the end of the three weeks, you leave, and we both go back to our lives." She slipped her hand carefully out from behind the pillow to shake on it. A gesture that he ignored, and instead he gave her a smack on the lips.

"Deal." His eyes glowed with wicked intent. "Unless you beg me to stay."

"I won't," she said, and meant it. At least that was what

she told herself. "I have a busy day today." She poked him in the chest, ignoring how it flexed under her touch. "Now move so I can get dressed."

Jace moved all right—right onto his back, folding his arms behind his head and leaning against the headboard. Charlotte tugged on the blankets, which were trapped under all two-hundred-plus pounds of him. He just smiled.

Undeterred, she smiled back. Charlotte had made a plan, her grown-up sexy plan, which included embracing her inner awesomeness and taking back control of her life. And she wasn't about to allow one more male to come between her and her master plan, even if he did make her knees weak.

With a well-practiced grin, she threw the sheets off, dropped the pillow to the ground, and made her way to the bathroom. From the bed, Jace let out a sound that was all male appreciation, so she added a little extra swing to her step as she went.

And why not? Jace was determined to stay, and she was determined to not lose sight of the big picture—which was living by her own rules. Which was why she stopped at the door and looked over her shoulder.

Jace was zeroed in on her backside, so she cleared her throat and waited as he slowly ran his gaze back up to meet hers, not a bit embarrassed that he'd been caught ogling. "Oh, by the way, I won't be home for dinner tonight," she said. "I have a date."

Not that an evening with Lionel was something to brag about, but the only way she was going to make it through these next few weeks with her heart intact was to get them on even ground.

* * *

"*You're* my date?" Charlotte asked as her parents' front door opened.

"You say that like Lionel is a better option," Ben said, looking more than offended. "At least you know I won't try to play foot doctor under the table." This was true, although Charlotte had come prepared this time, wearing her knee-high boots. "And I don't look like I run a funeral home."

No, Ben looked like a true Southern gentleman in a pair of dark gray slacks, a blue button-up, and a coordinating tie.

"So unless you're planning on ending the night with a game of doctor, then this isn't a date." He looked her up and down and smiled. "You bring your lab coat?"

"No," she hissed, then peeked over his shoulder, relieved to find the foyer free and clear of any relatives. "And don't let my mom know this isn't a real date. If telling her that you were already taken wasn't enough to thwart her matchmaker skills, then she might ignore my wishes and call Lionel."

"Too late," he said, opening the door and letting her inside. "He's already in the study."

"Great." Charlotte groaned, her boots suddenly feeling flimsy. She shrugged out of her coat, and Ben, always the gentleman, took it. She looked him up and down and a plan started forming in her mind.

"He's talking to *my* date," he said. "The leggy redhead from HR who, by the way, has already asked if my stethoscope and I would like to have a sleepover."

Damn it, her ankles were toast.

"You should host a little doctor-patient sleepover yourself," he said, guiding her down the hallway toward the dining room. "Or maybe have that mechanic come give you a tune-up."

Charlotte kept walking, but her heart skipped several

beats. She thought back to that morning, having Jace in her bed, and felt her legs tremble. He'd given her an ultimatum and she'd caved, so easily it was embarrassing.

Charlotte had enough people standing in the way of her goals, yet one plea combined with those deep-blue pools looking at her as though she were everything, and she'd so readily accepted her fate.

Charlotte stopped right outside of the closed double doors. "Did you mean what you said? About why we didn't work out?"

Ben let out a long sigh and turned to face her. They'd had this conversation before, but he'd never had a name to go with their breakup. "You have dated exactly one person since you came home from Atlanta, and that was just because I was familiar and parent-approved."

"Between the new pediatric ward and the Grow Clinic, I haven't had time to date," she said, surprised at how easily the excuse rolled off her tongue. Even more surprised at the empty ping she felt when saying it.

"Well, you might want to find some time before that wound-tight-with-no-fun-in-sight scowl you've got going on becomes permanent."

"I have fun. And I am not scowling." To prove it she looked over at him and smiled serenely.

"God, that's even worse." He grimaced. "All I am saying is that I can't remember the last time I saw you let go, offer up a real expression that wasn't tempered for someone else's benefit, like you did in your office the other day with the mechanic. I forgot that Charlotte existed, the fiery, stubborn girl I met in med school who didn't apologize for how she lived her life."

Charlotte opened her mouth to tell Ben just how wrong he was. That *that* wasn't fire he saw, that was frustration, irritation, and, okay, so there was a lot of chemistry. But he wasn't done.

"You've spent so much time trying to please everyone else you are barely living. You are good at playing nice. You do it with your parents, the hospital board, your patients. With me."

"Nothing is wrong with nice," she defended.

"Nice is boring, Charlotte," he said quietly. "If it weren't, you and I would have worked out. But neither of us wants boring, which is why I am here with a twenty-something former gymnast who likes to twist herself into a pretzel." She smacked him again and he laughed. "Life isn't a degree, Charlotte, it doesn't come with a course outline, so stop worrying about coloring in the lines and live a little."

Maybe he was right. Maybe she had been constructing reasons to avoid putting herself out there, to avoid creating waves. And maybe spending these next few weeks with Jace, letting go of their past, would give her the courage needed to take the final step for a full future.

The mahogany doors slid open and Reginald Holden the Third stepped forward, pulling Charlotte in for a hug.

"Glad you made it, honey."

"Me too," she said, and she meant it. Even though she was still angry at him for trampling inside her lines, something they would discuss before the night was over, more than anything she wanted to move forward and really live. And maybe that meant sharing some of the responsibility so that she had time for that life she was so excited to get to.

"I was just telling everyone about my trip to Nashville," he said, stepping back, and Charlotte could see that by everyone he meant the entire medical board. "I convinced

Mr. Neil and the entire Mercy Alliance board to come to the Founder's Day Fair."

Then again, maybe karma wasn't on the same page.

* * *

Jace was shoulder deep in the exhaust system—more correctly, what was left of it—when his cell buzzed. Wiping his hands on his pants he hit speaker.

"You're late," Brett greeted. "Hattie is already here, Payton has been asking every ten seconds where Uncle Jace is, and Joie is pulling the brisket out of the oven in five minutes. *Mom's* brisket, which means she spent all day tending to *that* instead of taking advantage of kid-free time to tend to me, so if you don't walk through that door in three minutes we're going to have issues."

"Shit." Jace grabbed the towel off the hood of the car and wiped his hands. He had completely lost track of time working on Hattie's car—and thinking about Charlotte.

And her damn date.

While he was pretty sure it was with the podiatrist her mother kept pairing her up with, he'd also heard that Dr. Perfect was to be in attendance. According to Hattie, Ben and Charlotte had given their relationship a second try after she came home, but it didn't go anywhere.

Which meant Ben could live. For now. If what Hattie said was true, and her gossip was as solid as gospel, then Charlotte had been the one who put on the breaks. That made sense, though, because why would Doogie Howser choose to be "friends" with a woman this amazing unless there was a "with benefits" added to that title.

And the only benefit the guy was going to get was his 401K. "I'm working on the car."

"Work on it tomorrow," Brett said.

"I'm covered in grease."

"I'm covered in baby slobber and quite possibly spit-up breast milk." He had Jace there. "Three minutes," he said then hung up. And since Jace was smart enough not to argue with a strung-out new dad, he headed to the bathroom to clean up.

Ten minutes later Jace pulled onto the same gravel road he'd walked a thousand times as a kid, cut the engine, and rested his head on the seatback. The moon was already visible over the trees, casting a light glow over Sugar Lake. Jace caught a reflection of himself in the front windshield. He was dirty, bone tired, and scared shitless.

Jace had always taken comfort in the saying that you could never really go home, but in that moment he was terrified to realize that maybe he actually had. Because even though his parents were gone and the house was no longer standing, every nostalgic feeling he'd been avoiding, every memory he'd buried for the past ten years came rushing back to him the second he opened the car door and the familiar scent of clean lake air, fresh-cut grass, and bluebells—his mama's favorite flower—gently blew by.

A deep longing rolled through him, but he set his jaw against it and grabbed the case of beer he'd picked up at Mable's Market off the passenger seat. It got stronger as he walked around back and went to the small dock that jutted out onto the lake. The night was crisp with fall, but so clear that every single star was visible, something he missed these past few years of being around all the city lights.

Standing near the edge of the dock felt like standing on the edge of something huge, and the longing shifted from an ache to something deeper. Something nostalgic and weighted. As if all he had to do was take one more step and everything would shift back to the way it was before. Before he lost his parents. No one could have anticipated the summer storm that destroyed their home, a chance lightning fire that tore through the McGraw ranch. But if Jace hadn't insisted on going back in the house to get his football gear, they wouldn't have also lost their parents.

Jace remembered the smell of the smoke, the taste of fear when his dad went back in for their mom, who was looking for Jace, and felt everything inside tighten until breathing became difficult.

He'd made a stupid, impulsive decision, and his family paid the price. Not that they ever blamed him. In true McGraw fashion, his family surrounded him, gave him the patience and understanding he needed to push through a difficult summer—and a hell-raising next few years. And when they saw Jace struggle to fit in, their love went so deep they gave him the room he needed to run.

Some days it felt as if he still running. Too tired to go there, he cracked open a beer and took a long, cold swallow, noticing the small dingy tapping the edge of the dock as the current moved. It was ugly as hell. Fire-engine red with a white racing stripe around the rim, the boat no bigger than a glorified wheelbarrow. Just the idea of cramming his body in that thing had him smiling.

Actually smiling... and it felt good.

He'd caught his first fish in that dingy, was so excited about the small-as-shit guppy that he tipped the boat and plunged himself and his dad into the water in the middle of November.

"Brett found it in the barn in pretty sorry shape," Cal said, coming to stand by Jace's side, as though sensing that his kid brother needed him. Jace reached down and handed him a bottle. With a nod of thanks, Cal twisted off the cap and took a pull. "He and I rebuilt it last summer, then the girls painted it to match an old photo Hattie had."

"You ever get Payton out on it?" Jace joked, although he didn't feel like laughing inside.

Cal gave him a long side look that was sheer joy, and Jace found himself wondering how Cal could be so light being here. "Every Saturday during fishing season."

"Really?" Jace couldn't hide the surprise in his voice. His niece who used to bake mud pies and take pride in skinned knees had become quite the young lady, trading in her shin guards for high heels and sparkles. Not that Payton didn't recently break the record for the fastest underarm pitch in three counties, but now she preferred to do it with painted lips and designer ponytails.

Cal's smile fell. "Payton's friend Mason likes fishing, so she has a renewed interest in the sport. He goes out with us a lot."

Holy shit. "Payton has a boyfriend?" When did this happen? Even crazier, if Cal knew, then how was the punk still breathing?

"Mason is a friend," Cal stressed the word until Jace though he'd run out of air. "Who happens to be male. Which means they can hang out in large groups of friends or with other adults or me—"

"You make them hang out with you?" Jace had forgotten how lethal his brother could look when he was pissy.

"—but no dating until she turns sixteen."

Jace fought the urge to laugh—fought it hard because Mason must have a pretty big set if he was willing to take on hanging out with Psycho Dad. "You know her birthday is in seven months."

"Which is why I haven't slept in over a year." He laughed then tipped the bottle back.

"Does it ever get easier?"

"Nope," Cal said, and Jace nodded. Neither spoke for a long moment, just silently stood there, sipping their beer. Two brothers and a lifetime of memories, staring out at the lake. "Been coming here every week for dinners for over a year, and I don't think it will ever get easier."

That was not what Jace wanted to hear. Every time he came back to Sugar the pressure grew until he thought his head would blow right off. When he left, it got even worse. So he'd tried his best to stay away.

Eyes still on the lake, Cal said, "But between you and me, I think you've made it a hell of a lot harder than it needs to be."

Jace waited for the lecture that usually followed, for Cal to point out that it was time to come home. But he just stood there, staring out at the lake and calmly sipping his beer.

When his eyes had finally acclimated to the darkness, he noticed a flicker of light across the lake near one of the old peach orchards. It was Charlotte's house, nestled between the trees, barely visible because of its isolated location. He couldn't see her car or her porch swing, or much of her house for that matter, but if he squinted hard enough and looked through the distant branches, he could make out the soft glow of her kitchen window, which was illuminated from the inside.

Jace looked at his watch and frowned. It was too early for her to call it a night. Unless her date had gone sensationally bad. That thought turned his frown right-side up. But the smile was short-lived, because what if it went sensationally good, and they'd skipped dinner altogether, heading home for dessert.

And he wasn't talking about the ice cream in the fucking freezer.

Shit.

"Everything working out okay?" Cal asked.

"What?" Jace asked, a little startled because he had already pulled his keys out of his pocket. He looked at his brother and, hoping he came off more causal than he felt, tried to figure out if Hattie had spilled the beans already.

Cal cocked his head. "The shop? What were you thinking about?"

Right, the shop. The *real* reason for this little bonding moment. "That Brett has a big mouth."

"Brett's worse than Hattie when it comes to gossip," Cal said with a smile. "How do you think I keep tabs on Payton and her goings-on?"

As long as he didn't put that kind of detective work into figuring out Jace's goings-on, they'd be good. Not that he had any goings-on at the moment, or even potential goings-on. But he was on a mission to change that. After he got rid of Dr. Fucking Perfect.

"So the loan's looking promising?" Cal asked.

After receiving that letter from the recorder's office it was looking better than it had in weeks. He'd be surprised it if wasn't a done deal. "As long as it comes through by the beginning of the month, I'm good to go."

The longing grew stronger, gnawed at his gut. The prospect of distance didn't hold the same power it once had.

"Or you could stay," Cal threw out.

"Atlanta Motorsports is in Atlanta." Atlanta had a lot going for it. In fact, it had everything he'd been looking for.

Except Charlotte.

"Open a shop here."

"I'm not just buying a building. I'm buying Dale's client list. And the name."

"You have as many connections as Dale. If not more.

Plus, people know your work, it carries more weight than a garage name," Cal said as though it were that easy. As though Jace could just uproot the business and make a go at running a high-end car shop in the middle of truck country.

"My network is in Atlanta," Jace said. "And how many Shelbys do you see driving around Sugar County?"

He knew how specialized Jace's job was, knew that the best shot Jace had at making this a success was to use the connections he had and to be located around people who had the kind of cars he wanted to work on. Which were in Atlanta.

"Your family is here," Cal said. "*You* belong here. Always have, you've just been too busy to realize it."

"I've been busy building a career." *Rebuilding my life.* "Just like you and Brett. I don't hear you giving him shit for playing tournaments all over the world."

"Because he always comes home when he's finished," Cal said.

"I'm back." He avoided the word *home*, because it felt like a lie.

"For how long? Two weeks? Three? Until it starts to get too hard and you bolt?" Cal slid Jace one of those all-knowing big brother BS looks and said, "Or until it starts to get too easy?"

His brother was so fucking wrong. And since he'd heard the same thing from practically everyone else in his life as of late, he felt a riptide of fury and frustration roll through him. "Until I figure things out with the garage."

And with Charlotte.

"Then it will be what? Another five years before we get you back?"

"Atlanta is only a few hours away." Something he had three weeks to convince Charlotte of. Because a few hours in the car didn't mean that he wasn't committed to her.

"With your track record, you might as well have bought the Beverly Hills location."

Jesus, his family wouldn't let up. Jace worked harder than anyone he knew. "If that's what it takes to make it, then yeah."

"That's a bullshit answer and you know it," Cal said calmly, but it was apparent that neither of them felt calm right then. Jace felt like packing up and heading across the lake. "You're good enough that people would ship you their engines wherever you live. Brett doesn't have just anyone work on his clubs, he sends them to the guy in that pro shop in Arizona."

"Sending a set of clubs off to get tinkered with is a hell of a lot different than sending an engine. Or a fucking car," Jace said, his emotions so close to the surface he felt them bubbling.

"All I'm saying is that I miss you. We all do." Cal let out a breath, and Jace watched as his brother's frustration faded into something warmer. Sadder. "You're a smart guy, Jace. If you wanted to make it work here then you'd figure it out."

A painful pulse started behind Jace's eyes because that was the question of the hour. Did he want to make it work here in Sugar? Last week he would have said hell no. But after Atlanta, after this morning with Charlotte, he wasn't sure. And that scared the shit out of him.

"Just think about it," Cal said. Brother-speak for *I love you*.

Cal finished his beer in a gulp then jerked his head toward the house. "Now, if I don't get you inside Joie will start fretting about dinner getting cold, then Brett will see we took the time to share a beer without him and lay into us both. And if you thought I was unhinged when I became a dad, wait until you see him. Guy doesn't get his beauty rest and he's as hormonal as Payton."

And since the last thing Jace wanted to do was make tonight any harder on the people he loved, he finished his beer and offered a smile that was in complete contrast to everything he was feeling inside.

He'd long ago learned that hiding the frustration and pain was easiest for everyone. And it was important to him that his brothers really believe he was happy. They'd lost as much as he had, maybe even more. Only they'd stuck around to piece the family back together.

So, happy Jace in full affect, he walked up the back porch and into the house.

He held that smile all the way down the hallway, past the dozens of pictures and memories, some of which he hadn't thought about in years. Others, the newer ones, he hadn't been around to create. And if that didn't piss off his lungs, then walking into that kitchen and seeing his family all gathered in one place, looking happy and at peace, did.

Joie was at the counter working on dinner with Hattie, who was mashing the potatoes and telling everyone the secret to fluffy spuds. Payton was snapping the beans with Brett, who was managing the salad and his baby girl. Lily Anne was managing to be the cutest kid ever with one slobbery hand balled up in her mouth while the other, quite the multitasker this one, was fisted in her daddy's hair.

"Uncle Jace," Payton squealed, and rushed over, wrapping her arms around his neck. She gave him a kiss on the cheek and he noticed that her lips were all glossy, like pink shimmery gloss that a woman would wear. "You're just in time to be my taste tester."

Jace cleared the emotion from his throat. "What am I tasting?" What he really wanted to ask was whose baking was he testing. The look on Brett's face, the one that said *run while you still can,* told him his niece was the chef in question.

Which meant heartburn, tooth chipping, or worse was highly possible.

Payton was a disaster in the kitchen, but that didn't stop her from trying. And trying. And, God help them all, trying. The poor kid couldn't even manage to make Jell-O without starting a fire.

"Butter pecan sandies. My favorite cookie for my favorite uncle," she said with a proud smile that no one with a heart could say no to, especially her *favorite* uncle.

"Did you hear that?" he said to the competition, who happened to be a born lady whisperer. "I'm her favorite."

"Have you tasted the cookies?" Brett asked, eyes on the cutting board. "No? Then I wouldn't go bragging just yet."

"They're good," Payton defended, and tilted her head for effect, which only managed to bring his attention to all the freshly cut layers of blonde hair that swished over her shoulders. No more ponytail, his girl was sporting a stylish do fit for a co-ed. "My best batch yet."

"I bet they are." Just like he bet she was sweetening him up, for what he wasn't sure, but knowing his niece and *that* look, it was certain.

"Thanks, baby," he said, and kissed her on the top of the head, noticing he didn't have to bend down all that far. Then he noticed her sandals, strappy and red with little gold clasps around the ankles and heels high enough to be considered strutting pumps.

What the hell?

"I'll grab you one." She fluttered toward the cooling rack.

"How about you make me a plate and we'll eat them on the porch swing after dinner, like we used to," he said, wanting to have some one-on-one time with his niece, as well as giving his stomach time to prepare.

Payton stopped and spun around, her face expressive. "Or we can go now."

"Or you can let the man take a breath before you start working your magic," Hattie chided. "Plus, he's got to get me that dish way up there." Wasting no time putting Jace to work, she pointed to a platter on the top shelf.

Balancing the case of beer in one hand, Jace easily grabbed the platter with the other. Setting it on the counter proved a little more difficult. Impossible, actually. It was like a raceway, with Payton going back and forth between her cookies and the oven, Brett placing salad fixings on the counter, and Joie moving all over the place. Jace felt like that sorry dingy out back, knocking up against the edge of the dock while his family ebbed and flowed as a unit.

Chest a little tight, he handed the platter to Hattie directly and took a step back—and out of the way.

Hattie locked on him, her white brows puckered as she studied him thoroughly. Jace leaned casually against the back wall, set the beer at his feet, and Hattie pursed her lips. "Do I need to pull that boot out of your backside?"

"No, ma'am."

"Good to hear." She set the platter on the counter with ease.

Cal picked up the case of beer and slid it in the fridge. "What did you do now?"

Nothing that he wanted to discuss in front of his entire family. Even though Jace wasn't a big talker, there wasn't much he kept from his brothers. But Charlotte, well, she was his. Always had been. And with gossip being what it was in this town, he didn't feel like sharing. Plus, *they* were a long story, a story he'd promised that morning he wouldn't share.

Not that he would even know where to begin, since not a soul in that room, except his nosy grandmother, knew about their history.

"What haven't I done?" he joked right as Brett hurdled toward him.

"Incoming," Brett said, flying baby Lily and her gummy smile though the air, making all kinds of propeller noises— and making Jace's chest her landing strip. "Hang with your uncle Jace for two seconds while Daddy gets the bread out of the oven," he cooed.

Lily Anne cooed back, then she giggled like everything in her world was right. Until Jace decided to get a better look at his niece and shifted her around to face him. She took one look at his scruffy face, her eyes went owly, and she let out a shriek that was car-alarm certified. Jace had to stretch his jaw just to pop his ears. He also had to move the baby out of kicking range, since her arms and legs were moving with intent. Not that anyone else seemed to notice, cue ball was wailing for all the woes in the world and the entire kitchen was business as usual.

Jace bounced, swayed, hummed, paced, tutted like Hattie used to when he was a kid while salads were tossed, plates and platters made their way to the table, and Lily kept wailing. It was surreal.

"Uh, bro, I think she's broken," Jace finally said, a thin sheen of sweat trickling down his back. Jace had spent time with exactly one baby over the years, Payton. And he was suddenly realizing that *that* was a lifetime and a pair of hooker heels ago.

"Nah, she's just teething," Cal said.

Teething? "She's already teething?" He peeked in the kid's mouth, which was wide open and midhowl, and yup, a sharp little white dagger poked through the front.

"Next time you pass through she'll be walking," Cal said, sticking his finger in her mouth.

Lily Anne instantly went silent, her eyes wide and assessing while she gummed the hell out of Cal's finger.

"And I'll be driving," Payton proclaimed, and Cal groaned something that, had Hattie heard, she would have gotten out the spoon.

"Hey, Jace, welcome home," Joie said, going on her toes to give him a sweet kiss on the cheek, and Lily one on the head. She looked at Cal and frowned. "Did you wash your hands?" Then to Brett, "Did he wash his hands?"

Brett looked up from the oven. "Come on, man, there is a teething ring in the freezer." He pointed with his mitted hand. "Like two feet from you."

Cal rolled his eyes and mouthed *amateurs,* but grabbed the teething ring and popped it in. Lily Anne continued to study Jace and to slurp, while a big stream of drool dripped off her chin and onto his shirt.

"I saw that, Cal," Joie said, picking up the brisket and making her way to the table. Brett intercepted her, trading in the heavy platter for the salad and giving her a kiss that made Payton gag.

"Sorry I'm late," Glory said. "Hey, Jace. You made it!"

Jace turned around to say hey back, but Glory was busy saying her *hey* to Cal, who was busy tangling himself around his fiancée.

"Gross," Payton said, but she was grinning like it was Christmas morning and she'd found a bright pink convertible under the tree. And who could blame her? After a lifetime of waiting for her mom to show up, Payton was finally getting what she wanted—a real family.

"Biscuits are done," Hattie said, and before his grandmother could say *Time to eat* everyone was already around the table, napkins in their lap, his brothers making googly eyes at their women. And Jace was still leaning against the wall wondering what had just happened.

Somehow over the past couple of years his brothers had found happiness. Managed to create the kind of homes their parents would have been proud of. And Jace was proud of them, too, he truly was. He just wondered what he was missing that they seemed to have figured out so easily. Over the past few years his brothers had found their way through the pain, managed to build amazing lives for themselves, and Jace was exactly where he'd been the day his parents died.

Surrounded by family and love, but completely alone.

Ignoring the urge to make up an excuse and head out, Jace did what he hadn't been able to do in over a decade. He took his seat at the family table. At least he assumed it was his seat since it was the only vacant one, and it was in the same exact spot as it had been when he was a kid.

Within seconds platters were being passed, Payton was talking about school, and Jace found himself silently in awe at the kind of connections that were happening. The kind that felt easy and warm and right. The kind you didn't have to work at, that just came with being family. And he knew that if he just let go, made the decision to stay, then maybe he, too, could be a part of it.

"Are you breathing yet?" Payton asked quietly, and Jace realized he wasn't breathing at all. He just silently sat, taking everything in. Wondering what Payton would be doing next time he—how did Cal put it, right—blew through. If Lily Anne would really be walking. Hell, if something didn't change she'd be talking. And he would have missed it.

Who knew what else he'd miss? Not only with his family, but with Charlotte, who would have fit right in around his family's table.

"Yeah." He managed.

"I wanted to ask you if you'd teach me to drive while you're here."

Jace looked at Cal to judge the exact size of the explosion that was about to go down. When Cal said nothing, just chewed a bite of brisket until it was dust, Jace said, "You gotta ask your dad about that."

"He says I can't get my permit until I know how to change a tire and my oil. So I figured who better to teach me than the best mechanic in racing. Right?" Jace wasn't sure about the *best* mechanic in racing, but he felt himself getting nice and buttered—and liking it. "Mason said that when I get my permit he'll teach me how to drive a stick."

"Mason needs to keep his stick to himself," Cal said. But instead of Payton storming out of the room and bursting into tears, her current MO, she calmly looked at Glory, who rested her hand on Cal's arm. And, *holy freaking hell*, Cal took a breath and said, "Maybe Jace would let you help out at the shop with Hattie's car. Show you the basics."

"You sure?" Jace asked, because Cal didn't sound sure. In fact, he sounded like he was considering cracking Mason's stick in two.

Cal looked from Glory, who was smiling for all the world like he was some kid getting the mom-approved nod for using good manners, to Brett, who was snickering, and back to Payton. "Fine. Uncle Jace can help you with the mechanics, and then you and I can take *my* truck out for a drive around the property."

"Really? Thanks, Daddy." Payton leaned across the table and kissed him on the cheek, as though that wasn't her plan all along.

Not that Jace was complaining. He actually found himself looking forward to working on the car with Payton, getting back some of that time he'd been missing out on. Being the kind of uncle he'd promised himself he'd be when she was born, and maybe passing along some of the love for cars he and his dad shared.

And maybe he'd figure out what to do with the pretty doctor across the lake.

Chapter 11

"What we are going to do is call Mercy Alliance, explain that although the fair won't be held at the clinic this year because it has never been held at the clinic, Sugar is still a sound investment," Charlotte said sternly—to her reflection in the bathroom mirror.

"*That* is what you should have said." She slipped her dress off, pulled on her flannel pajamas, then narrowed her gaze. "Not that brown-nosing speech you made about teamwork and the good old Holden touch." Next she let her hair free from its bobby pins and leaned against the counter—getting up close and personal with herself. "You are a chicken, Charlotte Holden. A big, fat, lying chicken. And a pushover."

When Charlotte was good and scolded, she gave one final disappointed huff then said, "No one likes a pushover, so time to get busy fixing that."

To that end, Charlotte marched into her bedroom in her pink fuzzy slippers and picked up the big, obtrusive duffel bag and work boots she'd found sitting next to the foot of her bed. Taking up her personal space. She'd had enough of controlling men messing with her plans for one night, so if Jace was determined to stay, he could stay on the couch. Which was where she ceremoniously dumped his things.

Feeling stronger by the second, she dusted her hands off and walked into the kitchen, heading straight for the freezer. She opened it up, scanned the interior, and—

"Damn it all to hell!" She slammed the freezer door.

Someone had eaten her last ice-cream bar. Okay, that someone had been *her*, but if she hadn't been so thrown off this morning by her unexpected houseguest, then railroaded by her parents in front of the *entire* hospital board, she would have remembered to pick some up at the store.

Only now she was home, in her pajamas, with no ice cream—and no ideas on how to fix something that was so obviously broken. Well, she had ideas, but since strangling her dad was illegal and egging his car would horrify her mother, Charlotte plopped down at the kitchen counter and said a really bad word. Really loud.

And then, because *that* was the same as acting grown-up, she said it again.

"Well, that's about the best welcome home I've ever had," Jace said from the kitchen doorway, looking big, edgy, wind-rumpled, and the right kind of dirty. "You know we could do that." He glanced over his shoulder toward the hallway that led to her bedroom, those bad-boy vibes he was so good a producing in full effect. "Or we can do this." He crossed the kitchen, that black cotton tee pulling just right across his chest as he set a paper bag on the island.

It clanked.

"We already played spin the bottle," she informed him in her most unaffected voice. "You won, remember?"

"Oh, I remember. Every moment of the night we met." His eyes went a deeper blue, and she knew that he was replaying every wicked thing they'd done that night. In slow motion. "Are you offering a rematch?" he asked in a tone that left her a little breathless.

His lips tilted up at the corners, and *great. Just great!* Now she was remembering that night. Remembering exactly what he'd won, how sweet his victory had been—for the both of them. "No."

"You sure about that?"

"Yes," she answered, but her voice quivered. Damn voice.

"If you're sure?" She nodded, because she wasn't sure, but she needed him to believe she was sure. He wasn't buying it, but he went on, "Then how about making it a float kind of night?"

He reached in the bag and—Lord almighty—pulled out a gallon of vanilla and a bottle of sarsaparilla. Her favorite. "I only brought one bottle, so your date will have to leave."

"There was no date," she sighed, feeling like the biggest fool in Sugar, and with residents named Skeeter and Rooster, that was saying a lot. "Dinner was a setup."

"Ah, a blind date then."

"Worse." It was a big, elaborate hoax for her father to announce the "good news" to the board and take the credit for Charlotte's hard work while dumping the gigantic aftermath in her lap.

"Worse than spin the bottle?" he joked.

"Worse." She tried to smile, but she just couldn't.

Jace walked around the island, turned her stool around, and stood between her legs. His hands went to her hips and hers went directly to those big shoulders of his, the ones that felt like they could carry all the weight in the world—even hers. "So we skip the bottle and go straight for the carton."

"Ice cream can't fix this."

"Maybe not, but I bet I can." He leaned past her and, pressing that *I can shoulder anything you want to give me* chest against her, grabbed a spoon out of the top drawer. Scooping out a big helping, he held it to her lips. "But a little ice cream never hurt."

She said nothing, and a flicker of challenge lit his expression. He slid the ice cream along her lips and a chill went up her spine that had nothing to do with frozen dessert. She loved it when he was like this, when she felt his strength mixed with a gentle understanding.

"Mmm." She took a bite and the big jerk grinned. He was right and he knew it. Ice cream did make it better. Or maybe it was that he was there, and she didn't have to come home and try to figure out how to fix this alone. Isn't that what Ben had said, that she had to give up control a little if she wanted a chance at something amazing?

"Good girl." He set the spoon on the counter, his hands immediately going back to her hips. "Now, what was so bad that you almost turned down ice cream?"

"The entire Mercy Alliance board is coming here, to Sugar, to partake in the Founder's Day Fair before they make a decision about the endowment."

Lord, saying it made it even more real. Made the panic she'd been keeping at bay wash over her. How had her father let this happen? While Charlotte struggled to add color to her black-and-white world, her father ran his world in the gray.

And any good belle could tell you that gray is not the new black, and it never would be, because no one looked good in gray. No one!

"And that's bad because?"

"Because they expect the fair to be held in the medical

center's parking lot as a token of the town's support for the advancement of medicine in our community."

"Isn't it always held on Maple Street?" He looked as confused as Charlotte's dad had been when she'd voiced the same concern.

"Not according to my mom. Who went on and on and on about how this town has rallied behind the center," she explained, picking up the spoon and scooping herself a bite. "Jace, she flat-out lied."

"Does that surprise you?"

"No." Sadly, it didn't. Not much that her parents did surprised her anymore. And wasn't that a sorry state. "But then she even implied that all the proceeds were going to the center, and my dad didn't correct her. When I tried, he said, "It's not like they're going to come to Sugar and check. Only..."

Oh God, she was going to be sick, so she shoved the mouthful in and waved the spoon for him to continue when a hunk of sweet, cold ice cream got momentarily lodged in her throat.

"They're coming to check."

She nodded, her eyes watering past the brain freeze. "I broached the idea about uprooting more than a century of tradition and moving it to the center with the Sugar Peaches last week. Even explained how moving it would make the parade longer, because we can put more cars on display in the lot than on Main Street." She shrugged. "We'll vote on it at tomorrow's meeting, but Darleen is seducing them with old-fashioned barn raising of Bluebell Hall dreams, and some of the older members are pretty set in their ways. It isn't looking like enough of them can be swayed. And why should they be?"

"Because that endowment can mean a lot to this town."

He stroked a finger lightly under her eyes, and she was surprised to discover just how close to real tears she was. "It means a lot to you, too." She sniffled and he scooted closer, his strength and warmth wrapping around her. "And I can't imagine that there isn't anyone on the planet you can't sway, Charlie. Sure, Bluebell Hall is flashy and a great sound bite for the gossip line, but you are all about heart. You turn that laser focus and soft heart on anyone and they'll be on your side. I promise."

"Not my dad."

"Again, your dad's an idiot," he said a bit dryly, and instead of defending him this time, Charlotte laughed. Okay, it was more of a snort, but after tonight she truly believed that her dad had a screw loose. "He is. Any person with a lick of sense would know that. Sure, he's good at schmoozing the clients, telling them what they want to hear, but you have so much passion and drive to do right in you, it's contagious," he said with such a level of awe in his voice that her knees went weak.

"You make everywhere you go a better place, Charlie. You show people how they can be the best part of themselves, how they can be the best part of other people's lives. You make the impossible a reality." His voice dropped to a smooth timbre when he said, "That's a special gift. Powerful, and damn impressive. People get a taste of that and they can't help but follow you."

His conviction was so strong, so unflappable Charlotte wanted to believe him. Wanted to believe what he saw in her was true. And she almost did, only to remember that she had given him all her best parts and he hadn't followed her.

He studied her for a long beat then slowly shook his head. "I was an idiot, too. But even idiots can learn from their mistakes."

"You weren't an idiot," she whispered, cupping his face and loving how rough his jaw was with the day's growth.

Jace was just hurting. And scared. Had been for years.

Having grown up surrounded by love the way he'd been, only to lose it all in one summer storm must have been paralyzing. But he never stopped to grieve like his brothers, at least not that Charlotte saw. He kept on moving as though his world hadn't been broken.

Most people in town thought Jace was wild, but Charlotte had come to understand that he was afraid of finding peace. Because he didn't think he deserved it. So he kept busy with the wrong friends, going down the wrong path—anything to avoid any kind of real attachments.

Then they'd had a chance meeting at a bar in Atlanta, where no one in the room knew their baggage, and things got serious fast between them. Jace asked the prissy hometown girl if he could buy her a drink, and to his surprise she ordered up a shot of Jack and enough tequila to throw a party, which they most certainly did. She laid one on him, right there in the bar, and they went from one night to forever in a matter of weeks, but when the dust settled Jace started looking for the next distraction. And at the first sign of happiness, he took off.

"Can I get that in writing?" he said, leaning into her hand.

"I thought you were going to help me fix this mess."

"Right, that part's easy, we just need to find a good reason." A smile crossed his face. "Parades are about floats and cars, and no one can say no to a fleet of fancy cars."

"A fleet of fancy cars?"

"Yep. I know a guy in Atlanta who collects rare classic cars and happens to love showing them off." He tightened his hand on her hip and gave a teasing squeeze. "Now, I can't imagine anyone on the board, including Darleen Vander, who would turn down riding in the parade in a souped-up roadster."

That was actually a great idea. There was a long tradition of Sugar Peach board members leading the parade in the back of a hay-filled wagon. The last few years some of the older members had opted out of riding along because the hay irritated their psoriasis, or the wagon was too much for their hips to handle. But if Charlotte could offer a stylish, comfortable alternative that happened to support moving the parade route, then Darleen would be outnumbered.

Except for the fact that she'd already stated the flaw in this plan. "The Peaches are about preserving tradition."

Jace shrugged. "Just because you move locations doesn't mean you have to lose tradition," he said softly. "Like every time I have a bad day, I bring home a carton of vanilla and bottle of sarsaparilla and drink my sarsaparilla float at the kitchen counter. Whatever counter I happened to be living at."

"You hate sarsaparilla," she said, remembering what a hard time he'd given her every time she'd ask him to bring a bottle home from the market.

"But you don't."

"Jace," she whispered, because if what he was saying was true, and Jace was a lot of things but he wasn't a liar, then on some of those nights when she couldn't get him out of her mind, just maybe he was sipping a float in another part of the country and thinking of her. Even right now, there he stood, right next to her, vanilla ice cream in hand, and she realized he'd only brought one bottle of sarsaparilla.

"Did you bring this for me?"

He looked into her eyes. His held a mix of raw uncertainty and relief. And something so heartbreakingly sad it had her reaching out to touch his arm. "I was hoping you'd be here, but I bought it for me." He blew out a long, shaky breath and ran a hand down the back of his neck. "I had dinner at Brett's."

"Jace," she said gently, taking his hand in hers.

All night she'd been sitting there wallowing in the disaster that was her family. Convinced that everything was over, that her dad had tossed away three years of hard work. And Jace had walked right into her drama, got shoulder deep, and told her how much she mattered, how special she was, and helped her find a solution. All the while his world was changing, too, since she was pretty sure he hadn't been back to Sugar since Brett built a house on their parents' property.

"When was the last time you went out to your parents' property?"

He laced his fingers through hers, running his thumb back and forth across the inside of her wrist, saying nothing for a long while. "The day I left for the army."

Charlotte thought about that for a moment, knowing that he'd enlisted the summer after he'd graduated high school. "You've never gone back? Not even once?"

"No. Never really saw the need. The house was gone, my parents were gone." He looked at her and gave a small smile. "But Brett and Joie have done a great job with the place. It looks just like the kind of place my mom would have built."

"Was that hard?"

His face creased, perplexed, as though he had to think about his answer, so she slid her free hand around his neck, gently gliding her fingers through the hair at the base of his neck. His eyes met hers and held. "Actually, tonight wasn't as hard as it could have been."

"Yeah?"

"Yeah." This time when he smiled Charlotte could see the exhaustion lining his eyes. In fact, everything about Jace seemed tired, the kind of bone-deep tired that came with letting go. With moving on after being stuck in the same place for so long.

"So you don't need a float?"

"No," he said, his mouth inches from hers. "I just need this."

He was going to kiss her. Charlotte saw it coming, saw the way his eyes slid closed as he got closer, but she didn't move. Didn't push him away, either. Nope, she just sat there as he closed the last little gap and took full possession of her mouth. Moaned when his hands slid around her, pulling her to the end of the stool and so fully against him that she could feel his heart pounding through his chest. Felt her body melt as he slowly took her night from awful to awfully hot with every seductive brush of the mouth.

She felt her resolve melt, too, right along with all of the ten thousand ideas why this was a bad idea. Because she needed this. Needed to let go and live. That was her plan, right? And if this was what living with Jace felt like, even if just for a brief moment of time, then she was game.

His lips were so incredibly soft, so purposeful and skilled, bringing her to a hard boil with the lightest of feather touches. His hands slid lower, cupping her butt and pulling her even closer, and she felt herself sigh when their body parts lined up perfectly.

Everything about them lined up perfectly, she thought as he continued to drive her right out of her mind. Not out of her dress, she noticed disappointedly, as his hands stayed firmly on the outside of the fabric. She shimmied even closer, sliding her hands up and under his shirt, and hello!

Muscles and more muscles. All bunched and coiled, tightening under her palms like they were about to snap— telling a very different story than the languid *We've got all night, darlin'* kisses he was giving. She was open to all night, she was even open to the three weeks. What she wasn't open to was him pulling back.

Which he did. The silly man gave her one more mind-blowing kiss, then stepped back.

"What are you doing?" she asked in a harsh breath.

He was breathing a little heavily, too, and his eyes were hot and zeroed in on her mouth as he spoke. "Dropping it back into first."

"What if I like overdrive?" she said, and then took his mouth again because after that kiss, after her night, first gear didn't work for her.

Jace sighed, actually it was more of a moan, and then rested his forehead against hers. "I promised that tonight was about helping you out. I want to stick to that promise."

"What if I need more help?" She grabbed his belt loops and yanked him close. "This kind of help."

"This kind of help hasn't lasted well for us," he explained, and she could hear the steel determination in his voice.

"Why do you get to make all the rules?"

"Because you only gave me three weeks. So as long as my boots are under your couch instead of the bed, kissing is all we're doing," he said, then with a quick kiss he headed toward the family room. " 'Night, Charlie."

Charlotte mumbled that bad word again, only this time it didn't make her feel better. So she dug into the carton of ice cream and decided it was a gallon kind of night.

* * *

Monday morning, Charlotte was up and out of the house and walking into work before the sun crested the hills—or before

Jace graced the house in his altogether. Charlotte knew that, like his military career, Jace preferred to go commando.

As often as possible.

Not the worst way to start the morning, she thought, remembering how his muscles felt rippling under her palms. But she was facing off with Darleen later today and needed to be as focused and collected as possible. Getting sucked into Jace's sexy bad-boy vortex wouldn't be a smart move. And Charlotte was smart. Courageous. Ready to fix her world.

The first crucial decision of the morning came down to an old-fashioned or a jelly-filled with pink sprinkles. Both lovely candidates. The first, her reliable go-to morning goodie choice, and the latter a risky surprise that could either be mouthwatering or a major disappointment. Charlotte knew this was an important decision, one she took her time with—while nibbling on a doughnut hole. Then another.

When she was positive that choosing between them would be impossible and unfair, she reached for a napkin.

"You know you want both."

Charlotte froze as that husky, trouble-filled voice slid over her. God, she loved that voice. Four years and her body still quivered every time she heard it. She'd hoped that annoying tic would have passed by now, but it only seemed to have become more acute with time.

She let out a deep breath, braced herself for impact, and turned around. Her affliction was worse than she'd originally thought, because Jace got better looking every time she saw him. Not only was he filling the doorway to the lunch room and giving off enough sexy man vibes to have her heart melting, but the man could fill out a pair of jeans like nobody's business. His dark hair was a little damp at the ends and crammed in a ball cap, scruff covered his jaw, and he was wearing a wrinkly black T-shirt that clung to his chest with a hint of perspiration. She would have thought that he'd run all the way here, except his breathing was sure and steady.

His smile, she couldn't help but notice, was twitching with amusement.

"I just need one." Who needed *two* doughnuts to start their day?

His amused gaze held hers. "But you *want* both."

She so did. "Two would make my butt too big."

"Not possible," he assured her in a tone that was so full of male appreciation it sent vibrations skittering though her body. "But to be safe, we can do a before-and-after inspection. A very hands-on experiment."

"That won't be necessary." Although her body said it was as necessary as breathing.

"If you change your mind, let me know. I've been told I have very efficient hands."

Which he'd ruthlessly used on her last night, only to get her all hot and bothered before handing her off to a gallon of ice cream. She put the jelly-filled back and grabbed the old-fashioned before setting it on the small breakfast table. She didn't sit, hoping he'd get the hint.

He didn't, instead leisurely sipping from one of the to-go cups in his hand.

"What are you doing here?"

"Morning ritual. Number five on the list." He handed her the other to-go cup. A warm, intoxicating blast of cool mint and steaming coffee teased her nose. "I heard you tear out of the driveway, so I hopped out of bed and decided to bring the caffeine to you."

Which explained the sleep-mussed hair and soft eyes. "Thank you. But I actually have to get to work, I have a full caseload today." She waved to the files awaiting her on the table.

"I can see that." Although his eyes were too busy staring at her mouth to even notice the stack of files. A small spark ignited under his intense gaze, heated until she felt her body vibrate as he slowly met her eyes. "Was it always like this?"

Charlotte wanted to pretend that she had no idea what he was talking about, but she couldn't ignore the pull. Because no, it had never been like this. Ever. When they'd married it had been the kind of heat that burned too hot and fast to sustain. But this time, she felt a slow simmer in her chest that was far more dangerous to her well-being.

"You should go," she said, hating how throaty she sounded. Hating that every time he came around she forgot her plan, forgot what she had worked so hard to create. Because every time he looked at her with those deep blue pools she remembered what it felt like to truly live.

"I will," he said, placing his cup on the table. "But before I do, number one on the list."

Jace took a step closer, close enough that she could smell the crisp morning on his skin. Close enough that delicious, bone-melting desire slid through her, which is when she discovered several things.

The first being that she didn't want him to go. Charlotte wanted him to pull up a chair and share his morning coffee with her, as though they did this every day. Even more unsettling, if Jace did go, she wanted to go with him. Which led to the last, and completely unacceptable, realization. She wanted to find out what number one on the list was. She wanted it more than her peppermint latte, more than a maple bar. She wanted it more than she wanted her next breath.

Not that she had time to take that breath, because Jace, good to his word, lowered his head and showed her exactly what he'd come there for. And work was the last thing on her mind. Not while his mouth gently worked hers as though he'd also been fantasizing about this all morning.

He teased the seam of her lips, and she gave a breathy little moan that would have been embarrassing had she not been distracted by the way his chest muscles felt under her exploring hands, how they moved and tensed as she ran her palm down to his flat stomach.

"Kissing is number one?" she breathed against his mouth when he pulled back.

"*No, daily* kisses is number two, listening to your partner's needs is number four. And the way you were staring at my mouth stated loud and clear you needed some loving, but since we're at your work I settled on a kiss."

"You're reading too much into this." His eyes dropped to her fingers, which were fiddling with the button of his jeans. She snatched them back.

"I don't think so," he said, nipping her lower lip, and yeah, she needed some loving all right. "And this," he breathed against her lips and her body went up in flames. "This is number one."

It happened so fast, Charlotte barely saw it coming. One moment they were hot and heavy, throwing gasoline on fire, the next his big arms were around her, pulling her toward him. Into him really, until she was engulfed in the safest place she'd ever been.

Because Jace might be a master kisser, but his hugs could change the world. Of that she was certain.

"I better let you get back to saving mankind," he said. With a final brush of the lips, he walked over to the counter and grabbed the jelly-filled and set it on her napkin. "Sometimes what you want is also what you need. Enjoy, Charlie."

Charlotte watched him walk away and had one last realization. Not only had Jace ruined other men for her, now he'd gone and ruined doughnuts, too. Because all she could think about was that hug.

Wrapping up the doughnuts for later, after the contact high wore off, she went to her office to handle some follow-up emails, then headed down the hall to see her first patient of the day. Scotty Clay, a nine-year-old who had a habit of liberating his "light saber" in public places. According to his chart, today he had freed Willie near the local junkyard to relieve himself—on an electric fence.

Glory looked up from the nurses' station as Charlotte approached. "Hey. Don't you have a Peaches meeting?"

"Not until noon."

"Then why did I see Darleen leading the Peaches toward the boardroom?"

A bad feeling crept over Charlotte. She had moved today's meeting from town hall to the clinic so that she would be able to make the meeting between patients. Darleen knew this, knew that if the meeting was held at a different time then Charlotte wouldn't be able to make it. Wouldn't be able to vote and, worse, present her case. *Damn!* "When was this?"

"About ten minutes ago."

Charlotte looked at the file in her hand, then at the waiting room. "Is Ben in yet?"

Glory shook her head. "He's working the late shift." She paused. "Your dad is the rotating physician for family practice today." *Double damn!* "Want me to call him?"

Charlotte sighed. They both knew what her father would say if Charlotte asked him to cover for her to take care of a Peaches meeting. Then again, it was because of her father that she was in this mess to begin with. "Yeah, tell him Clay Scott is waiting in exam room four and I will be back in an hour."

"Do I tell him why?"

"No." Charlotte headed toward the boardroom, then turned back around. "Only if he asks."

"He's going to ask, which means I'll be the messenger," Glory explained, not looking happy about it. "The last messenger was sentenced to a week in podiatry with Lionel. The one before that was fired."

"You won't get fired," Charlotte promised, thinking that the first girl actually got off easier. "Just tell him I am handling something for the Mercy Alliance project. Oh, and can you upload the Reasons to Pick Sugar Medical PowerPoint on my laptop to the center's so I can pull it up in the boardroom?"

The twenty bullet-point reasons she'd compiled in an effort to sway the board, while polishing off the gallon of ice cream last night.

"So you want me to upload personal stuff on the company cloud *and* lie to your dad?" Glory laughed. "You so owe me."

"Saturday night. Drinks on me," Charlotte promised, and tried to hand off the folder.

Glory didn't take it, instead crossing her arms. "Oh, I don't want drinks, Doctor. I want details. All of them. Like where Jace was last night."

"He was at home." Not a lie.

"His truck was at Cal's, but when I left for work this morning I noticed *he* wasn't there."

Great. Charlotte had been hoping that no one would notice Jace wasn't in the guest room. Then again, this was Sugar. Secrets were harder to keep than a pot full of gold.

"Did anyone else notice?"

"Not yet. And I can help you keep it that way if you let me know what's going on."

"Fine. But you're buying the drinks then." Charlotte tossed the file on the nurses' station and quickly made her way to the elevator. She took it to the top floor. The conference room sat at the corner of the building, offering a beautiful view of the town of Sugar. When she stepped inside, twenty sets of eyes turned to focus on her—including a pair of wide, surprised, *I am so caught* eyes.

Charlotte smiled. Darleen stood at the head of the table, Golden Peach in hand, presentation board propped up behind her, and frowned.

"Sorry I am late," Charlotte said, making her way to the front. Eyes on Darleen, she sweetly asked, "Or is it that you're all early?" She held her hand out for the Golden Peach. "Thanks for covering for me until I could get away."

"No problem." Darleen handed over the Peach—and the meeting—with a sweet smile. "I was just getting started on the agenda."

Charlotte looked at the poster board facing the room, which showed a Photoshopped image of Bluebell Hall looking ready to host a ball, at the half-dozen poster boards stacked behind it, then down at the agenda on the table. It listed the order of business, and not surprisingly the only two items up for discussion were the parade route, conveniently mapping out a route that ended on Maple Street, and the recipient for the funds raised. "Item one under suggestions, Bluebell Hall. I wasn't aware that Bluebell was an official candidate."

Darleen looked out at the group—and they were all looking back, rapt by the drama that was about to unfold. She cleared her throat. "Well, it was mentioned at the board meeting, so I assumed it would go on the agenda."

"We all know what assuming can make you," Hattie said from the table. "And I thought we were here to talk about the new parade route, not changing the recipients this late in the game."

"If we have time to consider altering the parade and fair location, then I don't see why we wouldn't be able to reconsider who benefits from this year's profits," Darleen said in a sugary voice.

"The girl is right," Mable, the oldest and most respected Peach in the room, said. She was also the senior adviser to the board, so her opinion was golden. "My suggestion is to allow Miss Charlotte to explain to us how moving the parade will benefit the town, then let's allow Ms. Darleen to propose why Bluebell Hall is a viable project."

"I think that's fair." Darleen beamed. "And since you are the current regent, I'll let you go first." She handed over the laser pointer and took her seat, several gasps and whispers rising in her wake.

Charlotte felt her forehead start to glisten. Darleen would pop a grandma's wheelchair tire if it meant getting one space closer in line. The only reason she would let someone else go first, especially Charlotte, was if she thought she'd already won the argument. The woman had an ace up her cashmere-capped sleeve, and that made Charlotte nervous.

"The girl acts like she's the only angel in God's choir," Hattie murmured loud enough to be heard in the ER. "She's already done finished her presentation."

Which meant the women had been successfully seduced by tales of ceiling-to-floor leaded windows, inlaid mahogany floors, and a sapphire-colored glass dome. Charlotte could feel the titillating energy in the air, see the twinkling promise of eternal glory residing behind each and every bifocal. Making her job that much harder.

The PowerPoint flickered on, a photo of a little girl in wheelchair smiling from inside the Grow Clinic lit the screen, and Charlotte stopped being nervous. Stopped caring about Bluebell Hall and her dad's flub-up and remembered

what Jace said. That if she led with her heart she couldn't go
wrong. And suddenly this wasn't about her versus Darleen,
it was about the town and the clinic. And helping families.

"I have wonderful news, so I would love to." Charlotte
used the laptop on the conference table and clicked to the
next screen. A map appeared. "Now, if you'll look at the pro-
posed route I have outlined here, you'll see that we are only
looking at adding a few blocks to the historical route. The
parade would take the same path our ancestors took, but it
would continue on until the Medical Center."

"What are those fancy cars there for?" Mable asked.

"I am so glad you asked." Because Darleen might be hiding an ace, but Charlotte had a Jace. And suddenly she didn't
feel so alone. "Jace McGraw knows a classic car collector in
Atlanta who is willing to loan us his collection for the parade. It will allow our board members to ride in the parade
without the hay problem, and attract more out-of-towners by
having the rare cars on display. More tourists mean more
money."

"My pa used to drive one of those," MeMaw Wilkes said
pointing to the Model T Charlotte had added to the map.
"We used to ride in it during the parade."

"There's a total of nine additional cars so far, so the only
concession is that the route be extended to allow room. Plus
ending the parade at the Center's parking lot will ensure that
the cars don't get scratched or dented and can remain on display."

"But the fair has always been on Maple Street," Summer
said, looking to Darleen who was giving her a sly thumbs
up. "If we move it, all of the foot traffic the shops count on
will move, too."

"I thought about that," Charlotte said, clicking to the next
slide. "Which is why I propose that we offer every sho

owner on Maple a free tent at the fair, a place where they can sell their wares and interact with the community."

"It would take care of that awful traffic jam," Mable said, and a few of the older members nodded. "Last year I couldn't even get into the shops because there were so many people and tents on the sidewalk."

"It also takes into consideration how our community is thriving," Charlotte said, running a red beam to the additional space. "The first Founder's Day Fair had seven families. Last year over three hundred local businesses and families participated, and an additional two thousand people came out for the fair. This day is to honor the people of Sugar, all of the people of Sugar, and Maple Street isn't big enough for our growing town."

A few murmurs of approval sounded, and Charlotte sighed in relief as some of the grayer heads began to nod. When Darleen didn't even mumble an objection or point out a flaw with the plan, Charlotte asked, "Are there any questions?" She paused, giving the members time for consideration. Nothing but smiles. "Great! Then, as the regent of the Sugar Peaches, I propose that we change the route of the parade to end at the Sugar Medical Center. All those in favor say aye."

A resounding aye went up and Charlotte blinked. Almost burst out in a giddy laugh. Could it really be that easy?

"Great," she said again, still in shock. "That's really great. I guess the next item up for consideration then is the recipient." And because part of winning the argument was going to come down to etiquette, Charlotte said, "Darleen, would you like to go first?"

Darleen stood, smoothed down her lavender shirt, and smiled. "Sure. I'll make this quick. I know that we have spent the past few years focusing on the Grow Clinic and the new pediatric ward. It is only natural that we'd want to spread the love, pick a new cause."

"I agree that we have focused a lot of time and money on the medical center," Mable said, and Charlotte felt her chest pinch. If Mable sided with Darleen then Charlotte was sunk. "Bluebell Hall will be there next year, and we're almost there with the center, so I think I speak for the rest of the board when I say it would need to be a really compelling reason to switch in the last leg of the race."

Charlotte sat back and smiled, wondering why she'd doubted her Peaches. They were about tradition, honor, and serving this wonderful community. They might be temporarily entertained by the idea of grandeur and glory, they were former debutantes after all, but when it came down to it, nothing could sway them from following their heart.

Darleen whipped her hair back and shot her shoulder out. "I have it on good authority that the Sons of the Revolution are telling everyone who will listen that *they* are going to revive old Blue."

Nothing except a good old-fashioned competition.

Chapter 12

⌒

One excruciatingly long hour later, Charlotte stood at the head of the table and tried her best to come off confident and unfazed, but truth be told, now that the board had reached its conclusion, she wasn't feeling all that well. The dough-nuts she'd eaten earlier had settled into a solid lump in her stomach, and the idea that she might go from front-runner to Darleen's runner-up was more than she could say grace over.

She wanted the board to vote her way, but Lord knew a girl didn't always get what she wanted.

Still, Charlotte had busted her backside for three years, dedicated her entire being to this town, the Peaches, and this center, so she was going to make it go the distance even if it killed her. Which her father might do for her if he heard that the Peaches were contemplating this year's benefactor.

"Have you reached a decision?" Charlotte asked with as much decorum as she could muster. After the two sides had presented their cases, the group had been split, right down the middle. So Mable suggested that Charlotte and Darleen wait in the hallway so that the members could voice their concerns without the pressure of pleasing either party.

Most of the senior board members had agreed with Charlotte that ending support when the Grow Clinic was weeks from reaching its goal didn't set the kind of example of follow through and dedication that the Peaches were known for. Others didn't feel the same. And it was the *others* Charlotte worried about. The ones who shared their last name or deepest secrets with Darleen.

"We have," Mable stood, surprisingly agile for a woman who was older than the town. "We have decided to postpone the decision until after the Founder's Day Fair."

"After the fair?" Charlotte asked, wondering when that elephant decided to crawl up and sit on her chest.

"It appears that the vote didn't come down to beneficiaries so much as leadership styles."

This did not sound good. "Is there concern about my ability to run this group?"

"You mean besides Ms. Vander?" Hattie asked.

"Yes, dear," Mable said diplomatically. "There is concern that some of your past ideas aren't in line with the forward direction some members feel is essential to the group." Wow, that stung. "There is also concern among those who want to focus the next few years on Bluebell Hall that you are not the best person to spearhead that project."

"I am not against resurrecting Bluebell Hall," Charlotte explained. She knew Darleen was after her spot, she just didn't think she could get enough support to make her any more annoying than a housefly. Charlotte had obviously underestimated the competition. "I just believe that taking on a project of that magnitude—"

"You mean like funding an entire pediatric ward and patient outreach center?" Darleen countered.

"Yes. But we didn't jump into that project, there was a lot of time and energy put into strategizing, gathering the facts."

"Facts that I have already presented." Darleen beamed, then pointed to her presentation, which Charlotte was certain had very skewed facts that would support the idiotic decision to jump into renovating Bluebell without further exploration. A move that would no doubt cost the Peaches everything—and Charlotte her job. Because there was no way they could resurrect it on their own. "So I don't see why this project is so different from yours?"

"The Peaches didn't build the new ward or the Grow Clinic," Charlotte said, then at the horrified gasps added, "although the Peaches were a big source of support, both financial and emotional, the town all pitched in for that center."

"And I believe that the town will pitch in with Old Blue!"

"What if they don't?" Charlotte put it out there, because if people were thinking about diving into the crazy pool with Darleen then someone needed to be the voice of reason. "What if they don't, and the money spent is just another few grand down the Blue money pit? Then what will the town think?"

"That we're as dumb as those big-city builders that came through here a few years back and lost the farm on that place," Hattie said, and a few concerned whispers formed. "Only we'd be losing the town's money."

"Not with the right leadership," Darleen countered. "Charlotte might not have faith in our abilities, but I sure do!"

"Which is why we have decided to divvy up the Founder's Day responsibilities between the two of you." Mable leveled Darleen with a glare, then picked up her reading glasses that were attached to a bedazzled chain and slid them on her nose. She glanced at her notes. "If you both agree, then Darleen will be handling the fair and Charlotte will handle the parade."

"Oh, that sounds perfect." Darleen said. "I already spoke to a guy in Atlanta who is willing to donate the booths this year." A guy who, Darleen failed to mention, Charlotte had introduced Darleen to. "And I love helping local businesses and families connect, just like my grandmother did when she became the first female councilwoman at town hall."

Saying her platform was upholding tradition would have been more subtle.

"Charlotte, you in agreement?" Mable asked, taking off her glasses. Charlotte nodded. "Then at the end of the weekend the board will hold a special meeting and vote. Whoever holds the title of regent will decide who gets the money."

Darleen smiled. "So whoever does the best job wins?" And since she already had the tents donated and the booth map outlined, thanks to Charlotte, Darleen's victory was looking strong.

"No, dear, the only way to compare apples to oranges is to measure their sweetness," Mable explained. "So whoever keeps the best interests of this town and our organization at heart will win."

"And if there is no clear winner?" Charlotte asked, because when it came to heart, she had this. But if it came down to looking busy, Darleen was a grand master.

"Then nothing changes for the board. You will remain regent, and the money will go to the beneficiary the board was going to approve last week. The Grow Clinic."

Darleen gave a disappointed gasp, and Charlotte felt her chest loosen a bit. This was hers to lose. And she had never lost to Darleen. She wasn't about to start now.

"That sounds fair," Charlotte said, knowing it would be

the best Founder's Day celebration Sugar had ever seen. Because not only was her position on the line, so was the endowment. If this fair came off more hick than heartwarming, Mercy Alliance would walk. And if Darleen triumphed, then the money would go to Bluebell Hall—and Mercy Alliance would think that the local support had dried up and they'd walk. "But the classic car display will fall under my direction."

"But that's going to be a big pull for tourists, and the display will be at the fairgrounds," Darleen argued. Then she softened her smile and turned all five-bazillion brownnosing watts on Mable. "I am friends with Jace, so I could just ring him up and get things going."

Like hell. "Actually, they will be in the parade, which means they fall into the transportation category, and therefore are in my category."

A loud commotion came from outside the door and what sounded like a herd of cattle tromping past caught everyone's attention. Charlotte raced around the table and reached for the handle when the door blew open and a terrified bleating echoed down the hall.

"Dr. Holden," June Ferguson said, obviously winded. Her face was flushed, her chest heaving, and her frosted hair was blown back as though she'd sprinted all the way from her farm.

"Ms. Ferguson." Charlotte took the older woman by the arm and guided her to a chair. "What seems to be the trouble?"

The words had no sooner left her lips when trouble came barreling through the door. Making some kind of battle cry, a white cotton ball on black sticks raced around the conference table, bouncing off legs riddled with arthritis and knocking over chairs. Sitting atop the streak of white, Charlotte caught a flash of red and black bobbing up and down and side to side as Woolamena went from skittish sheep to bucking bronco.

Ba-aah! Woolamena wailed so hard her back feet came off the ground, then her front. And that's when Charlotte noticed the wet white ring around the sheep's mouth.

"It's rabid," Darleen cried, climbing on top of the conference table. Followed by utter hysteria. Pearls started clacking, and twenty sets of pastel-colored pumps headed for higher ground. Some climbed on their chairs, other shielded themselves with their sweaters.

"She's not rabid," June said, fanning herself. "According to an article I saw on Facebook, she's going through the third phase of loss."

"Anger," Charlotte said, slipping her belt off her dress just in case she needed a leash.

"Poor thing can't think straight she's so angry. I was hoping we could move onto the bargaining part, but a trough of vanilla bean didn't help."

As sad as that was, having angry livestock in her hospital didn't help, either. "How long has she been like this?"

"Since morning training."

"I take it this isn't normal?"

"Nothing's been normal since that tumbleweed of a bull left town," June explained. "Everything was fine at practice, we did calisthenics, a little Zumba, then I took her to the new track we had built in the back pasture, thinking it would be a nice surprise, help her get her mind off her heart. Only, we got there and she started doing this."

June gestured to the sheep, who was running circles around herself, nipping at the red and black puppet-like sock attached around her belly to her back.

"It took three ranch hands and six gallons of ice cream

to get her in the truck and drive her here. Three blocks from Maple she jumped out and I had to herd her here."

Charlotte cautiously stepped toward the sheep. "What's on her?"

"That's Jockey Man Jack," June explained. "He's Woolamena's rider for the Scurry. My great-grandmother crocheted him out of yarn spun from her biggest male. Jack's maiden race was atop the first Ferguson sheep scurry champion back in nineteen-oh-nine. He's been riding our champions ever since."

"Even Woolamena?" Charlotte asked, stepping aside right as the champion in question bucked past and into the table leg.

"Yup, all six wins," June said, her voice thick with confusion and fear. "Which is why I brought him out as a treat. To help up her game. Before the devil tarnished my baby's fleece, dress runs would get her in the competitive spirit."

Woolamena snapped her head back and forth until she got the momentum needed to crane it as far as it would go. With a satisfied grunt, she sank her teeth into Jockey Man Jack's lower quadrant, and one whip of the head had him airborne. Everyone watched as the crocheted man flew across the room and hit the wall, his stuffing spilling to the carpet.

Woolamena peeled her lips back, showing off her extremely large teeth, then made a raspberry sound. Clearly exhausted, she sat back on her haunches and let out a tired little bleat.

Sadly, Charlotte understood the sheep's frustration. "If some male had promised me a greener pasture, then cut out without so much as a good-bye, I wouldn't trust any man riding on my back." She picked up the tattered jockey, his pants sagging to his ankles. "I think the solution is simple. Lose the Jack."

"Watch your words," June said in horror, her hands clasping her heart. "Every scurry has to have a jockey to enter, and Jockey Man Jack has led every sheep scurrier in our family since before the dawn of time."

"Well, this sheep doesn't want some old-fashioned cotton-for-brains man telling her what to do," Charlotte said. "So my professional opinion is to dump the sock man."

"Then she can't race!"

Woolamena had to race. Mr. Neil was coming out specifically to see her race. However, this wasn't her problem. Not anymore. "Actually, this is more of Darleen's area of expertise since she is now heading up the fair."

"Oh, no." Darleen, still kneeling on the table, shook her head violently. "The sheep scurry is all about getting from one place to the next the fastest, which is clearly a transportation issue, and therefore your problem."

"Plus, you're her doctor!" June said, tears in her eyes. "What kind of doctor passes her problems onto someone else?"

Charlotte's father immediately came to mind.

Charlotte looked at Woolamena, who looked back with big, trusting black eyes. "Bring her by my place after work."

* * *

It was late afternoon before Jace headed into town. He'd spent part of his day on the phone, burning through his network of collectors and trying to find a couple of guys willing to donate their cars for a day—not nearly as easy a job as he'd let on last night. And the rest of it was spent thinking about breakfast with Charlotte.

Okay, so outside of the doughnut holes she had inhaled

they hadn't really done much eating. But he considered their first morning tradition a success.

As a result, he'd accomplished jack shit on Hattie's car. So when he pulled into the lot and saw a group of ladies sitting by the door, he swore. They weren't just any ladies, but young, twittering, teen ladies dressed in cheerleader skirts and fancy sneakers. Then he saw Payton holding court and got a bad feeling in his chest. He threw his car into park and called Cal.

"I said I'd help Payton," Jace snapped when Cal answered. "Not half the fucking cheer team."

"Girls this age are like locusts, you know that. They move in swarms. You invite one and they all show up," Cal said, and the fucker was laughing. "You scared?"

"And man enough to admit it." Just looking at them bouncing up and down and flicking their ponytails side to side gave him a headache. "What the hell am I supposed to do with a gaggle of teens for the next hour?"

"Two hours," Cal corrected. "And you'll figure it out."

Jace disconnected and opened his door. On cue, Payton squealed and came racing over. "Uncle Jace!"

He was barely out of the car when she threw her arms around him in a sweet hug, and Jace decided that it could not be all that bad. Then someone yelled, "Group hug," and Jace found himself suffocating in perfume and spray glitter.

When the lovefest broke up, Payton introduced each and every girl by name, grade, and squad ranking with perfect southern etiquette. Jace wasn't sure what being a "flyer" meant, but he understood that for his niece, the only underclassman in the group, this was a big deal.

"And this is my uncle Jace! He is not only the best uncle ever, but he is also the best mechanic in racing," she said, hanging on his arm as though being his niece made her special, and damn if his chest didn't puff out a little.

He couldn't help it. Cal was the stellar single dad and hometown hero, Brett was as big a celebrity athlete as one could get. All Jace had ever been was a problem. Only, Payton was looking up at him as if he were in the same league as his brothers. And it felt good.

"I don't know about the best," Jace said, feeling himself flush a little. "But I know my way around a car."

"Are you going to teach us how to hot-wire a car?" Ashley, a pocket-size redhead with big green eyes and freckles asked. "Or rebuild an engine?"

"Um, I was thinking we'd start with something a little more basic."

"Basic," Ashley said, sounding disappointed.

"I bet whatever he has planned is going to be awesome," Payton said, her eyes pleading with him to bring on the awesome.

Jace had once found himself in the pits at one of the most dangerous raceways in the country, facing down eight hundred horsepower of runaway steel as it barreled right for him and his crew. The car had been on fire and spinning out of control. It took out two hydronic jacks and a couple tons of tires before sending Jace and two of his crewmates to the ER.

He'd been less terrified in that moment than he was now looking at his niece who was banking so much hope on him making this day the talk of the lunchroom tomorrow. Only changing out spark plugs didn't sound lunchroom worthy.

"Oh, it will be awesome," he said.

Payton beamed.

The girls cheered.

Jace took his time, sizing up the girls—stalling for genius

to strike. Nothing happened. He hoped that since they were mostly older, maybe a few of them had licenses and had worked on cars with their dads. And Jace had learned when working with some of the most difficult clients in mechanics, if he wanted to meet expectations he had to ask the right questions. "Raise your hand if you've ever changed a tire."

Not a hand went up.

"Put air in a tire?" Nothing but crickets. "Pumped gas?" *Okay*... "Reprogrammed the stereo?"

"I hooked my iPhone up to the car's Bluetooth so what we could practice to beats. Does that count?" This from Lacy, the almost breaking six-foot blonde of the group who had a temporary SHS tattoo on her cheek.

"For today it will."

All of the hands went in the air telling him jack shit about the girls, except they got creative when push came to shove. Which gave him an idea. "Okay, let's start with what you hope to take away from this lesson. Why are you here?"

"Oh, that's easy." Payton's eyes got big, her smile went electric, and Jace felt himself relax. *Easy* was a great word. Easy was what he was looking for today. Hell, an easy day with his niece and her friends, sharing stories and reconnecting, was exactly what he hoped to get out of this.

That was what working under the hood was about. That was what constituted most of his memories with his dad. And it was something he was excited to share with Payton. If getting back on the same page with his niece, making a connection that would last over two hundred miles, meant getting to know her friends in the process, even better.

"We want to be efficient, independent driving members of society," Payton said with a sweet smile.

"We want to be car babes," Lacy supplied as though *that* was an okay title to aspire to.

Jace would have thought the girl was joking if his niece's expression hadn't gone from role-model niece to *I'm so fucked* in two seconds flat. The girl had explaining to do. "Car babes, huh?"

Payton studied her shoes.

Lacy beamed. "Yup. After reading several *Maxim,* *Cosmo*, and *Men's Health* articles, we've figured out that men are into the three *C*'s. Cheerleaders, cars, and, well…" Lacy looked down at—*oh hell no*—the letters stretching across the front of her uniform and smiled.

Jace did his best to stare the girl in the eyes. "You want me to teach you about cars so you can impress some guys?"

All six heads bobbled in perfect unison, because, just his luck, they were finally on the same page.

* * *

Two hours and eleven minutes later, Jace leaned over the hood, staring down at the Stingray's engine, taking in the blessedly quiet garage. Each girl had successfully balanced a tire, checked the oil, and, as a team, taken off the valve covers on the Stingray and jump-started one of Spencer's cars. Although they were more concerned with who got to pick the radio station than the actual placement of the cables, they all left with a better understanding of car safety—and with enough grease under their nails that Jace didn't think they'd be back anytime soon.

Everyone came out a winner.

"Want to hand me the gasket?" Jace asked, figuring that at least she could pitch in after bamboozling him.

"What does it look like?" Payton asked.

"It's a black rubber rectangle with four circles cut out."

Payton looked at a complete loss. "It's sitting next to the torque wrench." Hell, if she didn't know what a gasket looked like, then... "It's the—"

"Big silver thingy sitting next to the big black thingy?" She held up the gasket and the torque wrench, then cracked a smile. "I might have said I came to be a car babe, but I was paying attention."

Jace smiled back. "So being a car babe isn't in your future?"

"Nah." *Thank God.* "I want to get my license. Bad. And that means proving to Daddy that I can change a flat and check my oil. Plus, Mason isn't into car babes. He says he's into me."

"Mason sounds like a smart guy," Jace said, loving how her cheeks went pink.

"He's the best." She beamed, and the next thing he knew Payton was sitting next to him on a rusty old stool she'd pulled over from the workbench.

That was all it took: Jace showing up and sticking around long enough, and suddenly his niece was looking at him like *he* was the best.

"He has this old truck he bought off Mr. Gregory, and it is always breaking down. So on the weekends he comes over and works on the car at Grandma's. We can't really date until I am sixteen because, well, you know Daddy." She rolled her eyes, and even though Jace agreed with her daddy wholeheartedly, he rolled his eyes with her. Which made her laugh.

And made him feel like a fucking superhero.

"Anyway, I sit on the porch steps while Mase works, and we talk about *everything.*" Apparently, *everything* was a ten syllables word in Payton's world. "But it would be cool if I could actually help him. You know?"

Oh, Jace knew. Knew how much two people could share while working on cars. With his dad, it was more about the journey than finishing the project. Sure, the conversation was great, but it was the unspoken moments that shaped Jace's life.

Like Jace, his dad wasn't a big talker. He said what needed to be said and didn't mince words. Yet every person in his world knew that they were loved.

"Your grandpa and I used to work on engines all the time," Jace said, and realized that this was the first time he'd talked to anyone about his dad in ages. "Sometimes it was a tractor or the neighbor's mower."

"What was the first thing you fixed?" Payton asked, handing him the gasket.

"I was twelve and decided to borrow Mr. Wilkes's John Deere," Jace said, smiling at the memory. He set the gasket in place, wiggling it around to ensure the fit was airtight. "It was parked out behind their barn, and my buddies talked me into taking it for a spin."

Payton's eyes went big. "You took a joyride in Mr. Wilkes's tractor?"

"Yes, ma'am. I was the coolest guy in the eighth grade for about two minutes, until I drove it right into a ditch and cracked the engine block. When my dad found out he walked me back to the scene of the crime and made me apologize." He let out a low whistle. "I was sentenced to an entire summer of hard time rebuilding that engine."

"That sucks."

"It wasn't so bad," he said, because—shit, now that he was talking he couldn't seem to stop. "Your granddad helped me every step of the way, teaching me what he knew. By the end of the summer I even taught him a few things. Not that he let me off easy. I had to pay for all the new parts out of my allowance. I was broke for the next two years, but my interest in engines was solid."

"I pretended I was tutoring a senior football player once, because I thought he was hot," Payton admitted, a little sass and a whole lot of teen drama in her tone. "Only, Dad found out, and I spent the rest of my summer washing down livestock at the feed store in town. And he made me wear a jumpsuit."

As far as Jace was concerned, the girl got off easy. And if the football player was still walking, then he had, too. But Jace was feeling too good about being her confidant to say anything.

"Jumpsuits aren't that bad," he teased, and Payton snorted.

"Then how come you're not wearing one?"

She had him there. The head gasket snapped into place, and Jace picked one of the bolts out of the box he'd set on the side rim of the car. "Grab that big silver thing and help me tighten this bolt."

Payton didn't hesitate, stepped up to the bumper, and tried to get the wrench around the bolt. Jace flipped it over and helped her get it into the correct position. "Now turn it this way until you hear a click. That is the wrench telling you it has the correct pressure."

Payton started turning, and when it clicked she stopped. But she didn't sit back down, she reached for the next bolt and started twisting. Painted nails or not, his niece was pretty good with a torque wrench.

"You know, when I was about your age my dad decided he wanted to fix up his dad's old car. This one."

"I saw the photos on Grandma's wall, but all I can make out is your backside sticking out of the hood." Payton laughed, and suddenly the heavy sense of loss he'd been carting around didn't feel so heavy. "She said you were a born grease monkey."

Jace paused, letting that process. "I think I am more of a guy who loves to solve puzzles, especially ones where I can get my hands dirty. It didn't hurt that I got to hang out with my dad, one on one, so I didn't have to compete with my brothers for his attention." Because Jace learned early on it was impossible to compete with the golden boy and the hometown hero. "When we were under the hood, it was my time."

And Jace could just be himself.

"So it was your thing and Grandpa's, huh?"

"You could say that." He handed her the next bolt, then causally threw out, "It could be our thing, too. If you want." And when Payton didn't seemed horrified at the idea of turning wrenches after school with her uncle, he added, "I could use the help. And when we get her running I'd even let you drive her." Payton's fingers froze and she looked up at him. "On private property, of course."

"Really? Omigod! That would be so cool," she said, and gave him a hug, an honest-to-God hug that didn't come with bouncing or squealing. She pulled back and went serious. "So we'd be partners, like you and Grandpa were?"

"You bet."

"Okay, because I was thinking cherry red is kind of outdated. Way too mainstream. Not to mention it wasn't an original color to the year."

"And you know that how?"

"Google." She pulled out her cell and a few swipes later flashed him the screen. "Look at this one. I found it online last night when I was looking at classic car sites to see what kind of car we'd be working on. It's sky blue and has a cream leather interior with matching blue piping on the seats. It is all the original paint and interior. I think if we restore this, then we should restore it right." She looked up at him, uncertainty in her eyes. "Don't you think?"

Was she kidding? His niece had been excited enough to search the Internet before coming today. They could paint it sparkly pink for all he cared.

Chapter 13

It was nearly ten by the time the front door creaked open. Jace bit back a smile, because Charlotte was sneaking in. Heels in one hand, a Fabric Farm bag dangling from the other, and guilt clinging to her like her wool coat.

"You're home late," Jace said from the couch, where he'd been waiting for her to come home.

Charlotte spun around, and the realization of being caught had her hand flying to her chest and her things crashing to the floor.

"You scared me," she said, and gasped.

"That's what sneaking will do to a person, set them on edge."

Charlotte picked up her shoes and the bag. "I have no idea what you're talking about."

"Ah, this is where I just smile and say, 'How was your day?' See, that was me considering my partner's needs." When Charlotte didn't answer the question, instead focusing on her bag, he held up a wineglass. She reached for it and he pulled it back. "You have to sit down and tell me about your day while you drink it. Sharing about one's day creates a connection."

She eyed him, then the small couch, then the wine. The wine won out, and she plopped down. He handed her the glass and filled it barely an inch. When she held the glass there, waiting for him to top it off, he said, "Talk and I will fill."

"Are you serious?" He quirked a brow. "Fine. I wasn't sneaking."

He filled it a tad more.

She huffed.

"I was taking a class." Now they were getting somewhere.

"What kind of class?"

"If I tell you, will you fill my glass to the top?" He thought about that for a moment then nodded. "I was taking a knitting class."

"You knit?" he asked, and when he went for the bag, she snatched it back. He held up the wine. "I'll top you off again."

She pushed the glass closer to him, then with an annoyed yet self-conscious expression, Charlotte pulled out a pathetic-looking six-inch square. And *bam*. That was all it took. The image cemented itself in his head, and he was screwed.

Jace had come home with a plan, a good one that included nothing more than showing Charlotte just how easy it was when they were together. That they could have a good time without the added pressure of sex or hashing out the past. But the contrast of her sitting on the couch in that uptight doctor getup next to those fucking heels while looking all domesticated with knitting needles and pink yarn was enough to sidetrack him.

Because Dr. Charlotte Holden, with all of her degrees and well-thought-out plans, was sexy as hell. A flustered Charlie McGraw, holding a sorry-as-shit-looking scarf or whatever it was she was attempting to knit was a different story altogether. That woman was so damn irresistible.

But he wanted more than a little nibble. He wanted the whole cake—icing and all. And that meant sticking to the plan. No sex before bonding, because if he wanted to convince Charlotte that they deserved that "more" he was after, then he knew getting naked before getting in her bed was a bad idea. According to the article in *Hitched* magazine, for a woman sex was a different form of connection.

Sex feels good. A connection, when nurtured, lasts forever.

He still wasn't sure what forever held, but he was certain that wherever it was he didn't want to go there without Charlotte.

"Don't laugh," she said. "It's for Woolamena. I'm making her a new jockey. Jockey Jane."

"She's pink."

"I-am-woman pink," Charlotte said, then told him about her plan for sheep scurry domination, her walls crumbling with each sentence. When she was finished, she leaned back and pulled her legs beneath her.

"Only in Sugar could the fate of the world come down to a sheep and my ability to knit a doll." She laughed. It was a great laugh. Deep and throaty, and so honest he had to laugh, too. And admit, silently to himself of course, that after everything he'd witnessed overseas, after living in a dozen big cities where no one gave a crap about their neighbors, it was refreshing to know that there were still towns like Sugar. Places where everyone cared enough to meddle and the biggest obstacle in sight was a man-hating sheep.

Not that Sugar was for Jace. But he could see why Charlotte had come home. Envied her, even, that she had the ability to come home. Because even if Jace moved back, he would never be able to find peace. And as far as he was concerned, home was where you were supposed to be at peace.

Although, sitting right there, sharing a glass of wine and his day with Charlotte, Jace felt more at peace than he had in a while.

Charlotte went silent and rested back against the couch. Jace tugged one foot out from beneath her, then the other, and placed them in his lap. He looked at her toes, painted a bright red, and with a smile started rubbing circles in her arch. "I got a call back about the cars."

"You did? Already?"

"Yup," he said, feeling kind of like a superhero. "I got two classics for people to ride in and one concept car, which should bring a nice crowd."

"How on earth did you get a concept car to come here to Sugar?"

"I called a friend of mine who is a collector, plus he owns a racing team. The classics are his, the concept car belongs to the team."

Charlotte thought about that for a long moment. "And what did you have to do to get that?"

"Agree to consult on a new high-performance engine they are experimenting with next season."

"In Atlanta?" she asked, and something about the way she said it had his hands stopping.

"Atlanta Motorsports is in Atlanta. So yeah, most of the projects I work on are in Atlanta."

"Makes sense," she finally said then closed her eyes and wiggled her toes for him to continue. He obliged. "I heard Payton came to visit you today."

Happy to accept her topic shift, Jace said, "She did. Thought she could impress some guy by pretending to be a car babe."

"Car babe?" She snorted. "Where do girls get these ideas?"

"From boys."

"Right, I remember now," she said, then moaned when he dug his fingers deeper into the pad of her foot, right below the big toe. It was her secret pleasure button, and when he hit it just right, applied the correct amount of pressure, while sliding his other hand up her calf and maybe a little higher for his own benefit, her eyes rolled back.

"God, that feels good."

Hell, yeah, it did, because every time he hit that spot, she pressed down on his spot. Hard. So he did it again and—

"Ah, Charlie, please tell me my boots are under your bed."

She slowly shook her head and damn it if he didn't feel like crying. He purposely hadn't checked, wishing like hell that after his visit this morning she'd reconsidered. Made a step in his direction. And damn, he was disappointed that she hadn't.

"Then you need to stop wiggling your foot." Her eyes slid down his body until they reached his lap, which was sporting a major bulge, and he saw the pulse in her neck pick up. She went to move her foot, but he held on to her ankle. "Just let me be the one giving the foot massage and we'll be good."

"You sure?"

No, he wasn't sure about anything anymore. Like why he was so bent on not having sex with the woman he loved, especially when she was making it clear by the way she was looking at him—as if he were her dessert and nightcap all rolled in one—that she was more than open to a little tangled sheets two-step.

Oh, he wanted sex, all right. But he also wanted naptime shenanigans, and daily hugs and kisses, and to go to bed together so that the next day, when she woke up all warm and soft with sleep, he was the lucky son of a bitch who got to put the good in her morning.

"Jace," she whispered, her voice making it clear that everything he was thinking was on his face.

"Why don't you tell me how you know about Payton's impromptu lesson?" Because talking about his family was a surefire cure for his hard-on.

Charlotte cleared her throat. "I worked the last half of my shift with Glory. She said Payton had sweet-talked you into teaching her how to drive."

"Oh no," Jace shook his head sternly. "I agreed to teach her how to change a tire and jump-start her car. Her daddy has the honors of the driving lesson, because if Payton is anything like her grandma, the day she gets her license this town will never be safe again."

Charlotte laughed. Jace did not. Hattie McGraw was the worst driver in the South. In fact, she had taken out more street signs and mailboxes than the entire Sugar High baseball team during a game of mailbox baseball.

"So let me get this straight," Charlotte said with a sweet smile. "You're teaching your niece how to change a tire, and you're the new instructor for the Car Maintenance 101 course, *and* you're on the Parade Committee for the Founder's Day Fair. That's an awful lot of pots to have your fingers in for a guy who gave up his residency."

He knew what she was doing. Trying to see just how committed he was to seeing this through. Even so, the idea that so many people were counting on him didn't go unheard. Which was why his heart shifted and his breathing changed pace.

Jace silently swore and waited. Waited for the panic to set in and the noose that had been wrapped around his neck since his parents died to slowly tighten. Only nothing happened. Maybe it was the wine or maybe it was the company, either way he didn't feel like burning rubber out of town.

At least not just yet.

"Not really," he said, testing her a little, too. "Seeing as I have a house and wife in town, it makes sense."

Charlotte didn't argue, didn't correct him, she just stared silently at him. Her lips were parted slightly, and her eyes were soft, imploring him. And his heart shifted again until that little slice of peace he'd felt earlier grew, and suddenly Jace didn't want to leave. Not if staying meant feeling like this forever.

Neither of them spoke, just letting his words and whatever feelings they evoked settle. The longer they sat here, the more flight they seem to gain. And even though they kept staring, waiting for the other to speak, nothing settled.

This was probably because Charlotte kept wiggling her foot.

Or maybe it was because he kept touching her legs. Higher and higher, he ran his fingers over her silky skin, loving how her breathing picked up. How her eyes dilated and zeroed in on his mouth. The longer she looked, the harder it seemed to stop, until the hunger in the room was palpable.

Jace wasn't sure who moved first, but suddenly they were both lying on her small-as-shit couch. Strike that. He was lying on the small-as-shit couch and Charlotte was lying on him. Her hands pushing up his shirt. Their mouths fused together so tight he'd need a crowbar to separate them. The way she kissed him, desperate and needy, told him that she did want more, she was just afraid of what came after the more.

And yeah, Jace being Jace, he couldn't seem to think past

right then, past sinking into her and staying there for a long time. Long enough to forget their past, forget the hurt, forget everything except how right it felt.

She shimmied a little, he sucked in a sharp breath. Then she shimmied some more, moving herself right up his secret spot and then back down. On her third pass Jace was about sure he was going to explode, so he gripped her ass to hold her still. Only the second his hands made contact with skin instead of her skirt he froze, long enough to give silent thanks for the best ass on the planet, then pulled her even closer, sure to do a thorough investigation of just how far her skirt had slid when she'd shimmied.

And *amen*, his fingers found the sweetest curve of skin and, what he could only imagine was a fuck-me red thong with some kind of bow nestled right above her cheeks. Except he didn't have to imagine for long, Charlotte did this little twisting action, taking her hips lower and her skirt higher until he was able to see that it wasn't a bow at all, but a little heart made of rhinestones on the band of her—*God yes*—fuck-me red thong.

And something about that stopped him short. Not the fuck-me red part, and sure as shit not the thong part, but the little sparkly heart. Because he didn't want her sparkly heart, he wanted the real one, and he wasn't going to get a shot at that here on the couch.

With great effort, and a promise that he would remove those panties with his teeth someday very soon, he pulled back so that their noses were still touching, their breaths were still mingling, and every other part of them was still connected.

Her panties still in place.

"Jace," she said, her eyes filled with confusion—and a dump truck full of lust.

"Are we moving my boots, Charlie?"

She paused, long enough for him to know that she wasn't ready. She was ready for sex, and maybe even sex in her bed, but she wasn't ready for more. His fault.

"I don't want to rush you," he whispered. "But that's my only rule."

With a smile that was all trouble, she leaned in and snagged his lower lip between her teeth, letting it go with a tug. "It's more fun when I make the rules."

"Agreed," he groaned, and her mouth was back on his, those sexy hips of hers on the move, slowly driving him insane.

"But," he managed, his hands slipping down to grip her sweet ass and hold her in place so that he could think with the right part of his anatomy. "The last time you were rule maker I didn't even get to walk you to your room. You distracted me with that mouth of yours, left me with my pants down and craving a nice cuddle moment, then evaded me for days, accused me of using a nice dinner as a precursor for sex, and told me to pretty much screw off."

"I was confused about what I wanted."

"You still are," he whispered, determined not to think about the fact that time was running out. There was less than two weeks before their agreement was up, two weeks until the annulment came in and she'd have to make a choice. He didn't have time to screw this up. "But I'm not. And for the first time in a long while I am trying to look past this moment, and God, baby, you aren't making it easy." He tightened his grip on that lush ass, then delivered a small brush of the lips. "I want you, so bad it aches. All. Day. Long."

"Me too," she whispered back, her hair a mess of tangles from his fingers, and her makeup smudged just enough to make her irresistible.

"But," he said again, his hands tightening again, because her hips were on the move. Again. "I need to make sure that before we go there, you understand that what I want goes beyond the physical. Beyond fun and exciting."

"I'm not sure I can give you that," she said in a tone that would have crushed him had he not heard the fear in her voice, seen the way her lips trembled slightly.

Calling himself a hundred different kinds of bastard, he ran his hands up her back to cup her face. "It's not you, Charlie, I know you can. You're just waiting on me to prove that I'm worth the risk."

Jace had stopped planning past tomorrow the same day he'd stopped seeking out deep connections—and Charlotte knew that. Had experienced it firsthand. It was what had her waffling. But Charlotte was different, always had been, which was how she managed to slip through his defenses and wiggle her way deep in his heart. So it was important to take a different approach this time. Start thinking about down the road instead of using the road as an escape.

He couldn't tell her that, he'd have to show her, and the idea that he might not get the chance made his stomach go a little squirrelly. "I'm willing to do whatever it takes, as long as you give me a chance to prove myself."

Afraid she might not give him the answer he desperately wanted, he kissed her gently. Then not so gently. Then he kissed her until his lips started tingling and his pulse was going haywire.

"I thought you said this wasn't going to happen," she whispered.

"I said *sex* wasn't going to happen. Tonight at least," he added with a grin. "I have nothing against making out until our lips go numb."

"Until our lips go numb, huh?"

"Or we catch fire. I'm open to either."

Charlotte gave him a sexy smile that said she was open to a little make-out session, too. Maybe even that second chance. And Jace hoped to God he didn't blow it again.

"We've never really kissed without it leading to sex," she said.

The first night they met in that bar, he'd sweet-talked her all the way home and straight into breakfast in bed. Nothing about them had ever been slow. And maybe that was part of the problem.

"Well, then I guess it's time we do that."

Her hands fisted in his shirt and she tugged—hard. "As long as you lose this."

"Is that an official rule?" he asked.

Her impatient tug was all the answer he needed.

Chapter 14

An irritating tapping pulled Charlotte from a lovely dream starring Mr. McGraw in nothing but tattoos and that crooked grin, using his skilled and crafty hands to slowly rev her engine.

Telling herself that the light peeking through the blinds was just the moon and not morning, Charlotte snuggled deeper into her pillow, determined to cross that finish line. Only the pillow snuggled back, nuzzling her neck and creating enough heat to warm her all the way through.

Her pillow also smelled amazing. Like sleepy, sexy, hot man.

She opened one eye and closed it against the bright sun. Yup, it was morning, and Jace's boots were still sitting by the door, which was why they were still twisted like a couple of pretzels on her couch. Instead of naked in her bed, where they would have been had she found the courage to leap.

Something that in the daylight, while nuzzled against his hard-muscled chest, seemed ridiculous. But the leap between inviting him into her home and inviting him into her bed was huge. Her bedroom was her sanctuary, and she was afraid that if she let him in too far, her sanctuary could easily become Jace.

A low tap sounded again, and before she could take further stock of the situation, sunlight flooded the room.

"Aw, Jesus," Ben said, and Charlotte's eyes flew open.

"Oh my God! Ben!" She tried to sit up, but her legs were intertwined with Jace's, and his hands were molded to her backside. Her nearly bare backside that was sticking out from beneath her skirt. She tried to tug it down around her legs, but Jace wouldn't move his hands. And Ben was staring. "Turn around!"

He did. But not until after she managed to secure her skirt, which was around her waist like a hula hoop, in a more useful position. "Put a sock on the door next time."

"Or you could knock." Charlotte did a quick pat down, relieved to find that, while Jace's shirt was wadded up on the floor, hers was securely in place.

"For the record, I did. Twice." Ben held up two fingers as though visual cues were necessary when communicating without eye contact. "When no one answered, I used the key."

Jace opened one eye. His hands were back on her butt. "He has a key?"

"Do you really want to talk about this now?" she whispered.

The other eye slid open and locked on. "I don't know, Charlie. Mr. M.D. over there has his own key while the house is on my credit report and I have to park my car across the lake."

"Oh for God's sake, he has my emergency key." Charlotte shoved off his chest, and Jace finally let go of her enough to free her. She stumbled to her feet. "Wait. Is it an emergency? Is it Kenny O'Neil?"

Kenny O'Neil was a thirteen-year-old patient waiting for a liver transplant. Not that Charlotte was the overseeing surgeon, but as his physician she was the glue that connected all of his doctors together. Made sure everyone was kept in the loop. Talked to his mother when things got hard, gave Kenny hope when things got unbearable. "Is he okay?"

"Kenny's fine," Ben said quietly.

"Thank God." She blew out a sigh of relief.

Ben peeked over his shoulder and, satisfied with Charlotte's state of dress, turned back to face her. "There was just a change in the caseload at work that I wanted to discuss with you." He paused, eyeing Jace, who was still sprawled out on the couch—shirtless—his hands behind his head as though he wasn't in any hurry to move. "In private. Patient-doctor confidentiality being what it is."

"Well, then I'll make myself scarce," Jace said, standing and stretching until every one of his muscles tightened and coiled. Then, to make a point, held it a second longer than necessary, sure to give everyone a clear look at just how big he was, before padding over.

To them.

Every time his bare feet hit the hardwood, he drew closer, as did Charlotte's breath. Even in the morning with his hair standing on end, his jaw rough with yesterday's growth and those deep blue eyes glossy with sleep, the man was gorgeous. *Especially then,* she thought. Because the big, invincible Jace McGraw, bad boy of Sugar, looked soft. Almost vulnerable.

Oh yeah, Charlotte had it bad.

Jace stopped right in front of her and winked. With a

quick smack to Charlotte's lips that had her toes turning and her face heating, he turned to welcome their company, who had to look way up to meet his gaze.

"Ben," he said. Not an ounce of welcome present.

"Jace."

There was a beat of silence, then another, followed by some weird eye twitching, and finally Ben nodded in what must have been some kind of secret guy-code because Jace made a low grunt then moseyed his way into the kitchen. "I'll just go rustle us up some breakfast while you two talk shop. You hungry, Ben? No? Okay then, be sure to leave your key by the door when you head out."

The kitchen sink turned on and Ben said, "Did he eat Paul Bunyan?"

"He's just big boned," Charlotte said, equally impressed with the way his broad shoulders rippled and dipped as he moved. The McGraw men were all big, but Jace was supersized.

"Well, now I know why you didn't answer my calls. Must have been some kind of engine problem." The big jerk had the nerve to snicker.

"Why are you here?"

His smile faded. "I wanted to give you a heads-up that I was assigned half your patient load for the week."

Shock hit hard and fast. Followed by confusion. "What? When?"

"This morning. I got an email from Reginald informing me that I would be handling a portion of your patients for the rest of the week," Ben said. "And from the stunned look on your face, I take it you weren't in agreement."

She couldn't speak, couldn't think, so she sat down on the couch, her heart beating so fast she was sure it would pop right out of her chest. "I didn't even know." She looked up at Ben, who was looking back with concern laced in his expression. "Why would he move my patients to you? Especially when I am on the schedule all week."

"I don't know," Ben said quietly. "But when I called in to see who was on my schedule for today, Glory told me that Reginald had instructed the nurses to hand over the rest of your patients to him."

"This makes no sense." Charlotte reached over the couch to grab her phone out of her purse. She scrolled through her activity.

A missed call from Ben. Three from her mother—and it was only seven thirty. Not a single call from her dad.

"Let me call him and figure out what's going on," she said more mildly than she felt. She dialed her dad's cell, every ring echoing in her chest until she felt like she was going to crack. On the fifth ring it went to voice mail. "Hey, Dad. I had a question about this week's schedule, if you could give me call back that would be great. Thanks. Love you."

She hung up and stared at the phone. Her dad had just reorganized her entire week and she'd ended the call with "Love you." Not that she didn't always end her calls with an endearment, but suddenly she realized how strange it sounded to say "I love you" to her boss. Because that was who she was calling, her boss.

Yet, neither of them were acting professional.

"I'm sure he had his reasons," Ben said, so incredibly reasonable that Charlotte almost agreed. Almost.

But something in her clicked.

Jace would have said her dad was being a controlling idiot. And he would have been right, because while the old Charlotte hoped that this was just some clerical mix-up, Charlotte 2.0 knew that this was just another example of her dad not taking her feelings into consideration, steamrolling over her life without regard to her at all.

"No reason is good enough to alter a doctor's schedule without consent." Had this been any other doctor on staff, her father wouldn't have meddled.

Ben paused, a bit surprised at her comment. Then chuckled. "I wholeheartedly agree. So when you figure out what you want to do, let me know, Doctor." The way he punctuated the statement was primed for his exit. Only he stood there, staring at her, his expression perplexed.

"What?" Charlotte felt the urge to smooth down her hair, make sure she was indeed wearing clothes.

"I always wondered what love would look like on you," he said softly. "It's a good look, Charlotte."

Ben shoved his hands in his pockets and, with a small smile, left. She stood there, watching Ben walk down the front steps, completely stunned. Not that she was in love with Jace—she'd admitted to herself long ago that she could never stop loving him. But that her love was so transparent.

Needing time to process, Charlotte sat back and closed her eyes. Her phone vibrated in her palm. She glanced at the screen and groaned.

"Not now." Only it was now or never, so after a settling inhale that did nothing to calm her nerves, she answered. "Morning, Dad."

Reginald didn't return the greeting. "Want to explain to me why there is a mob of sheep eating all of the vegetation around the clinic and huge segments of the main parking lot are blocked off? Patients are parking on Maple Street and walking!"

"That's what happens when you tell everyone that the Founder's Day Fair will be held at the hospital," she explained, wondering just how many sheep made up a mob, and if they were in the clinic or just in the parking lot. Then she wondered if Woolamena was there and if she was feeling better. "They need to prep the location. Scout out places for the booths and racetrack. And the mob needs to feel out the land."

"They need to understand this is a place of business." He sounded annoyed and exasperated, as though Charlotte was the one who had disrupted his carefully orchestrated world. "I can't get anything done with the sheep charging patients and people asking the staff a dozen questions a minute about bathroom facilities and if we have a freezer big enough to hold the ice cream for the Pie à la Mode booth. I am trying to run a hospital, Charlotte, not a damn ladies' club."

Charlotte ignored the burn his statement left. "Then let Darleen know she needs to come back at another time."

"I tried," he explained. "That woman doesn't do well with the word *no*."

Actually, Darleen didn't do well with losing, either, but Charlotte kept that to herself. She quite liked the idea of her father and Darleen butting heads for a few weeks. They were perfectly suited to drive each other insane—creating less time to drive *her* insane.

"Which is why I need you to get down here, so you can straighten this all out," he explained in a tone that left no room for argument.

Too bad for him, Charlotte was in the mood to argue. She was emotional and confused and a little unraveled at the edges. "Sorry, Dad. I can't do that today. I have Kenny O'Neil coming in for tests at noon, plus a new patient was sent over from Magnolia Falls needing a second opinion. My schedule is booked."

"Ben can handle the second opinion and Kenny," he said, completely discounting the fact that the doctor had wanted Charlotte to give the second opinion because he valued her in-

put. Not that Ben wasn't a great doctor, he was, but Charlotte
was the best doctor for this particular patient.

Charlotte was quiet for a moment, gathering her courage.
Trying to find ground in the middle of the emotional hurri-
cane brewing in her core. Trying to silence the obedient little
girl wanting her dad's approval. Trying to be the person she
knew she was capable of being.

"That mess is not mine to clean up," she explained.
Thankfully her voice didn't betray the fact that her hands
were shaking. "And you should have talked to me before re-
arranging my schedule."

"I was trying to make your week easier," he said as
though *she* was being the unreasonable one. "Let Ben handle
your patients or not, I don't care, as long as the parade of
chaos is under control by end of day."

That was it. No explanation, no apology for changing her
schedule without consulting her. Even worse, her dad had no
idea that what he'd done was wrong.

"I will come in when my shift starts. At noon, as a doctor,
not a social planner," she clarified, proud of herself.

She could hear her father's shock through the phone. He
was used to her being a yes-girl. Depended on her being a
yes-girl. Only Charlotte was tired of being that girl, tired of
being overlooked, overworked, and underappreciated.

"You'll need to handle Darleen yourself, Dad. I can give
you her number, if that makes it easier," she said, and silently
cringed at the last part. God, when had she become such a
brownnoser?

"What would make it easier is for you to remember that
this is a family business, Charlotte. Which means that there
is no room for ego or pride," said the most egotistical and
prideful man Charlotte knew. "Going above and beyond is
how we have maintained a successful and respected medi

cal practice at a time when clinics like ours are closing up. It is how your mother and I provided the kind of lifestyle you were fortunate enough to have."

"I understand that, Dad, and I—"

"Good, because this week, I need you to step up, do what needs to be done to insure that Mercy Alliance signs on that line. If it means planning a fair, then I suggest you get your mother on the phone, throw one of your little meetings, whatever the hell you have to do so I can do my job." Reginald disconnected.

Charlotte stared at the screen, waiting for the anger to come, for the injustice to settle. It didn't. The only emotion she felt was this big hole of disappointment in her chest that was slowly sucking the life out of her. And she knew that if she didn't do something soon, it would be too late.

She didn't mind stepping up or even getting dirty. There wasn't much she wouldn't do if it meant making Sugar Medical a success, meant getting the townspeople here the best medical care available. But her job wasn't cleaning up someone else's mess.

She set her phone on the coffee table and looked up to see a shadow move out of the corner of her eye. A good-looking, beautifully built shadow with crystal blue eyes and an understanding smile that made everything inside of her still.

"You okay?"

She cleared her throat, trying to hide the emotion pushing its way up. "I'm fine."

"You're a terrible liar, Charlie," he said, and she laughed, strangled and a little desperate, but it was better than crying. "Because your face is saying that call totally sucked."

"I am. And it did." There went that laugh again. Oh God, was that tears she heard in her voice? "It totally sucked."

Jace pushed off the wall and walked closer. His body

moved like a predator's stalking its prey, but his eyes were open and unguarded, full of concern. For her. Which made the urge to cry even stronger. So she dropped her gaze to his chest, a safer place than those understanding blue pools, except now her mouth was watering, because all she could think about was how that broad, strong body had held her close all night. Taken her mind off the terrible day and made her feel safe. A feeling she desperately wanted to experience again.

"Want to talk about it?" he asked quietly.

"I'm fine, really," she lied, because who wanted to admit that they were a coward? Especially to a man who had shoulders big enough to balance the world and all its problems? But the second he was within arm's length, she caved like a weepy meringue.

"You're holding out on me, Charlie."

She shook her head, only to have it turn to a nod midshake, because she was holding out. Big-time. And not just about the call. Charlotte was letting her fear of failing, her fear of disappointing people, stop her from living. And wasn't that the point of all of this? To live a life without regrets? To find some kind of balance?

Unable to resist the pull and needing to feel his touch, she stood and slid her arms around his middle. And God, his arms closed around her, and she decided that was where she wanted to spend the day. Right there, tucked into his warm body.

As though sensing her needs, Jace pulled her closer wrapping himself all the way around her, and she felt his warmth and support radiate through every cell. A six-foot four hard-bodied, protective male wrapped around her was exactly what she needed. Charlotte nuzzled her face into his neck and breathed him in. He smelled so good, she did again, and again, until her heart was beating to the steady rhythm of his and the urge to cry was replaced with acceptance.

He didn't press her to answer his question. Didn't pry or rush her. Just patiently held her, his hand easing up and down her spine in comforting passes, giving her the time she needed to think things through. Make a plan.

She had forgotten that about Jace. He didn't judge or demand or push, he was a nurturer at heart. Patient and gentle and soft at his core. Funny thing to say about a man who was the size of a mountain. But he lived to take care of the people he loved, even if sometimes he went about it the wrong way. And in that moment, she could almost believe he loved her enough to make everything okay.

She knew she should let go, take a step back, and get it under control. She was an emotional hot mess, primed to make epically stupid decisions. But she'd forgotten how nice it felt to be taken care of, to have someone else be the strong one, so she held on.

He held her back, and when she was no longer afraid she'd crumble, she asked, "Do you ever wish you could be someone else?"

"Every day." No hesitation, no apologies. Nope, Jace McGraw spoke those words like he was an expert on the subject, and something about that appealed to her.

She looked up. "And what do you do?"

He brushed her hair behind her ear, his thumb grazing her cheek. "Remind myself that I can be anyone I want. That nothing defines me but myself. Not the past, or people's misconceptions, nothing but me. And if that doesn't work I pretend that it did."

"Does it work? Pretending?" she asked, because even the way the word fell from her lips felt bold and reckless and so incredibly freeing that a thrilling giddiness bubbled up in-side of her.

"Sometimes," he whispered, and there was something about the weariness in his tone, the strain bracketing his mouth, and the shadows that were always right beneath the surface that pulled her all the way in, broke through her fear and her walls. Because like her, Jace had struggled to bal-ance happiness with outside expectations, and he'd won. But being home was a reminder of who he'd once been.

"Who do you want to be right now?" she asked.

"The guy who makes you smile." He cupped her cheek and she leaned into his hand. "Who do you want to be, Charlie?"

"The woman you married," she admitted, hating that her throat tightened around the words. "I want to be the woman who was driven and focused and liked to bowl, even though my best game was a sixty-eight. The woman who wasn' afraid to say no, or yes, or scream when I was mad. I want to be the woman I am proud of and not the woman who make people proud." Now that she was started, she realized tha there were so many things she'd wanted and denied hersel because it wasn't polite or proper or, God forbid, perfect.

And she was staring one down.

Which left her two options. Go into work, establish peac in the parking lot, and make her dad pleased. But she kne how that would turn out, had been living that life for nearl thirty years. Even when she'd been with Jace her paren had weighed in on her every decision. If they hadn't, sh wouldn't have hidden their relationship just because they married so fast. Or because she'd married someone wh didn't fit the mold of what a Holden should be.

The other option was to give herself over to the exper ence with Jace, give him that "more" he was asking for, an give *them* a chance. A real chance to see where it could lead.

Option one was the safe choice. But the only way she was going to be that woman she'd described, find happiness and balance, was with Jace.

He might not be the safe choice, but the way her heart fluttered when she was around him and her body melted when she touched him told her that he was the right one. No question. She didn't know for how long or what the fallout would be when he left, but she knew she couldn't walk away. She was already in too deep. And making his chosen zip code a prerequisite, putting more expectations and guidelines on what he could give, what he had to become for her to accept his offer, wouldn't be fair.

To either of them.

Jace had asked for one thing. Just one. And Charlotte had countered with a grocery list of demands, all of which he accepted without question. So she would put that same faith in him, give herself over to the experience, risk the heartache for the chance at that elusive *more*.

"Right now I want to be the woman who shares your morning coffee," she said, walking over to grab his boots. "After I go put these in the bedroom."

Chapter 15

❧

A light breeze shifted through the fog and across Suga
Lake, rustling the willows that sat on the bank and sending
leaves from the distant oak trees fluttering down in a fire
colored snowfall. There was a stillness to the world—the
only sound was the boat gently gliding through the water
Charlotte skimmed her fingers across the top layer of water
watching it ripple all the way to the shoreline and lap agains
her dock.

"It's like we are the only two people in the world," sh
said, looking at her house, which butted up against a sma
channel off Sugar Lake. With her nearest neighbor separate
by a grove of peach trees, it was secluded and peaceful—an
exactly what she'd needed right then.

"I call it the Sugar experience without all of the chatter
he said, and Charlotte turned to smile at him, only to fin
he was looking back, not an ounce of amusement in h
expression. There was a heaviness clouding his eyes, an
underneath a resigned acceptance that tugged at her heart.

"Is this how you've been getting to my house unseen?"

"Yup," Jace said, like it was no big deal, driving the oars through the water, the muscles in his arms bunching and coiling with every stroke. "I park my truck at Cal's then paddle over at night. In the morning I paddle back, get in my truck, and drive into town. Very stealthy if you ask me."

It was also very sweet that he was doing all of that to protect her privacy. So she felt awful admitting, "Glory knows. About you sneaking over here. And about Atlanta."

"Well, shit," he said on a tired chuckle. "All this sneaking around and you went ahead and took an ad out in the *Penny-Saver*."

"I only told Glory, because she kind of figured it out, like Ben. Trust me, they won't tell a soul." She had complete faith in her friends. Since moving back to Sugar, Charlotte had forged some wonderful relationships with some extraordinary people, Glory topping that list. And she trusted them implicitly.

"She doesn't have to tell a soul, just her soul mate. And then Cal will tell Brett, because when those two get together they gossip like a bunch of old grannies. Gabbing about kids, wives, and family, everything under the sun." He paused, letting the ores dangle. "Or under their sun, and baby, that includes me and mine."

A warm tingle started low in her belly at the mention of her being his. "As long as Hattie doesn't find out—"

"About that."

"Please tell me your grandmother doesn't know about Atlanta. Or the *stairwell*," she whispered the last part, knowing that if it was true she couldn't look Hattie in the eye ever again.

"God no," he said, and shivered, equally horrified by the idea. "Just about the annulment." Right, because *that* was *so* much better. "The original letter sent from the recorder's office about the misfiling went to the house. She signed for it and, being Hattie, ignored the big Jace printed on the envelope and just acknowledged the McGraw part."

"She opened it and then kept her mouth shut?" That ranked a ginormous zero on the believability chart.

"She never even mentioned a word of it to me until last week. She claims she was giving us time to figure things out."

"Four years is a long time to keep a secret." A flutter of unease and a whole lot of guilt lodged in her chest at the statement. It got stronger when she realized Jace was still deceiving his family, rowing across Sugar Lake every day. Twice a day. Just because of her rules.

So was she.

Sure, the thought of everyone thinking they were shacking up sounded about as fun as a root canal. Telling everyone the truth, only to have him leave and have everyone give her the *Oh, poor Charlotte* look for the rest of eternity sounded even worse. But asking the man she'd married to lie to his family was beyond selfish.

"You don't have to keep rowing across the lake," she said, adopting as much conviction as she could. She even straightened her shoulders. "I don't care what people say."

Eyes on her, he set the ores inside the boat and let it glide with the current, back toward her dock. "Yes, you do, and that's okay."

God, she *was* transparent. "I don't want to care."

"I know," he said in a gentle way that had her going all melty. "But caring is who you are. You care about how it would affect your parents, your ability to do your job, your ability to move forward in this town. And those are all important things."

"But what about what you want?"

"I want to show you I'm worth the risk. That's all. I'm not here to prove to anyone else who I am except for you. So as long as you know the truth and what's real, the rest of it doesn't matter."

"Ah-huh, then why did you kiss me in front of Ben?" she asked, because she didn't buy what he was selling.

Jace shrugged a shoulder, just one, but it still jostled the boat. "He'd already seen my hands on your ass. In case he was too distracted by that thong to notice my hands there, I wanted to make myself clear."

She laughed. "Because he has a key?"

He leaned forward, their knees brushing, and as he shifted closer she could see the God's honest truth in his eyes. "Because I'm not him, Charlie."

Her chest tightened for the man who was so strong but carried so much pain. Pain he wore on his skin, in his stance, to hide the wounded boy beneath.

"I don't have fancy degrees or season tickets to the opera. I don't golf or have a membership in some exclusive club that doesn't revolve around engines or horsepower," he explained. "And I have nothing in common with your family. And that scares me."

It should scare Charlotte, too, but it didn't. It was exhilarating. She liked that Jace was different, that he saw beauty in the simple things in life. That he would rather watch a movie in bed than go to a gala, swing a fishing rod over a golf club, and would never consider hiring someone to work on his house, because getting down and dirty didn't bother him. She liked that he was the kind of man who'd spend an entire afternoon teaching a bunch of old ladies how to change a tire and his down-time fixing a car to make his grandma happy—even though Charlotte knew being home was tearing him up inside.

And she loved that he loved to take care of people—to take care of her.

"If I wanted to be with someone like you described, I'd be with Ben," she said quietly. "But that's not what I want."

"What do you want?"

She wanted someone who believed in her, challenged her, recognized just how hard she'd worked to get to where she was, and treated her as though what she did mattered. As though *she* mattered.

"You," she said, leaning over and covering his mouth with hers. "For as long as I can have you."

He groaned as his arms came around her, so big, and yet they managed to hold her softly against him. He took his time, exploring her mouth in a way that was coaxing and equally giving. Charlotte felt a shiver start way down in her toes and slide deliciously up her entire spine.

"Are you cold?" he asked.

No, she was just experiencing McGraw overload. "My reaction to daily kisses."

"I'd hug you, but I'm afraid we'd topple the boat."

Instead of opting to head straight to bed when she'd moved his things into her room, an invitation the old Jace would've taken, he'd told her to get showered and dress warmly. Then he'd surprised her by having their morning coffee out on his dad's old boat. Although the word *boat* made it sound a lot bigger than it was. This was more of a dingy, with two rickety bench seats that faced each other and left barely enough room for one adult, let alone the both of them. Yet it was the perfect size for a romantic morning cruise around the lake since their knees were forced to fit together like puzzle pieces, and their thighs brushed every time the wind picked up or one of them shifted.

"This should help." He wrapped a blanket over their legs, then pulled a thermos out of the paper bag he'd loaded and opened the lid. He watched her watching him, and with a cute smile he wafted the steam her way. The heavenly aroma of steaming peppermint mixed with the chilled morning air, and her eyes slid shut in ecstasy. He handed her the thermos, and just when she thought her world couldn't get any better, he reached back in the bag for his second surprise—whipped cream.

"Is that for the coffee, or are we starting new morning ritual?" she asked with a teasing smile.

"I'm open to either."

"I have a surprise, too." She passed him the thermos, and he added a generous spray of whipped goodness as she dug through her own bag.

"A string bikini?" he asked hopefully, taking a sip of coffee. "The kind that have those sexy peekaboo butts?"

"Better." She pulled out his copy of *Hitched* magazine. She flipped to the page she'd dog-eared that morning and showed him.

" 'Ten questions every couple should ask before saying I Do ' " he read, then met her gaze. "I'll answer first. 'You spread out over the hood of my Chevelle, in nothing but moonlight, pearls, and my racing jacket.' " His studied her, his expression confused, then he shook his head. "Nope. Lose the jacket, just you on my car. Hair down. Wavy and kind of sex-rumpled."

"Sex-rumpled?"

"Oh yeah," he said in a tone that was all male appreciation. "Don't forget the pearls."

She found her hand straying to the strand of pearls at her neck. They had originally belonged to her great-great-grandmother, Rose Holden, and had been passed down to

Charlotte the day she'd turned sixteen. If she was lucky enough to have a daughter then she'd pass them on as well.

"That's not how this works. We ask each other questions. Questions from the list." She held up the magazine.

He opened his mouth and she could tell by the wicked twinkle in his eye as he stared at the pearls that he wasn't done with his fantasy. Then said, "This is a boring game."

"It's your magazine," she pointed out. "You treated the other article as law, I thought this would be fun."

"My list had words like *shenanigans* and *sexcapades*. Yours uses"—he took the magazine, perused the questions, and handed it back—"*comfort zones* and *emotional needs*." With a heartfelt sigh, he rowed them a little closer to shore. "Does it at least say that we ask them while in a string bikini with a peekaboo butt?"

She flipped the magazine back over and pretended to study it thoroughly. "Nope. Sorry."

"Too bad. That would have been a good rule."

"I don't know if you could pull off peekaboo bottoms."

His eyes went the length of her. "I'd be willing to suffer the humiliation to see you in one."

Charlotte felt her cheeks heat up, and not just the ones on her face. "First question." She paused. "Do you want to ask first or be asked?"

"I'm easy," he said, and she rolled her eyes.

"I'll find a fun one." She went to the middle of the list. "Okay, here's one. 'If you could be any superhero, who would it be?' " She shoved the magazine in her bag with a disappointed huff. "You're right, this is boring. And the questions are too easy."

"It was just getting good, and that's not an easy question at all."

He sounded so confident that Charlotte snorted. "Side-swipe. That red Transformer. A Lamborghini one minute, a crime-fighting robot with pile drivers for arms and a rocket pack the next. Fast, dangerous, and can fly. Every boy's dream."

It was not, however, every boy's favorite superhero. Charlotte didn't even know if a Transformer counted as a superhero, but it was Jace's favorite.

"How the hell did you know that?" he asked, his expression clearly one of confusion, but Charlotte could also see a hint of shyness in there. Her big badass was flustered over the comment.

"You sat behind me every week in Sunday school and I overheard you telling Brett that you wanted one for Christmas. I didn't know who Sideswipe was so I went home and asked my dad to buy me one when he went to Atlanta. It took every penny of allowance I had saved up."

"Impressive," he said gently, studying her as if trying to read between the lines of what she was saying about the past and how it connected to the now. "Now tell me why a girl who was into Barbie bought a car robot?"

"First off, Barbie is amazing," she said, glaring at him when he went to laugh. "She was a gorgeous blonde with big boobs and mile-long legs who managed to fly to the moon, get her PhD, serve overseas, save baby dolphins, wield a hammer, surf, speak a zillion languages, raise a sister, and still hold court at every party in town. She did all of that while having to prove she wasn't a bimbo. How many male superheroes can say that?"

"Not a single one I can think of," he said, understanding lacing his expression at the similarities between Barbie and Charlotte, and now it was Charlotte's turn to blush. "She is beyond impressive." He said it as though *she* were impressive, and not just because she knew his favorite superhero. "But you still didn't say why you were interested in what toy I was playing with."

She sighed. It was silly that after all these years she'd never admitted her crush. They'd been together such a short time and were too busy talking about the future and trying to figure out the present to even get into the past. "Why else would a girl spend her allowance to buy a toy car for a boy?"

"You bought it for me?"

"I was going to give it to you for Christmas, in the Secret Santa gift exchange because," and here it went, "I thought you were cute."

"Cute, huh?" he said, tugging on her ankle, the boat swaying with his movement. "I never got it."

"I know," the disappointed little girl in her who had come up with the perfect plan sighed. "I went to put it under the tree, then I heard you got it as a present from your mom and I hid it in my bag."

"You could have told me, I would have been more into your pigtails than a toy car anyway." He teased and she cocked a disbelieving brow. "Okay, probably not, but now I would." He ran his hand under the blanket and up her leg. "How old were you?"

"I was in the fifth grade and you were in fourth. You had this cute spiky hair, and your mom had dressed you in Brett's old suit, which was two inches too short in the legs."

He laughed. "I remember that. It was for Christmas pictures, and the week before I tore a hole through my church pants scaling the playground fence. I was too afraid to tell my mom, so when Sunday came and there was no time to get new ones, I got Brett's hand-me-downs." He met her gaze. "You remembered all that?"

"You fascinated me," she admitted. "You were always up to something, getting into some kind of trouble, but you were also so sweet with your mom and grandma."

"I drove my mom crazy," he said with a raw laugh.

Charlotte found his hand under the blanket and linked their fingers. "I once overheard our moms talking. It was after you got caught trying to saddle Mr. Ferguson's bull."

"Brett bet me that I couldn't stay on for eight seconds," he explained as though a bet was all the reason he needed to mount one of the most dangerous bulls in Sugar County. "I lasted nine."

"You also drove him through their fence and into my granddad's garden. But instead of apologizing for your behavior, your mom said that you were a beautiful reminder that the best things in life don't always come with instruction manuals. She admitted that while your curiosity and determination would get you into trouble, she knew it would also be your greatest strength, and out of all her boys, you were the one who was the most like your dad."

Jace swallowed hard, then stared out over the water, taking in the houses dotting the shoreline across the lake, his face reflective and unsure. After a long moment, he said, "She used to tell me I was just like my dad, but I figured she said that to all of us kids."

Charlotte tugged his hand, waiting until he looked at her. "She said you got your fascination for trouble from him, that it allowed you to play as hard as you loved, and it was her favorite part of you."

That was actually what had peaked Charlotte's interest. Sure, her parents loved her, but they were never affectionate or outward with their feelings. She didn't grow up in a home that embraced hugging or gave easy compliments. Until Jace, the only kind of love she knew was complicated, based around milestones and achievements, and always left her feeling empty.

Lost.

But the McGraws, they loved big and loud. And Jace was no exception.

"Thank you," he said, not bothering to hide his gratitude or emotion. "I really needed to hear that." He cleared his throat, and glancing down at the article he scanned the page a few times, then looked up. "My turn. Did you know I was in the bar before I offered to buy you a drink?"

"That isn't one of the questions." She snatched the magazine back.

"No, but you're right, we know the answers to these," he said. "So we're getting creative. I'm good at creative." As she well knew. "So spill, I have it on good authority that you knew I was in the bar before I offered to buy you a drink."

Embarrassing fact number one: Charlotte not only knew he was in the bar, she went to the bar knowing he was going to be there.

"Molly from the Gas and Go told me you were in town for the race." Wanting to catch a glimpse of her childhood crush all grown up, she convinced her roommate to go with her, ditched the pearls and angora for denim and cowgirl boots, and went on a manhunt.

He let loose a low whistle. "Oh my, Miss Peach, were you stalking me?"

"No," she lied. "I wanted to see what you'd turned out like."

Which brought her to embarrassing fact number two. When Jace walked in that door, crush didn't begin to describe what she felt. Jace had become the man she'd always known he'd be. Big, badass, clouded in mystery, and so incredibly sexy it took everything she had to play it cool. Let him see her and approach her, which took an agonizing hour.

"And?" He held out his arms, flexed those guns, and shot a set of double-barred dimples her way.

"What do you think?" she said. "I let you buy me a drink, and I went home with you."

It was the first real risk she'd ever taken. The first time she'd ever gone after what she wanted without regard to her parents' opinion. And it was the most exhilarating thing she'd ever experienced. Being with Jace was like skydiving naked through a tropical storm.

"Are you telling me you picked up a man up at a bar? Wearing a teeny-tiny skirt and shitkickers?"

"Yes. And since there is no room on this boat for your ego to get any larger, my turn." She picked a question. "This is a two-parter. Who was your first kiss and your best kiss?"

He ran a hand over his chin, and she could hear the rustle of his stubble. "First kiss. Eighth grader, Holy Cleavage Hanna Jacobs, behind Mable's Market. She tasted like watermelon lip gloss and let me cop a feel. She stuffed her bra. It shattered my little world."

"Eighth grade, really?" She laughed. "I have you beat by a year. I never would have taken you for a late bloomer."

"I was in the fifth grade, Hanna was in eighth." He waggled a brow, and Charlotte could practically feel the boat sink with the added weight of his ego. Then he got serious. "Best kiss. You. In the backseat of my sixty-seven Camaro the night we met. I had no idea they taught girls like you how to kiss like that."

"What do you mean 'girls like me'?" she asked, and okay, if she was being honest, Charlotte had never kissed a man like that before, never understood before Jace that kissing was more than foreplay. With Jace, kissing was as sensual as sex. It wasn't a side dish or a precursor, he treated it like the main dish. And there was something so intoxicating about that she gave herself over to it.

"Look at you, baby. You are *that* woman. Beautiful, classy, put together in all the right ways—don't look at me like that, I'm not done yet." He scooted closer, linking their hands and bringing hers to his mouth. "You're also sexy and funny and sweet and the kind of woman every guy dreams of marrying."

Charlotte froze at his words. Waited for the bitterness to creep in, for the anger and frustration she felt whenever she thought of their marriage. Instead she felt connected in a way that was new to her. New to them.

"I'm also a terrible cook," she added, afraid that he was about to add *perfect* to that list. "And I couldn't carry a tune even if it was in a bag."

"Trust me, baby, when I say I know. You can't bake worth a shit, either."

"Hey!" She tried to jerk her hand back but he held it to his lips, pressed a gentle kiss to her palm that had her bones melting. "You love my cinnamon snap cookies." He made a face that looked like death warmed over and she laughed. "They can't be that bad."

"Worse," he said. "But you kiss like an angel and have the best ass I have ever had the pleasure of groping." To prove it he slid his hands around her, getting two palms full and scooted her close, his knees parting to make way for her.

The boat rocked, a little water sloshing inside, and she froze, afraid it would capsize. Now that she thought about it, this rickety old dingy was one wrong move from toppling. And the water looked cold.

"And when you're nervous you do this thing with your lower lip that gets me hard." His gaze dropped her mouth and held. "Yeah, that right there. You do it when you're turned on, too."

She put her hand to her mouth to cover the tell, but Jace caught her wrist, stopping her before she could finish. He trapped it against his chest, which was so hard she could feel the steady beat through his shirt. "Don't hide who you are, Charlie. Not from me. Not from anyone."

He said it as though it was that easy, as though she could just decide she was ready to be brave and courage would magically appear. And she wanted that, so desperately, because pretending for so long had become exhausting. Confusing.

"What if I don't know who I am?" she admitted, because although she was some of the things he mentioned, she didn't know how to reconcile the person she wanted to be with the person he was describing. She had spent so much of her life trying to be who she thought she should be, she wasn't sure who she was anymore. All she knew was that she wanted to be that woman he was describing, the woman she saw when she looked through his eyes.

"Baby, you're a blonde bombshell with a killer rack and mile-long legs who has the heart and the smarts to take over the world. You can fly to the moon, deliver a baby, save a kid's life, save the town from itself, and still hold court at every party in town. Just so long as you don't serve those cinnamon snap cookies," he said, and she tried to laugh past her tight throat.

"You don't have to decide who you want to be, you just have to decide what you want to do with all of those superpowers you've got in there." He tapped her chest, right above her melting heart. "So what's it going to be?"

In her professional life Charlotte was confident, composed, able to make a life-or-death decision in the blink of an eye. In her personal life she was so afraid of disappointing others that she hesitated to put herself out there. That hesitation left room for doubt in herself and in her ability to make the right choices, and so she sat in limbo. Waiting for her life to begin, too scared to take the first step.

But Jace was right. If she was going to live without regrets, she needed to be fearless. Channel the woman who kissed her secret crush in the back of his Camaro. Who saw something special and went for it.

"I want to be all of those things." She stood up and the boat shifted dangerously under the change in weight distribution. "And more."

"Whoa!" Jace gripped the rim of the dingy and tried to balance it out. "If you're not careful, you'll rock the boat and we'll both go in headfirst."

Charlotte kicked off one shoe, then the other. Next came her socks. "I'm starting to realize that headfirst is the only way this will work."

* * *

Headfirst worked for him, Jace thought, as Charlotte's sweater, which was peach and soft-looking with little white buttons going up the center, hit the deck. Because that meant she was standing in the middle of his boat in a bright pink lacy bra, which did nothing to hide the fact that it was cold out, and a pair of hip-hugging jeans.

She hooked her thumbs into the belt loops of the jeans and, hello, a simple slide down those mile-long legs later and Jace was staring at the sexiest pair of barely-there peekaboo panties. Also bright pink and lace.

"I know it's not bikini bottoms, but they'll do." She laughed, which he should have guessed was her subtle way of telling him they were going to go for a swim, because without warning she reached up to her ponytail, pulled out the rubber band, and said, "Hair down, right?" then jumped.

Right off the fucking boat. Vanishing beneath the surface, but not before giving him an inspiring view of that world-class ass he loved.

Jace held his breath until she surfaced, then he held it a little longer because, *man,* she was amazing. Hair loose and sticking to her skin, lips moist and glistening, her face lit with giddy mischief. And there was something about the way the water reflected in her big green eyes, making him want to dive in, headfirst like she said, and never come up.

"Is it cold?"

"Nope." She cupped her hands and made a wave of water that hit the side of the boat. "It's perfect."

"I can see the goose bumps from here."

She laughed and went under again. This time when she surfaced she was right next to the boat, and her hands weren't empty. Nope, seductress Barbie held two balls of wet pink lace, which she tossed into the boat. "Does it matter?"

"Hell no," he said, untying his boots.

"Good." Her tone was pure temptation. "Because my fantasy is you, in nothing but lake water, giving me a religious experience that has me moaning the Lord's name." She rested her arms on the edge of the boat and whispered, "And I'm not talking about a Southern baptism."

She pushed off to swim backward, giving him an unobstructed view of her front and rocking a whole lot more than the boat. The playful looks and let's-get-naughty tone were too much, winding around him and driving him completely insane.

He'd told her he needed more, and she informed him in the most creative way that she was not only open to more,

but that she wanted to go after it headfirst. Which was fine
by him, since that finally, *finally,* put them both on the same
page and, as far as he was concerned, was something to celebrate. With steamy, hot, lake sex.

Sure, it sounded like something a bored debutante
would do with the local hell-raiser, but Charlotte wasn't a
bored debutante, and he was no longer that hell-raiser. So
he would have her moaning all right.

As soon as he got his damn boots off.

In a frantic attempt to undo his pants, he nearly capsized
the dingy, and Charlotte laughed. Then after he ransacked
every single pocket looking for—bingo!—a condom, all of
his clothes joined hers at the bottom of the boat, and she
stopped laughing altogether. Because he gave her a look that
meant *it was on,* then dove in.

Headfirst.

The second he broke the surface the little remaining oxygen left his lungs, because damn, it was cold. And this was
it. The moment he'd been waiting for. But he'd swum this
lake in fall before, without the promise of a creative way to
get warm or the promise of more. And he'd survived. He
could do it again, only this time when he surfaced he'd be
holding on to forever.

As though his body could pick her out in the million gallons of water, he came up right next to what he'd been looking for. He could feel her legs, smooth and elegant, brushing
against his as she treaded water. Other things brushed too as
she slowly glided closer until he could see the water droplets
clinging to her long lashes and the way her lips parted when
his hands settled on her hips.

He ran one palm up her side and around her back and she
shivered. "You're freezing."

"I figured you could find a way to keep us warm." Her

arms slid around his neck, and her legs drifted around his middle. They moved with the current as he kept them afloat, every ripple of water bringing them closer together, bringing her soft body flush with his.

"Like this?" He ran his hands down the impossibly soft skin of her back, and lower, until he molded them to her bare ass, taking a cheek in each hand. World-class indeed.

She shivered again as, little by little, he steered her closer and even closer still, until the sensation of their slick skin sliding back and forth was enough to create a spark of heat that flashed in her eyes.

"Warmer," she mused, threading her fingers through his hair and scattering droplets of cold water down his neck. "Definitely warmer."

"I was going for inferno." And to prove it he kissed her, his lips gliding over her frozen ones, slow and deep, and like accelerant on a match, she ignited. She was laying a kiss on him that was needy, erotic, and so raw he forgot to keep kicking, and it took them both under, the water closing over their heads.

Instead of stopping, Charlotte's eyes opened and met his, and as she smiled her hands tightened in his hair. And then, holy hell, she kissed him as the water caved in around them, the bubbles sliding over, between, past them, until they were so deep he couldn't see the surface. Until his lungs were burning and the urge to inhale was so strong he was convinced they were both going to pass out from sheer need and lack of oxygen.

Even then they both held on, knowing that when they broke the surface everything would be different. Or maybe this was, once again, him hoping that things would be different. Maybe Charlotte was just enjoying the hell out of their kiss.

Nope, she felt it, too. It was right there in the way she held him, the way she curled herself around and into him, all of the things she hadn't said were on the surface, for some-one who knew what to look for.

And Jace knew what to look for. And fucking loved what he saw.

She was drinking him in as though he was more neces-sary than breathing. One hand gripped his head as though she'd rather drown with him than let go, while the other nim-bly made its way south.

Jace did the only thing he could, he held on tight and slowly started kicking for them both. Easing them toward the surface without breaking contact. And when they came up they were closer to the dock than the boat, which worked for him.

He guided them under the wood platform and up against the weathered pylon. The crisp autumn air moved off the lake and wrapped around them, rustling the leaves nearby and sending scattered shards of sunlight through the cracks between the slats of the dock.

Able to touch the bottom, Jace pinned her body between the pylon and his chest, then stood. Water sluiced off them like a waterfall. Hands still firmly on her ass, he rested his forehead against her so they could both take in air. "Are we hot yet?"

With a soft smile she kissed him, her mouth moving in a languid but confident manner. And those nimble fingers, they stroked him from base to tip and back again, and just when he thought his legs would buckle, she positioned him at her slick heat. "Hot, yes. But I thought we were going for inferno."

"I need to get the condom on," he said, thanking, miracle of miracles, that it wasn't at the bottom of the lake, and knowing it had been sheer survival instinct in action that allowed him to maintain hold. But he had, and thank Christ he had, because even though they were submerged in freezing cold water, she was ready.

And he was more than ready. "But I need to get us to dry land."

"Okay," she moaned, her hands back to making promises he wasn't sure he'd be able to hold out long enough to collect on. "Fast."

"Baby, you keep on doing that and I guarantee it will be lightning fast." Only she didn't slow down, she wrapped her hand around him. So he let his hands do a little wandering of their own, loving how her skin felt wet and slick under her palms. How hard her nipples budded from the cold, and how they budded even harder at his touch.

"You are so fucking amazing," he said, and she tightened her grip slightly, then squeezed. He was going to come right there, in her hand.

"I refuse to wait here all day."

Jace froze. Charlotte froze, too, her eyes meeting his and widening, because although the person speaking was female it sure as hell wasn't Charlotte.

There was a bang at the front door, then, "I know you're in there."

Darleen? Jace mouthed slowly, making sure to raise a brow so she understood his question.

Charlotte nodded and closed her eyes. *I am so sorry,* she mouthed back.

He caught her face and delivered a gentle kiss because, *God*, he didn't want her feeling guilty about things she had no control over. *It's okay. She'll leave soon.*

What if she doesn't?

She will.

She had to. Her appearance left them stranded under the dock, with Charlotte's breasts bared for his viewing pleasure and her hands wrapped around him. He watched the panic growing in her expression, and he wanted so badly to make this okay. To make it so that something that started out as amazing didn't end in disaster.

He weighed their options. Getting back in the boat would cause too much noise, and going onto dry land wasn't going to happen. Which left staying put, with his dick millimeters from sinking into home, with Charlotte naked and shivering— no longer from need.

He pulled her close and she nuzzled against his neck. His hands moved up and down trying to keep the chill from settling.

"You aren't going to win this, and you know it," Darleen hollered.

Charlotte's breathing changed, or maybe it was her heartbeat, but he felt the shift through his body. Felt her body relax and her lips open on his skin. Then there was the slight rotating of her hips against him, and he felt sweat bead on his forehead.

"I can hear your cell ringing inside the house," Darleen accused.

A small smile tugged Charlotte's lips, and her hands softened as she leaned in and, using every one of her superpowers to draw him in, captured his mouth.

"I mean it, Charlotte." *Bang bang bang.* "Open up. Or answer my calls. Or I call the rest of the board."

And she kissed him, slow and deliberate, taking her time to rebuild the heat. She didn't close her eyes so he didn't, either, instead watching the connection pool while they made out ten feet from one of the biggest bigmouths in town, who was threatening to kick down her door.

Only Charlotte wasn't scared. Nope, she released his mouth and slowly rose up and slid down the outside of his length, doing that thing with her lower lip. On purpose. She was completely, totally, one hundred percent turned on. Showing no signs of slowing down.

Condom, he reminded her, gripping her hips before she drove them both home.

Pill, she mouthed back a little sassy and, God bless her, Charlotte was indeed a master planner, because she turned what was a problem of epic proportions without a variable solution into the sexiest fantasy he could have ever imagined.

She rose up, all the way up, so fucking high that her breasts grazed his chest, then his chin, then his mouth and, without making a single ripple in the water, slid back down.

All.

The.

Way.

Down.

Taking him in one fluid, excruciatingly slow, and completely mind-blowing thrust.

Jace's hips jerked up, how could they not? He had Dr. Charlotte Holden naked and panting, under a dock in fucking Sugar Lake. This was better than in his Camaro. Better than stairwell sex. Better than anything he'd ever experienced, because it was more. Sure, it was hot and erotic, but it was about connection and sharing, being open to all the possibilities that could come.

And just when he thought he'd die from the pleasure, she did it again and he had to amend his previous statement. The second pass was even better, because it meant they'd gone even further down that path, only the water lapped at the movement, gently but enough to splash against the far pylon.

He gripped her hips and, holding her still, put a finger to her lips. *Shhhhh.* A move Charlotte clearly took to heart since she sucked his finger in her mouth while tightening her muscles—all of her muscles—around him in a move that rewrote the book on seduction.

Fuck! Sweat beaded on his forehead from the strain of not moving. Because how could she do that move and expect him to stay still?

"Was that a statement or a command?" she whispered against his ear, making sure her lips grazed the outer shell.

"You're playing with fire," he said, equally as hushed.

"I like the heat." She also liked to nip, because her teeth sank into his lobe, and it was game fucking on.

Message received so loud and clear he didn't need a manual on communication to understand. He'd gotten it wrong all these years. His prim little miss wasn't looking for a bad boy to show her trouble, she was looking for a partner in crime—someone who matched her in every way. And suddenly Jace didn't feel so lost. With her, right here in Sugar, he actually felt as if he belonged. As if his fascination with trouble was an asset, a shared foundation that led to a deeper understanding. Of each other.

To prove to her that he was more than up to that challenge, he showed her a few things from his wild-card résumé that had her biting back a moan.

She released a wicked smile and, yup, Miss Peach was a closeted exhibitionist who got off on making trouble. And God's honest truth, with her, so did he.

He moved, slow and sure, at first, all the way out, then sank back in, and Charlotte's head fell back against the pylon. She watched him through hazy eyes as he ducked his head to kiss down her neck to her chest and finally those perfect tens.

"Fine!" Darleen said, right as Charlotte let out a little purr. Then a bigger one. "I'll go to the source, and if you need help with the parade, make sure to lose my number!"

Darleen's heels clacked across the porch and down the steps, allowing Jace to up the pressure, the pace, until Charlotte was panting. Biting her lip to keep from screaming.

"God, more," she hissed. Her legs tightened around his middle, and she crushed her mouth to his.

He gave her more as the sound of crunching gravel got farther and farther away, and the sound of Charlotte's moans came closer and closer together. And then, halla-fucking-lujah, all he could hear was the water lapping, their bodies sliding, and Charlotte exploded around him. Her hands gripped his shoulders, and her legs strangled all the air from his lungs as she fought for purchase, and with one final surge right when she tightened, he followed her over, kissing her to keep from crying out.

He wanted to hear her scream "Oh God" almost as much as he wanted to hear her scream "Fuck me, Jace." But what he wanted more was to carry her into the house, up into the master bath for a hot shower. Then round two, only this time he'd wake up with her in his arms.

Instead he heard a ringing. Coming from the dingy. His phone. With great effort Charlotte pulled her head off his shoulder and met his gaze. The dingy was twenty feet from them, visible from the dock and close enough that anyone who was looking—and he knew that if his phone blew up Darleen would be looking—could see their clothes strewn around the bottom.

It rang again, and Jace held his breath because those heels they'd thought were gone clicked back over, closer and closer with every ring. Charlotte looked up at him, her hair a wet ness, her eyes wide and pleading with him to make it better.

The phone gave one final ring, then blessed silence.

"Um, yeah, hi, Jace, it's Darleen. Darleen Vander." She paused and he could hear the confusion in her voice. "I was calling to see if I could swing by the shop, maybe take you to lunch so I can pick your brain about all those cars we have coming. I can't map out the fair until I have numbers, so anytime you could spare would be appreciated. 'Bye now."

She disconnected and Jace held still. Between the most intense sex of his life and waiting for his phone to chirp with a voice mail, he was certain he was going to have a heart attack. He could feel Charlotte's pulse skyrocketing, too. So he took her face between his hands and gave her a gentle, *we got this* kiss, and to his amazement she kissed him back, *I know.*

His phone chirped, but it was muffled by the distance and could have been a bird or something else. Darleen waited another few seconds, then with a huff she clicked her way back to the car.

When her engine started Jace let himself breathe. He dropped his head to Charlotte's shoulder and said, "That was close."

"I know. It makes me rethink things," she said so seriously he paused, because no way in hell was she putting on the breaks now. Sure, they almost got caught, and yeah, it would have caused some serious issues around town. Nothing they couldn't handle. But when he looked up she was smiling and his heart did a little ping-pong action in his chest. "Maybe we should stick with your list. Naptime shenanigans sounds dryer and warmer."

Chapter 16

⟨decorative flourish⟩

Jace had repaired some of the most damaged cars in racing history. He'd designed a next-generation fuel injection system, built engines from the block up, and in under sixty seconds repaired ones on their last lap. He knew how to plan for the win and make split-second decisions to guarantee one. What he didn't know how to do was manage a teenage girl picking out car colors.

"I like the sky blue," Payton said, holding the sample and studying the way the sun reflected off of it, as though this decision would become one of historical significance. She held up the second sample and paused. "But this other blue is a bit brighter. More Tiffany."

Harvey, an old-timer who'd been painting cars since before the Stingray was invented and still ran one of the best auto-body restoration shops in the country, looked at Jace, his eyes glazed over with confusion. And maybe a touch of hopelessness.

Jace shrugged. He had no idea who Tiffany was or how

she weighed in on the decision. All Jace knew was that Harvey had done him a solid driving all the way out here just to look at the car, bring color samples, and give them a fair bid. And an hour to decide between two shades of blue wasn't the way to repay his generosity.

Jace had dropped the seat frames off at the upholstery restorer yesterday, when Charlotte had gone to work after naptime shenanigans, and until the guy knew what color to match the blue piping, he was at a standstill. And with the parade just over a week away, every day was crucial.

"So which one will it be, honey?" he asked Payton, trying to sound encouraging rather than irritated. "The original blue or Tiffany's blue?"

"I love the Tiffany blue. Don't you?"

"Um, sure." At this point he didn't care.

"It goes really well with the cream accents." She paused, and Jace was about to say, "Great, Tiffany it is," when she sighed like the entire fate of her generation rested on this one decision. "But the original sky blue would bring up the value of the car."

A point that was made at the beginning of this hourlong debate.

"And it brings out the light-blue flecks in your eyes," she said, holding the samples up to his face as if they were fabric swatches.

Harvey sat down. Jace wanted to sit, too, but was afraid Payton would take that as a sign of weakness and bring back options three and four—which they'd eliminated twenty minutes ago. So he stood firm. "I'm not going to be driving this, Hattie is. So pick whatever you think matches the fleck in her eyes."

She let out a long-winded sigh, and so did Jace, because he'd heard that sigh before. About ten minutes ago. So he took a seat on the tailgate of a pickup that was in for servicing.

"I need to see them inside once more," she said. "See how they look under the fluorescent lights."

"You bet." Because cars were examined under fluorescent lighting so often.

When Payton was inside, Jace turned to Harvey. "Sorry about this."

To his surprise Harvey waved a dismissive hand. Then he pulled out a toothpick and stuck it between his teeth, rolling it around. "Girl wants to get it right, I say let her have her fun."

"Even if her fun lasts all day?" Jace joked.

"It's a sign of character, shows she was raised to go after what she wants." Harvey slid the toothpick to the back of his mouth to chew in it. "Son, part of being a man is waiting on a woman. I've spent the last forty years waiting on my woman, and I wouldn't change a thing, because a woman who won't settle is the one worth waiting for."

Jace looked inside the far bay at Payton, holding up one sample and taking a selfie with her cell, and something inside Jace softened. So what if she was taking a year to make a decision, if she posted it on Instagram to see what Tiffany thought, he was spending time with his niece, passing on the love of cars that his dad instilled in him.

Sure, her first visit to the garage had been to impress her boyfriend. Scratch that: her friend who was a boy but not a boyfriend. But she'd come every day after practice and put in the sweat and hours. Helped him finish up the engine, flush out the radiator, even change the oil, never once complaining about her dirty fingers or chipped nails.

And she talked. The entire time. About school, cheerleading, colleges, boys, if she should cut her hair or leave it long, if her lipstick matched her complexion. She even talked about how much fun she had when he took her camping a few summers back, and how she wanted to go again. He'd learned more about Payton and, as sad as it was, his family, in the few hours they'd shared under the hood than he had in the past fifteen years. So, yeah, he'd wait. Just like he'd happily wait on that front porch swing forever if it meant spending even a second with Charlotte.

"You got another one of those?" Jace asked, pointing to Harvey's mouth. Harvey pulled out a plastic container filed with toothpicks. "Thanks. And thanks for coming out. I know it's a bit of a drive for you."

"Well, I was hoping to bend your ear about a 426 Hemi."

"Yours?" Jace picked one and stuck it in his mouth, then leaned back and let himself enjoy the moment with Payton. He had nowhere he needed to go, nothing he needed to do, except sit back and do some good old-fashioned small talk with an old-timer about the king of engines.

"Belongs to a friend of mine. He wants to get it rebuilt. It's been sitting in his garage for fifty years. Stock condition, can you imagine?" Yes, Jace could. His fingers tingled at the thought. "He finally has the time now that he's retired, but his hands don't work the way they used to. Told him I'd see if you were interested."

The chance to work on a factory 426 Hemi was every gearhead's dream. Plus, Harvey had done him a huge favor coming out today and promising to get a week's paint job done in three days. The least he could do was take a look at the guy's engine. Only...

"I'm leaving after Founder's Day to open a garage in Atlanta."

"Heard about that. Hattie's right proud, telling everyone how her boy's made it big, handling Ferraris and whatnot."

Jace wanted to say that he was a damn good engine specialist and that to most people "making it big" meant owning
a Ferrari. Only people in Sugar were different, and when one
of theirs made something of themselves, whether they were
under the hood or holding the trophy, people took pride in
that.

Jace had seen it in the way people looked at his brothers,
but he'd never stopped to think that people would be proud
of him. And now that he was on the receiving end of that
kind of praise, here in his hometown, he wasn't sure how to
respond. "I like what I do."

"Are you only interested in fancy engine work?" Harvey
asked. "Or are you open to classic restorations?"

"Both."

"I bet he'd ship it to you." Harvey rolled the toothpick
back and forth. "Also, I belong to the Dixie Rumblers."

The Dixie Rumblers was a classic muscle car collectors
club that had members all over the South. Mostly old-timers,
but Jace's dad had been a member, even taken him to a few
meetings and shows as a kid.

"Some of the members are getting up there in age,"
Harvey said disgustedly, as though *he,* who looked as
though he'd walked the earth with Jesus, wasn't one of
those men. "They want to enjoy the ride but don't have the
patience to put in the work. But with Alan Parson moving
to Palm Beach, we're short an engine guy. I brought your
name up at the last meeting as a potential replacement."

Blown away by Harvey's support, it took Jace a minute
to respond. "An endorsement from you means a lot, but do
they know which McGraw you were talking about?"

Jace hadn't seen any of those guys since he was a teen
and got busted taking a little joyride around Sugar Lake in
a sweet '69 Camaro SS—that belonged to the Ramblers'

president. Jace joined the army, the old-timer dropped the charges, but he wasn't so sure they'd want him tinkering with their collection. "Not sure my reputation with them is so solid."

"Your reputation under the hood is widely known and all that matters, son," Harvey said, and Jace let that sink in. "Hell, when I brought up your name as a replacement, they all started clucking like a bunch of churchwomen."

As humbling as it was startling, it got Jace thinking that maybe he had been away too long. Or maybe he'd been away just long enough to finally miss home.

It also got him thinking about how many Ramblers hired outside help when rebuilding and maintaining their cars. And how many of them had stock Hemis just sitting in the barn, waiting to be worked on, because turning wrenches with these old-timers to restore forgotten history would be amazing. Then he wondered if working on classic engines would give him the same thrill and satisfaction as high-performance engines.

It was a toss-up.

Then again, isn't that what Charlotte had done? She'd walked away from a glamorous job in Atlanta, where she was at the forefront of medical advancement, and managed to come home and find her place. Sure, the place hadn't existed when she moved back. But instead of chasing a dream, she dug deep and built her own right here in her hometown, surrounded by her friends and family.

That took guts. And a lot of hard work. But Charlotte never shied away from a challenge, which was why there were a half-dozen pathetic-looking Jockey Janes sitting on the couch. The ability to do the undoable time and again was an admirable trait.

"Do you think you could corral a few of the Ramblers

into driving some debutantes in the Founder's Day Parade next Sunday?" Jace asked. "There's also going to be small car show at the fair where they can display their cars. So far there is a '64 Bellaire, a '59 Caddie, and two concept cars."

Harvey nodded. "The single fellas will hear debutantes and sign up, the others will sign up because McGraw's son is asking."

"That's it?" Jaced asked. "Just like that?"

Harvey clapped Jace on the shoulder. "Son, debutantes aside, those fellas would wet themselves if they knew you'd be there to talk shop. Share a few of your stories. It doesn't get any bigger around these parts than you."

Jace was going to have to ask Harvey to repeat that last statement next time Brett was around, but for now he said, "I'll give you the number of the woman running the parade before you leave."

Harvey let out a gravelly laugh. "It always comes down to a woman."

A fact Jace was starting to understand a little more every day. But instead of feeling suffocated by the implications, he actually took peace in it.

"The tallies are in," Payton said proudly, walking out of the garage waving her cell. "The final decision is sky blue. It is original to the car, which is important in restoration."

She hopped up on the tailgate and rested her head on Jace's shoulder, and he couldn't help but smile. Payton hadn't only been listening, she'd cared enough about their project to put her mark on it. They'd created some memories and, more importantly, a bond that went beyond him being that fly-by-night fun uncle. And every time Hattie took her car out for a spin, Payton was going to remember the time she helped her uncle restore it.

"And the cheer team agreed." She looked up at him—to

put the sample next to his face again. "It makes you look friendlier. More approachable."

"Friendlier? I'm a friendly guy," he said, a little hurt.

Payton made a sound that implied he was, in fact, not friendly or approachable and she was really banking on the sky blue. It was the tattoos, he decided, until she reached up and smoothed out the creases in his forehead and he realized he'd been scowling.

He flashed a grin. "Is that better?"

Payton put a finger to her lips, deep in thought. "Maybe shirts in a color other than black would help. And ones that don't show all your muscles."

He'd consider other colors, but he'd consult Charlotte on the whole muscle thing later, seeing as how he caught her staring at his arms all the time. Or maybe it was his ink?

A theory he was more than willing to test—while naked in her bed.

*　*　*

By early Thursday morning, Sugar Medical Center was a hospital in transition. What had been the back parking lot for the past ninety years was slowly taking shape to become the new and improved Founder's Day fairgrounds. The empty field beyond had become the new sheep scurry track and course. Which explained the half-dozen tractors, the piles of boards, and the army of excited Sugar residents already hard at work assembling the fences for the holding pens, even though the sun was barely cresting.

It also explained the warm lump of wool nestled at her feet. Mrs. Ferguson, excited that Woolamena had moved into the fifth stage of loss, the Upward Turn, thought it best if she could watch the new tract being erected. Hoping a change of location would give Woolamena the push she needed to work through the loss, she'd loaded up her motor home and set up camp right outside the track's starting line.

When Charlotte told her this wasn't a campground but a hospital, the older woman agreed and asked if she could park her motor home outside Charlotte's house, then went on and on about the serene lake view being therapeutic. So Charlotte had agreed to let Mrs. Ferguson park on the field, with the understanding that she couldn't let the sheep wander around the facility or eat the vegetation. Which was how Charlotte ended up on girlfriend duty when Mrs. Ferguson went into town to stock up on ice cream.

Just in case.

To make sure that the sheep didn't get into trouble, Charlotte tied the pathetic scarf she'd used as a practice run yesterday to leash the animal to her hip. On the up side, Woolamena seemed to like the new pink yarn, nuzzling it and coating it with her scent.

"Think of this new track as a fresh start," Charlotte said.

Woolamena peeked out from beneath the sign-up table to watch the first wall of the pens go up and let go an agreeable *baa-ah.*

"Hey, ladies," Glory said, slipping through the back flap of the pop-up tent Cal lent them, otherwise known as Command Central. She gave the sheep a pet to the ears and then looked at Charlotte. "I managed to push your first three appointments forward and your last three back an hour."

Charlotte looked at the schedule Glory had created and exhaled. "This will be tight."

"It's going to suck, but it gives you from seven until nine to organize the volunteers, then Joie can take over. And it frees up an hour before lunch, giving you two hours to oversee the installation of the sheep scurry track." Which was exactly what she'd asked Glory to accomplish. But nine patients in two hours?

As though sensing the growing panic in Charlotte, Glory added, "I can always call the on-call doctor and see if—"

"Nope, Ben's on call today." And was going hiking with the twenty-something pretzel from HR. Not that Charlotte would choose the coed for Ben, but he seemed happy, and who was she to judge? She'd done the skinny-dipping free-for-all under a dock, with a potential witness. A memory that still made her good parts tingle.

She had managed to balance medical school, working full-time, and interning at a local hospital. She could handle her job and a silly fair.

Besides, she owed Ben. He'd been covering for her for the past two weeks, the man deserved to spend his free day being free. Not picking up the Holden slack. "This is really great. And I'll be fine."

Glory looked over Charlotte's shoulder and gave a worried expression. "You sure?"

"Positive." Charlotte even gave her most assertive nod to prove it. Woolamena stirred at her feet.

"Okay," Glory dragged out, still not meeting Charlotte's eyes. "But call me if you change your mind."

Still so positive that she had this, Charlotte stacked the parade route and lineup order she'd compiled and printed out last night in case people had questions, and, after making sure her booth was ready to go, she turned around and let out a "Lord have mercy" when she saw a swarm of women headed toward the booth.

Not just women. Miss Peaches. It was as though every Miss Peach from the dawn of time until the present had amassed in pearls and purpose. Charlotte felt a genuine smile take over.

Baa-ah.

"Thank you all for coming," she said, blown away at the sign of support. Many of the Peaches in the crowd had been disappointed that they weren't jumping into renovating Bluebell Hall, so the fact that they had shown up this early, braving the cold, the mud, and broken fingernails, touched her. "We can use all the help we can get. If you all just make a line, I can get you signed up for the team you are interested in."

"Perfect," an older woman with meaty hands and meatier hips said, stepping out from the front of the pack. It was Etta Jayne, owner of the local bar, The Saddle Rack, and Miss Peach 1954. "I would like to sign up to ride in one of those fancy cars."

Charlotte paused, trying to make sense of what the older woman was asking. "I can give you a list of what cars and floats go where for the parade, if that's what you mean." Charlotte held up her color-coordinated sheet.

Etta Jayne pointed toward the first of the classic cars on the list. "I want to be in that one. Riding shotgun."

"Shotgun don't mean you get to carry your shotgun, Etta Jayne," MeMaw Wilkes snapped, elbowing her way to the front.

"The hell it doesn't."

"It's just a saying," MeMaw argued, and, ignoring Etta Jayne's mumbling about checking the history books, turned to Charlotte. "I want to sign up, too, only I want to ride in whatever car that good-looking McGraw boy is driving. The single one."

"You mean, Jace?"

"Yup, the muscly one with the big arms and tight buns."

"I think he's driving his grandma," she said, guessing that after all the time he spent on the car he'd want to be the one to parade Hattie around. Then again, driving in the parade was as close to an "I'm moving back" sign as one could get in Sugar. So maybe not.

"Well, then put me in that car," MeMaw said. "I can still hang on to his arm from the backseat."

Charlotte didn't get to explain that the car didn't have a backseat, nor was it one of the show cars, because someone hollered out, "Me too."

"There are a few extra seats in the classic cars," Charlotte explained. "As for who is riding in them, that hasn't been decided yet."

"Well, decision made," Etta Jayne said, as though there would be no further argument. "First come, first served. And since I'm here first, sign me up."

A wave of frenzy took over the crowd as women started pushing forward to be next in line. Woolamena, smart girl, smashed her entire body under the table and started nibbling on the yarn leash.

"Hang on!" Charlotte held up a silencing hand, wishing she'd made time to grab a cup of coffee before leaving the house. But it had still been dark and the tight-bunned McGraw with the big arms was sleeping peacefully in her bed—naked and sated after a long night of considering each and every one of his partner's needs—so Charlotte had been as quiet as possible when leaving. "This booth is for volunteers. How many of you are here to help build the sheep track?" Nothing. "How many of you are here to ride in one of the classic cars?"

Every single hand went up.

"Well, as you all know, due to the limited number of cars there is only enough room for the board members and the current Miss Peach," Charlotte told the group, and was met with hostile glares.

"We were told that there were extra seats," Jelly Lou said

rolling forward in her wheelchair. "So we gave up our seats on the tractors to the Sons of the Confederation."

Charlotte stopped breathing. She told her lungs to take in oxygen, but they weren't listening. "You gave up your seats?"

"Sure," MeMaw said. "When we heard you had extra room, we thought we'd let those men suffer sore bottoms and hives while we ride in style."

This couldn't be happening. Sure, there were a *few* extra seats. Two to be exact, and of course Charlotte would gladly give up her seat, but that left a few dozen former Miss Peaches without seats in the parade. And the Miss Peaches always, *always* opened the parade. It was tradition. There was the current Miss Peach Court on their beautiful float, followed by two tractors pulling a living legacy of women who paved the road for each generation, riding on horse-drawn trailers.

"There aren't enough seats for everyone," Charlotte admitted, and an explosion of disgruntled and panicked questions filled the air.

"Then how are we going to be in the parade?"

"What about my walker? I can't walk down Maple with my walker!"

"Sorry for the misunderstanding," Darleen said, coming forward with a big grin. "When I never heard back about the number of cars, I just assumed that all of the cars you had on that fancy presentation were coming."

"Those were just examples." Which Darleen knew. "And I texted you yesterday. Told you that there were three cars. *Three*, Darleen!"

"Unfortunately you texted me *after* I ran into Mable. She was so excited about riding in one of the cars because of her hip, I said in passing it would be nice if the former

Miss Peaches could ride in style, too." Darleen looked at the crowd and gave an innocent shrug. "You know how news travels in Sugar."

She also knew how Darleen worked, and if Charlotte didn't fix this mess, all of those women standing in line would vote to have Charlotte *im*-peached. That hot wave of panic was back, so intense Charlotte thought she was going to be sick.

Adopting a calm and competent *if I can save a life I can save this parade* composure, she addressed the crowd. "This is not a big deal. If you could all hang tight for just one minute, I'll take care of this." And with a confident smile, she boldly strutted out through the back flap of the tent, across the lawn, and around the corner of the building—with Woolamena trailing behind her with a long pink scarf.

Hidden from prying eyes, Charlotte collapsed against the wall. The cold morning dew on the exterior wall seeped through her clothes, and the rough edges of the bricks pressed into her bare legs. Resting her palms on her thighs, she dropped her head between her knees.

Woolamena sat on her feet and went back to nibbling the leash.

"Oh God," she breathed in. Then out. Then back in.

Watching her breath crystalize didn't help. Nothing could help because this situation was so beyond fixing. Short of finding two new tractors and trailers, which none of the ladies would want to ride on now that they'd been offered shiny chrome carriages with sexy drivers, she was screwed.

So. Incredibly. Screwed.

"Oh God," she breathed again.

"Is that your way of telling me you want another religious experience?"

Charlotte opened her eyes right as a pair of worn work

boots came into view. Her gaze followed the boots to a pair of jeans, button fly to be exact, finally higher to the most magnificent biceps in the county, and her belly gave a little flip. Because Jace was standing there, looking like a warm blanket on a cold autumn morning.

Baa-ah.

"Morning to you, too," Jace said, bending down to pet the sheep.

"Oh, she's kind of shy around men."

Woolamena flopped to her side, her little legs sticking up like roadkill, so Jace could access her belly. Traitor.

"She likes me fine," Jace countered, giving the sheep a rubdown so thorough even Charlotte felt her soft underside showing.

"Bad boys with lethal smiles are her weakness," Charlotte sighed, glaring at Woolamena who was too busy sucking up Jace's affections and sighing in ecstasy to be offended.

"Lethal, huh?" Jace stood, and flashed her a grin so lethal it should be registered. "Sounds like someone else I know."

She smiled back, she couldn't help it. Jace had walked into what she'd believed to be a battleground, yet with a single smile he brought everything into perspective. "I thought you were getting Hattie's car ready to paint today."

"I am," he said, extending a steaming cup of coffee. "But you left before we could do our morning ritual."

She took a sip and nearly wept. "I so needed this." Remembering her promise to not hold back, she stepped over Woolamena and into Jace, sliding her arms around his middle. "I need this more, though."

"Mmmmm," he said, pulling her into him and resting his cheek on her head. "Me too."

She listened to the steady beat of his heart, felt the panic ease out of her body, and enjoyed the feeling of being held.

Having support. To her surprise, Jace's hugs were more intimate than anything she'd ever felt with another man.

Minutes passed, and admitting that she could stand there for a year and never get her fill she said, "I'm hiding." He chuckled, and she felt it vibrate through her entire body. "There is a line of bitter Peaches around that corner."

"I saw. They seem pretty hostile."

"I know." Charlotte heard the grumblings all the way around the corner. She dropped her head to his chest. "I have an insane schedule, my dad isn't talking to me, Darleen is out to win, and if I don't come up with a better option than a tractor-drawn trailer they might lynch me." She snuggled deeper. "I should have stayed in bed."

"I agree." The husky tone in his voice told her exactly what they'd have spent their morning doing.

She looked up, and for just a second Charlotte considered, instead of facing the swarm, rising up on her toes and claiming her daily kiss. Of course, kissing would lead to touching, which would lead to shenanigans and eventually sexcapades. And a sexcapade sounded so much nicer than disappointing a bunch of women she admired.

"Later." He kissed her lightly, then released her. "Because although I am more than interested to find out what is making you nibble that lower lip, that mob isn't going away. So how can I help?"

His willingness to help was beyond sweet. Most men would rather get a limb severed than be willing walk into a den of disgruntled former pageant queens. Not Jace. He shoved up his sleeves and got to work, doing whatever was needed to make her day easier.

Charlotte explained the situation, leaving out the part where Darleen was torpedoing her. By the time she got to the angry swarm and how there was no way she could make this parade special for those women anymore, she became aware of the way Jace was watching her—the quiet understanding in his eyes, how his face softened with patience as though he didn't have a full day in the garage waiting for him.

Jace listened to each and every complaint she had. Never once judging or dismissing the importance the situation held for her, he just ran his hands up and down her spine in comforting passes while she unloaded. When she was done, he gave her another kiss, this one a little longer and with enough tongue to leave her nipples hard, and said, "How many cars do you need?"

Chapter 17

Saturday afternoon, Jace stood in front of the Car Maintenance 101 class. They'd burned through jump-starting a car, so he was eating up time with some fun backwoods diagnostics for common car problems. They'd covered how to check the tread on their tires using a penny, how to check the tire pressure without a gauge, and were in the final stages of how to fill your radiator if you're out of coolant. All tricks his dad had taught him early on.

"So if it gets too hot and I don't have even a drop of water on me I can use this?" Darleen asked, and somehow managed to make a benign question sound like a proposition.

"As long as it's cold and not sweetened, you should be good," Jace said, looking at the women gathered around three different cars, taking turns pouring iced tea into the radiator.

"Then this only works if I'm in Yankee country," Hattie said, peeking her head out from under the hood of the blue pickup. "Because no Southerner would make tea that wasn't sweet."

A few *Amens* and *God's truths* went up, and Darleen leaned in and whispered, "Mine is always sweet. Sweetest in three counties. In fact, I just made a batch if you wanted to come by tonight. Catch up."

"I thought Tribble had a game," he reminded her.

She shrugged. "Change of plans. So you free?"

"Thanks for the invite, but I've got plans."

"Tomorrow?" She put her hand to her chest. "That's right. Family dinner at the McGraws. How about after?"

"Actually I'm pretty booked." Until forever, he wanted to say, but knew better than to rile a territorial cougar. Darleen didn't take well to being told no.

"I'm sorry to hear that. I know you don't get home often." She gave him a look that was equal parts sweet and sting. "At least you got in some lake-time fun."

Jace went as still as a stone, trying to decipher exactly what she was saying. And what she wasn't saying. Only, unlike Charlotte, the woman had an impeccable poker face. And he didn't mean that as a compliment.

"I know how much you McGraw men like to fish," she finished, and before Jace could respond a hand went up in the far bay.

"We have a question," MeMaw said from beside a mid-nineties Chevy sedan.

"Perfect," Jace said, striding over to MeMaw Wilkes and Dottie Ryan, both longtime family friends and both smiling too widely for his liking. But he could handle whatever they threw at him, as long as it got him away from Darleen. "What can I help you with?"

"We were wondering if you could show us where the dipstick is," MeMaw asked, and her gaze dropped to his crotch. Dottie snickered with delight. "In case I need to check my oil."

Jace had no idea what they were up to—no good, knowing those two—but he wasn't about to accuse a couple of woman who had changed his diapers of asking him to drop trou. So he grabbed a rag off the bench and leaned under the hood. "If you want to keep your hands clean, use a rag to pull the dipstick out, which is located right—Ow!"

Jace looked over his shoulder. Someone pinched his butt. Actually, it was more of a pinch, pat, squeeze combo. But there was definite contact made. Not that the women were fessing up, since they were looking for all the world like they were innocent grandmas.

"Thank you," MeMaw said. "For being so gracious."

Not sure how to respond, he straightened and addressed the entire class. "All right, ladies. That ends our lesson today. Remember, next Saturday will be our last class," he said, and something about that didn't settle right.

"Are we going to go over techniques for proper lubrication?" MeMaw asked.

He shot her a stern look, not that it helped. Dottie was back to snickering. "We will be going over how to not get bamboozled by a mechanic. So bring a pen and pad to take notes."

Someone mentioned something about enough time to hit happy hour before coupon bingo started, and the room emptied pretty quickly. Darleen was straggling behind, finding every reason she could to be alone with him—something he did not want to happen.

So he caught up with Jelly Lou, who was trying to wheel herself out of the garage while clutching her electric lug-nut changer.

"Let me walk you out." He grabbed the Sunday school teacher's handles and wheeled her outside.

"Sure is pretty," Jelly Lou said, taking in downtown.

The sky was bright orange with inky swirls, painting the autumn leaves and extending well beyond town and into the wide-open countryside. Jace had seen sunsets from every side of the world, but nothing got to him like the sun setting over Sugar.

"Sure is."

He pushed her down the cobblestone sidewalk and to her car, giving Darleen a cordial nod as they exited. When they reached it, Jelly Lou looked up at him and smiled. "Thank you for helping me out."

"Let me get your door," he said, taking her keys and opening the driver's side.

"Always the gentleman," she said. "Even when you were little, you had this courteous way about you."

"My parents were strict when it came to manners," he said, helping her get in the car.

"That might be true, but your chivalry seemed to come from inside. Like you love to care for your loved ones." She reached out a bony hand and gave his cheek a pat. "You get that from your mama, you know?"

Jace knew his mother had the ability to love unlike anyone else he'd ever encountered. Her hugs, even the way she looked at a person, carried a power that was magical. Around her, Jace felt as though nothing bad could happen.

"She had the gift of caring and passed it along to you," she said, but something about how she was looking at him told him her statement wasn't out of obligation, the way most people say sweet things. Jelly Lou said it as though she was just stating a fact and Jace happened to be there to hear it.

"Now don't go getting shy on me," she laughed, giving his cheek a little pat. "I didn't mean to embarrass you. It

was just my way of saying I miss your mama and I'm happy
you're home. We need more people like you around, is all."
And before he could say a word to the contrary, she added,
"I think that Darleen has left, so it's safe to go back inside
now."

Jace laughed. "Was I that obvious?"

"No, but Darleen was never good at hiding when she was
on the hunt for a new husband. And I don't think Hattie
would be too happy about her landing you as husband number four."

"There is no chance of that."

"I didn't imagine there would be," Jelly Lou said. "Now,
you have a good night."

"You too, Ms. Mann." He closed her door and strapped
her chair to the rack affixed to the back of her car. He
smacked the truck twice and raised a hand as Jelly Lou
pulled onto Maple Street. He watched her brake lights turn
after town hall and tried to remember when he'd last passed
time gabbing with people who knew his entire family history. Before coming back to Sugar, he couldn't remember a
single one.

Jace hadn't expected to be chased out of town, but he
sure hadn't expected the warm welcome he'd received.
Maybe the only one harboring issues about the past was
him. Because as far as he could tell, his return brought up
happy memories for people.

Not the devastating ones he'd clung to for so long.

* * *

By the end of the weekend, Charlotte found that balancing
her patient load while planning a parade was harder than
it sounded. After word spread that Woolamena was living

onsite, all of the other entrants, afraid that the champion was gaining an unfair advantage by memorizing the new track, decided to board their sheep as close to the start line as possible—turning the back field into a zoo of sorts. Her younger patients, catching wind of the pop-up petting zoo, came down with various symptoms that miraculously disappeared as soon as they saw the sheep. And since Charlotte was no closer to getting Jockey Jane to hold her stuffing, the lunchroom at the hospital had turned into an impromptu knitting club meeting ground.

"Loosen up on your yarn," Hattie said, holding up what looked like a pair of baby booties and showing off her perfect stitches. She was plump and squat, and in electric green tennis shoes and a yellow tracksuit and with her white bristle hair she resembled a pineapple. "You look as if you're about to strangle the needles."

"That's nothing," Ms. Pearl said, her fingers moving with speed and accuracy. The woman wasn't even looking at her hands and she was making more progress than Charlotte. "Yesterday, the girl yanked her stitches so tight, Jockey Jane's face fell in on itself. Looked like one of those dried apple–face dolls."

"This isn't how I wanted to spend my lunch break, either." Charlotte looked at her progress and set Jane in her lap. She could feel the panic set in, gaining ground with every day that passed, taking her closer to Founder's Day. Closer to Jace's departure date. "How could I make it through four years of medical school, top of my class, yet I can't knit a silly doll?"

"I don't know, dear," Ms. Pearl said. "But I've knitted me an entire tanning top in the time it's taken you to knit one row." Charlotte had no idea what a tanning top was, even when Mrs. Pearl held up what appeared to be two triangles attached by a braided rope. Then she molded it to her saggy cleavage and Charlotte got the picture. "No tan lines."

"Why don't you all clear out and let me help the girl," Hattie said, making shooing gestures with her hand. "The way you're watching over her shoulder, it's no wonder she can't figure out a head from a backside."

Charlotte watched in horror as the other women packed up their canvas bags and waddled out. She hadn't been alone with Hattie since she'd discovered that her grandmother-in-law was privy to being her grandmother-in-law. Survival by avoidance, Charlotte liked to think of it. A difficult task since the entire downtown area was roughly the size of two football fields.

"Actually, I have to get back to work," Charlotte said, standing. "Crazy workload today."

"Sit your tush down," Hattie said knowingly, her fingers still working magic with the yarn. "You don't have a patient for another ten minutes. I checked with Glory before coming in."

Charlotte would have to remind Glory that her schedule wasn't for public consumption. *Not that it would do her any good now*, she thought, taking a seat and picking up her needles.

"Good, now close your eyes and try it again."

Charlotte looked at her raw fingers and chipped nails and wondered how she was supposed to knit a straight line with her eyes closed when she couldn't manage to do it with them open, but she did as she was told. Because she had to get this right.

Had to.

"There you go," Hattie said, with gentle encouragement. "Now don't think about it, just picture what you want it to look like all done and let your fingers go to work."

Her fingers ached, and the yarn burned as it slid back and forth over the angry skin, but a few minutes later she opened her eyes, and, "Oh my word!"

The first thing she noticed was that she was calm, her heart wasn't racing, and her palms weren't sweating. The second thing she noticed was that she'd knitted two lines. Two straight pink lines with even tension.

"I did it! Look at them." She held up the yarn. "They're beautiful!"

"Now don't go calling the President, you did two rows," Hattie said.

"But they are perfect rows." The second the statement left her lips, Charlotte wanted to take it back. She had unintentionally "perfected" herself into a corner. Expectations were set, the pressure was on, and she was going to be sick. "I don't know how I did that. Or if I can do it again."

"Sure you can," Hattie said, taking the yarn from her and doing the next row. "You've been knitting so much your hands know exactly what they're supposed to do."

"They didn't earlier." Earlier they hadn't even known they were crushing poor Jane's face.

"You were too busy staring at each stitch to see the whole piece. With your eyes closed you weren't thinking about what was on the needle, what came next, you were thinking about what it would look like on Woolamena's back. Do that for a day or two, then call me and we'll get busy on the doll."

And with that Hattie put her needles and yarn in her quilted bag and stood. As if she were going to leave. Without interrogating Charlotte about the annulment. Which was so unlike Hattie it made sweat bead on Charlotte's forehead.

And when the older woman made it to the exit, Charlotte jerked to her feet. "Don't you want an explanation of what happened between me and Jace?"

"Nope," Hattie said, popping that *P* hard, which made Charlotte's right eye twitch.

"Are you sure? Because if I were in your situation I think I'd want an explanation."

Hattie turned around and set her bag on the counter. "Child, I imagine you have enough people weighing in on you two without adding my opinion to the mix."

Charlotte felt a mix of guilt and regret flood her face. "Actually, outside of you, I don't think anyone else knows. At least the marriage part." She let out a deep sigh. It felt good to talk to someone about this mess. To open up. "And I'm sorry I asked Jace to keep it from his family."

"If he wanted us to know, he would have told us. Plus, with a mother like yours, I wouldn't expect you to be able to make a decision without her trying to give her stamp, even if she doesn't know the facts." Hattie laid a soft hand on Charlotte's arm. "Jace is a good boy, with a big heart. Bigger than most, so it makes him moody. Been running for so long I don't think he knows what it feels like to stand still."

That was Charlotte's biggest fear.

"Do you think he'll be happy in Atlanta? Happy enough to stay?"

Hattie shrugged a very old, very tired shoulder. "Don' know, but it shouldn't matter."

"What do you mean?" As far as Charlotte was concerned, that was all that mattered. What if they could make it work with him in Atlanta and her in Sugar, or if she followed him there, then what? In a few months, few years, would he pack up and move again? Expect her to pick u the pieces again? "Did you come here to tell me I should follow him?"

"I came here to teach you how to knit, dear." Hattie stepped closer, and Charlotte could smell the polyester fibers of Hattie's jogging suit. "You were the one who wanted to have a come-to-Jesus moment in the lunchroom."

Charlotte choked out a laugh. "I know. I just wonder sometimes if I gave up too easily. Had too many rules and expectations for it to work."

"First off, you've worked hard to build yourself a home here. Don't throw that away. Second, any man who would let you is not a man at all, even if I did raise him." Hattie took both of Charlotte's hands in her own, holding on in that soft steel way that grandmothers did. And suddenly, Charlotte didn't feel as though she was talking to a neighbor, she felt as if she was talking to family. "And here's the most important part, so listen up. If Jace is gonna run, that's on him. Not you. But how I see it, he done tuckered himself out a few years back."

Charlotte felt her throat tighten. "Then why hasn't he come home? Why did he wait until there was a problem to show up? And why now, after all these years, did he decide to finally come back only to start a new life in Atlanta?"

"He's waiting for somebody to tell him it's okay," Hattie said gently. "That after everything that's happened, he's welcome home."

"Then tell him that," Charlotte said, wondering if it was that easy why they'd waited so long. "Tell him you want him to come home."

Because she did. More than anything. She wasn't sure how they'd make it work, but she knew with a certainty that if Jace went to Atlanta he'd never find his way back to Sugar. He was so used to running, if he didn't find a reason to stay now, then she didn't think he'd ever find one.

Hattie's eyes went shiny with emotion, and when she gave a small smile, Charlotte felt every ounce of love the older woman had for her youngest grandson. "I'm not his home anymore, child. You are."

Chapter 18

Charlotte pushed open her bedroom door and, giving herself three minutes of peace, collapsed on the bed. She had seen a steady stream of patients until she clocked out at five fifteen. Except for the knitting break, she had been on her feet since six that morning. And was expected at her mother's in just under an hour for Sunday dinner.

She had enough time to change and pick up a bottle of wine. According to her mother, Charlotte's date for the evening preferred a good French Bordeaux. Except a quick glance in her closet, which consisted of picking her head three inches off the mattress, reminded her that every suitable outfit she owned was in the hamper. She dropped her head back with an exasperated sigh. The fair was exactly one week away, and at the pace she was keeping she wasn't sure she'd make it.

Something had to give. She was afraid it would be her mornings with Jace—which had come to be the second-best part of her day. The best part being number ten on the "Keeping It Sizzling after Singlehood" list:

ALWAYS GO TO BED TOGETHER

But thinking about bedtime got her thinking about how much time they had left together. One week. Seven short days and their time would be up, the annulment would be complete, and if Jace lived up to his promise, he would leave.

Unless she asked him to stay.

Hattie's words had weighed heavily on Charlotte all afternoon, making her question if that was really all it would take. Her asking. It also gave her pause, because if a real man wouldn't ask her to sacrifice her career, then how could she ask him to sacrifice his?

Knowing there was no easy answer and that she'd exceeded her three minutes, she slipped off a heel and flung it across the room. It landed in the hamper and then she saw the steam coming out from beneath the bathroom door.

Someone was in her shower.

Sitting up, she glanced around, going still when she noticed a pair of worn work boots peeking out from beneath the bed, and suddenly she wasn't tired. In fact, the sound of water spraying her porcelain tub had every cell of Charlotte humming with electricity.

The smart decision, her brain said, would be to put her shoe back on and go to her mother's for dinner—like she did every Sunday night. And endure yet another blind date, as she'd also done every Sunday since her return from Atlanta. One would think her mother would have exhausted her network of suitable bachelors in the county by now, but Babette was very resourceful when it came to marrying off her only daughter.

Then the shower turned off and her nipples registered

that, on the other side of that door, Jace was hot and slick with water. Apparently her nipples were in charge, because instead of looking for a dinner dress, she slipped off her current dress, then her bra and panties, and lay back on the bed.

The only thing waiting for her at dinner was the county coroner and a night filled with suffocating expectations.

"I'll take what's behind door number two," she said to herself, feeling bold. And extremely naughty. A heady combination.

It was as exciting as cutting fifth period to go make out with your superhot boyfriend on his motorcycle. Not that Charlotte had ever cut a class in her life, or that Jace owned a motorcycle, but if she had and he did, she was positive that this was what it would feel like.

Daring. Erotic. A real time-of-your-life adventure.

Every second that passed her body coiled tighter with anticipation, her breasts got heavier, until the sheets felt so good against her sensitive skin she thought she'd go up in flames. She turned on her side, then realized her boobs looked perkier when she was propped up against the headboard. Only resting against her updo made her neck kink.

Charlotte sat up, uncoiled her hair, pins flying everywhere, and, remembering Jace's bed-rumpled request, gave t a few tosses and then lay back, feeling a bit nervous now. But just when she started to feel the hesitation build the bathroom door opened.

A wall of fog rolled out—not that it hampered her view. And what a view it was. Jace came out in nothing but a owel, which was conveniently tossed over his shoulder, and vent to the closet, giving her an unobstructed view of his ackside, which was so firm she was convinced it could detect a speeding bullet. One hand rested flat against the closet frame and he shook his head, sending droplets of water scattering to the floor in a move that was all male.

As if sensing a shift in the force, he looked over his broad shoulder, the one that had a tribal tattoo that started at his pec and wrapped over and down to his shoulder blade, and his eyes immediately locked on hers, a mix of wry amusement and raw hunger so intense her mouth went dry. Which was the exact opposite of what was happening down below.

"You're home," she said, trying desperately to sound casual, as though she hadn't just implied that this was his home. Even though there was nothing she wanted more.

"You're naked."

"Except for the pearls." Charlotte slipped a finger under the strand and ran it back and forth. Jace's eyes zeroed in with laser precision and followed her every move. So she trailed a little lower, letting her pinky graze over the top of her cleavage, dipping ever so briefly into the valley.

"Is that what you're wearing to dinner?" he asked. "Your date might feel overdressed."

"My date is Andy Mosby," she said. "I don't think he'll mind."

"Isn't he the guy who got busted hiding in the women's locker room with a video camera?"

"At the senior center," she clarified. "But his dad is a congressman now."

He grinned. "Well, there is that."

"How was your day?" she asked, light and breezy, doing a little visual assessment of her own. There wasn't a woman alive who could resist perusing merchandise as beautifully sculpted as his.

"Getting better by the second." And he was getting bigger by the second.

The towel hit the floor and she saw him coming, watched

as he stalked closer, his gaze dipping from her eyes to her breasts, to her thighs and back, but nothing prepared her for the jolt of awareness that shot through her when he took one of her feet in his hand and rested it on his rock-hard abs. Leaving her completely exposed, and him erotically rubbing her arch.

His thumb trailed up her instep and back to her heel, sending a zillion volts of high-powered hormones rushing though her body.

"What are you doing?" she whispered, getting lost in the sensation of his hands on her body, stoking a hunger so intense her eyes wanted to slide shut in ecstasy.

"I heard you had a long day." Bypassing her heels, he trailed a single finger up her calf to her knee, then dug deep on the return. Her body tingled everywhere he touched.

"Who did you hear that from? Hattie?" Jace raised a single brow. "We had a talk. I told her about how sorry I was for asking you to keep everything a secret and that if you wanted to tell your family I think you should."

"I don't want to talk about my family right now," he said, his voice rough.

"What do you want to do?" Charlotte asked, surprised at how her body responded. She never considered herself a dirty talker, in fact, she rarely talked during sex. But right then, with this man, she wanted nothing more than for him to tell her in exquisite, minute detail exactly what he wanted to do.

"Too many things to list."

"Give me the highlights." *Preferably the dirty ones.*

His expression was one of welcome surprise, then it turned to molten lava. "I've had a list in my head that's been building for the past four years. At the top of my list is you in my car, but you already knew that."

"With pearls." She slid her fingers down the strand.

He groaned, but his hands never stopped moving, down and back up, roaming over every inch and molding his hands to her curves. Soft at first, then deepening the pressure as he moved higher, teasing closer and closer to command central with each stroke. "Then there's the one with you straddling me in that denim skirt you had on the night at the bar, while I'm driving my Chevelle."

"We already did that one."

He flashed her a heart-melting smile. "I know, but I'd like a replay."

"Me too." She picked up her left foot, the one that was still on the bed, and ran her big toe up his concrete stomach, to his chest. Then ever so slowly back down his smooth, wet skin and rippling muscles. "Do all of them involve cars?"

Trapping her foot an inch before things got interesting, he thought about that for a moment. "I'll skip to some of the pages without cars. Like you in your lab coat looking all doctorly, with red fuck-me pumps, and me on the exam table."

"I don't own those kind of shoes," she said, her breath catching when he brought her foot to his mouth and nipped her toe.

"I'll buy you some for my birthday," he said, and a warm thrill settled in her heart that he was making plans, which included more of this, seven months out.

"Oh, my latest one," he said, placing a hot, openmouth kiss on the inside of her ankle. "It comes in at number two. It's a good one." Another kiss, this one lower. "I get home from work to find you. Naked. On the front porch swing. Knitting needles in hand."

Charlotte laughed when she realized he was dead serious. "Knitting needles comes in at number two?"

"Fuck, yeah," he said earnestly. "There is something about you looking all domestic that gets me going." Another kiss, this one with teeth. "But tonight, I'm going with number three. The She Works Hard for Her Money move." He stopped rubbing her feet. "Don't laugh, hear me out."

Charlotte smothered her giggle with a cough. "Completely open mind."

His talented fingers rubbed and stroked until she was nearly sobbing with pleasure. "You come home from a long day at work to find me, your dashing husband."

"Dashing?" She shook her head. "*Dashing* sounds like Matthew Crawley from *Downton Abbey*. You're more lethally sexy, like a big, sexy beefcake." He frowned. "Or a sex pistol," she offered.

"Sex pistol." He tried out the title and then gave a satisfied shrug. "All right, your sex pistol of a husband gently takes off one heel, then the next, then lifts you onto the island."

"What am I wearing?" she wanted to know, because even though this was his fantasy, she needed to get the whole picture.

"That yellow dress you used to have. The one you wore to your interview at Atlanta Memorial."

Her eyes must have shown her surprise that he had remembered a dress she'd worn exactly once, because he said, "Yeah, that one. With the scalloped top that showed the right amount of cleavage, the tiny belt that could be used for more than cinching in the waist, and that skirt." He blew out a breath, which Charlotte felt slide all the way to her core. "That prim skirt that floated down to the knees. So proper, but when you walked it swayed, giving a flash of those legs of yours. Made you look like a naughty schoolteacher."

Charlotte found herself nodding, and breathing more heavily than usual. And he hadn't even gotten to the good part.

"You're wearing that while I rub your feet, hitting all the right spots, until you are so relaxed you're game for anything. Then I slowly work my way up your thighs." His hands drifted higher, deliberately past her ankles, her knees, the sensitive inside of her thighs quivering under his calloused touch, and higher still until she thought she'd combust from the building pressure. "First with my hands." The tips of his fingers grazed her with a featherlight touch, and she arched up, digging her feet into his stomach, trying to get closer to his touch. "Then my mouth." He trailed a single finger up the middle of her, sending her pulse racing to the moon and back. "Until you're screaming."

"A religious experience?" she asked on a ragged breath. Because she could almost see the promised land in the near distance, coming in to claim her.

"Oh no," he said, slipping his hands back down to her ankles. God, he felt good, but she wanted to tell him he was going the wrong way. "This time the only name you're going to be screaming is mine."

He tugged. One minute she was leaning against the headboard, her heart pounding from anticipation, the next she was flat on her back, her legs dangling off the end of the bed, and Jace was pinning her to the bed with his big body. His hands rested next to her head, his mouth was flush with her ear.

"And Charlie, I'm going to have you screaming my name over and over again, until you pass out from the pleasure," he said, with so much alpha-male confidence she believed him. "And then I'm going to coax you awake, slowly and gently, only to start back at the beginning until you're screaming again. And come morning you're going to be so sated that getting out of bed will be hard work."

And before Charlotte could say that yes, she liked that idea very much, he was on the move, kissing and biting, his magical mouth working its way down her body. All the way down, taking his time about it, too, making sure to hit every trigger and lick every button until—

"Jace!" she cried as his warm tongue passed through the promised land with a one-way ticket to heaven when his fingers got involved, deliberate and talented, taking her higher and higher and so unbearably high that she was quivering from head to toe.

He sank his finger in even deeper, a soft, long stroke, followed by a not so soft one, going so exquisitely deep it was as if her entire body held its breath. Waiting.

Anticipating.

And Jace delivered, the man always delivered, going for a full withdrawal before sinking back in as he licked and worshipped her so thoroughly she was gasping his name. More like chanting. It was embarrassing, really, in a matter of minutes he had her shaking so hard she was certain her body would come apart. Then gave one final lick and twisted his fingers just how he knew she liked it, and she came apart. Her vision narrowed, her breathing turned nonexistent, and a pleasure so intense rocked her until she exploded.

"Oh, Jace, yes," she heard herself cry out, then she was pretty sure she lost consciousness for a brief moment. And that at some point she'd gripped his head and held him there because when she finally came, too, Jace was standing at the foot of the bed, his hair on end from her fingers, her legs dangling lifelessly to the floor.

He gave her a slow, sexy-as-hell grin. "Not counting that rythmic chanting you were doing there at the end, I believe you screamed my name twice. And I haven't even kissed you yet." He pulled up one leg, then the other, locking them behind his back, positioning their bodies so that all their best parts were perfectly aligned. "At least not on the mouth."

The smug male look he was wearing had her preparing for him to enter her in one hard thrust. She was praying it would be one hard thrust. But instead he leaned over her and gently brushed her lips with his, in a kiss that was so breathtakingly tender she felt her throat tighten. Cupping her face, he kissed her eyelids, her cheek, the tip of her nose.

"Jace," she whispered, looking up into his eyes.

"I love it when you scream out my name," he said, giving her another kiss, this one just as tender, but it seemed to last forever. "But when you say it like that, it slays me. Completely and shamelessly slays me."

He kissed her again so she said it again, but what she really meant was *I love you.* Yet no matter how many times she tried to say it, all that came out was his name.

Too overcome by the way he was holding her, how reverently his hands, those deliciously rough and demanding hands, softened to form to her every curve, to realize that they were already moving together—making love.

Mouth on hers, Jace cradled her to him, one hand cupping her face, the other her bottom, pressing them so close that they were sharing the same space, the same breath as their bodies slid against each other, creating a beautiful friction and connection that she had never experienced before. Not even with Jace. He wasn't being delicate or giving her the debutante treatment, this was different. He was different. Raw and all-encompassing, as though he couldn't get close enough, deep enough.

As though he couldn't get enough.

He didn't withdraw or release his grip, just loved her over

and over with short, urgent thrusts, until she felt what she feared were tears—blurring the lines until there were none to be found. No rules or hesitation or fear. Just the two of them, open and vulnerable, unafraid of the possible fallout.

Because whatever the fallout was, it would be worth this moment. This time together.

The way he made her feel as he kissed her, cherished her with his hands. Down her neck to her breast, as though memorizing the shape of her waist and hips, then back up to her face.

"Jace," she said again, and when he pulled back enough to meet her gaze, their bodies so slick with heat they were moving in perfect synch, she went all in. Because it was exactly what he'd promised, a religious experience where she was too tired to fight anymore.

As she looked deep into his eyes, she could feel herself being pulled, while simultaneously being freed with every stroke. She gracefully gave in to the promise and adoration he showed in his gaze, when he brought her to the point of no return and her body tightened around his, then released.

Jace caught her gasp with his mouth as he came with her, and whatever little piece of Charlotte she'd been holding back she handed over. Freely.

A few minutes passed before Charlotte was confident that she could speak without embarrassing herself. She opened her eyes to find Jace propped up on one elbow, smiling down at her. "You're beautiful when you let go like that."

"I feel beautiful when I let go with you," she admitted, her heart beating so fast she could feel it reaching out for his.

He looked at her mouth and groaned. "Before you start waving that lower lip at me, I need to tell you that you are probably late to your parents'. I know I talked a big game, one I would love to finish, but I'm pretty sure they were expecting you right about now," he said, his fingers dancing across her stomach.

"Don't you have to go to Brett's?" He gave her a noncommittal shrug.

"Then I'm right where I want to be." And there was nothing noncommittal about the way she felt, or the way he was looking at her.

With unsure expectancy in his eyes, he asked, "Are you sure?"

She'd never been more sure of anything in her life. Because although she'd promised to go in headfirst, she was pretty sure that she had just jumped in heart first. And she could have sworn when Jace pulled her in close, cradling her against him as if he was finally home, that he had, too.

* * *

After a long day, Jace wanted nothing more than to go home and play another round of She Works Hard for Her Money. Charlotte had chosen the perfect dress, which Jace had been dreaming about all day—only she wasn't home. And Cal and Brett had each texted him nine thousand times, which was how he found himself at the local watering hole, crammed into a too small booth between his two older brothers.

"I'm already on my second glass," Cal said. "You'd better catch up."

Jace looked at Brett, who held up his soda. "I'm the designated driver."

The Saddle Rack, a leave-your-shitkickers at the door and your cash on the counter kind of place, was already packed. Classic country was playing on the jukebox, the Falcons were on the giant plasma screens, and the bar was shoulder-to-shoulder cashmere and pearls. It seemed that the Sugar Peaches had called an emergency meeting, which meant that the lovely Dr. Holden was holding court in a pretty cream dress that was fitted at the waist but flared out at the hem to flirt around her knees. It wasn't *the* dress, but close enough, and it was flirting with him all right, brushing sexily back and forth and calling out, teasing him until he was half hard.

Too bad its owner wasn't as breezy, he thought, taking a swig of beer, since she looked as if she was about ready to stab Darleen with her knitting needles.

"How's the car coming?" Brett asked.

Jace took one last look, then dragged his attention to his brother. "The paint's been ordered, Harvey loaded up the car on his truck about an hour ago, and if all goes well it should be delivered to the upholstery shop Thursday and back to us Saturday morning." Which gave Jace a few hours after his last class to give her one final inspection and make her parade-ready. A tough timeline, but if everyone did their job, not impossible, something to celebrate.

Or so he thought.

"But you didn't call me to talk about the car." Or grab a celebratory beer.

Jace had walked in to find a full pitcher and Cal's ugly mug, and he knew this wasn't a simple shoot-the-shit bro night. And by the storm brewing in Cal's eyes, it most likely had something to do with him skipping family night. "Is this about dinner last night? Because I called Joie, explained that I couldn't make it, but could do Wednesday."

He was even thinking of asking Charlotte if she wanted to go.

"I'm good, bro." Brett sat back and sipped his soda. "I'm just here to play referee." Brett looked at Cal. Cal said nothing. Brett sighed and said, "He heard you're helping Charlotte out with the Founder's Day parade."

"Is that a problem?" Jace asked, sensing that it was.

"Are you still set on leaving next week?" Cal asked.

"That's the plan."

Cal leaned forward. "Then yeah, it might be, since I also heard you're taking day trips and sharing bunks with her, too."

Jace's pulse idled. "Where did you hear that?"

He waited for Cal to answer, but the uncomfortable silence stretched on. *Not a surprise,* Jace thought, knowing he'd been lucky to keep his brothers in the dark this long. And if there was one thing Cal hated, it was being kept in the dark. A residual tick from having one's wife walk out on him for another man.

Which was why he'd planned on telling them later that week. Only someone had beat him to the punch.

"I can't believe I expected Hattie to keep it quiet." He should have known, in this town secrets were as precious as babies, whoever had bragging rights was bound to flap their lips. And if Hattie told Cal, and Cal told Brett, then that left the question, who the hell else knew?

"Hattie knows?" Cal asked in disgust, and Jace held in a groan.

"Yeah, you might have wanted to keep that to yourself," Brett whispered. "I had my suspicions when the dingy went MIA and Cal had channeled that big-brother oracle shit he does, but you just confirmed it."

"I was going to tell you," Jace said, then wondered if he was telling the truth. He'd never mentioned the marriage because Charlotte had her reasons, justified reasons, looking back, but when he'd come home or taken her to Atlanta what had stopped him then?

"Payton went to your room to talk about cars last night and found an empty bed. When you weren't back by breakfast she freaked," Cal said, running a hand down his face. "If you want to play sleepover with a lady, fine, just don't do it with Glory's boss and pretend you're sleeping at my house. Come on, bro, we're all too old to be sneaking out windows. And Payton is too smart not to figure out what you're doing, and maybe try it on her own someday."

Jace hadn't thought that far. Never for a second did he stop to consider how it would affect the rest of his family. "I should have been straight up with you."

"All right then, here's your chance." Cal pulled out a thick manila envelope and slid it across the table. Jace looked at the names typed across the front and everything suddenly became real.

Mr. and Mrs. Jace McGraw
18526 Sugar Lake Circle
Sugar, Georgia 30359

"Doesn't anyone in this family respect address labels?" He looked over to make sure Charlotte wasn't looking back, then palmed the package and tucked the envelope under the table. The second his hands made contact, though, his stomach turned. He'd known the annulment was coming, he just hadn't expected it until later in the week.

And after last night he was hoping it would never come.

Yet there it was, sitting in his lap, as concrete as the weight in his chest. Everything he'd wanted, had come to Sugar to achieve, was just a signature away.

"I didn't open it. I should have, but I didn't." Cal said. "Hattie kept asking if I checked the mail, which meant she was checking the mail, most likely for something that wasn't

addressed to her. So when I saw a contract-size envelope
from the county recorder's office in Atlanta made out to you
and the missus I decided to hand deliver it myself."

"Thanks," Jace said, wishing Hattie had found it and hid
it from him like she had the other one because then he
wouldn't have to tell Charlotte that the annulment was in.
And she could end their marriage a week early.

"Is that what you and Charlotte went to Atlanta for?"
Brett asked. "To get married?"

"No." Jace flipped his ball cap backward and ran a hand
down his face. "Not even close."

"Then why are you spending time at the pretty doctor's
house?" Brett wanted to know, and the disappointment in
his voice damn near took Jace under. Had him regretting not
telling them earlier, because they deserved to know. And he
needed advice, bad. Who better to give it than the two men
who had sworn off love, only to find it here in Sugar?

Jace looked over at Charlotte. She was pressed and
primped and holding court, and she was so damn perfect for
him his chest hurt. "Four years ago Charlotte and I filed for
an annulment."

"Rewind," Brett said. "Because when the hell did *you* get
married?"

"About three weeks before we filed to end it. Only there
was a mix-up with the paperwork, and, well," he gestured to
the contract in his lap, "we're still married. For another few
days anyway."

"I need a beer." Brett took Jace's mug and drained it in
one swallow.

"Better?" Jace asked.

"Hell no," Brett said, looking appalled. "You're married
man. To the hottest doctor in town. And you're moving to
Atlanta?"

Yeah, that pretty much summed it up.

"I need another beer." Brett reached for Cal's.

Cal smacked his hand away. "Back up and start at the beginning."

Jace did, not leaving anything out. And when he got to the part about Charlotte's job in Atlanta and the rumored lawsuit with Dylan McAdams, he felt like he was going through it all over again. After that story broke, Jace's arrest photos had been everywhere. It would have cost her that job, no question. But looking at how things turned out, he knew in his gut that it was a bad move. She'd left Atlanta anyway.

Only she'd left alone and heartbroken.

"So you need the annulment to get the loan?" Cal asked after Jace finished.

Jace nodded and Brett let out a low whistle. "Then it's either the garage or the girl?"

"It's more complicated than that," Jace felt the need to say, because when phrased that way it didn't even sound like there was a choice to be made.

"Then let me uncomplicate it," Cal said leaning in on his elbows. "Are you going to sign it?"

"I don't know." Charlotte had agreed to three weeks. At the end, if he couldn't convince her for more, then he wasn't sure what he'd do.

"Do you love her?" Brett asked, and Jace shot him a hard look. "Right, you married her."

"Charlotte's it," Jace admitted, finding himself watching her again. No matter how hard he tried, he was always drawn back in, like a moth to the flame. But this time she was watching back.

Oh, her eyes weren't on him just then, so to anyone else Dr. Charlotte Holden, current regent of the Sugar Peaches, appeared to be hard at work doing Peachy things. But to someone who knew her, someone like, say, Jace, who knew that every time she ran her finger over her pearls, or nibbled that lower lip, she was flirting. But that flirting quickly became foreplay when she scooted her sweet ass around the table so she had to bend way over to point to something on the other side, causing her prim and proper skirt to ride up the back of her thighs.

It didn't reveal much, but just enough to remind Jace that hidden under that Sunday dress was one hell of a sexy woman who had a penchant for trouble. "For me, she's it. Always has been."

Always would be.

"Does she know that?" Cal asked.

"Still working on that part." Which was why he needed every day he'd been promised.

Brett laughed. "Right, because nothing says I love you like moving two hundred miles away." Jace opened his mouth to explain that he was figuring that part out, had a few ideas spinning in his head, only Brett, being the girl he was, wasn't done bitching. "And before you go saying that Atlanta Motorsports is your dream, acknowledge that you came up with that dream when we were kids. Sitting on mom's shag rug, eating Popsicles while playing with your Hot Wheels in our tighty-whities."

"Sure, but that doesn't invalidate it."

"You were seven." He grabbed a cocktail napkin and scribbled a rudimentary car on it and held it up. "Boy's dream." Then pointed to Charlotte. "Man's dream."

"Who the hell are you to talk? You call your loafers cleat and hit little balls with a stick. How manly is that?" he pointed out. But Brett had a point, working on exotic cars had been a kid's dream, and he'd lived out most of it. Buying Atlanta Motorsports seemed like the next logical step. The again, thinking logically never seemed to work that well for him.

Brett shrugged. "Joie thinks golf is sexy."

And Charlotte thought Jace with his unfriendly tattoos and unapproachable demeanor was sexy. She'd also thought, at one point, that he was a sound bet.

Him.

Jace McGraw.

The guy who spent most of his youth running wild and his teen years chasing trouble. The guy who cut out after graduation, then cut out on her when things got complicated. The same guy whose unwillingness to listen cost his parents their lives.

Charlotte looked at *that* guy and promised *him* forever. And what a lucky SOB he was, because once again Charlotte was giving him a chance to be the kind of man she deserved. A man like his brothers. A man like his dad.

She was also giving him a prime view of those mile-long legs again. And yet he was thinking of moving away.

Cal laughed and sat back. "Ah, shit, bro. I know that look."

"What look?" he asked, wondering if he was frowning again.

"The one that says you're screwed and you know it." Cal refilled both mugs to the top. "I bet there will be other garages in your future, but when it comes to the right woman, you usually only get one shot, damn lucky if you get two. But I guarantee you won't get a third."

Jace lifted his beer. "To not blowing it."

Cal held up his beer in salute, and Brett put his hands out as if calling a foul on the play. "How come when I fuck up, you're all 'man up, bro' over a bowl of cereal? But when he fucks up you buy him a beer?"

"I always liked him better," Cal said, and Jace toasted to that.

*   *   *

Charlotte slid her panties into her purse and did her best not to giggle. But she couldn't quite pull it off as she smoothed down her skirt, knowing that underneath she was commando. Jace's favorite color. Better yet, it came with a matching bra.

Her hair looked sexy. She'd taken it down and used the hand dryer in the ladies' room to achieve that tousled, bed-rumpled look he seemed to be so fond of. A quick swipe of the lips and she was set.

She loved when a plan came together. Loved even more when she got to move all the pieces around so that something that should have been a pipe dream suddenly became the clear choice. And tonight that had happened, Jace had made it happen for her, and she couldn't wait to show him just how appreciative she was.

She had watched him the entire evening, her body hyper-aware of his from the second he walked into the bar. It was as if they'd had an entire conversation, yet they hadn't exchanged a single word. So when he dropped some money on the table and started saying his good-byes, she quickly ended the meeting and headed toward the bathroom. A quick glance told her he was still at the table, so she snuck out the back.

Wanting to surprise him, she ran across the parking lot, cursing her heels as the clicked on the pavement. She made a dash across Maple Street and toward Kiss My Glass, where she'd parked her car. Conveniently right next to his. Only when she reached the little secluded parking lot off the back of the garage and got past the blinding security light did she realize that she wasn't alone.

Jace, of course. Looking like a dark and alluring sex pistol standing in front of his manly car, feet crossed at the ankles, that heavenly butt leisurely resting against the hood. The same hood she'd wanted to be splayed across when he came out.

"You beat me," she said, a little winded from the sprint, the adrenaline making her legs wobble. Or maybe that was the testosterone wafting off of him.

"I'm stealthy like that," he said, his breathing perfectly regulated. She was gasping like a beached whale and he was cool as ice, looking for all the world like a guy who made a habit of rescuing women from dark parking lots. "You in those heels, not so stealthy. I heard you heading for the back door even before you stood."

She'd have to work on that. "I was coming out to talk to you."

The night was cool and refreshing on her heated skin, and the breeze brushed gently against her bare legs, rustling the skirt of her dress as she closed the distance. The man in front of her rustled everything else, including her defenses, as his eyes dropped the length of her and back up.

"No underwear usually means that you want to do more than talk." He grinned.

Her hand dropped to cover command central. "How did you know?"

"I'm that good." His hands immediately went to her hips, then around the back, pulling her between his thighs. "Next time you wear cream with nothing beneath, don't stand in front of a streetlight." Lurking beneath the breezy tone was a subtle possessive quality that made her mouth water and her thighs quiver.

Without a word she leaned in and snagged his lower lip. She didn't need to start slow, they'd been teasing each other for the past hour, so she went straight for serious and quickly moved into demanding. They were so close that a piece of dental floss wouldn't fit between them.

Not that Jace seemed to mind, he was pretty wound up himself. He was grabbing her backside plastered flush against her front side, and when he started sucking on her neck she heard a desperate groan.

It was throaty and needy. And hers. "Jace."

And at the sound, he pulled back and gave her a smoking-hot look. "I love these talks of ours."

"Me too," she said, tugging him back down for another kiss. Because the man knew how to kiss—knew how to do a lot more, too. Like make her world easier. Which was the reason she'd come out here. "Is there something you forgot to tell me?"

His face went carefully blank.

"I had lunch with Harvey today," she said, and couldn't help the hero worship she felt. "He has ten cars confirmed. Ten cars means that every single former Miss Peach and board member will get to ride in style. We even have room for a few of the nurses from the hospital."

He smiled, genuine and open. "Was that what the meeting was about tonight?"

"Yeah. Darleen tried to say that she couldn't accommodate ten additional cars, but she was overruled. The board is so excited and happy with the results. For the first time in weeks everyone seemed to be looking forward to the parade," she said, running a hand down his chest. "And that's all because of you."

She wrapped her arms around him and melted into his body. "Thank you, Jace."

His arms came around her, and it felt as if she was snuggled in a big, warm, man cocoon. They stayed like that for a long moment, silently holding each other. Then she felt his quick intake of breath, heard his heart pick up pace, and he said, "My brothers know."

She pulled back and smiled. "I'm glad."

"You're not mad?"

"At what? That you don't have to lie to your family anymore?" she asked, now knowing that had been the topic of heated conversation she'd witnessed earlier in the bar. Guilt hit hard. "I'm just sorry that I made coming home even more stressful."

"It was my choice to wait. I own that," he said. "I just waited a little too long, but it all worked out." He paused, his eyes studying hers for a long, introspective moment. "Do you think maybe we should tell your parents? Get it out in the open before—"

"No." She could tell her quick response hurt him, so she reached up to cup his face. "What I meant was, yes, I want to tell them. It is just that telling my mom would be like pinning it to the community bulletin board." And this wasn't about her parents. Their opinions of Jace or who Charlotte loved didn't matter. Not anymore. Charlotte was going after what made her happy, and he was standing right in front of her.

But she didn't want her personal life to complicate her professional one. There were too many people counting on her. So if she could keep them separate for just a little while longer she was confident it would all work out. It had to.

"We said we'd give it until Sunday," she reminded him, and he stiffened. Which made not one ounce of sense. It was his idea. "I need the parade to be over, the Peaches to weigh in, and the endowment to be secure." Then she would know what Jace's plans were, so she could make her own, and hopefully they'd make some together. But Sunday wasn't that far off, and the realization that it could all end in just a few short days had a bead of panic rising up.

"We give it until Sunday, but then we will figure this out." He reached out to pull her closer, and Charlotte immediately curled herself into him, breathing in his scent and trying to remind herself that they still had time. Not a lot, but enough.

At least that's what Charlotte hoped.

Chapter 19

"Grandma's barricaded herself in the Stingray," Payton said, rushing up to him. "She said she wants to take it for a drive, and if anyone other than her grandson attempts to get behind the wheel she'd call on Mr. Smith and Mr. Wesson."

Jace looked at the crowded parking lot, packed full with coat-clad volunteers sipping hot cocoa and coffee, who had dared the morning chill to come and help prep for tomorrow's fair. Jace was in charge of the directing the classic cars into their spots, which were due to arrive any minute.

"Let me call Charlotte." Who was supposed to be putting the final touches on Jockey Jane. With Hattie.

"That's who she's threatening," Payton explained, her ponytail bobbing as she talked. Since she was running the refreshments booth with her team, she was in her cheer outfit, which was all but tempting frostbite. "Charlotte was at the Fabric Farm when she saw Harvey waiting out front of the garage. Spencer wasn't at work yet, so Charlotte went over to let him in and Hattie followed and started up the car.

Harvey tried to reason with her, you know, her having a suspended license and all, and that's when she started waving her purse."

Which held Mr. Smith and Mr. Wesson.

Jace didn't bother to ask how the information had gone from Charlotte to Harvey to his niece and instead focused his attention on the clipboard in his hand that had a detailed and color-coded list of cars and their designated spots. Then he looked at his phone and saw two missed calls from Harvey.

Great. He promised Charlotte that he'd handle the car delivery so she could focus on her knitting. But there was no way he could leave her to fend off Hattie and expect there to still be a functioning car when he returned.

If he left he was screwed. If he stayed he was screwed. He was sensing some sick, twisted pattern.

"I can help," Payton said, all sweet and innocently. "I mean if you want, I can go take Grandma for a spin."

Jace snorted. "Your dad would kill us both. Only me he'd kill slowly."

"Yeah," she said, knowing he was telling the truth. "Plus, we haven't done a leak check yet, and it would suck to blow up the engine after we just spent so much time rebuilding it."

His gaze slowly rose to his niece. To really look at her, and what he saw staring back had him grinning.

"What?" Arms crossed. "I totally listened to everything you said. I might not be a gearhead like you, but I know enough about cars to hang with Mason."

"You probably know more than Mason," he said, damn proud. "Which is why I'm giving you this." He handed her the list. "You need to match each car to the chalked number on each parking spot. Scan it and tell me if you have any questions."

She got three lines down, and two big eyes peeked up at him over the clipboard. "Omigod! You have a Shelby coming? Mase is going to freak!" The sparkle in her expression said she might freak a little herself.

"Yup," he said, taking in the awesomeness that he and Payton now shared a common interest. That he'd managed to do something no one else in his family had—pass on his dad's love of cars. "If they arrive before I get back, my buddy's name is Drew, just point him to where each car is supposed to park."

"Are you serious?" she squealed, and Jace gave her a big hug because she was so damn cute.

"What? You didn't think I wasn't paying attention to you paying attention?" he said, and she laughed. "Thanks, kiddo, you're doing me a solid."

"Solid enough to take Grandma for a spin?" she asked, but Jace was already on the move.

It took him approximately four minutes at a steady sprint to make it to Kiss My Glass. When he arrived Hattie was sitting in the driver's seat, arms folded—scowl dialed to Scrooge. Charlotte was sitting on the concrete slab in the middle of the bay, eyes closed, calmly knitting while effectively blocking Hattie's escape. And Harvey, man of the world, had positioned himself as far away from the drama as possible, leaning against the workbench, sucking on a toothpick.

"Hey, Harvey," Jace said, making his way into the garage. "How's it going?"

"Not bad. Need to get moving, though."

Jace removed his hat and wiped off his brow with the back of his hand. "Give me a minute."

Harvey looked at the circus in the bay. "You'll need more than that."

"Morning," Charlotte said when he got closer.

That was it. No yelling or rolling of the eyes, none of those big theatrics or guilt trips most women he knew would do when forced to deal with batshit crazy in-laws. She just looked up at him with a sweet "Morning" and an even sweeter smile.

"You're knitting?"

"You're staring," she whispered, then proudly held up the doll. It was pink, lopsided, but nearly finished. "After this I just have to stuff, stitch up the hole, and she will be a fully functioning member of Team Woolamena."

He squatted down, balancing on the balls of his feet. "Did I mention how sexy you look knitting?" he whispered back.

She sent him a secret smile.

"Sorry if she"—he waved a hand at Hattie—"complicated your day."

"Are you kidding? I carry needles and nasal syringes in my lab coat and corral sick kids for a living. This was nothing. Plus, Hattie's actually been a big help. Giving me tips and pointers." She lowered her voice. "From the driver's seat, of course."

Jace actually felt himself relax enough to laugh. Two things he found himself doing a lot around Charlotte. "Wouldn't expect any different."

"I'm right here," Hattie snapped. "No sense talking about me like I'm dead."

"Don't tempt me. The day's still young." Jace straightened and finally looked at the car he'd been jonesing on since he was a teen. With a low whistle he circled it, appreciating every hard-won detail. The soft curve of the frame, the two-toned leather seats, the white-rimmed tires he'd had shipped in from a place in Detroit. He knew that it was even better under the hood.

"Payton was right," he said, running a hand over the fender. "Sky blue is the perfect color." He met Hattie's gaze, which was shiny and full of pride. "Dad would have loved this."

"Would have been over the moon." Hattie patted the seat next to her in that *Come here, son* kind of way that reminded Jace of summers as a small boy, sitting on his grandma's lap and watching the day float by.

He was too big to sit on her lap anymore, but he wanted to be right there with Hattie when he took in this moment, so he opened the door and swung himself in. It took a little negotiating to get his legs inside, but he managed. The leather melted around his frame, and the smell of new car and fresh oil greeted him as he leaned his head back.

Heaven.

Then her fragile frame settled against his bigger one and everything fell into place. He was right back there, on the front porch, swinging with his grandma and telling stories.

"They did a great job on the dash," he said quietly. "And look at your radio. Payton and I refurbished the original one so it works again." Every part of this car belonged. Not one thing he and Payton used went against the integrity of the original design. "I can't believe this made it through a fire."

"I can," Hattie said, her voice shaking. She placed something in his palm and closed his fingers around it, and suddenly Jace knew that they weren't talking about the car. "Your dad loved this car because you loved this car. It was something that the two of you shared. My Ray left it to his son, and your daddy intended to do the same. Only life got in the way and plans changed, but it's time now."

"Grandma." He cleared his throat and tried again. "You can't give me Dad's car."

"Sure I can," she said. "And after we take it for a little test drive, real slow down Maple so everyone can see, you can drive me home. Just be sure to pick me up in time for the parade tomorrow."

"You want me to drive you in the parade?" He had assumed that after she accepted the fact that she wasn't driving herself she'd want Cal to do it.

"With all those fancy cars, a lady does what she needs to make a splash," she said, patting her spiky hair. "And cruising through town with a Ferrari driver as a chauffeur, it doesn't get any more big city than that."

"You know I don't own one. I just work on their engines."

Hattie seemed unconcerned with this. "Put on your Ferrari hat, wear a shirt that shows off those guns, and people will think you're that sexy Tom Selleck."

"Tom Selleck didn't really own that car. It was just a show."

"Well, then," she patted his hand. "I guess I'll have to drive through town with my favorite grandson."

"Brett's your favorite, and he and Cal might want to have a say in what happens to the car."

"We had our say," Cal said from behind, and Jace turned to find both of his brothers standing in the middle of the garage. "We want it to go to you."

"Why?" Jace asked, completely floored. Sure, he had a connection to it and loved cars, but this car was one of the few things that belonged to their dad to make it out of the fire. Why would they want to give that to someone who might not be here in a week's time?

"You dare question the favorite grandson?" Brett laughed, then he was back to being serious. "It's always been yours, Jace. From the time we were kids. Remember Mom used to load up a backpack and you'd camp in the damn thing instead of in the tent with us?"

Jace had forgotten about that. "It was warmer in the

garage than the tent. I was just being smart." He was also hanging with his dad. Because when the other guys fell asleep he'd sneak into the garage and his dad would come out and they'd make their own camp, right there on the garage floor. "Wait. Was this a setup?"

Cal and Brett both smiled.

Hattie took his hand and gave it a kiss. "I asked you to stay and fix the car because I wanted you to finally finish what you and your dad started. Hoped that maybe it would help you find some kind of peace in the storm."

He'd found more than he could ever verbalize. That car had given him a relationship with his niece, rekindled one with his dad, and brought him closer to his family—closer to knowing who he was and who he could be. Most importantly, it kept him here in Sugar, provided the time he needed with Charlotte.

He looked at his dad's old radio and smiled, wondering if maybe it was his old man's last attempt to bring him home.

"Thank you." He pulled Hattie in for a hug.

"You hug just like your mama."

"I've been hearing that a lot lately." His eyes found Charlotte, who had moved to the side of the garage, as though giving him and his brothers space while making sure she was there for him.

"I hate to break up this touching family fest, but Kiss My Glass is an official No Family Drama zone. So can you and your family go hug it out somewhere that doesn't smell up my garage?" Spencer said, coming out of her office. She was wearing a sleek red dress, red heels, and had some kind of flower fastened to her hair.

"What are you wearing?" Jace asked, because he'd never seen Spencer in anything but boots and jeans.

"A dress. Normal attire for a date."

"You wearing that"—Jace waved a hand at the flower—"to the range?"

"I am taking a salsa class, not that it's any of your business." She handed Jace an envelope. "Here."

He took out the paper and unfolded what looked like a billing statement. For a thousand bucks. "What's this?"

"Rent," she explained. "Due by the fifteenth. Because I am so generous, I prorated it."

"But you were letting me *borrow* the bay. A bay you weren't using," he reminded her.

"Brett hasn't done any kind of advanced thinking past changing diapers and hitting golf balls, but he's still paying on his student loans." Spencer smiled then punched him in the arm. "If you aren't cleared out by midmonth, it doubles. Thank you for coming," she said dryly as she walked away. "Have a nice day."

* * *

Charlotte slid into a vacant spot behind the finish line just as the last of the sheep were put in the starting cages. She was supposed to be working the Grow Clinic booth over by the classic car display, handing out pens and bumper stickers, but she wanted Woolamena to be able to see her when the mayor fired the start gun and the gates opened. Woolamena was counting on her and she didn't want to let her down.

Plus focusing on someone else's issues made it more difficult to dwell on her own. Like today was Sunday, their three weeks were almost up, and Jace could be leaving any day.

"Isn't it exciting, dear?" Dottie Ryan, owner of Sugar Savings and Loan said from beside her. The woman was tall, bony, and had a pair of binoculars pressed to her face. "I bet all my tickets on Wooly Bully. I'll be taking home a jar of this year's Great Sugar Jam-Off winner."

"I thought they threw out all the jams because people were concerned that they weren't safe for consumption," Charlotte said.

"They did, so they're handing out jars of Skeeter's peach bombs instead. Every person who picks the winner gets two jars."

Peach bombs were sliced peaches marinated in bathtub moonshine. A Skeeter specialty, because he stored them in quart-size Kerr jars that pop when they're sealed. With hundred-proof moonshine and slices of kumquats, no wonder so many people had turned out.

"Well, it's a bad bet," Charlotte said. "Woolamena is going to take it."

"Woolamena's the long shot." Dottie looked around, and when she was sure no one was listening, she leaned in, "I heard she's been having man troubles. Something about a stud who moved on to a younger prize. Drowned her woes in calories and people are claiming she's too plump to win."

Charlotte leaned in close, too, and whispered, "Real women have curves, Ms. Ryan. So do winners. It gives them padding for when they bust through the competition. So when that gate opens, I'd take a step back, because Woolamena is going to destroy the competition, and she might even take out that fence right there."

With horrified eyes, Dottie took a big step back.

Charlotte grinned and watched as the mayor approached the podium. He looked out at the crowd that had gathered, and he smiled. The parking lot, which had been completely shut down for the fair, and the back field were packed with families. Because of the addition of the classic cars, there were more tourists than usual. It was as if most of Sugar and the surrounding towns had turned out for the Founder's Day Fair, and not one of them was about to miss the Sheep Scurry and Trials.

No longer were people milling about, sipping sweet tea and ogling the concept car. They were all gathered around the racetrack, waiting with their team's button pinned to their chest, all hoping they'd picked the winner.

Hoping that they made the right bet.

With a deep breath, Charlotte ran a finger over her button, Woolamena the Warrior, then searched for the white speck in the distance with a pink dot on her back. She was standing at the front of her cage, her little black face pressed against the metal fence, hooves grinding the dirt.

"You got this, girl," Charlotte whispered.

And she did. Woolamena was almost there, almost ready to move on, and Charlotte knew that this race was a test. One she was determined to help her friend pass. Because next came acceptance and healing, and they were both more than ready for that.

Charlotte didn't hear Jace approach, but suddenly she felt him. Bigger than life and standing right behind her. "Is she ready?"

"I think so," she said, looking over her shoulder, her mouth going dry.

Jace was dressed in his usual jeans and boots, but today he'd swapped out the standard black tee for a button-down Light blue, to match his new car, and undone at the cuffs and collar. And his ball cap for mirrored aviator glasses, taking that dark guardian thing he had going on to a whole new level.

"I brought this." He held out an ice-cream bar from the hospital vending machine. "For inspiration."

"Thank you." She unwrapped the bar and took a bite. "Mmmmm. That is so good."

"Ah, I actually brought it for Woolanema," he said, and Charlotte froze, tongue midlick.

"Oh." Resisting the urge to lick the melting drop on the stick, she pulled the wrapper back up.

"I figured if she panicked, knowing an ice-cream reward would be waiting at the end might motivate her to finish. But you have a little on you. Right"—he leaned in as though he was going to lick it right off, then hesitated and pointed to his own lower lip—"there."

It had been like this all day. Jace had been supportive and encouraging, and completely remote. Always around, but floating in the background. He hadn't touched her once, not even a hug when she first saw him at the parade lineup. She knew that it was her fault. That he was keeping his distance because there were people everywhere and one touch would get people speculating, but suddenly she didn't care. Because no matter how perfect the day got, and it had gone pretty dang perfect so far, if she did say so herself, it felt hollow.

As if reading her mind, he leaned in and said, "The spooks from Mercy Alliance are a few feet to your left with Reginald, who has had his eye on us since the moment I walked over." Then handed her a napkin from his shirt pocket.

She wiped her mouth and looked to her left and had to laugh. Jace was right, Mr. Neil and his starched entourage looked like a bunch of CIA agents in the middle of a hoedown. And Reginald Holden the Third, he didn't stand out per se but he also didn't seem to belong. He held himself as though he wasn't a part of the community, but the overseer. A *position that, although self-appointed, must be lonely,* she thought, then wondered what he'd do if she went over and hugged him.

In front of everyone.

She snorted. Even though a hug was exactly what he needed, her dad wouldn't know what to do with such a public outpouring of affection. So she smiled and wiggled her fingers his way.

He gave a nod, not necessarily a friendly nod but better than nothing. Then he went back to watching the sheep.

"I just wanted to say good luck," Jace said.

Charlotte turned around to say that they didn't need luck, that she and Woolamena were going to be just fine regardless of the outcome, but Jace was gone.

"He promised the cheer team he would be the *O* in their victory line during the race, if they gave up the quest to be car babes," Glory said with a smile. "I'm told there will be pompoms involved. Don't worry, Cal is on hand with a camera."

Charlotte tried to smile, but she couldn't bring herself to do it.

"You haven't asked him to stay, have you," Glory said.

She shook her head. "I didn't want these few weeks to be about him leaving, put expectations on him that were unfair. They don't just offer garages like this to anyone. It's a huge deal and something he should be proud of."

From what Charlotte had gathered from Harvey and Drew, Jace was beyond talented in his field. One of the best He'd busted his hump to get to this point, and, just like her he was one step from realizing his goal. "And I would never ask him to sacrifice that. I just keep telling myself that we can make this work, that Atlanta is just a few hours away Right?"

"Right," Glory said, but her voice held the same concern Charlotte felt deep down.

"Has he said anything to Cal? About his plans?"

"Just that he's figuring things out."

A small bead of hope flared. Jace was a master problem solver, able to take a bunch of stray parts and make them purr. That, combined with her planning skills, made them unbeatable, or so she kept telling herself.

"But he still wants to go? To Atlanta?" Because that was the only reason she'd held off on asking him to stay. She knew if she did he would. And then one day he might regret his decision—and leave.

"He hasn't said anything about changing plans," Glory said gently. "To be honest, I don't think he knows what he wants." At Charlotte's defeated sigh, Glory bumped her with her hip. "I do know that he loves you, though, that much is obvious."

Charlotte took comfort in that, and hoped that this time love would be enough.

"Ladies and gentlemen," the mayor's voice boomed through the hospital's intercom and into the crowd. "Welcome to the one hundred and sixty-ninth annual Sugar County Sheep Scurry and Trials."

Charlotte's gaze traveled the length of the track to find Woolamena, who was, *oh God no*, staring out the side of her pen—at a big black silhouette in the far pasture.

Charlotte grabbed the binoculars from Dottie. It wasn't Diablo but a tractor. The way the sun hit it from behind, highlighting the deer antler emblem attached to the hood, it could be construed as a bull.

The mayor lifted his gun high above his head. "Let the curry begin."

Everyone pressed forward as the shot exploded through the air. The gates swung open and the floor vibrated beneath the crowd's feet as forty-four hooves pounded the ground at once—forty-four, not forty-eight, since Woolamena was still staring longingly out at the field.

"Plumpies never win," Dottie said.

"Want to bet?" Charlotte ripped the wrapper off the ice-cream bar and pushed her way to the fence. Waving it high above her head she yelled, "Show them your roar, Woolamena!"

Woolamena's head turned toward Charlotte, who was waving that white bar for all she was worth. She looked back at the tractor, then back to Charlotte, and she knew the second Woolamena found her voice.

A loud *baa-ah* echoed over the roar of the crowd and Woolamena dropped low to the ground, so low that when she took off she appeared to be flying. Eyes locked on the prize, she shot past sheep after sheep, all male, all twice her size and twice as strong. Jockey Jane was strapped to her back, pressed against her rump from the velocity, her glittery pink shoes slapping Woolamena's flank.

It took less than a minute to catch the leader, Wooly Bully, who pressed himself aggressively against the side of the track, trying to intimidate and block Woolamena.

"Go for the goods," June screamed from the sidelines. She was wearing a Boys Intimidate and Women Castrate T-shirt.

Woolamena got even lower, pressing herself under Bully's big legs and taking him out at the knees. He stumbled and she charged forward, pushing right past the competition, the finish line, and the podium, not stopping until she was at the fence.

Dottie screamed and jumped back, but Charlotte dropped to her knees and shoved the bar through the boards.

"Lord almighty, the sheep understood you, didn't she?" Dottie asked from a careful distance, gazing at the animal as though she was now divine.

"No, I think ice cream is a pretty powerful motivator

she said, petting Woolamena as, sides heaving, she gobbled down that bar. Muzzle white from the treat, the sheep lifted her head and then butted the fence.

Dottie leaped back, hand on her chest as though staring down the Reaper himself. Charlotte reached in and gave Woolamena a scratch behind the ear, taking the movement for what it was. A wooly high five.

With one last butt to the palm, Woolamena strutted her rump right past the podium and Bully, who was watching.

"That was more fun than the Kentucky Derby," Mr. Neil said, and the rest of the board members laughed. "I only wish I'd bet on the winning sheep."

Charlotte stood, her cheeks hurting from the strain of smiling so hard. "Woolamena might be the smallest of the entries, but she's scrappy."

"I always say bet on the incumbent. Winning is in their blood," Reginald said, and Charlotte wanted to gag. A wink to the board would have been more subtle.

"I think even if this had been Woolamena's first race she would have taken it," Charlotte said.

"Why is that?" Mr. Neil asked.

Charlotte looked at Woolamena, strutting up and down the track like a queen, and she felt her eyes water. "She was the smallest and youngest one out there, and she had to prove to herself that she deserved a win. That's a pretty compelling motivation, one that's hard to beat."

Even more compelling than ice cream.

"I agree," Mr. Neil said with a smile. "Kind of like this town. The support Sugar Medical has instilled among the residents is almost as compelling as the way you approach medicine. And you, Dr. Holden, are a breath of fresh air." It took Charlotte a long moment to realize that he was addressing her and not her father.

"Thank you, sir," she said. "I love what I do and I love this town. It's home to me."

"A compelling motivation as well," he said. "Which is why I am pleased to tell you that, while the board needs to finalize the details, it is safe to say that as soon as the Grow Clinic is open and running, the funds will be wired. In five years' time we will reassess the endowment."

"You're going to fund us for five years?" Charlotte asked, her heart in her throat, because she'd expected to have to reapply every year until they had a proven track record.

"We want the staff practicing medicine, not researching grants and funding. Plus, I believe strongly that this clinic shows great promise, a promise we'd like to invest in for the long term." Mr. Neil took Charlotte's hand, but she went in for a hug. It wasn't professional, and she was certain her father was shooting her disapproving glances even as she did it, but this wasn't a business deal to her. This was a partnership, one that started from a shared interest and solidified when Sugar showed them their heart.

"We won't let you down, Mr. Neil."

Chapter 20

⌒

Jace watched with satisfaction as Charlotte ended the hug and took the suit's hand, pumping it excitedly. She was trying to play it professional, but he knew she was a mess of emotions inside. She had done it. He could tell by the body language that she'd gotten her money. And he couldn't be more proud.

"Next time could you give us a little kick, maybe spirit fingers?" Spencer said, ruffling Jace's pom-poms. Okay, they were Payton's, but he promised he'd hold on to them.

"Here's the money." He handed her a thick envelope. He was standing behind the concept car display, making sure people abided by the No TOUCHING sign. "Thanks for letting me *borrow* the bay."

Spencer ignored his sarcasm and took the envelope. She paused at its weight then opened it. "What, is it all in ones?"

"A thousand of 'em," he said. "Just like you requested."

"Yeah, well, if you're even a dollar off I will find you."

Jace looked down at the woman, who came to his

chest, and laughed. "I have a good foot and a hundred pounds on you."

"I have a gun and I know how to use it." She looked up at him and smiled. "Plus, I'd be scared if you didn't have that dopey-as-shit look on your face," Spencer said slowly, enunciating every word as though Jace was talking to someone with the emotional control of a hormonal teenage girl.

"This is a smile, you should try it sometime." And to demonstrate what a real smile consisted of, he flashed his whites her way. "This is because Charlotte landed the endowment."

"No shit," Spencer said, giving him an insincere smile as though they were twelve and in middle school. "Good for her. So then why are you over here and she is over there and you have both been pretending all day that you have no idea what the other one's *O* face looks like?"

Jesus. "Who told you?"

"You just did. I kind of assumed after yesterday with that heartwarming moment in the garage, but there was a little doubt. You and the doctor?" She paused on that for a moment, then shrugged. "Who would have guessed?" Spencer's face went slack at something over Jace's shoulder. She ducked down, using him as a shield. "No way. This is not happening. Hide me."

Jace looked over his shoulder to see Ben in a pair of Dockers and a freaking tie walking toward him. Jace looked at Spencer and laughed. "Seriously? You went dancing with Dr. Perfect?"

"What?" Her brows drew together, then she peeked through the gap between his arm and side. "No, the other one."

A quick glance told him that his friend was avoiding Sheriff Jackson Duncan. "You hooked up with the sheriff?"

"No!"

"Liar." He raised his hand and waved. "Hey, JD."

Spencer yanked it down. "Okay, we didn't hook up. I went to the salsa class and my date was a no-show, but lo and behold, guess who likes to tango three nights a week?"

"JD?" Jackson Duncan was a brawler with a permit to carry. He liked to hunt and box and, before he earned a badge, the occasional bar fight.

"Yup. And he saw me there, sitting all pathetic with a freaking flower in my hair. And." She shivered. "He asked me to dance. Talk about a dick move."

"Total dick move," Jace deadpanned, giving her a WTF look. "Well, time to pull out your dance card, he's headed over."

With a squeak she dove behind the display holding the car's specs. "Don't stare at me, that's as bad as me screaming polo."

"You owe me, Spencer," Jace said, then turned around. "Hey, JD. Ben."

Jackson gave Jace a side bro hug. Ben and Jace exchanged cordial glances.

"Good to see you. I heard you were back." Jackson's walkie-talkie cut in and he listened and sighed. "Let's grab a beer later. It seems I need to go arrest my grandma. She assaulted some guy with her peaches."

Jace didn't bother to ask for clarification, just agreed to a beer. Then he turned to Ben, who had decided to stay—and chat? Apparently, he wanted to play friends. "Are you leaving town?"

Or not. "That's always been the plan."

Ben looked over at Charlotte, who was still deep in conversation with Mr. Neil. "Is she going with you?"

Jace went still. "No. Why, did she say she was?" Because that would be fan-fucking-tastic. He'd been racking his brain trying to come up with a plan that would work for both of them. All he'd managed was a splitting headache. Then he remembered. "I am positive you guys got the money for the clinic. She'd be crazy to leave now."

"Then none of this makes sense," Ben said, not nearly as excited as one should be to discover that they'd just landed a few mil. With a sigh he met Jace's gaze. "Do you love her?"

"With everything that I am."

Ben nodded, as though his answer hurt but he respected it. "Then no matter what happens, don't let her leave. She's worked her ass off for this clinic, and she deserves to see it through."

"I agree."

"Good, because Reginald just offered me the position of medical director at the Grow Clinic," Ben said. "And the only reason he'd do that was if Charlotte was leaving."

*   *   *

The sun was starting to set when Charlotte finally finished her shift at the booth. Handing out the bumper stickers that said OUR DOCTORS GIVE GOOD SUGAR, she went in search of some ice cream. The Sugar Gun and Ammo Club was selling soft-serve cones dipped in chocolate. She was going to bring one to Jace, who was still acting as security at the car show, and tell him the exciting news.

Celebrate with the one person she'd wanted to have by her side when she shook Mr. Neil's hand.

She stopped next to the DOUBLE BARRELED AND DOUBLE DIPPED banner dancing with the breeze when a familiar sizzle shimmer down her spine. She slowly turned to find Jace.

Waiting for her.

He stood by the side entrance to the medical center, propping up the entire building with his shoulder, and had two chocolate-dipped cones in hand. His shirt was untucked, his face dark with the day's stubble, and even though his sunglasses hid his eyes, when he took a lick from the cone it was as if telling her his plans for later.

Her knees wobbled.

She gave him a smile, a real one that came all the way from her soul, and headed over. "How was the car show—whoa…"

Jace handed her the ice cream, grabbed her wrist, and tugged her around the corner behind some delivery trucks, and into the loading dock behind the clinic.

"Jace, what are you—"

That was all she managed before he sank his free hand into her hair, pinned her to the wall with his body, and fused his mouth to hers. He tilted her face, aligning it perfectly, before taking the kiss deeper.

Only deep didn't even begin to describe it. Jace consumed her, took her right out of her head, and over the edge. She lost herself in the sensation of being wanted, the wave of desire and need that washed over her.

This was what she'd needed all day. Connection. Passion. Heat.

Jace.

She tried to pull him closer and balance her ice-cream cone, a difficult task but she managed. She considered the physics behind pulling off his shirt while holding the cone, then decided to screw the cone and dropped it, right as the kiss ended.

"You dropped your cone," he said—to her mouth.

"I can get another. We can get it to go," she said suggestively.

"Best idea yet, but Payton is only covering my break. I am on car-watching duty until Drew comes to pick up the cars at nine. Rain check?"

"I have to make sure that all the tents get returned. Which means I can't cash in the rain check until late." She let out a breath. "I missed you today. Missed this."

"Me too," he said against her mouth, giving her what must have been the kiss to end all kisses. Soft, hungry, and better than ice cream. "I've been dying to get my hands on you all day."

"Me too."

He liked that answer, his boyish grin said as much. He nuzzled her for a moment, then sat down on the edge of the loading dock, pulling her onto his lap. He took a lick of his cone, making a big deal about how good it was, then when she was pouting offered it to her. And sharing was *way* better than having her own cone.

"Everyone is talking about you and your new car," she said, referring to the parade, which because of Jace and his "favors" had been one of the most well-received parades in recent years. And every board member had made a point during the day to tell her so.

Well, every Peach except Darleen.

"Everyone's talking about how Hattie flipped the sheriff the finger when he refused to let her use the portable siren on the car," he said, making himself right at home, his hand roaming her body as she took another lick of the cone.

"No, I think they were talking about how nice it was to see you in the parade," she said, telling him the God's honest truth. "How sweet you were to provide all of those fancy cars for the parade, including your dad's, and how because of you the parade was perfect."

"I'm far from sweet, Charlie." Slowly he slid the su

glasses down to the end of his nose and his deep-blue eyes locked on hers. "And we both know that the parade was perfect because of you. The idea was yours, the execution was yours, and the volunteers, the town, even the Peaches, all came together to make this happen because of you. You made the parade about this town and its residents, and I bet they will be talking about this fair for years."

Unsure what to say to such a statement, she held his gaze. Hers went little blurry with emotion, his remained unguarded and unwavering. "Thank you," she finally whispered. "Today was important, and what you said…" She shook her head and swallowed. "That was—"

"Don't say sweet."

She didn't say anything at all, just smiled. He smiled, too, then leaned forward and went after the cone—with his teeth.

"We got the endowment." *Wow*, saying that, to him, made it all the more real. The money, the confidence, the hands-off approach Mercy was willing to take. All of it. "Five years, Jace. They gave me five years to make a go of this."

"I never doubted you," he said, but something changed in his tone. "Never once. You deserve this, Charlie. You deserve to make it exactly how you imagined it."

She nodded. "I know. I do. I really do." And when she said it she believed it.

She hadn't just lost Jace four years ago, she'd lost her job and her identity. But today she'd managed to finally let go of all the what-could-have-beens that came with thinking about her time in Atlanta. Let go of expectations and accepted that everything turned out the way it was supposed to.

She rested her head on his shoulder. "And in a few weeks the doors will open and I will be Dr. Charlotte Holden. Medical Director of the Grow Clinic."

"Yes, you will be." There was so much conviction in his voice her heart melted.

"And all because I found my voice."

"You roared," he said, resting his head on hers.

She closed her eyes. "Oh, my word, you heard that?"

"Baby, the whole town heard." He laughed, and she decided she liked the endearment *baby*. She liked anything that came from Jace. "If we ever put our kids in Little League, remind me never to let you coach."

Her heart stopped at his statement. His stopped, too. She felt it as she lifted her head to look at him. "Did you say our kids?"

"Huh, I guess I did." And he didn't even look like he wanted to run.

* * *

It was well after eight by the time Drew loaded up his cars. Jace thanked his buddy, and after promising him a cold one when he got back to Atlanta, he headed toward Sugar Lake. He didn't go to Charlotte's, though. Nope, he went west straight for her father's house. He didn't know what kind of sick game her old man was playing, but Jace was going to make sure that whatever happened, Charlotte was on the winning team.

There were three types of homes on Sugar Lake, some newer builds like his brothers', but most were like Charlotte's, modest family homes that had been built around the turn of the century—the nineteenth century. Jace pulled into the driveway of the third kind, a twenty-thousand-square-foot three-story Greek Revival mansion, which was on the water only because back in the day that was where the cotton plantation ended. With its marble columns, crisp white clap board siding, and sweeping front staircase, it stood as a living reminder of just how powerful and rich in history Charlotte's roots were.

Reaching the end of the quarter-mile magnolia and oak-lined drive, Jace parked next to the family's Rolls-Royce. He took in the car, which most likely cost more than his entire net worth, and felt the tension knot in his neck. He wasn't unaccustomed to nice things; his parents had done more than all right for themselves. And the McGraw name carried a weight that only added to his résumé. But in Sugar there was money, and then there was Holden money, and there were several zeroes and former politicians separating the two.

Jace climbed out of his Chevelle and saw Reginald Holden the Third sitting in a rocking chair on the porch. Backlit by the porch light, he appeared imposing. Formidable. But Jace wasn't intimidated in the slightest, because he knew better than most that appearances didn't mean jack shit.

Take him, for example. He was built like a tank, had a record, enough ink for an entire platoon, and tended to scare small children. Yet he would rather cut off his arm than hurt someone he cared about.

Reginald might look like a man to be respected, admired even, but Jace knew that anyone who could treat their daughter the way he did was nothing but a bully. Or maybe he was scared that if Charlotte found her own success she wouldn't need him anymore. Either way made him a coward.

Jace walked up the front steps, his boots clicking against the whitewashed wooden slats.

"Have a seat," Reginald said, pointing to the chair across from his. In the middle there was a small beverage table that held a china tray with a crystal decanter and two tumblers. Filled with scotch. No ice.

"You were expecting someone?" Jace asked, taking a seat.

"You," he said, picking up the tumbler in offering. Jace waved it off and Reginald sat back with a shrug. "After I saw you talking with Ben earlier, I figured it would either be you or my daughter."

"Why did you offer the position to Ben without talking to Charlotte?" he wanted to know.

"Charlotte was on the list of candidates, a short list, but there was a list." He took a sip of his scotch. "Her becoming the medical director wasn't a given."

"Bullshit. Everyone knew that Charlotte was going to be the medical director. Even Ben. She raised the money for the new ward, came up with the plan and treatments for the Grow Clinic, even secured an endowment when you couldn't. So yeah, she might not be the only one qualified for the position, but you know she is the most qualified."

"A few weeks ago, I couldn't have agreed with you more."

"Then what happened between then and offering Ben the position?" Jace asked, wondering if the older man's answer would hurt as much as he thought it would. He didn't care if Charlotte's parents liked him, but Charlotte would. She cared about everyone in her world, and in the best possible way. She had a huge heart and always took others' feelings into account. It was what he loved most about her.

So if something was important to Charlotte then Jace would make it a priority, but he couldn't help it if this guy hated his guts. And that made him nervous.

Reginald swirled the liquid around the side of the tumbler and laughed. "It's not what you're thinking. Are you the person I would have chosen for the great-great-granddaughter of a former United States Vice President?" He paused dramatically. "It is clear you care for her, but no, you weren' what I would have chosen. But she is an adult who makes her own choices. And she chose." He sipped his scotch and looked out at the lake.

A zillion stars reflected off the water's surface, expanding and stretching as the water rippled against the shoreline. As calm and peaceful as it was, Jace felt anything but. He watched Reginald watching the water, swirling his drink, acting as though his answer would suffice, and a hot, bitter roll of frustration pounded Jace's head.

"You're going to crush her," he said, at a complete and total loss. "Absolutely crush her world, and you're acting like you don't care. Like this is nothing more than replacing the battery in your car."

"I care, Mr. McGraw," he said, a fire to his tone, the first sign of emotion he'd seen from the guy so far. "As a doctor and medical director, I am charged with caring. For this town, my family, the clinic, a rich legacy that I refuse to tarnish. Do you know a doctor's most important asset?"

Jace thought about the thousands of hours Charlotte spent studying, interning, treating patients. How many mentors she trained under and how much she put into finding the right solutions for tough problems. "Dedication."

"No. It's truth," he said. "People rely on doctors to tell them the truth, even if the prognosis is a long, suffering death. Because truth builds trust, and if a patient doesn't trust their doctor we can't do our job, regardless of how talented and dedicated we are."

Reginald leaned forward and set down his glass. "My daughter chose to elope and keep it a secret."

"She had her reasons," Jace said. For the life of him he couldn't remember any at the moment, but she'd had them. A whole spreadsheet full.

Reginald chuckled. "I'm sure she did, my wife being at

the top of the list. Yet she still had a choice, and had the annulment gone through no one would be the wiser. But it didn't, and she came home, began practicing at the hospital, building a reputation, building trust within her patients and the staff, even convinced a prestigious nonprofit to invest millions of dollars. All the while pretending to be single, dating, mostly men her mother shoved on her, asking for people to put faith in her assessments, to be honest with her, and yet she was living a lie."

"How did you find out?"

Reginald offered Jace the tumbler again, and this time he took it. He had a sinking feeling he'd need the entire decanter by the time this conversation was over.

"Last week Charlotte refused to come in early, and one of her ladies' group friends asked me if the facilities would be made available to the public on the day of the fair. I told her to ask my daughter, who she informed me was fishing. With you." He eyed Jace. "Charlotte doesn't fish, doesn't even own a boat. But I had seen yours docked at her house. Remembering how you left town and wanting to make sure you weren't fishing for gold in my family's pond, I did some calling around. Imagine my surprise when I discovered you two weren't just having an unsavory fling. Did you know marriage certificates are public record?"

He knew. It was how the whole loan mess stared to begin with.

"It didn't take long after that to discover the annulment filings. Two. Thankfully, it looks as though the second one will come through."

"She made a mistake," Jace said. "She was hurt and upset when she came home. I can't blame her for wanting to deal with the heartache in her own way." That he was the cause of the heartache killed him.

"I know, and as her father I want to make everything better," he said, and Jace believed him. Holden might be a grade-A dick, but deep down he loved his daughter. "However, as the director of the hospital, I understand that I serve a small, conservative Southern town, and I can't risk her personal choices affecting patients' or investors' faith in our ability to treat them. Or be honest."

Jace closed his eyes and let that wash over him. He wanted to argue that no one would give a shit, but Holden knew his clients, knew how things worked in small towns. Even small towns like Sugar, where they can forgive a guy like Jace. Charlotte's dad was right, there was the potential for fallout, but Jace knew that there was more of a chance of forgiveness.

Carrying out a lie takes time and commitment, and yet it only takes a second for a lie to hurt. Forgiveness, he learned, worked the same way. It took time.

Which was something he was desperately short on.

"If Charlotte was really out of the running you wouldn't have wasted your evening talking with me," Jace said, calling the man's bluff. "So what needs to happen for Charlotte to wake up tomorrow as the newly appointed medical director of the Grow Clinic?"

"Promise me that your secret marriage never surfaces," her father said. "It wouldn't just hurt her professional reputation, but it would affect her standing in the community. Especially with the families of the people she has dated since her return."

Jace polished off his scotch and stood. He meant what he'd said to his brothers, there wasn't much he wouldn't do if it meant securing Charlotte's happiness. Even if it meant sacrificing his own.

* * *

It was nearly midnight when Charlotte dragged her aching feet through the front door. The fair was over, the parking lot cleared out, and she had a gallon of mint chip in the freezer. She considered calling in that rain check, then decided she'd rather crawl into bed with Jace and just snuggle.

Only her bed was empty.

Jace had taken off shortly after the cars had been loaded on their trailers. He said he had an errand to run, then he was going home to wait for her. Maybe check another fantasy off his list.

"Jace," she called out, checking the bathroom. Empty. He wasn't downstairs, she would have seen him.

She checked the guest room, the downstairs bathroom, and found herself back in her bathroom, checking the shower. "Jace?"

Nothing.

She sat on the toilet to remove her shoes, and, thinking that he must be at that garage or maybe out with his brothers pulled out her phone. She was about to hit his speed-dial number when she noticed the sink.

It was practically empty.

His toothbrush was gone. She fumbled with the side drawer, the drawer she'd cleared out for him, but it was empty as well. Kind of like the feeling starting at the pit of her stomach. She pulled it all the way out, dumping it on the counter.

"No." No razor. No deodorant. No body spray that made him smell like a Scottish laird from one of her romance novels. Nothing. Even the box of ribbed-for-her-pleasure condoms he'd brought with him. Gone.

Convincing herself that there must be some mistake—

they'd talked about Little League and rain checks, both things that implied going the distance—she ran into the bedroom and yanked open the closet. Nothing Jace-related.

Then everything inside of her went cold and Charlotte spun around. Racing to the bed she hit her knees. She looked behind the bedpost, lifted the bed skirt, even checked behind the pillows that had fallen on the floor.

She found nothing. Nothing to still that sharp ball of ice swirling in her stomach. Nothing to stop the panic from rising. Because his boots, the ones he'd been so adamant about, were gone.

She blinked her eyes and waited for them to clear, afraid that because her heart was pounding so hard it was causing her to become disoriented. Because that was what panic did, it flooded your system with cortisol, which raised your heart rate and blood pressure and could, under extreme situations, impair your judgment and comprehension.

That's what it had to be, because what she was seeing couldn't be comprehended. For the empty bathroom and closet she could come up with some rational explanation. He was doing laundry, toothpaste exploded in his bathroom drawer and he had to buy new things, a dog ate his boots. All sound, rational reasons when compared to the alternative.

No, what was limiting her lungs' ability to work at full capacity was the stack of papers sitting on the nightstand. Who knew that printed paper, ink, and a staple could be so detrimental to one's heart, but the signature at the bottom, right above JACE DONOVAN MCGRAW, carried enough lethal force to rip her heart right out of her chest.

She looked down to see if her chest was still moving, and it looked fine, which she chalked up to the cortisol again. Because she could feel a gaping hole in there, raw and painful, the ache so deep she was sure it was a fatal wound, but when she looked down she saw nothing. Just the neckline of her top and her great-great-grandmother Rose Holden's strand of pearls.

Which she was certain would go to her cousin Joyce in Magnolia Falls, because if she did manage to survive this, it was certain now that she wouldn't have a daughter to pass it on to.

Charlotte closed her eyes, squeezed them shut as tightly as possible, and that's when she remembered her phone on the dresser. With shaky legs, she made her way over and picked it up. Then she took a photo of the annulment and the signature and hit send.

Setting the phone on the end table, she sat on the bed and waited. Every second she waited the dread built and questions flew at her, to which she had no answers. None.

A few seconds, or maybe a few hours later, she heard a muffled vibration against the top of her 1789 Thomas Affleck Chippendale nightstand that she'd picked up at an auction in Atlanta a few years back. She looked at the phone and knew it would hold the answer to at least one question.

Only her fingers wouldn't pick it up, all she could manage was a single finger swipe over the screen. Her whole body shook when it lit up. Taking a breath, she looked at the screen and saw that there weren't possibly enough words to make her understand. Five, maybe ten words is a small explanation, surely not big enough to be considered world-shattering. She took heart in that. Until she read the message: I WILL EXPLAIN. I LOVE YOU. —J

Charlotte read it again, hoping that it would make sense And then she didn't want it to make sense, because he'd explained to her once before why he had to leave, and it didn't change things. Didn't make the pain any less debilitating.

She knew what it felt like to only have part of the answers, and she didn't want to go through that ever again. Jace might be a runner, but he wasn't a liar, and if he said he'd explain, then she was going to give him the chance.

So she waited, on her bed, in her dress and pearls, for him to come home. For him to explain away the hurt and the sadness and the big hollow space in her chest that grew with every breath. She waited until it hurt too much to stay upright, until the sun started to crest the hills, and when the time came and passed for their morning ritual, Charlotte couldn't wait anymore.

And that was when she let the tears take over.

Chapter 21

It was past nine in the morning when Charlotte finally dragged herself into the clinic, her body rebelling from what felt like an endless night. She'd managed to change clothes and cover up some of the shadows under her eyes, but the grief she saw every time she looked in the mirror—unfortunately there was nothing she could do about that.

She reached the third floor and saw Glory standing at the nurses' station and wondered if she had made the right decision.

With everything she needed to do to prepare for the endowment, hiding in her house for a week and crying into a gallon of ice cream wasn't an option. Neither was facing his family. Not after they knew everything. She didn't want to spend her morning fielding questions of where Jace was, if he'd left town, and how she was holding up. Charlotte had enough questions of her own to deal with, so she headed the other direction.

Nope, she didn't want to talk to anyone, just go into her

office, see her patients, and then go home. Only she remembered that Joie was coming in today for Lily Anne's checkup, so she turned right instead of left and went to find Ben. To ask him to handle Joie's appointment.

Because the only thing more painful than the questions would be to know that he'd cared enough to give his family the answers she desperately needed.

She tapped on Ben's door then let herself in. He was sitting at his desk looking handsome and familiar and safe. His head was free of a hat, no scruff on his chin—he looked, in a word, dashing.

"Oh God." She was crying, which seemed impossible since there should be no way her tear ducts could produce more fluid.

"Charlotte?" Ben gave her one look, then he was on his feet and taking her by the shoulders. "He told you. What a son of a bitch! Whoa, are you going to pass out on me? Here, sit down."

She didn't want to sit. Not after that. "He told *you?*"

"Yeah," Ben said, fussing over her and looking a little too panicked for a man who had started his career as an army medic. "Yesterday. At the fair."

"He told you yesterday? At the fair? That he was leaving?" she asked, going from shock to denial to pissed off in less than twelve hours.

"Why are you repeating everything I say?" Then Ben closed his mouth and cocked his head to the side. "And what are *you* talking about?"

"What are you talking about?" she countered, but Ben remained tight-lipped. "Ben, I have spent the last twelve hours crying because of a man. I am tired, and hungry, and angry. And a little on edge, because castration is sounding reasonable and right about now I'm not really choosy about my subject."

Ben dropped his head with defeat. "Okay, but sit first." She did, then skewered him with a glare. "Your dad offered me the medical director position yesterday."

And just when Charlotte thought she couldn't feel any more pain, she took another hit. It welled up in the pit of her stomach, coiling tighter and tighter until she was sure she would crumble. Or snap. "Why?"

"Honestly, I don't know," Ben said softly. "I assumed it was because you were getting serious with your mechanic, but then this morning your dad told me that the position was to be yours, and if and when the time came for a new medical director I would be his top choice, then he asked me not to mention any of this to you. I assumed Jace convinced you to stay."

"I was never leaving, and . . . Wait? Jace knew about this?" Red-hot frustration laced with sadness rushed through her veins as she thought back to yesterday at the loading dock, when Jace had been so determined she'd get the promotion. So adamant that she would see her dream fulfilled.

"Yeah, I told him that I wouldn't take the position. That if you were staying in Sugar that it was yours," Ben said. "He promised that you wouldn't leave."

Some of that pain she'd been carrying seemed to fade, to make room for the guilt. She could only imagine what Jace had felt, the conclusions he would have come to—most of them true. She knew Jace, knew how protective he was of the people he loved, and he loved her—enough to walk if it meant her getting the promotion.

Part of her was mad, so incredibly mad that he didn't consult her. That he once again made the decision for her, had chosen the noble path instead of the right one. Then she remembered what Hattie had said, that she was his home. Yet she'd never even given him a key. She'd shared her bed, her shower, her problems, her responsibilities. But when he'd asked to share in her world, be in her family, she'd told him no.

The McGraws didn't hide their love or put restrictions on it or save it for a special day. They celebrated it, paraded it through town in a flashy car.

"Where's my dad?" Charlotte asked.

"He's in the conference room. I guess the Sugar Peaches are here to talk about who will get the Founder's Day pot."

Charlotte stood and flapped her hands in the air. "How is it that I am a sixth-generation doctor, graduated top of my class, head of pediatrics, and a two-time regent of the Sugar Peaches, and yet people seem to think I don't need to be informed when important decisions are being made?"

Ben's hands covered his boys. "Are you going to castrate me?"

"Not today," she said, and marched straight down the hall to the conference room. She burst through the door to find the hospital's board on one side of the table, the Sugar Peaches on the other, her mother clutching her pearls in the middle, and Darleen holding the Golden Peach.

Although the moment she walked in everyone turned to stare at her.

"I'm glad you're all here," she said, clapping her hands and taking her place at the head of the table, taking the Golden Peach from Darleen. "I must have missed the memo."

"We were just getting started," her father said. "It seems there is a question about who will receive the donations collected at the fair."

"The terms of the agreement were that if the parade and sheep scurry went well, then I would remain regent and the decision would be mine." She looked at the board. "Correct?"

"That's what I heard," Hattie said, giving Charlotte a supportive wink. "So I think this is all a waste of time. Give the pot to the Grow Clinic so we can all go home. I've got a pie in the oven."

"That would be nice," Mabel said. "But there have been some concerns voiced about people withholding pertinent information and, well, mixed-up priorities."

All eyes went to Darleen, who took that as her cue to speak. She pressed down her skirt and took in a deep breath as though about ready to give a speech on how she was going to cure world hunger. "Charlotte purposefully waited to give me the number of cars that were coming to the show, which made it impossible for me to plot out how many tents we had room for."

"But the whole day was a success," Babette said, and sent Charlotte a proud smile. "In fact, my daughter's efforts resulted in a nineteen percent increase from last year's total earnings. I know, I tallied the money myself this morning."

Babette took a stack of spreadsheets and divvied them up. As they made their way around the room, impressed whispers began circling.

"Why does everyone assume that *she* is responsible?" Darleen said, her bony finger pointed at Charlotte. "We all chipped in. In fact, I bet if we divided what money came from her part and what came from my part, I'd be the winner."

"You told people where to put up booths," Hattie said with a dismissive wave. "How hard is that? Plus, this is about the community, not about winning."

"Exactly." Darleen clapped her hands with delight. "This is about the community, which is why we have all sacrificed a lot of time and energy to make this amazing. But what Charlotte didn't tell you was that if her clinic doesn't get the pot, then Mr. Neil and those fancy city boys wouldn't invest either. She used us and didn't say a word, which is not very forthcoming or neighborly."

At the horrified gasps, Charlotte held up a hand. "Both times I ran for regent, I made it clear that my platform centered on the medical center and the Grow Clinic. Both times you elected me on that platform, so yes, while Mercy Alliance is intent on ensuring that the local support won't dry up, that requirement came *after* we had already put the Grow Clinic on the table as the recipient."

Charlotte glared at her father, as if to say just how complicated he'd made things. He had the decency to look embarrassed.

"Maybe I should have been more forthcoming," she admitted. "But we have never required other organizations to disclose their financial partnering."

"Okay," Darleen said, hands on hips. "Explain why, while we were all scrambling to get the fair stepped up and organized, *you* were making whoopee with *her* grandson." This time the pointer went to Hattie, and shocked gasps, and a few titillated ones, filled the room.

"I don't understand," her mother said to her father as though she needed him to explain the theory behind time travel. "I thought Cal was marrying that nurse."

"Not now, Babette," Reginald said, running a hand down his face. With an exhausted sigh he leaned back in the chair and closed his eyes. Everything about him looked tired. Sad. And suddenly Charlotte saw a side of her father that she hadn't known existed. He was disappointed. Not in her, but in himself.

For not protecting her? For putting her in this position? She wasn't sure.

Her mother, on the other hand, almost delighted in the fact that Charlotte might be marrying Cal. Darleen was delighted that she'd won. But it was Hattie who drew Charlotte in.

Hattie with her spiky hair and loud tracksuits and mama bear love for her family, who was silently waiting for Charlotte to explain. Explain that Charlotte Holden, local MD and former Miss Peach, loved her youngest grandson. Then give that love what it deserved, what he deserved.

To be claimed by her.

Charlotte had been so angry when he walked out that she never considered why someone walks to begin with. Because they don't know where they belong. Even though Jace belonged to her, with her, she'd never told him that. Never gave him any reason to believe that it was the two of them through the good times *and* the bad.

Sure, he'd run, but she'd known he was a runner when she married him. And she'd taken a vow to bring him home.

"I didn't come here today to argue over who did what with you, Darleen," she said, and Darleen rolled her eyes. "I came here as the current regent to inform the board of two decisions. The first, I will do my duty as your elected officer and put forward to the board that all of the proceeds from the Founder's Day pot go to the Grow Center."

"You can't do that," Darleen said. "She can't do that!"

"As your elected leader, I can and just did." Charlotte looked back at the board. "Which brings me to my next point. Effective immediately I will be stepping down as regent."

Confusion erupted as everyone started talking over one another.

"Did she say she'd quitting? My hearing's acting up!"

"Lord have mercy, if she quits we're stuck with Darleen!"

"She must be delirious from all that whoopee!"

"One time I had whoopee so long I got confused, forgot who I was."

Charlotte wasn't confused. Not at all. She knew exactly what she wanted, and this was the last step.

"Nope. Not happening! Do you hear me?" Darleen crossed her arms, shaking her head as though that alone had the power to make it not true. "There is no way you are re-signing, because I am *im*-peaching you."

"You can't *im*-peach anyone," Dottie chided. "Plus, the girl already resigned."

"But if she resigns then I get to be regent by default," Darleen screamed, knowing that the only way she'd ever be voted in as regent was if Charlotte wasn't the opposition. "And I am not a default leader!"

"Honey, that's the only way you'd ever get it." Hattie took Darleen's hand and yanked her back when she went to grab the Golden Peach. "And before you start shooting spit and making more enemies, remember that while you get the po-sition by default today, come January we have to reelect you. And I'm already voting for the other guy."

Darleen opened her mouth only to look at the disapprov-ing faces and take her seat. Even crossed her legs and folded her hands politely on the conference table, but she didn't look happy about it.

"Now," Mable said, sliding the Golden Peach back to-ward herself for safekeeping. "As the adviser I want to en-courage you to reconsider. You have done so much for this group and are an asset we'd hate to lose."

"You women gave me more than you could ever guess," Charlotte said thickly. "But you all deserve a leader who has the time to put your needs and this organization first. And after today I can't do that. If I am promoted to medical direc-tor of the Grow Clinic, that will need all of my professional attention." Charlotte shifted her focus to her father and the hospital board. "If not, then I will be leaving Sugar and taking a position at Atlanta Memorial."

That made her father nervous. Without Charlotte, the medical center would be floundering at a time when the Grow Clinic needed to be sound. She wasn't just the idea behind the clinic, she was the heart, the warrior who kept pushing through all the noes until they found their yes. The doctors who had come on board, the staff who had spent the last year training to be a part of a ground-breaking center, were all there because of Charlotte.

They would have a hard time replacing her, but finding herself a new job would be easy. She was still close with her former boss and knew they'd take her back in an instant Maybe not in the position she'd had, but she could work her way back in no time.

"Charlotte," Reginald said with a softness that made her want to say yes to whatever he asked. "Regardless of what the board decides, you know that you will always have a position here with Sugar Medical."

Good thing Charlotte wasn't a yes-girl anymore. She wasn't open to handouts or being overlooked. She wanted what she deserved.

"Actually, I'm not here as Charlotte, I'm here as Dr. Holden," she corrected, surprised to see a hint of admiration flash in her father's eyes. "And there is only one position am interested in, and it is the one I am the most qualified for. I have worked hard for this town and this hospital, and no one else can run the Grow Clinic better. Mercy Alliance sees that, the staff sees that, but if this board can't see what bring to the table then I need to go somewhere that can."

"You can't leave." He father stood, and actually appeared distraught. "You are a Holden. Your place is here."

And even though the girl in Charlotte, who longed for her father to understand and accept her without question, wanted so badly for her place to be beside her father, the older, *I Am Woman* Charlotte, who had recently learned what was important, wanted to weep for the man whose entire identity and purpose was defined by expectations of dead ancestors.

"I love you, Dad, but I belong where I can make the biggest difference. I belong with people who believe in me and what I can give." She paused and found herself smiling. "Hell, I belong with my husband."

And if there was one thing that could upstage a living-in-sin story, it was a four-time former Miss Peach using foul language when announcing news that she'd gotten hitched.

"You're married?" her mother said over the chaos. "Did she say she's married?"

"Yes, I did, Mom. I married an amazing man I love." Charlotte looked over at Hattie who was a bit shiny in the eyes. "Which makes me a McGraw. Now, if you'll excuse me, I need to go bring my husband home."

Unable to remain silent a second longer, Darleen shot to her feet, and her first words as regent were, "Wait, she gets the money, the honorable you-were-the-best-regent-we've-ever-had farewell, *and* the last McGraw?"

And as Charlotte walked out the door to find her husband, she heard her mother ask, "If she's not married to Cal, and the golf player married that Yankee last year, then…Oh my word. Did she marry the one with the tattoos?" Her mother hissed the last word as though she was talking about the evil himself.

"He's got a record, too," Hattie said, and although Charlotte couldn't see her face, she could hear the pride in her grandmother-in-law's voice. Because when McGraws loved, was a soul-deep, all-in, no-exceptions kind of thing.

And Charlotte would be crazy to let that walk out of her life.

*   *   *

Jace was pacing the back bay at Kiss My Glass Tow and Tires. Spencer was in her office taking her sweet-ass time, typing every letter with her pointer fingers, knowing that it was driving him insane.

"Your fifteen minutes ended fifteen minutes ago," he hollered.

"Keep talking and it will take fifteen more," Spencer hollered back.

Jace ran a hand down his face. He'd never felt so much pressure in his life. He'd received exactly seven texts in the last two minutes, six telling him Charlotte was on her way and one from Ben that just read: YOU'RE A PUSSY.

Truer words had never been texted before. Last night, after talking to Charlotte's dad, Jace knew that the only way to salvage her life here was to leave. He still hadn't figured out a plan, hadn't figured out how they would see each other, and the drive-by relationship that they were looking at wasn't worth her losing everything. Because it wouldn't just be her job. The second Charlotte found out that her dad, the guy who was supposed to be in her corner no matter what, had offered her position to Ben, she'd lose her belief in herself—and she'd worked too damn hard to find it again only to lose it in the next breath.

So he'd gone back to her house, packed up his things, signed the annulment, and headed for the county line. Only to stop when he got there and realize what he was leaving behind.

He'd found something he'd long ago given up expecting

to find—home. And he'd found it in his family, and his hometown, and even with his niece. Most importantly, he'd found it with Charlotte.

Jace plopped down on the stool and hung his head in his hands. Charlotte, with her big heart and grand life plans, had somehow looked beyond his reputation and troubled track record and offered her heart to the riskiest bet in town.

And he'd run.

"If I were her I'd shoot you first, then ask you what the hell," Spencer said, coming out of the office, a stack of newly printed papers in her hand. "If she did, it would make my life easier."

"Hers, too," Jace admitted.

"Well, in case you live." Spencer handed over the contract that had taken her longer to type than the Bible.

Jace flipped through it, skimmed the highlights, signing it when he was satisfied. "This is fair."

"Yay me," Spencer said, then looked over his shoulder. "A friendly reminder, you are in a family drama, marital dispute, and gun-free zone." She patted the gun on her hip. "So if you feel the need, take him outside first. Blood is a bitch to get out of concrete."

Jace turned around and his breath caught and he knew he'd made the right decision in coming back to Sugar last night.

Charlotte was standing at the entry to the bay looking so damn beautiful his chest ached. She was in one of her flowy dresses, a soft green that matched her eyes, and the sun was reflecting off her hair, which was down and spilling over her shoulders.

She was holding the annulment.

"Hey," she said, her voice calm and reserved. "I was looking for a mechanic."

"A mechanic," he repeated, the blood pounding in his head so loud he was certain he misunderstood.

"Yeah, about three or so weeks ago I came in looking for new tires, but I ended up getting an entire life overhaul. Only, last night it sputtered to a stop, and I'd like him to explain so I can get a refund."

Jace had no idea what to make of this, so he asked, "A refund?"

"And that's my cue," Spencer said. "I'm not sure if 'refund' is couples' code for sex or if this is a fight. Either way I'm officially creeped out." Spencer grabbed the contract, then a doughnut from the box, and headed into her office. "Thank you for coming. Have a nice day."

The door slammed and he was alone with the woman he loved. And there was nowhere to run.

* * *

Charlotte walked over to her husband, stopping when she was close enough to see the gentle shadows beneath his eyes, and the uncertainty and utter desolation in those intense blue pools. Jace might have an impeccable poker face but he wasn't hiding anything right then.

"I ran," he admitted. "I saw what you had created here and God, I wanted to be a part of that, a part of your world, but then I talked to your father and realized that the foundation you built was crumbling. Because of me. So I went home to talk to you, then I saw your kitchen table and bedroom and pictures on the wall, everything we'd talked about building, and I couldn't take that from you. Couldn't take your family from you. So I ran. I wish I could tell you different."

Jace looked so alone, so incredibly lost, Charlotte wanted

to reach out and hold him. Tell him that she loved him, but she knew the second they made contact she'd lose it. And this was too important.

"I waited," she said quietly. "All night. I never gave up, knowing that you had to have a good explanation, a good reason for doing what you did. But morning came and I made coffee and you never came. Then I realized that you did have a reason. You had the best reason, but I was afraid I was too late."

"Please don't say that, baby," Jace said, his face falling. "I panicked because I didn't have a plan. Not one that could give you everything you deserve."

"I deserve to have a say," she said quietly.

"I know, and that's why I'm asking you to sign that." He touched the rim of the annulment and her heart sank. That was not what she wanted to hear. "Look, I fucked up. From the start it was one mistake after another. Ah, Jesus." He ran a shaky hand down his face and grimaced. "That sounded so much better in my head, it really did. What I mean is I want to do this right. For you. You deserve for me to get this right."

The sweetness in his voice made it hard to swallow.

"Jace—" she managed.

"No, please let me finish," he begged, and even though it broke her heart she let him. "A lot of people depend on you in this town, and I want to be the kind of guy you can depend on. And I don't want a drive-by relationship. I want our first date to not be in some dive and I want it to end with a kiss at the front door. Maybe tongue, maybe not." He paused, shoved his hands in his pockets, and they trembled he was so nervous. "Probably tongue. But I want to court you, and date you, get to know your family and friends. I want to pick you up for lunch, and build little inside jokes, and bring you flowers at work. And when the time is right, I want to take you for a ride around town in my car with a sign on the back that says *I just got hitched to the hot doctor*. And I want to do that here, in Sugar, full-time."

"But what about the garage in Atlanta?" He'd worked so hard, she didn't want him to give that up.

"Atlanta doesn't have you."

"I don't want that," she admitted, then met his gaze, hers strong and steady. His crumbled right in front of her so she took his free hand and laced it with hers.

For most of Charlotte's life, acceptance and love had to be earned, it was doled out according to achievement. Not with Jace. From the beginning he had embraced her for who she was. Even now he was trying to give her the ridiculous courtship she'd always said she wanted, because he knew it wasn't ridiculous to her. He'd given her the wonderful gift of unconditional acceptance, a gift that changed her life, and now it was time to give that gift back to him.

"I want you to have your dream garage, and I want the marriage we have."

"But people will know that we kept it a secret," he said. "It could cost you the position."

"I choose you, Jace," she said, her voice shaking. "I choose you over a job or a title or even my family. I choose you for exactly who you are and where you've been. I choose your hugs and naptime shenanigans. I choose the guy who remembered what dress I wore to my interview and the guy who smiles when he talks about his nieces but frowns when he talks about anyone else in his family."

She stepped forward and placed a hand on his chest, and she felt him shudder. "I choose you because I love you. I love that you rebuilt your dad's car, punched some jerk out for mistreating his girlfriend, and I love that everything with you feels like a great adventure. But most of all, Jace McGraw, I love that you love so deeply and intensely that sometimes you have to run just to breathe."

She stepped even closer so he could see the conviction in her eyes. "But know that no matter how far you run, I will be right next to you. I let you walk away once and it was the biggest mistake of my life." She cupped his cheek, which was rough against her hand. But the look in his eyes was soft enough to melt her heart. "You're my home, Jace. Let me be yours. Wherever that is."

"I love you," he said, relief in his tone. "I have loved you every single second of every single day for the past four years. Maybe even longer. But when I saw you in that bar, wearing those boots, I knew you were trouble, knew that one taste and I'd be a goner."

He lifted their twined hands to his mouth and kissed her fingers. "Everything is sweeter with you. I love you, Charlie. You are my home. My everything."

Charlotte felt her eyes tear up and her heart expand with love. She took the annulment and tossed it over her shoulder, then went up on her toes and showed him just how sweet she could be.

When she pulled back he asked, "When you said you 'didn't want that,' did you mean just the dating part or staying in Sugar?"

"I want to be wherever life takes us," she admitted, loving the way his arms circled her waist, holding her as though he'd never let go.

"Thank God," he said. "I just signed a year lease with Spencer to rent out half her shop. If I renege she might shoot me."

"You're opening your shop here?"

He shrugged. "Seems like I am a pretty big deal. I already

have three teams who want to hire me to consult and send me their engines. Even if I live in Sugar. Go figure." He smiled. "Now, you still want to talk about that refund?"

She returned his smile, her heart so light she felt as if she were flying. She didn't know exactly what the future held but that was the part she was the most excited about. Life with Jace would be unpredictable, and messy, and beautifully full. "Yup. I want my three or so weeks back. But with lots of public displays of affection."

"How about I take your three or so weeks and match you with forever," he said, pulling her to him for the first daily kiss of the rest of their lives.

Epilogue

A month later

Charlotte stood at the top of the steps, looking down at Jace. It was the beginning of December, and a light dusting of snow covered the ground and the dock, making the day more magical than Charlotte could have imagined.

And Jace, he looked even more handsome than she could have imagined, too. He was dressed in black slacks, a sky-blue button-down that fit his big, built body to perfection, a tie, and a black leather riding jacket, taking the whole lethal GQ to mouthwatering levels.

Her very own sex pistol.

"What are you doing here?" she asked, pulling her coat tightly around her. "You aren't supposed to see me yet."

Charlotte had kept her dress over at Glory's so Jace would stop snooping through the closet. She'd caught him on three separate occasions trying to peek in the canvas dress bag, and she didn't want to give him a fourth shot. Not when she wanted today to go perfectly.

"And miss our morning ritual?" He held up two to-go

cups. "Plus, I wanted to be the first to see you," he said with a smile that was all trouble.

She liked trouble, as he well knew, which was why she slowly undid the belt of her coat. With a secret smile all her own, she stopped. "Unless you'd like to do the honors?"

Jace was on her in two seconds flat, setting the mugs on the porch rail. His hands made themselves comfortable at her waist, his eyes were on her mouth. He leaned in for a nuzzle then stopped and pulled back. Eyes narrowed. "You smell like mint? Did you start without me?"

"No, I had ice cream for breakfast," she said. "It's a big day, you know."

"Oh, I know." His eyes went the length of her, and he ran a finger over her coat's belt. "May I, Doctor?"

Charlotte put her hands on his shoulders and watched as he slowly untied the belt, then eased his fingers between the layers and popped the first button. Then the second. And the higher he got the harder she was breathing.

"Last one," he said. His fingers hovered over her breast. Eyes on her, he popped it and the coat fell open and she heard the air whoosh out of his lungs. Her lungs were whooshing, too, the desire on his face did that to her.

"Do you like the dress?" she whispered when he just kept staring.

"Savoring. Need a minute."

She did him one even better, she took the lapels of the coat and pulled it all the way open, giving him a view that he'd remember until the day he died. His eyes roamed over her, then his hands, exploring every single inch of the dress.

He got to her waist and ran his palms over the little bow and then up to touch the delicate scalloped neckline.

"Just like I remembered," he said.

"I made it from memory." He looked up at her words, his eyes heavy-lidded. "No knitting needles, but there was some hand stitching involved in the hemline. And I assure you it was all very domestic."

"I do love domestic," he said, scooping her up off the porch to cradle her to his chiseled chest. "But domestic will have to wait until quitting time, because right now, Doctor, you are running late for your first day of work."

Jace walked her down the steps and ceremoniously placed her in the front seat of his Stingray. He leaned over, strapped her in, spending a little longer than necessary with the buckle, then gave her one hell of a good-morning kiss. "And we can't have the new medical director late for the grand opening of the clinic."

Jace shut her door then walked around the car. He climbed in and handed her an insulated lunch sack—it was I-am-woman pink. "What's this?"

With that boyish grin she loved, he opened the bag and inside were all of her favorites. He pointed to the peanut butter and banana sandwich and peach. "For lunch. And for after." He held up a doughnut, then pulled four quarters out of the side pocket, the exact amount needed for an ice-cream bar. "In case *after* isn't enough for you."

A flash of blue lace caught her eye in the bottom of the bag. She pulled out the fabric, a sky-blue G-string dangling from her fingers, and sent him a sidelong glance. "And that's this for?"

"The ride home," he said with so much heat her body shimmered. "Now hold on, I only have six minutes to get you across town so you can cut the ribbon, and I want to take a slow drive down Maple Street first, to show off my smoking-hot wife."

"I love you, Jace."

"I love you, Dr. McGraw." Jace cranked the engine and let it purr. "One taste and I knew you were it. You were home," he said as he stepped on the gas and they sped down the road and toward the best forever she could have ever dreamed.

Romance blooms in a charming
small town in Marina Adair's
LAST KISS OF SUMMER.

Read on for a preview.

Chapter 1

Kennedy Sinclair had taken only two steps toward her new life and already her toes were beginning to pinch.

"I don't think I have what it takes," she admitted, ploping down on the changing room bench to loosen the buckles on her new *Comme Il Faut* ballroom dance shoes, sighing as the blood rushed back to her feet. The red satin straps were trouble enough—looping tightly around the ankle and pulling across the tops of her toes, pinching off all circulation—but the heels were the real problem. Staggering toothpicks that added enough height to cause light-headedness and excessive teetering. A result, no doubt, of attempting to perform aerobic activity in depleted oxygen zones.

Or her body's preference for practical.

Too bad for her feet, she was done with practical. At least for the summer, she thought, taking in her matching cardigan set, glasses, and hair secured with a pencil at the back of her neck. Sure, right then, she supposed she resembled the bookkeeper that she was. But in a week's time, the summer semester at the culinary school she did bookkeeping for would end and she would be in Argentina—spending the next few months in the most exciting way possible.

Getting engaged.

"Engaged," she whispered to herself. A warm bubble of giddiness bounced around her stomach and tickled her heart.

Her boyfriend of four years, Philip, had been selected for an educational exchange program, teaching elevated Southern cuisine for the fall semester at one of the top culinary schools in South America. Not that anyone was surprised by the honor. Philip was handsome, charismatic and the youngest master chef at Le Cordon Bleu School in Atlanta. In addition to being the perfect boyfriend—he scored a solid 9.9 on the compatibility test she gave him on their first date—he was so dedicated to his career that he'd elevated the school to worldwide acclaim.

Sometimes he was almost too dedicated. Not that there was anything wrong with that. Dedicated people tended to be reliable and stable. They had the ability to see things through—something her perpetually unemployed mother could benefit from. But lately Philip had spent so much time heating up his teaching kitchen, he couldn't even manage a simple tangled-sheets stir-fry when he got home.

So when he asked Kennedy to go with him to Argentina days after she'd found a sizing slip to her favorite vintage jewelry shop, she'd nearly exploded into tears. And had been walking around in a bliss-induced haze ever since.

She'd once read that traveling together ignites romance and intimacy between couples, opens the lines of communication, and builds healthy relationships. So it was the perfect time for them to reconnect, to take their relationship to that next level in an exotic land—to make that commitment into forever.

For her to have a long-overdue orgasm.

What better way to embrace what was to come, than with a new pair of shoes that made her feel sexy, spontaneous, and exotic. Daring even. There hadn't been a lot of opportunity for that in her life. She'd been too busy trying to find a safe harbor in an unpredictable childhood, which left her a little uptight. Okay, she was obsessed with organization and order, but now that she had a secure future ahead of her, and a stable man by her side, it was time to push the comfort of their relationship a little and experiment with new things.

Standing again, precariously balanced on her heels, she looked at her toes in the changing room mirror, then to the sensible cream flats she'd been dancing in for the past few months they'd been taking lessons. The flats matched her outfit—and her future if she didn't do something now to spice it up.

A loud thump sounded from the changing room beside her, followed by a low moan. Thinking someone had teetered right out of their heels, Kennedy pressed her ear to the wall.

"Is everything okay in there?" she asked, dropping to her knees when the only response was another thump, this one vibrating the wall between them.

A similar pair of mile-high red heels stood on the other side of the divider, fastened around a set of gorgeous tanned legs, which had a little gold anklet with an orchid charm dangling.

Oh my God! It was their tango teacher, Gloria. The woman who had inspired Kennedy to come to class early and try on the red shoes in the first place. The twenty-two-year-old Latin ballroom champion had legs to her neck, enough hip action to tempt the pope, and wore raw sex appeal like most women wore perfume.

And speaking of hip action!

Kennedy covered her eyes, then peeked through the cracks of her fingers to watch as a pair of black and white, very classy, very masculine, wing-tipped shoes stepped toe to toe with the red heels, one of which lifted off the ground to lightly trace up the outside edge of her partner's leg and wrap around in a perfect *caricia*.

The wing tips stepped even closer, another thump ensued, then Kennedy heard the telltale sound of a zipper lowering.

Frozen, Kennedy watched as the wing tips started rocking in a perfect T-A-N-G-O rhythm, working toward, what Kennedy *knew*, would be a standing O. Back and forth they swayed as the soft moans turned louder and the panting drifted under the dressing room door.

Kennedy found her hands were a little sweaty because for the first time in her life, she didn't have the right answer. Should she sneak out of the room and run for it?

A good choice, except she'd never been all that graceful and didn't have a sneaky bone in her body. Even worse, the hinges on the changing room door squeaked when she had come in, and getting caught would make for an awkward class. And she really loved their class.

It was the one hour a week when she had Philip all t

herself, his undivided attention as he'd swept her across the floor, making her feel elegant and feminine. For a woman born with the coordination of a gazelle in snowshoes, it was something of a feat—something she wasn't willing to lose.

Which left hiding until they finished. An option that rather intrigued her. In fact, Kennedy felt embarrassed, intrigued, and a little bit naughty all at the same time. She also felt a tinge of disappointment, which started in her chest and moved up into her throat, because leaving the lights on was as kinky as Philip got. So this might be as close as Kennedy would ever be to a standing-O-Tango.

With that sobering realization, she took a seat, pulled her knees to her chest, and stared at the wall. Which was all kinds of ridiculous.

It wasn't as if she could see anything through the wood divider, but sitting there in her red shoes gave her the courage to imagine. Only she didn't have to imagine much since the thumping got louder—and so did the dancing duo next door.

"*Ai, papi*," Gloria said, her accent making every vowel sound like a promise. "You are such a good *lo-bar*."

"Uh," was all Mr. *Lo-bar* said. A single release of air that was neither sexy nor expected from an experienced Latin Lover. It was more of an admission that he'd had all he could handle. Not that Kennedy was judging—she had crested her comfort level about two moans back.

"Yes! Yes, *papi*," Gloria mewed and Kennedy closed her eyes. She had to. She was a private person by nature and tried her best to respect others' privacy, so the guilt began to build low in her belly. But before it could settle, Gloria cried out. "Just like *zat*, *Phil-ep*."

Kennedy's eves flew open and the guilt quickly faded to confusion and finally shock. She climbed on the bench to get a look at this Latin lover *Phil-ep* who uttered a simple "Uh" in the throes of passion.

Breath left her body as her heart tried to adjust, to make room for the familiar ache of disappointment pressing in. Because there on the other side of the divider, with his pants around his ankles and another woman around his waist, was the man she lived with, the man she'd planned to spend the rest of her life with, executing moves with Gloria that told Kennedy this wasn't their first tango.

No, it appeared that *Phil-ep* was just exotic people's talk for a cheating, rat bastard of a boyfriend, and suddenly the past few months made sense. His shift in schedule, his sudden interest in "extra" dance classes, the way he pretended to be asleep when Kennedy would snuggle up behind him at night.

She didn't remember making a sound, or maybe the blood rushing through her ears made it hard to hear, but suddenly Philip looked up—and froze. At least she thought it was Philip. Right height, right build, right piercing blue eyes behind wire-rimmed glasses, but he looked different somehow.

"What are you doing here," was all he said. No "I'm sorry," or "Whoops, I tripped and accidentally ended up having sex with another woman," or "Please forgive me." Just "What are you doing here," as though this were somehow her fault.

Maybe it was. What kind of woman didn't know when her boyfriend was sleeping with someone else?

The kind who puts all her eggs in the wrong basket. A trait that had been passed down from Sinclair mother to

Sinclair daughter for five generations. A trait that Kennedy had spent a lifetime trying to overcome, without much luck.

Until today.

"You know what, *Phil-ep?* I have no idea what I'm doing here," she said then stepped off the bench.

Grabbing her purse, she walked out of the changing room, proud that she wasn't toppling over in the heels.

"Wait," Philip said and she heard a lot of rustling of fabric from his stall, but she didn't stop, refused to wait. She'd waited four years for him to pop the question, four years for him to take her on a vacation, to show her the world like he'd promised, and now she was tired of waiting.

Only Philip had always been an efficient dresser and incredibly quick, as Gloria must already know, so he was out of his stall and in front of her before she could make her escape.

"Let's talk about this."

"I am a visual learner, Philip, I think I understand. Tab A, slot B, no further explanation needed." Plus, there was nothing he could say that could make this any less painful—or more humiliating.

"I didn't mean for it to end this way."

Except that, she thought, her heart beating so fast she was afraid it would pop right out of her chest. He'd just broken up with her, in a public dressing room, with his fly down and his mistress listening to every word.

Part of her wanted to ask *why?* Why did everyone else always seem to move on before she got the memo that it was over?

"Well, it didn't end 'this way,'" she said. "Because I reject your pathetic breakup since I broke up with you the second you became *Mr. Lo-bar.*"

He stuffed his hands in his pockets, only to remove them when he realized his fly parted. "I never meant to hurt you, Kennedy. It's just that we're so"—he looked at her starched pants and shirt and sighed—"solid."

"Most people would think that solid was a good thing." It was one of her biggest strengths, right along with reliable, steady, accountable.

The look he gave her said that he wasn't most people; that he was no longer looking for solid. Maybe he never had been. Maybe she'd been nothing more than someone to fill the gap between life's high points. A position Kennedy knew well.

"It is, but we've become so predictable"—he shrugged—"boring."

"Excuse me?" she said, the words getting caught on the humiliation that was clogging her throat.

"There is a color-coded, itemized itinerary for our Argentina trip on the fridge." He said it like that was a bad thing. "With Gloria, everything is fun and unexpected and new. Exciting."

Kennedy wanted to argue that she could be fun and exciting, too, try new things. *She* was the one who submitted his application for Argentina—not that *she* was going anymore. *She* had signed them up for dance classes. But then she thought of Gloria and her Latin moves and impulsive tendencies, and figured Philip wasn't willing to settle for classes anymore when he could have the real thing.

"With her, *I'm* exciting," he added.

"Exciting?" she asked, heavy on the sarcasm. The man

thought golfing without a caddy was living on the edge. "You need a humidifier to sleep at night."

At one time Kennedy had thought he'd needed her, too. Just last semester he told her how he slept better, breathed easier, had less stress in his day knowing that she had his back at work and she'd be there when he got home.

Every cell of Kennedy froze in sheer horror because— *oh my God*—she was his humidifier. Kennedy Sinclair, winner of Berkeley's esteemed THE WORLD'S YOUR ABACUS award, was a certified life humidifier. Ironic because in that moment, with her whole *solid* world crashing down around her, she found it hard to breathe.

* * *

Whoever said one could never really go home obviously wasn't a Sinclair, because later that night, with all of her worldly possessions in the trunk, a bag of mostly eaten cookies in her lap, and a light dusting of powdered sugar everywhere in between, Kennedy pulled into her grandmother's drive. She'd made this journey a thousand times as a kid, the inevitable walk of shame to Grandma's house whenever her mother's world fell apart.

Only now that she was an adult, making the same pilgrimage felt so much worse. Maybe because it was *her* world falling apart or maybe because instead of packing for her first big adventure—which didn't come from a book or movie—she was once again packing up her entire life, forced to start over.

It was as if Sinclair women were destined to wind up alone and displaced. A disturbing thought, since Kennedy had done everything right, everything in her power to avoid ending up like her mother. The right school, right profession, right man. Yet there she was, single, homeless, and as of tomorrow, unemployed.

From a job she really loved. Balancing books at a culinary institute was the only way to blend her profession and her hobby—baking sweets.

Shoving another cookie in her mouth, Kennedy bent down to pop the trunk, crumbs falling out of God knew where and littering the floorboard. Wiping her mouth on the sleeve of her hoodie, she stepped out of the car, grabbed her suitcase, and walked up the brick pathway to the modest-sized Queen Anne–style house.

Even before her feet hit the landing, she knew Grandma Edna had stayed up and was waiting for her arrival. The "dreaming swing," which hung in the corner of the porch, was moving idly. Perched happily inside with Amos and Andy, her two cats, was Edna Sinclair.

All soft curves and frosted tips, she wore a teal house robe, matching crocheted slippers, and a warm smile. She also had a single strip of toilet paper wrapped around her curlers and secured with bobby pins.

"I'm home," Kennedy said, dropping her suitcase on the welcome mat, which read, WENT BIG AND CAME HOME.

"Figured it was either that or I was about to be robbed." Edna glanced at Kennedy's black hoodie pulled over her head and yoga pants. "Glad it's you, seeing as I made cookies and the boys don't like to share none."

The "boys" sent her their best *disrupt our pet time and we will pee on your bed* glare.

"I made cookies, too." She held up the bag, which was surprisingly light, and joined her grandmother on the swing. They both had to scoot down to accommodate

Andy's swishing tail. "Snacked on them on the way over."

"I can see that," Edna said, brushing at Kennedy's shoulder and unleashing an avalanche of crumbs onto Amos's back. He growled, his little whiskers doing double time.

"Snowball cookies." Kennedy rubbed at a large cluster of crumbs that had collected in her cleavage, but it made only a white smear, so she shrugged and gave up. "They're Philip's favorite. I made a batch while I was packing."

"Did you leave him any?"

Kennedy shook her head. "Just a dirty kitchen. And my resignation."

"That was nice of you." Edna patted her knee and Kennedy's eyes started to burn. "Most women would have assumed letting the air out of his tires was word enough."

Most Sinclair women would have shot first, asked questions second, and then let him pull up his pants after they felt they'd been properly heard. But Kennedy had always been the more reserved one in her family.

"I wrote it in Sharpie across all of his dry cleaning that I had just picked up," she admitted.

"There's that creative, passionate girl I know," Edna said and an unexpected flicker of excitement ignited at her grandmother's words. No one had called her creative and passionate since she was a girl. Instead of being embarrassed by her impulsive behavior, she gave in to it, surprised at how liberating it felt.

Almost as powerful an emotion as the choking fear of not knowing what was next. Of how she was expected to pick up and move on—again.

Torn between laughing and crying, Kennedy settled on

staring out at the Georgia sky and letting the gentle evening breeze be her guide. Like Kennedy, Edna lived in the greater Atlanta area, which meant that the city lights snuffed out most of the stars, leaving an inky blanket over the city. But tonight, there were a few bold ones whose twinkle was bright enough to break through the night and be seen. And for some reason that made Kennedy smile.

"I miss that girl," Edna said, wrapping a pudgy arm around Kennedy's shoulder and pulling her close.

"I do, too." Without hesitation, Kennedy snuggled in deeper, wrapping her arms around Edna's middle and breathing in the familiar scent of cinnamon and vanilla and everything that was safe. One sniff and Kennedy felt her smile crumble and the tears well up.

"They were doing it during the light of day against the wall of a dressing room," she whispered. "With their shoes on. He's never asked me to keep my shoes on."

"Of course he didn't," Edna cooed. "You're a respectable woman who knows the value of a good pair of shoes."

Oh God. Even her grandmother thought she was respectable, and everyone knew that *respectable* was just another word for boring. And boring people wound up living in their childhood bedroom at thirty with the neighborhood crazy cat lady as their roommate. "What if I wanted to keep my shoes on?"

"With what he's been stepping in lately, you should count yourself lucky," her grandma cooed.

"Gloria's the lucky one. He's taking her to Argentina next week." And there went the tears.

She tried to hold them back, but sitting there in her grandmother's arms, once again being the one snuffed out by something—or someone—bigger and brighter, brought back every time her mom had taken off with some guy on some other adventure, leaving Kennedy at home.

"He's the one who cheated, the one who lied, and he still gets to go teach in Argentina, and cross something off his bucket list. And I am stuck in another life time-out." A realization that not only sucked, but also challenged every belief she'd ever held dear. Including the belief in herself.

"That just means you get to check something off your *own* list now."

"That was my list. Argentina was *my* dream." Then it became their dream, and somehow Philip would get to be the one to live it.

"Ah, child, then find a new dream, something fun that doesn't include listening to all that wheezing the jackass does when he gets excited," Edna said, stroking Kennedy's hair.

Kennedy chuckled. "One time he snored so loud, our neighbors thought we were doing it all night."

"Probably thought he'd taken one of those blue pills," Edna said in the same tone she'd read a bedtime story. "Philip doesn't strike me as the most resilient man."

He wasn't, but Kennedy hadn't been interested in sprinters; she was looking for someone who was slow and steady. Only her best chance at going the distance had handed his baton to another woman.

"How can I have any fun when I know he's out there living his life, having shoes on while making whoopee, and tangoing all over my future?"

A future Kennedy had worked so hard to make safe. With a man she thought she could trust.

Edna tsked. "Even as a little bit of a thing, you were so

busy making checks and balances, you let the fun pass you by. Maybe this was God's way of saying you need to let go of the future you planned, and take some time to taste the icing."

The size of a large child, Kennedy still was a little bit of a thing who didn't know the first thing about life's icing. Hadn't had the luxury. Between her unstable childhood then working toward gaining fiscal stability, she hadn't had a lot of time for dreaming, let alone something that whimsical. Sadly, the closest she'd ever come to eating the icing was a fun four years working the morning shifts at a little bakery near campus to put herself through business school.

"I wouldn't even know where to start," she admitted, her voice thick with emotion.

"How about with one of these?" Edna pulled an old journal out from beside her and set it on Kennedy's lap. It was pink, pocket sized, had a well-worn spine and a picture of a cupcake with sprinkles on the cover.

The hurt and disappointment had settled so deep inside, it had turned into aching numbness by the time she'd walked out of her downtown loft for the last time, so she assumed any more pain would be impossible. Yet as she clicked open the gold-plated latch, which was rusty from years of neglect, and saw the swirly handwriting at the top, her chest tightened further.

This disappointment felt different, as though it originated from someplace old and forgotten, and it packed the kind of punch that made speaking impossible.

Kennedy wasn't sure how she managed to let herself stray so far from her life's goal. She hadn't felt the kind of hope and excitement that was apparent in the words she'd written since she discovered that while most people were looking for a copilot to happiness, not everyone had what it took to be more than just a brief stopover. Sadly for Kennedy, she'd figured out early on which category she fell into.

"'Life's short so eat the icing first,'" she read as her finger traced lightly over the words on the first page. Edna had given it to her the summer she'd turned thirteen, when Candice Sinclair had taken off with a truck driver from Ashland, leaving a brokenhearted Kennedy behind with her grandmother.

Kennedy was still naive enough to believe that one day her mother would take her along. That one day the two of them would see the country together like Candice promised. By July, Kennedy had realized that if she were going to live an exciting life, then she'd have to make it happen herself. And she took the *icing first* rule to heart and entered an apple and rhubarb pie in the State Fair. She'd found the recipe in an old cookbook, and Edna had spent hours with her in the kitchen helping her perfect it. Her entry won third place in the junior category, earning her two tickets to the theater in Atlanta. Something she'd always wanted to do, but her grandmother could never afford.

"Look at you, set to take on the world," Edna said, pointing to a photo of Kennedy as a teen. She stood in front of a table filled with winning cakes, lanky and still finding her feet, but the smile she wore was so bright, it burned Kennedy's heart.

She was wearing her favorite blue summer dress that her grandmother had made especially for the fair, and pinned to the front was a third place ribbon.

"I thought I lost this recipe," Kennedy said, looking at the swirly writing on the adjacent page. She'd also forgotten how excited she'd felt when she'd won that ribbon. It was as if she'd finally found some kind of tangible proof that maybe she was special.

Kennedy turned the page and a watery smile spread across her face. There was a photo of her grandma dressed like the queen, wearing pearls, white gloves, and a hat fit for a royal wedding.

"I borrowed the pearls from Pastor Cunningham's wife, and the gloves from Mabel," Edna said, nostalgia lacing her voice.

"You made me that dress," Kennedy said. She'd loved that dress, wore it until it went from midi to mini, and Edna said she was giving too much away for free.

"It's still in the attic."

Beneath each photo was the sweet creation that made that moment possible. A three-tier coconut cake, a recipe straight from her grandmother's Southern roots, that she made the following year. It took second place and she won high tea at the Ritz-Carlton in Atlanta.

It was her fourth attempt, though, a perfect Southern apple and red currant pie with a Georgia pecan crust, that took first place, then took her on a six-week Down Home Sweets journey at the local culinary school, cementing her fascination with small town living, Southern eats, and a deep love for baking.

Kennedy carefully thumbed through the pages of photos capturing some of the most precious moments of her childhood, the respective recipes that made it all possible. Ignoring the photo of her and Edna cooking snowball cookies in their pajamas on Christmas morning, since that recipe would now forever be connected to that rat-fink *lo-bar* and his pathetic "Uh" in the throws of passion, she stopped when she found what she was looking for. At the back of the journal was an extensive and itemized list she'd assembled, her LIFE'S ICING list, which indexed every recipe she wanted to try, every competition she wanted to enter, and every goal she wanted to accomplish, complete with coordinating check boxes.

Not a single one was marked off.

With a shaky breath, Kennedy flipped the page and scanned each item, stopping midway through when her heart gave a little stir.

☐ 39. Make a *Rogel torta* with *dulce de leche*.

She wasn't sure that she had quite mastered the flair for creating the soft, but crumbly texture of that variation of dulce de leche in the Confections of South America class he took over the summer. Let alone something as intricate as the layers of puff pastry required to make one of Argentina's most treasured desserts. But since Philip had robbed her of checking off the first and most important recipe on her list, a *Five-Tiered Wedding Cake*, she was taking what he could get. Because somewhere along the way she'd forgotten that she needed to be in charge of her own destiny.

She remembered it now.

"What I need is a job." One that would allow her to get new apartment, get back on her feet. Although she had some savings, she needed to make sure her bank account had enough padding so that when she started writing those checks, they didn't bounce.

"Already got you one lined up," Edna said, handing her a printout of a job listing for a pie shop. "It comes with a little frosting, too."

"What's this?"

"Sweetie Pies," Edna said, snatching the paper back and flipping to the next page to display several photos of a quaint brick storefront and their award-winning pies, including the five-pound Deep Dish HumDinger. Between the sixteen Gold Tins hanging in the window and the title of "Best Apple Pie in the Country," the two women in the photo were undoubtedly looking for a true, down-home baker. Kennedy was sadly neither.

"My old friend Fiona owns it with her sister-in-law. She e-mailed me that ad."

"You called her? About me?"

"Of course I did."

"When?" Kennedy's life was still shoved in her trunk.

"The second you said you were heading home," Edna tutted. "Picked up the phone to see if she was looking for some help for the harvest season. Even told her that my granddaughter is a college graduate with a fancy degree from a fancy school, and works at Le Cordon Bleu."

Kennedy was the first Sinclair to finish college, something that gave Edna bragging rights on her side of town. Because people who grew up in this neighborhood seldom got out. But Kennedy had, and there was no way she could go back.

"I worked in an office at Le Cordon Bleu. Writing checks and balancing payroll, not baking pies," Kennedy reminded her grandmother.

"You bake on the weekends, take classes every chance you get," Edna said. "And still manage to win awards."

"I was a teenager, it was the junior category, at the Georgia State Fair." Kennedy looked at the picture of the shop again. It was exactly what she'd dreamed of working in when she'd been a girl. Charming, welcoming, and looked like a mother's kitchen should look—sweet, warm, and a safe place to land. Then she read the address and her head started to pound. "The shop is in Washington State?"

"Destiny Bay. It's a little town on the southern border of Washington, nestled between the Cascades and the Pacific Ocean. Known for apples and, since Fi started baking, pies. It's the perfect place for you to find a new future."

"Destiny Bay?" It sounded perfect. Even the way it rolled off the lips implied it was the kind of place she could go and forget about her problems at home. Create a new life.

Only running away was a classic Candice move, and Kennedy would rather take dance classes from Gloria than be like her mother. Then again, she didn't really have a home any longer, so it wasn't as though she would be techically running away. "Isn't that where you met Grandpa Harvey?"

"I met him in Seattle, near where I grew up, but followed him all the way to Destiny Bay, where he got down on one knee, right there in the middle of town, with a bouquet of spring posies and his mama's ring." Edna sighed dreamily, as if remembering the day, and Kennedy gave in to the romantic nature of her story. "Met Fiona there, too, she was my maid of honor, my best friend, and the person who took me in when Harvey moved to Tuscaloosa, making it clear it was a journey for one. Fi gave me a job selling apples on her family's plantation so I wouldn't starve to death."

Kennedy sat up and shook all that romantic naïveté right off.

She was a finance girl, not a frivolous girl—and baking pies in the meantime to get over a broken heart only prolonged getting her life back on track. And kept the Sinclair curse alive and well. Which was why she refused the urge to make a life-changing decision because of a man.

"I don't want to spend the last few weeks of my summer baking pies. I need to buckle down and find a new job."

"Oh, you wouldn't just be baking, honey." Edna leaned in and lowered her voice as though she was imparting a national secret. "I have it on good word that Fi isn't looking for short-term help, she and her sister-in-law co-own it and are looking to pass on their legacy. They're looking for a strong-willed, sensible woman, who loves baking and is brave enough to carve out a little slice of life's pie for herself."

"And there aren't any of those in their hometown?"

Edna laughed. "Fi's got herself a slew of nephews, and Paula a son, but not a single female in the family. And Paula's got the arthritis, which is why Fi's still baking pie every day even though she's got more miles on her than my old DeSoto. She's ready to slow down and retire, and Paula needs to give her joints a rest and go on that cruise they've been blabbering on about. They're just waiting for the right owner to come along."

Now it was Kennedy's turn to laugh. "And you think that's me?"

"I think this is one of those opportunities we always talked about, where with a little courage and a lot of hard work, you can change your life."

Kennedy felt her throat tighten. How many times had

she sat right there on the porch swing and wished she could change? Her situation, her options... her life.

And she had.

It'd taken years of hard work and perseverance, but Kennedy had created that new life she dreamed of. A posh downtown apartment, a respectable job, and a man who represented everything her childhood and upbringing lacked.

Only as fate would have it, Philip found her lacking, and Kennedy had lost it all.

Nope. Courage wasn't the problem. Neither was hard work. Kennedy hadn't figured out the difference between an option and an opportunity—between loyalty and love.

"We don't know if it would be a change for the better," Kennedy said.

"That's what's so exciting," Edna said, her eyes lit with excitement. "You can either spend the rest of your life like I did, pushing someone else's pencils and dreams, and end up right here on this front porch, or you could start making some of your own come true."

A strange lightness filled her belly, warming the parts of her soul that had moments ago felt hollow, because suddenly the ridiculous idea didn't seem so ridiculous.

Kennedy had gone into business because she loved the idea of owing her own company, building something of her own that no one could take from her. And this opportunity seemed to combine her two loves with what she was trained to do. But there was one thing Kennedy couldn't seem to get past.

She rested her head on Edna's shoulder and admitted, "I can't even plan my own life, let alone a business." Especially a pie shop in small town Washington.

"Honey, you came out of the womb planning. It's what you do."

A slow panic started to churn in her stomach, moving faster and faster, until she regretted eating three dozen snowballs. Because wasn't that exactly what Philip had said?

"She's willing to sell it to you for a bargain." Edna pulled out a packet from underneath Amos, who let loose a throaty growl, and handed it over. "She almost sold it last year to another buyer, but changed her mind when the woman started talking franchising. Here is the contract she'd had drawn up, told me to have you look it over and give her a call if you were interested."

Kennedy straightened and flipped through the papers. F and Edna had both gone through a hassle putting this to gether so quickly; it was the least she could do.

She took her time, read every word, and decided that i was a standard sales agreement, straightforward and easy to understand. Then she reached the overview of the finan cials and felt her eyes bulge a little. "Her pie shop mad more money last year than Philip did."

"And it was a slow year since they closed up for te weeks last spring to take one of those senior trips t Alaska," Edna said, sounding wistful.

Kennedy looked over at the woman who had raised he and felt her heart turn over. The dreamy look on her fac over the idea of a vacation was a painful reminder of ju how much Edna had sacrificed. She'd spent some of he best years raising Kennedy, and most of her retiremen savings sending Kennedy to Georgia Tech. Kennedy wa diligent about paying her grandmother back, but with he student loans and bills, it was slow coming. Owning th business could change all of that.

"How much is she asking?"

Her grandmother rattled off a number.

"That's it?" Not that it wasn't a lot of money. It was. In fact, it would nearly wipe out Kennedy's entire life savings. But based on the shop's financials, the price seemed extremely low. Which meant either that Edna needed to get her hearing aid checked, or Fi wasn't being honest about the profits.

"Oh, that's the down payment, honey. But since Fi owns the property outright, she's willing to carry the note so you can pay her in monthly installments, with a small balloon payment due at the end of every fiscal year. She also said she'll sell you a few acres' worth of her special apples at cost for the lifetime of the shop and let you stay in her caretaker's house for six months rent-free, so you can get the apartment above the shop cleaned up."

"It comes with an apartment?" This deal couldn't get any sweeter. Having an apartment would allow her to save up enough money for a down payment on her own home someday—one that didn't have a live-in heartbreak waiting to happen.

One that belonged to her.

"The store, the apartment, her recipes, supplies, and name are all yours if you say yes." Edna smiled. "Did I mention Fi's apple pie is a sixteen-time Gold Tin winner?"

Kennedy gasped. Only the highest honor any pie could receive, and it explained the incredible numbers. It was too good to be true, which in Kennedy's world meant it was.

"What's the catch?" Kennedy asked, her eyes narrowing. "And what happens if I can't pull it off? Or I can't make a balloon payment?"

"No catch. But if you default on the payments, the shop

passes back to Fi," Edna said as if the word *default* were no big deal. As if it didn't cause perspiration to break out on Kennedy's hands and her stomach to roll with unease. After a lifetime of being passed back and forth, only to eventually be passed over by the people who were supposed to love her forever, it was terrifying.

And sure, money would be filtering in for her half of the condo she and Philip had shared. But she had no idea when he could make that happen or how much it would even be worth—details she wasn't ready to face. And money she couldn't rely on.

"Look at you, already planning yourself right out of an opportunity," Edna said softly, taking Kennedy's hand in her frail one, and giving a pat that connected with every insecurity Kennedy tried so desperately to control. "The worst that can happen is that it doesn't work out, you check a few things off your list, get a chance to live in a new and exciting place, and have memories that will last a lifetime."

In true Sinclair fashion, Edna completely overlooked that she'd also wind up broke and homeless. Then again, Kennedy was already the latter, and she'd spent most of her life being the former. But she'd never been a failure—until now.

She felt the familiar crushing disappointment close in but refused to let it take hold. Because, while the setback caused from her chaotic childhood were out of her control, she'd chosen the path with Philip.

And she could choose a new path, a path of her own, she told herself, because more than her fear of failing was the fear that she'd be sidelined for the rest of her life. Spend her career behind a desk, managing other people's dreams and never stepping out to go after something of her own.

Maybe this was her chance. Sure, it didn't come in the package that Kennedy expected, but sometimes the best opportunities presented themselves in the most unexpected ways. And hadn't she just been wishing for some excitement in her simple life?

Kennedy pulled her phone from her sweatshirt pocket, and swallowing down all the *what-if*s that would normally have her wearing out her cream ballet flats, she clicked on the selfie mode of her camera and said, "Smile, Grandma. I need a new photo to go next to my snowball cookies."

"Of you covered in crumbs and crying?"

"Nope, of me going after a little icing." And Kennedy snapped the photo.

Chapter 2

Kennedy was so tired, she wasn't sure what day it wa when she finally saw the giant pie-shaped sign that said SWEETIE PIES. But the second she stepped out onto the cob blestone sidewalk and took in the crisp costal air, all th stress and worry she'd been carrying for the past four day and twenty-five hundred miles vanished.

The daylight was long gone, but a million twinkl lights lit up nearly every storefront on Main Street, whil gas lamps lined the sidewalks, casting a warm glow ove the town square. Every shop had a brick face, a brightl colored awning, and an array of flowers on the window sills.

Kennedy closed her eyes, and if she listened har enough, she could hear seagulls squawking and wave crashing against the rocks in the distance.

"You were right, Grandma," Kennedy whispered und her breath. Destiny Bay was warm and welcoming, and th exact kind of safe landing Kennedy desperately needed. A place she could find her footing, build her business, and plan for a future.

Her future. Her life. The way she imagined it without the restrictions of others.

Feeling courageous and adventurous, two things that had been lacking in years past, Kennedy grabbed her purse and slipped inside the bakery, a warm blast of cinnamon and tart apples greeting her.

Sweetie Pies looked like a turn-of-the-twentieth-century bakery with white iron garden tables, pies stacked in the leaded glass window display, and floor-to-ceiling shelves housing a collection of antique flour tins from around the world. And hanging above the display cases and punch key register were sixteen photos of Fi and her Gold Tin, a snapshot to commemorate each one of her wins.

A reputation of excellence Kennedy vowed to continue.

The bakery was full of customers, some still in their coats waiting to be helped, others relaxing with family or friends at tables while sharing pie and smiling and greeting one another, inquiring about plans for the weekend, how the family was doing, and if they would be in town for the Gold Tin Apple Pie Competition, as though everyone here was one big family.

Kennedy didn't have a lot of experience with family, even little ones, so when the woman next to her smiled and said, "Good evening," then pulled out the chair as if offering to share her table, Kennedy smiled back, then did what any big city girl would do—took a seat at the counter, kept her eyes on the chalkboard menu, and avoided eye contact.

"What can I get you?" a twentysomething co-ed in a

GAMMA GAMMA SIGMA T-shirt asked, holding a pot of coffee. Just watching the steam waft up into the air was enough to make Kennedy yawn.

"I would love a mocha. Double shot with extra whip?"

The woman offered up an amused smile. "We have leaded and unleaded, but I can add a ton of sugar and some whipped cream if that helps."

"Double whip?" Kennedy asked hopefully.

"You bet." The woman grabbed a mug and set it on the counter. "Any pie?"

"Yes." Kennedy looked back at the menu then reminded herself that this trip was all about adventure, being courageous and taking the unknown path. "Surprise me, though. Oh, and I'm here to see Fiona."

A bright smile lit the woman's face, and she patted her hair down. "You must be Kennedy. I'm Lauren, the sometimes baker, sometimes cashier for the shop," she said, sticking out her hand. "Fi told me you'd be stopping by but I could have sworn she said you'd be here day after tomorrow."

"I got here faster than expected." The moment Kennedy had crossed that Georgia border, she decided there was no going back. She was going to go big or go broke—but there was no going back to her old home. She'd have to find a new one. No matter what.

"I think Fi's already left for the night. It's Channing Tatum Week at the senior center and tonight's showing is The Vow. Which is why there is a serious lack of silver hair here." Lauren laughed. "Fi said she was leaving early to get a front row seat. Didn't want to have to use her glasses to see his butt."

"That's a butt not to be missed," Kennedy said with

wicked grin, then she looked at the unfamiliar inky sky out-side and a small chill settled on her shoulders. "She didn't leave a key for me by any chance?"

Lauren glanced around. "I didn't see one, but let me check in the kitchen."

"That would be great."

"I'll be back with your side of whip." Lauren slid a piece of pie across the counter that was nine inches tall and filled the entire plate. "And this is on the house. Fi's HumDinger."

The pie that had started it all.

Mouth watering with anticipation, Kennedy forked off a small slice and lifted it to her nose, impressed with how it held together. She took a sniff, the sweet and tangy scent causing her to sigh. She slid the fork in and—

"Oh my God," she moaned as it melted against her tongue and sent her taste buds into an orgasmic frenzy. This is better than sex."

"My pie's a prize winner, I'll give you that. But better than sex? Honey, you must be doing it wrong."

Kennedy opened her eyes to find a pistol of a woman in a red SWEETIE PIES apron with spiky white hair, cherry-red bifocals, and a name tag identifying her as Fiona. She was squat, floured, and pushing eighty. She took one look at Kennedy and said, "You must be Edna's girl."

Even though the woman seemed as cuddly as a por-cupine, Kennedy found herself smiling at the comparison. People were always saying she had her grandmother's baby blues. "Was it my eyes that gave me away?"

"It was your hips." Fi's eyes dropped to Kennedy's backside. "Hope you're not one of those bakers who sam-ple the wears all day long."

"No," Kennedy lied, resisting the urge to peek at her butt.

"Good because I won't have people sampling my product," Fi said. "And why are you so early?"

"I decided not to stop in Montana and drove straight through." A decision she was starting to question.

"That's a long haul," she said suspiciously. "Now, being early is fine, but being late won't fly. Not with me. I run a tight ship. You must have been excited to get here."

"I was." Only now that she was here, little bits of doubt began to creep back in. It started when she realized that half the town was in this bakery, and she didn't know a single soul, and it grew when Fiona pulled out a contract and set it on the counter.

"Now, sign this and I'll take you on a quick tour of the place."

"What's this?" Kennedy asked, still holding to that smile as if her sanity depended on it. Because it wasn't the contract Kennedy had signed; it was an application.

"I need a list of your references," Fi said matter-of-factly. "Need to know who I'm working with. Knowledge is power," she said as if it were a Saturday morning commercial, "plus, it creates positive working conditions."

Kennedy was all for positive conditions, but there was no way she was filling out an application for the business she now owned.

Leaving Georgia to move to Destiny Bay had been impulsive and brave, and she knew there would be consequences. She just didn't expect being steamrolled by a grannie with a 'tude to be one of them.

"I only wanted to have a chance to learn the ropes before you left," Kennedy said diplomatically, even though she wasn't feeling very diplomatic at the moment. "However, if you would prefer, I can come back in two days as expected."

"Leave?" Fi laughed. "Honey, I'm not leaving. Didn't your grandma tell you, me and Paula are staying on. We're going to help you run the bakery. Teach the only other person in the world who has the right to bake my HumDinger what the secret is behind it."

"It must have slipped her mind." Something that she'd take up with Edna later. "But I don't recall it in the contract."

"We can add it if not." The older woman waved a hand as if the contract were an ever-changing agreement. "Right under the part where I agreed to sell you three acres of my best apples at wholesale."

"Plus, Sweetie Pies isn't Sweetie Pies without Fi," a woman two seats down said, gaining her a few nods from the counter, and a "Just ask anyone" from a table by the display. And suddenly Kennedy felt as if she were interviewing—for a place in this town.

She looked out at the customers, chatting like family and bonding over pie and coffee, and that doubt became full-blown panic. The people in this town obviously had decades of shared history, and with history came loyalty.

Kennedy had a history, too. A history that warned her she had nothing but the deed to a pie shop, and if the people of Destiny Bay were forced to choose, that they'd choose their own. Once again leaving Kennedy the odd man out.

A position she'd spent her life trying to escape, and never managing to succeed. Until now. Today marked a new start, her chance to be a part of something larger. And if that meant she had to open herself up to others, even stubborn old ladies, then so be it.

Straightening her shoulders, Kennedy adopted her most professional smile and said, "Of course it isn't, which is why I was hoping you ladies would share your experience with me. I want to be a part of this town, leave my mark, and sharing with me the secrets to your success would help with the transition of ownership. I want to make everything as smooth as possible for the community."

Before Kennedy had even finished, Fi said, "I don't pour coffee, don't work weekends, and I'm not filling out an application."

"Oh," Kennedy said quickly. "I think you misunderstood, I just meant—"

"Did you hear that, Paula? The girl's keeping us on."

"Isn't that just wonderful," Paula said, coming through the swinging kitchen doors. Even though she was at least a decade younger, she walked slower than Fi, leaning heavily on a cane. But she had a smile that warmed the room. "Working with us is going to be as easy as pie. Just you wait."

* * *

Whoever came up with the phrase *easy as pie* obviously never had to shell their own pecans, Kennedy thought as she lifted the side cutter and carefully snipped the pecan hull. The trick was to cut off the ends of the shell and no her fingers—an important lesson she learned yesterday.

The sun was beginning to set over the lush peaks of the Cascade Range, casting a warm glow over Main Street and the historic downtown, when Kennedy flipped the CLOSE sign, ending her first full week as the owner of Sweetie Pies.

She looked around the empty shop, then to the sold-out display case. A strange lightness bubbled up from beneath her chest. She had pie orders up the wazoo, enough dough to cover the Great Smoky Mountains, and hadn't cried over *Phil-ep* once since she'd moved.

She'd been too busy baking her way toward success. Independence. A real life. And it felt good. Liberating even.

So what if she'd gained a few pounds sampling the merchandise? She loved, *loved*, baking. No spreadsheets, no unattainable expectations, and absolutely no one else's agenda to distract her. Nothing but her and a never-ending stream of possibilities in sight. Not to mention sweets.

Pies, turnovers, deep dish, and cobblers; Kennedy was an equal opportunity baker—and taster. Anything that made her shop smell sweet and homey. It didn't take a genius to explain the appeal. Before living with Edna, there hadn't been a lot of sweet and homey in Kennedy's life. And she'd fought tooth and nail for any opportunity that had come her way. Which made her driven and determined.

A good trait to have since business had been going so well she didn't have enough apples or shelled pecans left in the barrel to make a single caramel apple pecan pie— let alone to fill the orders for tomorrow. Which explained the fifty-pound order of pecans and apples she'd had delivered today. Kennedy had no idea how expensive heirloom apples were, or just how difficult pecans were to hull.

So when the mini-apple turnover, sitting all by its lonesome on the top shelf of the display case, started silently calling her name, she ignored it, grabbed the NUT BUSTER apron her grandma had sent with the last shipment of pecans, and got hulling.

Thirty minutes later, the sun had vanished and she sadly had enough pecans to decorate a cupcake. She might love baking, but hulling could suck it. Her fingers were raw, her nails destroyed, and her arm muscles were getting quite the workout. Good thing for her, busting nuts was a skill she was determined to acquire in her new chapter.

A rustle sounded from the back of the kitchen, scaring the life out of her and causing the sliders to jab her palm, slicing the skin. More immediate than the threat of blood was the shadow that could easily belong to Thor coming through her back door.

A big and arrogant shadow because, yeah, it was definitely a man creeping into her shop and stomping all over her fresh start. Although he wasn't creeping so much as smugly moseying—as if *he* owned the place. As if he had every right to help himself to her safe.

Indignant irritation pulsing through her, Kennedy considered saying that she was closed and pointing to the sign on the window, but her burglar obviously knew that since he used the back door. The *locked* back door.

Plus, he was built like one of those MMA fighters with broad shoulders and double-barreled biceps who went by names like The Undertaker or Tank of Terror. In fact, his only hope of sneaking into or out of any place unseen was if it were pitch black and he had a small planet shielding him.

Kennedy grabbed her phone from her apron pocket to dial 911 when Tank bypassed the safe altogether to grab—

Oh, hell no.

Her last six apple pies. Which had been sold, lovingly boxed, and promised to Fi's favorite granddaughter, Elle.

Nothing pissed Kennedy off more than breaking a promise. Nothing except someone playing her for a fool. That the someone in question was a smug man set on burgling away the good in her week only added to her fury.

Acting on pure instinct, Kennedy grabbed the massive rolling pin off the counter. She might not be a trained ninja, but she'd seen *Xena: Warrior Princess* enough times to know how to handle herself. Doing some creeping of her own, she walked right up behind Tank and stuck the handle of the rolling pin in his back—hard.

"Hands off my pies, big guy," she said, then realized he wasn't just big. He was massive. And smelled really good. Like fresh-chopped wood, hot summer nights, and really bad decisions.

She half expected Tank to spin around and do some kind of complicated roundhouse, karate chop to the throat combination to disarm her. Only he kept his hands on her pies and looked over his shoulder, his blue eyes twinkling with confidence as he took in her ponytail to her pink toes, and everything in between.

With his dark wavy hair, the perfect amount of scruff, and a smile that was all swagger and charm, the man didn't need brute strength.

She cleared here throat. "I mean it. One wrong move and I shoot."

"Don't shoot, I'm just trying to figure out what the right moves are, so you wouldn't be so offended by the idea of my hands on your pies." He said it with a grin that was all eye candy and sexy swagger.

It was one of those *Sorry, babe, couldn't help myself* movements that her mom's boyfriends used every time they got caught with someone else's lipstick on their collar.

The same flash of white that Philip gave when he'd come home too tired to tango in the sheets. Only this man knew how to do it right, knew how to do it so that a girl went weak in the knees.

Not that her weak knees had anything to do with *him*. Or that grin. Nope, they were tingling because he had broken into her shop and touched her pies.

Kennedy jabbed him harder with the rolling pin, distracted when it bounced off his muscles. "The right move would be to set my pies on the counter and put your hands in the air."

"Or what?" He turned around, slowly, until her "gun" was pressing into his chest. His eyes dropped to take in her not-so-lethal rolling pin, and when they made their way back up, he didn't look scared at all. He looked amused. "You going to flour me, sweetness?"

"No." She held up her phone, snapped his picture, and waited for his amusement to turn to fear. It didn't. "I'm going to call the cops and report a break-in in process," she said, channeling her inner *NYPD Blue*. "And if you try to run, I will just show them your picture."

"No need," he said, stepping back, not to flee the scene, but to rest a hip against the counter. He casually set her pie boxes down—right beside him. "The nearest *cops* are in Tacoma." He threw up air quotes. "A good couple hours away. Around here, we have a sheriff, and his name is Dudley. He carries a badge and a gun made of metal that shoots bullets, not flour."

"I know Dudley," she said, still holding the rolling pin out, just in case he got any ideas, while she looked for the sheriff's contact info. "He's a good customer. I even have his cell number."

"How about that," Tank said but didn't sound impressed. He reached for the pie boxes again, and without thinking, Kennedy jumped forward and smacked his hand with the rolling pin.

"Ow!" He jerked his hand back and shook out the sting.

Kennedy had the sudden urge to apologize, but swallowed it quickly. She didn't ask him to break in and mess with her day. He did that all on his own. "Keep your hands where I can see them." She waved the pin for emphasis.

"Jesus, I was reaching for the sales slip," he said, snatching it off the box. "Suspicious much?"

With men? Always.

"I don't know. Were you about to walk off with the last six pies and not pay?"

He thought about that for a moment and shrugged. "Fi doesn't charge me."

"Do I look like Fi to you?"

His lips twitched in a way that had her thighs doing some twitching of their own. "Not that I can see. But a quick inspection of your pies will tell me all I need to know." He stuck out his hand with the sales slip. "I'm Luke, by the way."

"I'm not interested." And her pies were taking a permanent vacation from charming men with knee-melting powers. "And I'm still calling the cops, so you can save those disarming dimples for someone who cares." She pointed the rolling pin in the general direction of his dimples.

"Wow, sexy and disarming, huh?" he said as if he wasn't fully aware of their power. "Are you hitting on me, sweetness?"

"You're confusing hitting-on with plain old hitting."

He ran a hand over his jaw; the scruff told Kennedy that his five o'clock was a long time past. "Jenny Miller hit me with a pear in the third grade. The next day she sent me a yes-or-no note." He leaned in and lowered his voice, his breath teasing by her earlobe. "Was all that rolling pin action Southern for flirting? Because up here all you have to do is say, 'Hey, Luke, I think you're sexy.'"

"I'm not flirting with you."

He cocked his head to the side and gave a smile that had her toes curling. "I think you are."

"I think charm clashes with prison orange."

"That might be so, but I bet it goes great with pie."

Warm zings dancing in her chest, Kennedy was too flustered to answer, so she scrolled through her phone to locate Dudley's number. With a grin of her own, she held up the cell so he could see the sheriff's name, put it on speaker and hit Call.

"Be sure when Dudley answers, you tell him I say h and that he still owes me a beer," Luke said, crossing one arm over the other. "Then tell him you are interrupting Thursday night poker to report someone touching you pies. I'm sure he'll get right on that call."

"I'm reporting someone *stealing* my pies," she corrected. "And if you'll stop talking, I'll ask him to go eas on you."

"Pe*can*, *pe*can," Luke said in that *tomato, tomah-t* tone, and just the word made her fingers ache. "And if yo admit you're hitting me was your way of flirting, I won press assault charges."

"Press charges?" Kennedy said as the phone ran; "You're the one who broke in, and you're built like a tan How could I have possibly assaulted you?"

"You look like you went a few rounds in the ring, you're swinging a rolling pin with intent, and your apron says NUT BUSTER. Who do you think Dudley will side with?"

That was when Kennedy noticed her burglar was dressed for the boardroom, not a ventilator shaft. His dark slacks, pressed blue button-up, and silk tie were way too *GQ* for a small town pie shop B and E. Then she looked down at her split knuckles, the smudges of blood on the rolling pin, and saw his point.

The phone stopped ringing and went to voice mail. With a frustrated sigh she dropped her head and silently started counting to ten. She'd made it to three when black dress shoes came into her view. By five, Luke was standing in front of her, his finger gently wrapped around hers—disconnecting the call. And sending one hell of a tingle up her arm. "How about you just admit you like me, and I promise to ask before touching your pies next time, so we can call it a day?"

"I like you almost as much as I like hulling pecans."

"You just haven't spent enough time with me yet." He looked at the cuts on her hands and let out a low, concerned whistle. When he spoke, his voice was soft, full of concern. "Look, I'm sorry about scaring you—"

"You didn't scare me—"

"That wasn't very neighborly of me and I apologize. It's late and you look tired, why don't we pick this up another time. Over drinks."

She must have been exhausted because the idea of a drink didn't seem so crazy. It had been a long week, she was looking at an even longer weekend, and it would be nice to celebrate her small success with someone. Too bad, she still had fifty pounds of pecans to crack, four dozen apple pies to make, and justice to serve. Too many numbers to fit into a single night.

She considered her options. While seeing Luke hauled off in cuffs would make her night, it wasn't worth falling so far behind schedule. Not when she wasn't so certain he'd even be arrested. He hadn't actually *stolen* anything and he might not look the part of a small town hick, but the way he tossed around the sheriff's name told her he was the real small town deal.

Destiny Bay wasn't much bigger than a speck on the map, but it was big on family, apples, and justice. In that order, meaning that having the first sometimes determined follow through on the last. Being a local good ol' boy was nearly as good as being related to the President in these parts.

Knowing that she was going to regret this come tomorrow, she looked at his big, strong hands and said, "I'll make you a deal. If you help me shell that bag of pecans and promise to never come back, I won't press charges." When he went to open his mouth, she added, "And any funny business happens and I call the cops."

He closed it. Then with a raised brow, he said, "Define *funny business*."

She lifted the rolling pin.

"No funny business," he said with a chuckle. "Got it."

"The tools are on the counter, the rolling pin is within reach. Do we have a deal?" He just stared at her a beat as though she were crazy. "Luke?"

"Yeah, we have a deal, but if I shell this whole bag, want a pie, made special for me. Hand delivered by the baker, which will be you."

"You hull that entire bag tonight, I'll name a pie after you and even feed it to you myself."

"If I hull the entire bag tonight, they won't be fresh come the weekend," he said as if he were a baking god. And maybe he was. The man had a certain Adonis appeal about him. "Proper nut care is important."

Kennedy did her best not to look amused, but then he smiled and damn if she didn't give in. "Fine, half now."

"And half this weekend." He rested his palms flat on the counter and leaned toward her.

His hands were huge. Big and strong and oh so capable. She forced her eyes back to his. "I won't hold my breath."

With a laugh, he walked over to the bags, lifting one as though it weighed nothing. He carried it into the back room and, ignoring her orders to set it back down, poured the entire bag into an ancient-looking machine sitting in the back of the kitchen that Kennedy had been using to hang her aprons on.

"What are you doing?" she demanded.

"Dreaming about what you'll be wearing when you feed me that pie."

She went to say that wasn't part of the deal, but he pushed the big red button and the machine sprang to life. Noisy gears ground back and forth as pecans were sucked into the machine and crunched.

"What's that?"

"Fi's Nut Buster," he said, leaning in to stick the sales slip to the front of her apron, his fingers purposefully grazing the T and B in NUT BUSTER. "By the way, I'm . Callahan, Fi's nephew." He pointed to the first name n the slip. "And I think she probably meant the letter L when she called in the order, not E-L-L-E." He tugged on her ponytail. "See you around, sweetness."

Maybe it was the boyish smile he added at the end, or the way he smelled the pies as he carried them out the door, but Kennedy did something she hadn't done in weeks.

She smiled back.

Book your next trip to a charming small town—and fall in love—with one of these swoony Forever contemporary romances!

THE SOULMATE PROJECT
by Reese Ryan

Emerie Roberts is tired of waiting for her best friend, Nick, to notice her. When she confesses her feelings at the town's annual New Year's Eve bonfire and he doesn't feel the same, she resolves to stop pining for him and move on. She hatches a seven-step plan to meet her love match and enlists her family and friends—including Nick—to help. So why does he seem hell-bent on sabotaging all her efforts?

HOME ON HOLLYHOCK LANE
by Heather McGovern

Though Dustin Long has been searching for a sense of home since childhood, that's not why he bought Hollyhock. He plans to flip the old miner's cottage and use the money to launch his construction business. And while every reno project comes with unexpected developments, CeCe Shipley beats them all—she's as headstrong as she is gorgeous. But as they collaborate to restore the cottage to its former glory, he realizes they're also building something new together. Could CeCe be the home Dustin's always wanted?

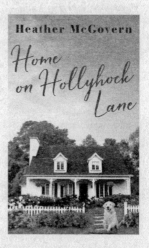

Connect with us at Facebook.com/ReadForeverPub

Discover bonus content and more on
read-forever.com

REUNION IN SUGAR LAKE
by Marina Adair

Pediatrician Charlotte Holden knows better than anyone that love leads only to heartbreak. Then sexy Jace McGraw blows back into her small town of Sugar, Georgia, and utters those three words every woman dreads: *We're still married*. The annulment went through years ago— or so she thought. But now Jace offers Charlotte a deal: He'll grant a discreet divorce in exchange for thirty days and nights of marriage. Easy as peach pie. Except this time, he isn't going to let her go without a fight.

FLIRTING WITH ALASKA
by Belle Calhoune

Caleb Stone isn't ready to give up his Hollywood dreams. But after a disastrous run on a reality dating show paints him as an unapologetic player, Caleb needs a little time and space to regroup. Luckily, his hometown of Moose Falls, Alaska, has both, plus a job helping his brothers run Yukon Cider. Even dialed down, Caleb's flirtatious vibes are a hit at work, except for one woman who seems completely, totally, frustratingly immune to his charms—the gorgeous new photographer for Yukon Cider's upcoming ad campaign.

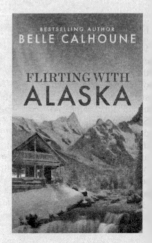

Meet your next favorite book with @ReadForeverPub on TikTok

SUNFLOWER COTTAGE ON HEART LAKE
by Sarah Robinson

Interior designer Amanda Riverswood is thirty-two years old and has never had a boyfriend. So this summer, she's going on a bunch of blind dates. Pro baseball pitcher Dominic Gage was on top of the world—until an injury sent him into retirement. Now, in the small town of Heart Lake, his plan is to sit on his dock not talking to anyone, especially not the cute girl next door. But when they begin to bond over late-night laughter about Amanda's failed dating attempts, will they see that there's more than friendship between them?

SNOWED IN FOR CHRISTMAS
by Jaqueline Snowe

Sorority mom Becca Fairfield has everything she needs to survive the blizzard: hot cocoa, plenty of books...and the memory of a steamy kiss. Only Becca's seriously underestimated this snow-pocalypse. So when Harrison Cooper—next-door neighbor, football coach, and the guy who acted mega-awkward after said kiss—offers her shelter, it only makes sense to accept. They'll just hang out, stay safe, and maybe indulge in a little R-rated cuddling. But are they keeping warm...or playing with fire?

AN AMISH CHRISTMAS MATCH
by Winnie Griggs

Phoebe Kropf knows everyone thinks she's accident-prone rather than an independent Amish woman. So she's determined to prove she's more than her shortcomings when she's asked to provide temporary Christmas help in nearby Sweetbrier Creek. Widower Seth Beiler is in over his head caring for his five motherless *brieder*. But he wasn't expecting a new housekeeper as unconventional—or lovely—as Phoebe. When the holiday season is at an end, will Seth convince her to stay…as part of their *familye*?

CHRISTMAS IN HARMONY HARBOR
by Debbie Mason

Instead of wrapping presents and decking the halls, Evangeline Christmas is worrying about saving her year-round holiday shop from powerful real estate developer Caine Elliot. She's risking everything on an unusual proposition she hopes the wickedly handsome CEO can't refuse. How hard can it be to fulfill three wishes from the Angel Tree in Evie's shop? Caine's certain he'll win and the property will be his by Christmas Eve. But a secret from Caine's childhood is about to threaten their merrily-ever-after.